THE GLUTTON

Also by A. K. Blakemore
The Manningtree Witches

The Glutton

A. K. BLAKEMORE

GRANTA

Granta Publications, 12 Addison Avenue, London W11 4QR

First published in Great Britain by Granta Books, 2023

Copyright © A. K. Blakemore, 2023

The moral right of A. K. Blakemore to be
identified as the author of this work under the Copyright,
Designs and Patents Act, 1988 has been asserted.

Image on page vi: French Republican Calendar of 1794, drawn
by Philibert-Louis Debucourt. Source: Wikimedia Commons.

A CIP catalogue record for this book is
available from the British Library.

2 4 6 8 9 7 5 3 1

ISBN 978 1 78378 919 1
eISBN 978 1 78378 920 7

www.granta.com

Typeset in Garamond by Patty Rennie

Printed and bound by CPI Group (UK) Ltd,
Croydon, CR0 4YY

for Edward, restless.

CALENDRIER RÉPUBLICAIN.

Author's Note

The action of this book begins and ends in September 1798 – renamed in the French Republican calendar as Vendémiaire [the name given to the first month of the autumn quarter] an VII [Year 7]. The Republican calendar was introduced by the French National Convention in 1793 and remained in use until 1805, representing a highly symbolic break with the days of the Ancien Régime that the revolutionary government had aimed to dismantle.

The twelve months of this calendar were named by the poet Philippe Fabre d'Églantine (1750–1794), who sought to suggest both the beauty of the changing seasons and the noble rhythms of agricultural labour through his designations. For instance, 'Vendémiaire' is derived from the Latin words *vinum* and *demere*, meaning 'grape gathering' or 'the grape harvest'.

... how then, while they all go rushing at such a pace, on unknown ways, with no bridle, towards no aim, can hurly-burly unutterable fail? For verily not Federation-rosepink is the colour of this Earth and her work: not by outbursts of noble-sentiment, but with far other ammunition, shall a man front the world.

—Thomas Carlyle

I Vendémiaire an VII

Hospice civil de l'Humanité
Versailles

To my esteemed colleague
Citizen-Doctor Jean-Pierre Dupuis,

It is with deep and long-held admiration that I write to you, although the circumstances that cause me to do so are strange indeed. Believing time to be of the essence in this matter, I pray that my brevity causes no affront.

Four days ago, a person of exceedingly poor and alarming appearance arrived at our hospital and was placed under my care. The name he uses for himself is Tarare, and he says that he was a soldier, and fought for the Republic in the north. He also asserts a past acquaintance with you, Citizen-Doctor Dupuis, though I can scarcely give credence to his account of himself. He can be no older than twenty-five, by his looks. He claims – and indeed, truly appears – to suffer greatly from some ailment that defies all diagnoses. His abdomen is distended and his skin is yellowed and atrabilious as one sees in cases of severe inanition, and he is convulsed by pains that render him unable to stand, and often unable to speak. He claims these pains are caused by a golden fork that he swallowed whole and that is – and here I quote the patient's vivid self-diagnosis *verbatim* – 'tearing him apart inside', although manual examination of the patient revealed no such foreign body, nor any other obvious obstruction to the gut.

His breathing has become laboured, and he will now take neither food nor water.

I believe he will soon die, and so does he. My sense of fraternal charity for this pitiful creature has overcome my natural temerity, and I am compelled to relay his desperate wish to see you and speak with you, knowing full well that your work may detain you in Paris. Although this poor Tarare may be beyond our healing art – he is certainly beyond mine – I believe it would ease his troubled and swift-departing spirit to see you once again, and bid you come, if you are able, as soon as you might.

Your humble servant,
Citizen-Doctor Alexis L. Tissier

I

Les paysans

[The Peasants]

IV Vendémiaire an VII

They look like grave-figures, the way they move along the dim corridors between the dim rooms. It is because their long habits hide the movements of their limbs and the muted shuffle of their feet on the bare stone tiles. Because their long habits disguise the movements of their limbs and the muted shuffle of their feet on the bare stone tiles, they look like they are gliding, as though it is some outside force that compels them along the dim corridors and between the dim rooms. They nod to one another when they pass.

Sister Perpetué supposes she must look the same way they do, because she wears the same long habit, and the same white cornette with the wide wings on top of her head. She supposes she must also look like it is some outside force compelling her along the dim passages and between the dim rooms, which, she supposes, in a sense, is true. Love? God? Love and God being one and the same, of course. There are crosses nailed to the walls to show it. There are sisters gliding along the halls in their white cornettes to show it.

It is – or was – the day of Autumn Crocus. It was raining outside, heavily, the last time she was able to look out of a window. Drowning the sooted cornice-work and the shy evening lights of the city. There are crosses nailed to the walls, but there are very few windows. The windows that there are, on this floor of the hospital, are very small, and barred. You can really lose your sense of time in this place. She knows what time it is now, though. She knows it is near midnight, because she has been called to the place where Sister Amandine watches the patient *who must always be watched.*

Sister Amandine is sitting upright in a chair in the corridor with a prayer book open in her black lap. You mustn't fall asleep, says Sister Amandine.

Why not? asks Sister Perpetué.

Always these stupid questions, says Sister Amandine. Because he must always be watched.

But you're looking at your book. Not watching him at all.

Sister Amandine closes the prayer book and presses her lips tightly together. The patient has been given laudanum, she says, for the pain. Now he is sleeping. And in any case, he is bound to his bed.

Why? asks Sister Perpetué. That was what I meant, she says. I meant, why are such precautions necessary? Citizen-Doctor Tissier says he is certainly dying.

Sister Amandine leans forward slowly in her chair, red, big-knuckled hands still sandwiched around her little prayer book. You mean you have not heard? she asks.

I have heard, Sister Perpetué says, things that could hardly be true. Could hardly be true if they were said of any man alive.

*

Sister Amandine putters away down the corridor with a yawn. And yes, with the movement of her limbs hidden, the shuffling of her feet muted, so that she appears to glide away, glide away across the flagstones to her narrow bed in the dormitories.

Sister Perpetué sits down. The chair faces the door of the patient's room. Sister Perpetué has heard that the man who lies in that room once ate a little child. There is more to it, of course. He worked up to eating a little child by eating other things first. Corks and stones. Snakes and eels. Dogs and cats, *alive*. She has heard how people would gather in the market squares and at the fêtes to watch him tear the bellies of puppies open with his bare teeth, there. Among the organ grinders and the girls with yellow flowers in their hair. Christian souls would come to watch him do those things.

He ate, she has heard, such quantities as seemed impossible. A whole bushel of apples, one after the other, hardly stopping, it was said, to breathe between bites. Three large meat pies and four gallons of milk, thirty pounds of beef lung and liver. Mesentery juices running down his chin. A medical marvel. He was a sight of rare, arresting hideousness, even in those times when severed heads were carried dripping through the streets to Vivat! and strewed tinsel.

He had not wanted to be what he was, whatever you might call it, because he had gone to a doctor, and he had said *cure me*. All this Sister Perpetué has heard. And the doctor had tried to cure him, with laudanum and eggs and enemas. But while the good doctor played with his leeches, the patient slunk around the shades of the hospital at night and discovered a new level of depravity there, where human meat lay prone, exposed, exuding—

Sister Perpetué wishes she had brought a prayer book herself. She rearranges her kirtle. She looks at her shoes. She examines her nails and finds them to be exactly as they ought to be, and exactly as the rest of her is: short, round, spotless. She looks up and down the corridor, left, then right. She looks at the patient's door again, which stands very slightly ajar – between door and jamb she can see nothing but void. A bar of black.

Having exhausted the possibilities for looking, Sister Perpetué begins to listen. In the court, the bell is rung for midnight, but after that there is nothing. A dripping noise, perhaps, from somewhere nearby. The hospital is old and the outside wills its way in, slowly. Drip. It could be rain in a pail, or blood in a basin. Either way, a dripping noise will hardly sustain her interest until matins. It is better, she tells herself, to spend the night here, alone, in peace, than in the dormitories. In the dormitories, where the patients are given numbers instead of names, and where their fitful breath sours the air, and the paupers with their speckled tongues wake crowing at the night. No. Here, she can be alone with her thoughts. She even says it aloud. It is better to be here than in the dormitories. She is a very bad nun. She thinks, for a moment, just for a little bit of fun, she will say that aloud, as well – *I am a very bad nun*. But she decides against it.

At the very furthest end of the corridor, there is a window. Sister Perpetué rises from her seat, takes a light from the alcove in the wall, and slowly moves toward it. She can see nothing because it is midnight, but the rain shills at the pane with a pleasing music. She lowers her head and presses it to the cold glass. It is then that she hears a sound behind her.

She turns on the spot. It was like creaking – or breathing, the sound. The corridor remains empty, the candle flames ensconced and unflickering, the doors all closed. Just as they were. Except, of course, for that one door, the fourth along. The patient's door. *He must always be watched*. What if the sound she heard was neither breathing nor creaking, but a call for assistance? She is a Sister of Charity, in her white cornette. Is it not her duty to mind those in her care? Slowly and noiselessly, she edges back down the corridor and returns to her seat, knitting her hands in her lap. Training her eyes on the little darkness disclosed of the occupied room, she listens. Yes – yes – she can hear it. He breathes. Slow and long, through his mouth. That famous mouth. She has heard of the great serpents of the Orient that can swallow men whole. Their lazy eyes. Their bright embossed hides conforming to the shapes of their prey as they wallow in the dirt, digesting.

Sister Perpetué is not a woman of science. Nor even, despite her current occupation, a woman of great medical knowledge. But she is aware of and abides by those biological precepts that appear self-evident. There is finite space within the body, a limit to what it can contain. What goes in must come out, some way, somehow. So *how* can all she has heard of this man be true? Thirty pounds of lungs and liver? Now, a child. That is something else. She supposes it is *possible* for a man to eat a child in one sitting, depending on the relative sizes of man and child. Some of the children in the hospital, starved and stick-limbed, can have no more meat on them than a large goose does. She thinks of the old kings of old days, your Henris, your Charlemagnes, who put bird within bird and roasted them whole, glazed in honey. But eating a child is not like eating a goose. Why? Because man was made in the image of God, and geese were not, and the body of a human being, of any human being, must therefore be honoured? Because a goose, or a chicken, cannot know salvation? She is pleased to have created some little discourse to occupy herself with. Noah, after the flood? *Everything that lives and moves about will be food for you. Just as I gave you the green plants, I now give you everything. Eat of my body*, demands Christ. Well. But there are other things, other passages, she is sure. Some prophecy concerning the Israelites, that, having forsaken God, they—

9

There. She hears the sound again, more pronounced this time, louder. Yes. It is a whine, a moan, and it is coming from the open door. From the patient. Sister Perpetué feels a shudder tickle through her skin. Are his teeth sharp by nature, like a dog's? Or perhaps he filed them to points. She slides the fingers of her right hand under her sleeve and pinches at the soft underside of her wrist. So thin, the veins vibrating underneath. It wouldn't take sharp teeth to break it. It wouldn't take much pressure at all.

There is another moan. Duty dictates she enter the room – or she could fetch Citizen-Doctor Tissier. He will be in his chamber, on the floor above. Sleeping, or sitting up with his books, perhaps. This is, after all, no ordinary patient. Perhaps Tissier would want to be summoned. She rises from her chair. She has turned her back to the door when she remembers – *he must always be watched*. She cannot leave. Frustration prongs at her belly. Perhaps fear.

Hello? Sister Perpetué calls, turning to the far end of the corridor. Is there anyone—? Silence. She knows before she can finish shaping the words that she is alone. Doctors asleep, Sisters pacing the feculent moonlit aisles of the dormitories and the paupers' ward, where the girls dragged from the river with stones weighting the pockets of their dirty frocks go to die in diminished grace under the dolomite eyes of Mother Superior. Alone. *For God has not given us a spirit of fear and timidity, but of power, love and self-discipline—*

Sister Perpetué opens the door and stands upon the threshold.

1772 – The Feast of St Lazare

Tarare's father dies the very same day that Tarare is born. It is the Feast of Saint Lazare, whom Jesus Christ raised from the grave after four days, and of his mild sisters Sainte Marthe and Sainte Marie de Béthanie. Everyone is drunk on sweet cider, and because everyone is drunk, Tarare's father will die.

Brawls are to be expected on feast days – on feast days and at weddings. The boys of one village bring cudgels and switches to beat the boys of the next village over, and it is all in good fun, their raising this bit of hell for themselves. A part of growing up, and of becoming men. Their fathers did it, and their grandfathers did it before that, in the old days, when half the meadows were covered thickly in trees, and wolves could talk and sometimes wore hats, and Martin Luther was no more than a sulphurous twinkle in the Devil's eye.

But today the brawl starts and it doesn't stop, because one of the boys, Tarare's father, pulls a knife. At least, Antoine saw something flashing in his hand. At least, Ignace bellowed A KNIFE! So now the boys are beating and beating the boy who pulled a knifesupposedly, Tarare's soon-to-be-father, and no one is prepared to intervene. The boys beat him for a while and then they stop. They spit at him where he lies on the ground, call him a black-tongued dog, a son of a whore, and then go off to find more cider.

Evening comes, stun-bright and violaceous. The boy, Tarare's father, stirs. He spits two pink teeth into the trampled grass, another into his trembling hand, and then climbs to his feet. He can hear the music of organ grinder and fiddle from the fête ground, a little way away. His head feels constricted, as though something has curled itself around it. He hugs his broken arm to his chest and sets out in a shambling jog toward what he thinks is home.

There are cows and horses standing about in the parched meadows. They watch the boy totter by, acutely nonplussed. His shadow wavers on the dusty path in front of him. The boy feels that if his body stopped moving even for a moment, if he stopped putting one foot in front of the other, his shadow would simply, soundlessly detach itself from his bulk and continue in a smooth, autonomous glide eastward, away from the setting sun. And that is what death would look like. He would slump on to his stomach and reach his swollen fingers out toward that indifferent adumbration as it slid further and further away across the field, across other fields, across the rooftops, and then eventually to the sea (the sea, which the boy has never seen), where it would be lost on the fretted silver among the other shadows of the other boys gone before their time. Oh well, he thinks. At least I drank and laughed. Oh well, he thinks. At least I did a bit of fucking, and it was good.

He trudges on.

By the time the boy reaches the village, he has become Tarare's father. An old woman is throwing the afterbirth to the pigs when she sees the youth limp toward her, then fall on to his side in the middle of the dirt road. She puts down her bloody bucket and screws her eyes against the flush of the evening sun. Over she goes to where the boy lies. She rolls him on to his back with her foot. She sees that the boy's face is livid and very swollen. The whites of his eyes are scarlet. The old woman sighs and goes back into the cottage, wiping her hands on her apron.

The cottage is just one room of mud and piled stone, oxlip and eglantine sheltering beneath the eaves without, a dog scratching at himself within. Inside the cottage they are gathered around the bed – which is just a straw mattress on the floor – deciding what Tarare's mother should do.

Tarare's mother is young. As much a girl as Tarare's father is a boy.

Jean is back from the fête, the old woman says. I think he's maybe dead.

Dead? repeats Tarare's mother, her mouth slack with the exhaustions of labour. She wants to sleep, but no one will let her sleep until she has decided what to do.

The old woman nods.

Go and check. For fuck's sake. *Maybe* dead. There is no *maybe* about *dead*. All this she says despite the exhaustions of labour.

The old woman sighs and goes back outside.

Now the midwife, who is holding the squalling baby in her arms, speaks. Very early on Saturday, she says, what you need to do is swaddle him tight and take him to the market. Before anyone else gets there. They'll find him and take him to the poor hospital. Done.

Or my son can take him to the Sisters in the city, says the neighbour-woman. The Sisters will take good care of the little one. Raise him up properly, good, God-fearing.

The old woman comes back inside. Not dead yet, she confirms. Will be soon.

They all look at her for further explanation.

His head is broken in pieces, she says, holding up her wrinkled hands. I felt it. And there's blood coming out his eyes.

They all look back at Tarare's mother. It is one thing to raise a bastard, but another thing to raise a dead man's bastard. She is herself an orphan, come down from the Morvan, where the cows are red and the wind-blown hillsides coloured with heather, and she has no one, no people of her own, and so they pity her. She is pretty, though, so they pity her less than they might. Her pretty head lolls back against the pillow. Can he speak? she asks. He really boils my piss sometimes.

(Tarare's father boils everyone's piss.)

He's still making noises, the old woman says. Wouldn't call it *speaking*.

Go back outside and ask him what our son should be named, says the young mother.

The old woman obliges.

The boy is lying on his back now, in the rutted road outside. When the old woman approaches, her shadow falls across his face, and the sensation of it is pleasantly cooling. He smacks his lips together, like he is trying to drink the old woman's shadow. She stands over him. She tells him he has a son now, you idiot, going and doing a thing like this when a girl has his baby in her, they are his mouths to feed and no one else's, but what will happen now? They will starve no doubt, the chit and the baby too, and anyway what should this baby boy be named, this baby who may as well be starved and dead already, having no father to make sure he is fed, what should they call him, this bastard whelped in sin, in sin and joy no doubt! Children these days! But now the boy can hear nothing, nothing but the faltering drub of his heart, and see nothing, nothing but the deep quiescent blue of the July dusk up above him, an eternity rested on the wide shoulders of proleptic stars, above the sweet village smells of strawberries and manure. He understands now that it was there, always there, and hears nothing the old woman says to him.

You just wait, says the midwife in the cottage, while the boy is dying. She bobs the baby in her sticky arms. This little problem won't be a little problem for long. He's so small. Won't make it through winter, mark my words.

And his head is too round, says the neighbour-woman, squinting at the baby with distaste. You ought to press on the sides a bit to make the shape better while his skull is still good and soft. The neighbour-woman reaches out her hands but the midwife slaps them away.

Tarare's mother sighs and closes her eyes and doesn't move even when a fat fly lands on her blood-streaked thigh, rubbing his black minikin hands together. The dog licks at his bits in the corner. Everyone is tired and everyone is hungry, and outside the little rag-covered window the fields are beginning to hum with night-time. Sweat and old copper. The midwife and the neighbour-woman exchange a grim look over their charge, who they begin to see will not be told, will not be guided, and who is about to hitch her cart to an idiot steed.

Fine, says the midwife, fine. She bends down to put the baby in his mother's arms. God help you, girl. At least he's sleeping now.

The old woman comes back inside. She shakes her head sadly. Crosses herself. He's dead.

The girl opens her eyes and tentatively wraps an arm around her infant's backside. Well? she asks. What did he say? About the name?

Nothing much, says the old woman. I don't think he rightly heard me.

But he said *something*?

The old woman could declare that the boy said anything then, and she knows it. She could say the boy chose for his son a fine and a usual name before he expired. A whole retinue of saints that it is good for a little boy to be named after troop before her mind's eye, lustrous in their robes of white and crimson, bearing the pearly wounds of martyrdom. Sébastien. Tomas. Or even Lazare, why not? But the old woman is honest. She shrugs. It sounded like... *Tarare*, she says. Like the village.

They all look at Tarare's mother again. People are not named after villages. Villages can be named after *people*, this is true, but not people like them. Bad people with hard lives. The midwife lights a candle. The puss moths begin to drift in through the window, drawn by the small flame.

Tarare, says the young girl. Tarare it is, then.

The neighbour throws up her hands. You can't be thinking of keeping him, Agnès. A bastard. *A bastard. A bastard.* There is a boy dead in the road!

And once again, they enumerate the possibilities, the avenues of dereliction. Leave him in the market, lots of girls do it! Send him to the Sisters in the city, two good meals a day, raised God-fearing, good!

But Tarare's mother will do none of these things. She had loved – still loves – the boy who lies dead in the rutted road outside. She hopes this love will pass inside her from father to son, like warm milk poured from pitcher to cup.

*

And some years pass, and each passes in the usual way, with the falling of the leaves to make a yellow clot in the rutted road where the boy died, and then the falling of the snow to cover over the yellow clot of fallen leaves with whiteness. Soon the people, who at first avoided standing in that place in the road where they know a boy to have died, still avoid standing in that place, but can't remember why. In the spring come the quiet grey-eyed men from the hills, and they go from door to door in the village, looking for a bowl of groats or a hay-bed in exchange for their afternoon's labour. Then the summer comes and the men from the hills follow the sun north over the fields where it tawnies the grain and ripens the grapes, and some of the older boys from the village go with them, to sleep piled like puppies under the mild-faced moon. Their absence is not regretted, because older boys eat too much.

Then one year the King, who is called Louis the Beloved (though even he does not know what he has done to earn so affectionate an appellation), dies. There is a new king, a six-teenth Louis, and he is crowned far away from the village, among painted sunrays – yellow, red and gold. Holy men anoint him with oil from the beak of a dove, and say *yes, the beautiful days will come.*

Little Tarare sits in his mother's lap and watches the crooked legs of drunken dancers comb the fire. The villagers drink cider and eat ash cakes with honey, and tripe sausages, and it is good. There is a great fire every night that summer. The women gather round it and sing loudly and badly of the angels in heaven, then softly of a sow asleep in a garden. They card wool and darn socks and twist straw into dollies for the small ones. Tarare sees how the women can never let their hands fall idle, how they work them until their muscles wear to strings, work their hands into ragged claws, so that to Tarare's young eyes they look like a tribe of great fire-worshipping birds, huddled there at the veillée in their black shawls.

He will remember this, a breast in his mouth and the great birds gathered by the great fire, after he forgets most of what follows. It is where he comes from.

V Vendémiaire an VII

Sister Perpetué opens the door and stands upon the threshold. She carries a little light, which at first illuminates much of nothing. But then, as her pupils dilate in the dark, she sees the wrought-iron bars of the narrow bedstead, and she sees between them – feet.

His feet, at least, do not look especially monstrous. They are white and bandaged. She moves closer, and her little light pools in the folds of the thin cotton blanket half-thrown from his body before it discloses to her the body itself. Sister Perpetué has observed that people expect to find the smell of death in a hospital – want to, in fact – strain their noses for it, to know what the smell of death is – but to her nose the hospital smells better than the street, where just as many holes and gashes, if not more, are left to fester. The hospital, for the most part, smells austerely of spirits and ammonia, the apologetic spice of laudanum. But here, yes, there is a new odour in her nose and mouth. One she finds offensive. The smell of that room is rotten, metabolic.

She is frightened, but she knows that it is right and good to be frightened of evil. She moves further into the room, and the candlelight throws the shadows of its meagre furnishings on to the stone wall. A spindly chair, a washstand. All the little things catch the flame, like they are waking up: scalpel, pliers, the brown glass of a bottle. Eyes winking in a cave. The patient is absolutely still. His face and his shoulders are turned away from her. On his right shoulder she sees the white embossed brand of a thief – V, voleur. His hair looks thin and greasy, but the colour of it, where it remains in patches on his scald head, is quite beautiful. A dark gold, lightened at the tips with the blanch of summers past. Sister Perpetué's own hair is fair, beneath her cornette, but she has never stood or sat long enough in the sun, uncovered, to know if the summer would turn it to floss, or raise freckles on her skin, as it has on the flesh of this sinister mendicant. This strange ghoul-thing that lies before her.

There are many things Sister Perpetué has never done.

The laudanum sits on a little table by the bedside, stoppered up, beside a dirty gauze. With a sudden and causeless rush of entitlement she sets the candle down, picks up the bottle, unstoppers it, wafting it beneath her nose. God – even the smell of it, big sweet. Somniferum. Brandy. Up through the throat to wobble on the inside of your head. Her cheeks flush and she feels her body reel. She grabs at the edge of the little table to steady herself. When the pale spots have ceased their gaudy fasciation behind her eyes, she sees, with horror, that the patient has turned in the bed, and now lies on his back, and his own eyes are opened.

He is looking at her.

His face should be round but the cheeks are sunken, gaunt. He has the slightly upturned nose that on a child or a woman might be charming, but that makes the face of a grown man somehow insolent-seeming, pretentious. Piggy? Or is she seeing what she expected to see in those dim-lit lineaments, the weak chin, the mess of blond fuzz on the upper lip? His eyes are exceptionally large. Fey, even, in their drugged blue-grey.

Those eyes rise from her face to her cornette. They are lovely weakling's eyes.

Do you like to hover above the beds of dying men with your wide white wings, to fright them? he asks. He speaks and then he groans, touching his left hand to the middle of his chest. He tries to raise his right hand, sees the manacle around his wrist, strikes it once, hard, against the bedstead, then swears.

Sister Perpetué flinches. She raises her own hand, self-consciously, to her cornette. The Sisters of Charity are here – she says, with as much conviction as she is able to muster – I, I am here to minister to the unfortunate and the infirm.

Well, says the patient, experimentally stretching first one leg and then the other, before turning his limpid eyes back to Sister Perpetué, minister, then.

His teeth are no more pointed than anyone else's. But they are disgusting – crumbling stumps in his livid gums, lustre-less as earth. The face does look young, once you have seen the cadaverous teeth and gums belonging to it. Sister Perpetué looks down at his body. Beneath his nightshirt, his chest is pale and hairless. The flesh swells plump between his hip bones, strangely and unnaturally distended, as though he carries a child. If her habit hides the movement of her limbs, she hopes it will also disguise the shudder precipitated by the look of his strange, pupal-pale body.

The man sees her horror. He seems to enjoy it, because he smiles a wide elastic smile. Would you like to look at me? he asks.

I am already looking at you, answers Sister Perpetué.

Then does it please you, to look at me?

She ignores him. Are you in pain? she asks.

Almost constantly, he says. Since before the Grand Republic.

But – he groans again, low and bubbling – I am not hungry now. See? That is something.

Citizen-Doctor Tissier says that you must eat or you will die, says Sister Perpetué.

The patient makes a croaking noise somewhere in the neighbourhood of laughter. Eat, he repeats, eat or die. Isn't that where all the trouble started? That a man must eat or die. So it seemed from where I was sitting. I know little of polity.

Your trouble, you mean? asks Sister Perpetué.

I mean the people. The homeland. *Patrie.* He shifts on the mattress. Where were you? Cosseted away in God's house, behind the thickest walls, when the blood was running wild? See. He has a look of pained smugness on his face. Everyone thinks I'm stupid. *My* trouble, *this* trouble – he presses a hangnailed finger to his chest – is because I ate a fork. A fucking fork.

If you don't want people to think you're stupid, you shouldn't eat forks. Sister Perpetué thinks this but does not say it. You ate a fork, which is the kind of thing a dog would do, and now you are dying like a dog. How does a person even eat a fork? Imagining the cold sapor of plated metal against the back of her throat makes her want to gag. The patient shifts on his mattress again, a shallow exhalation guttering into a hiss of pain.

She cannot help herself. It comes. You really ate a fork? she asks.

I'll tell you, little novice, the patient says. But I want some more of that stuff – he rolls his wide eyes toward the laudanum – and I want to piss.

Which first?

Piss first.

Sister Perpetué fetches the pail from underneath the bed and carefully rolls the patient on to his side. Halfway through this operation she becomes extremely conscious of the fact that she is touching him. She can feel the bone through the meagre, yielding flesh of his arm. *He is sick, like so many others,* she thinks to herself. *And it is our duty to care without discrimination.* But the senses will discriminate, even if the heart does not, and although there are very few abjections of the body the Sister has not had cause to see and to smell, there is something uniquely repellent about this man. She sees the sweat beading on his neck. Now he lies on his side and fumbles with his trousers, drawing his nightshirt up, and she sees also the folds of loose, stretched-out skin around his belly, like you see on the body of a woman who has borne children. When his member flops worm-like from under this lapel of flesh, she looks away. Urine spatters weakly in the pail. The patient groans. Then he laughs.

Oh, do I distress you, Sister? he asks. There is mockery in his voice.

When she turns back to take the pail away the patient has not covered himself, but lies there with his middle uncovered, grinning scampishly up at her, with his small nose and moon-shiny eyes, holding himself in his dirty hand as guilelessly as a child. Carefully, she disposes of the pail's contents. Threads of blood taint his dark, rancid-smelling urine. She will tell Doctor Tissier.

I asked, he says, do I distress you?

Sister Perpetué returns to the bedstead and rolls the patient on to his back. You seem to enjoy provoking revulsion, she says.

It's a living, says the patient. Do you know who I am?

You are a very sick man, she replies. I need know no more than that.

As Sister Perpetué reaches to rearrange the coverlet, he grasps at her wrist. I am Tarare, he says. The Great Tarare. The Glutton of Lyon. The Hercules of the Gullet. The Bottomless Man. The Beast. So I have been called, he says.

1778

In Tarare's village, everyone is your mother, as in everyone chides you if you dawdle, as in everyone boxes you if you are caught stealing. Everyone laughs at you if you fall over and skin your knee and cry like a girl, a boy who is really a girl. Everyone knows you are the bastard son of the dead man who pulled a knife on the Feast of Saint Lazare. *Get up Tarare! Two left feet. He'd trip over the Holy Ghost! Dumb as a calf at a doorway.*

Tarare is Tarare. Tarare is a name that means nothing, is a nonsense. For this reason, everyone remembers it – both curse and blessing. In the village, they say, *There is Tarare. There goes Tarare. Cute little bastard. Does he not know what he is?*

What he is is a happy child, although he has no special reason to be one. He greets every day in the village – which is really a collection of one-roomed cottages of daub and wood slumping around the stone church as though they are themselves at prayer – with a smile as blank and open as a hilltop. All who meet him comment on his jollity, which makes him beloved by most, and, because his happiness is so innocent, so seemingly egregious, despised by some. Who would claim the luxury of a big heart, or the bijou of a smile, when he is raised on a diet of boiled grass and stale bread? *He should rightly be miserable,* think those who despise him, *like I am.*

A big heart – Tarare has one and shows it carelessly. The sight of blood, or the sound of a death knell in the spire of the little stone church will cause tears to flow. He cries when the geese have their necks wrung. He cries when the lambs get to the wild cherry tree and poison themselves eating the hard pink windfall berries. People don't like it because a child's tears make them feel guilty for doing the things that they have to do. Things that aren't pretty, things that no one enjoys, but that nonetheless have to be done. Things like slitting throats and dubbing cockscombs. *Who does the boy think he is? SaintFuckingFrançois? Above the spilling of blood?*

One spring morning, a vagrant Auvergnate with a child clinging to her stinking skirts and another swelling under her apron comes begging at the cottage stoop. Tarare's mother is away washing smalls at the river, and Tarare gives the Auvergnate a whole loaf of bread and a flask of cider, and the Auvergnate goes away practically singing, calling out God bless Tarare! God and Our Lady watch over the little man! – and when Tarare's mother comes back he tells her proudly what he has done.

She beats him with a switch, then takes him to the abbé in the little stone church to be fixed.

The little stone church smells so good, of old waxed pine and sweet incense of balsam. His mother waits outside, huffing and stamping her foot, while Tarare, his face wet with tears and his backside blazing from the switch, settles into the pew beside the abbé. The abbé musses Tarare's hair and gives him a liard and tells him not to cry.

The spirit of charity is commendable, the abbé tells him. God loves a cheerful giver, it is true. And yet, beware of practising your righteousness before others in order that you might be seen by them, for then you will have no reward from Our Father who is in Heaven.

Tarare gazes at the old abbé uncomprehendingly, his upper lip shiny with snot.

The abbé sighs. And yet, he says, when the winter comes, one must howl with the wolves. Do you understand me, Tarare? One must howl with the wolves.

Tarare does not understand him.

Tarare's mother decides to become a whore, because what else could she become, besides blind from lacemaking in a cellar, or else syphilitic from nursing another woman's babies? Sometimes it is the men in the village she whores for, but it is better in the springtime when the itinerants come from the mountains, because if they have wives, she doesn't know their faces or their names.

The punters come to the cottage after night falls, smelling of beer and toil and peat, and Tarare's mother says Go outside, Tarare, as the baker or the wheelwright or the farmer's boy with the harelip sits on the mattress easing off his boots, Go outside and be quiet.

And Tarare does as he is told. Sometimes he sits on the kitchen step and counts the leaves of grass between his bare feet. Sometimes he sneaks away to the neighbour's sty to watch the pigs sleep, the dreams shifting in their plump, almost luminous bodies. Of what does a pig dream? he wonders. Of chestnuts and long summers, he thinks. Of running wild in the leaf-drunk light of the dead forests that had once covered everything, everything, from the mountains in the east to the sea far in the west, where the Kings of Joy with falcons on their fists and glass bells on their horses' bridles had ridden out to hunt. He knows the stories of the old times well. He has heard them told at the veillée by the women who were themselves very old, although still younger than the times they told stories of.

Perhaps, Tarare thinks, his father's father's father had watched this pig's father's father's father sleep, bristly and ancient, just like this. And time would pass and he would hear the baker or the wheelwright or the farmer's boy with the harelip slip out of the cottage through the back door, and he would go back inside and climb into bed beside his mother, the bed which now smelled of beer and toil and peat and something else, something Tarare didn't yet know to name, and his mother would pat his head and draw him in to her body and she would be so warm. The warmest thing Tarare knew.

He would climb up inside her if he could. Be just a curl of something, a bit of matter, enduring no disturbance but the sleepy beating of her most-known heart.

*

Sinful, says Sister Perpetué. To go on like that, to . . . to practise in such a manner, in a bed shared with her own child. She shakes her head. Her cheeks are flushed.

Where would you have had her *practise*? asks Tarare. In the fields? In the barns in the fields? In the market square? He sneers. The laudanum has made his eyes bright, and the corner of his lip curls downward, but his speech is fluent and his face is animated now that the pain is dulled. Needs must, he shrugs. And in the winter, when the cold came, with the rain and snow, I would pretend to be asleep when the men came and they would do it right next to me. I would lie as still as I could on the mattress, and they would rut and jostle there, right next to me. Sometimes I snuck a look through the tail of my eye and I would see them on top of her, pawing at her shift, patting their hands on her tits and their mouths on her neck, and I remember seeing that they, the men, had hair on their arses, just like the pigs did—

The chair squeals. Sister Perpetué rises to her feet, her whole face scarlet. Stop, she says.

The patient gazes up at her, seemingly abashed. My sincerest apologies, Sister, he says. I meant no offence. He inclines his patchy head.

Yes, you did, says Sister Perpetué. You enjoy the discomfort you provoke, she says, it is quite clear to me. Besides, she adds, knitting her hands in front of her body, I don't see what this has to do with the fork.

I told you it was a long story, Tarare pouts.

And full of sin, I expect?

Oh, every kind you can imagine. Probably some you can't. Then again – his eyes trail down her body. He chuckles from his dry throat. I've heard stories about nuns.

Tentatively, Sister Perpetué draws the chair back in. She must remember the manacle around his wrist, and his livid, bleeding gums. What is in front of her is a cannibal, a killer. Perhaps only a few days left before he arrives in Hell to brazen fanfare, to have his heart opened out by rotten teeth, again and again, forever, where frightful black fire burns. She feels a chill. Outside in the court the bell is rung again. Two, three in the morning? She could not say.

I like stories, says the killer.

Some can be edifying, Sister Perpetué concedes. But Mother Superior says the peasants pay too much mind to their tales of giants and talking foxes and not enough to the word of God. They lack, she says, for spiritual nourishment, as much as for any other kind.

Your Mother Superior sounds like a cunt, says the killer.

I can leave, you know, snaps Sister Perpetué, half-rising from the seat—

Sorry, sorry, he mutters, splaying his palms in submission.

Sister Perpetué realises that more than anything, the patient, the killer, does not want to be left alone. He wants to be listened to, to disburden himself in some way. She sinks back into her chair. It occurs to her, with a vertiginous rush, that not only could she leave him all alone with his stories of sin and his mocking looks, but she could do anything else she wanted to him, too. They are alone in that little room, that cell. She could get on top of him and fuck him. She could jugulate him with the shiny scalpel that rests by the bedside. It is a good feeling, but she doesn't like that she has it. She wonders if priests ever have a like feeling when they are called to deathbeds. She doesn't suppose she will ever know.

I can send for a priest – she says – if you wish to—

Oh, Christ, no, groans the patient. Just sit.

So she sits.

The killer moistens his lips. Have you ever heard the tale of the Peasant La Ramée? he asks.

She shakes her head.

The killer smiles. Long ago there was a princess, he says. As you would expect, she was beautiful, and very rich . . . and as you might not, with her wealth and her great beauty, she was sad and serious. Her father, the King, worried. He paid acrobats and jesters in pied jackets to come from all over the land to entertain her, and bought green-feathered parrots who spoke, who told her jokes. But none of these things could lift her spirits. None of these things even raised a smile on her lovely sour face. So the King sent out a letter across the land, and the letter said that any man who could make the princess laugh could marry her and live in the castle, and would someday be king. And the dukes and the counts rode in from all over the country with bells on their hats, and cloth puppets, and their best jokes scribbled down and stuffed in their pockets. They lined up in the King's great hall and one after the other they performed their mummers' shows and stumbled through their jokes. But the princess didn't laugh. She didn't even smile, to see all these great men of the kingdom showing their painted arses and walking on their hands. And last of all, there came a peasant – the killer smiles here – there came a peasant, just like me, and he was called La Ramée. And he was dirty and he stank. He stood there among the perfumed lords and he scratched his beard, and out from it jumped a hundred little black fleas. La Ramée whispered to the fleas, and up they jumped on to the King, and on to the courtiers, and on to the lords, and they began to bite them all over, and dash about under their fine clothes, so the King and the courtiers and the lords screeched and began to dance, dance wildly, slapping at their jewelled sides, shaking and wobbling their bellies. And the princess smiled. Then the princess howled with laughter.

So La Ramée won the princess's hand?

No! laughs the killer. The King will not abide his daughter marrying a peasant! So he reneges on his word, welches on his deal. He chooses a fine foreign prince and tells his daughter she must marry him instead. But when the princess objects, the King proposes a new game: both the prince and La Ramée will spend a night in bed with the princess, and afterwards she can choose whomever she likes best. After all, this King is thinking, what princess could abide the touch of a stinking peasant, so covered in fleas? La Ramée goes first, and all is well enough. The second night it is the prince's turn. The peasant La Ramée waits. He waits until they get going, then he whispers to his fleas, and sends them under the door of the princess's chamber, on to the bed, and then straight up the prince's arsehole. The next morning, the prince looks embarrassed and the princess flustered. Did you enjoy your evening? asks the King. Is not the prince a fine and virile man? The princess shrugs. I don't know, Father, says she – he seemed a little overexcitable. You would think he had never been with a woman before!

Sister Perpetué laughs, despite herself. She may be a Sister of Charity, but she is no innocent. She has seen the groundskeeper and the laundry girl at work on each other behind the outbuildings. She gets the idea.

How is that – the killer says, smiling triumphantly – for spiritual nourishment?

Very poor indeed, says Sister Perpetué. There is no moral to it whatsoever.

I don't know, says the killer. La Ramée is clever, you see. He uses the gifts God gave him.

God gave him fleas?

God gave him guile.

That he uses in a deception, counters Sister Perpetué.

That he uses, says the killer, to right a wrong that is done to him. The King reneged on his word, after all. The killer settles back into his pillow, grinning.

Well, says Sister Perpetué. I will admit that it is an amusing story, if not a very edifying one. Where did you learn it?

Can't remember. Can you read?

Yes.

Can you write?

I've never tried. Maybe.

Perhaps you can write my story down somewhere. He closes

his eyes and tents his hands over his chest, with a chuckle. *The Great Tarare.* My own little blue book for sale at Monsieur Dessein's. It would please me.

The memoirs of a cannibal, she thinks. But who would wish to read such a thing?

1780

The summer of 1780 is a hideous summer. Every second hour of the night a person wakes up half-stifled. Beyond the shade of the beech trees, nailed to the white-hot cross of the sun – which will remit itself only to hailstorm – haircracks of blue electricity flicker over the mountains. The nettles throw their spined arms windward, the sheep scream in the meadows. The storms drop stones as big as quails' eggs.

Tarare lies awake all night to a noise like iron-shod demons jumping on the roof while his mother and the vintner the slaughterman the porter rut on the mattress beside him, whispering disgusting things in each other's ears.

The hail tears the ripening vines from the trellises and breaks the grain. The heat of the morning cooks the battered fruit of their summer's labour where it lies in the field, so that every garden and every orchard smells like a compôte. Black flies rove in thick swarms over this unprecedented feast, murmurations almost solid, and children drop their toys in the road and run when they hear the drone of their approach. The baker is struck on the head with a hailstone and *dies*. Actually *dies*. It is a death so infelicitous, so darkly jinxed-seeming, that there is hardly any weeping at his funeral, just nervous laughter and wide, uncomprehending eyes. And everyone, in their sprigged cottons and Sunday hats, lines up to kiss the baker's widow and the baker's orphan, then goes away as quickly as they can.

Tarare's mother is pregnant again. She lets out her three gowns. She takes no men to her bed – or perhaps none want her – with the new thing puffing under her flesh. So there is no meat, not even tripe. Tarare tramps in his clogs to the edge of the wood at the bottom of the village, where the metallic light of July is dappled, softer, and there he gathers acorns and sorrel and clover to pad their groats (the clover gives him bellyaches, but bellyaches are better than the pangs of hunger, he supposes). He begs a bruised capon from a lanky man who returns from market with a brace on his shoulder. They make a week's feast of the tender grass-fed meat. A little fat, a little lard, black bread.

One bright September morning, Tarare wakes to find the mattress sopping wet. His mother is positioned in a splay-kneed hunch, and she puffs out her cheeks, and she says Tarare, Tarare – go now Tarare, fetch the midwife, and the neighbour-woman. Quickly.

And Tarare does as he is bidden. The midwife and the neighbour-woman and the neighbour-woman's sister all come, with looks of sardonic amusement on their faces. They send Tarare out, and he skulks around the garden, by the onion patch for a little while, chewing on stems, listening to his mother's moaning, her Mother Mary! Her Shit-shit-shit, agh! – and then he goes down to the stream to find spadefoot toads to pet and be kind to. He returns in the evening with three acorns, a newt and a rusted ladies' shoe buckle in his pocket, to find that he has a sister. A newt and a sister in the same day! His excitement is palpable. He goes to kiss his mother on her sweaty forehead and she tells him to leave her alone, she is tired.

This time it is the dog that eats the afterbirth.

The midwife holds the baby, and the neighbour-woman and

the neighbour-woman's sister all huddle around to get a good look, but they can apprehend no firm evidence of authorship in the infant's pink and shrivelled face.

Shame, sighs the midwife. We'll have to wait until she's older.

So Tarare's mother decides to become a wet nurse, because what else can she become, besides blind from lacemaking in a cellar? The meneur comes from the city in a big cart pulled by a beautiful piebald pony, and hands over two more babies, trussed and dozing, to Tarare's mother. She will be paid ten livres each to care for them until they are three years old, or until they die, whichever comes first.

They'll be asleep for a little while yet, says the meneur, pressing his tricorn on to his head and climbing back into the cart. I gave them some wine to stop them squalling on the road.

Tarare's mother takes the babies into the house, one under each arm. Tarare stays by the wagon. He strokes the piebald pony's cheek. I like your horse, he tells the meneur.

It isn't a horse, idiot, says the meneur, spitting at the verge.

I like it anyway, says Tarare, rubbing his cheek against the piebald's soft velveteen nose. Where do babies come from? he asks.

The meneur laughs and grabs at his reins. From the loose cunts of Lyon, boy, he says. Can't work a loom with a whelp at tit.

What's a loom?

It's a giant spider made of wood, says the meneur. You should hear the roar of them in the afternoons, eh, on the Croix-Rousse? A thousand thousand spiders, spitting lovely silks and nipping off girls' fingers. The meneur laughs and slaps at his knee. If he knew how to write, he would have done – well, and long into the night.

What's a cunt?

You, says the meneur. I'm leaving now. If I give you a liard, will you let go of my pony, little cunt? Or I'll run you over. Crush your little cunt feet. Either way, doesn't bother me.

And the meneur gives Tarare a liard and Tarare watches the cart roll away into the afternoon sunshine, along the wide white road that leads north, straight as a chine. He wants very much to follow, to walk his cunt feet all the way to see the wooden spiders of the city of Lyon. But he can't, because he is too young. Instead he goes back inside the house and prises up a floorboard in the corner to hide his liard in his usual hiding place, with the rusted ladies' shoe buckle and the dead newt.

And soon it is winter again, and everyone thinks everything is going to get worse forever, because it certainly won't get better or stay the same. An immutable law of nature being – as gentlemen-scholars of Paris are saying at this time – flux. The price of bread rises. The harvest is scarcely large enough to be named such because of the summer storms, and because the men, when they should have been in the fields, were called away by the Seigneur to fix a toy bridge on his estate. The black bird-women of the veillée curse the Seigneur and spit into the flickering fire. They curse the Seigneur's well-fed wife and children too, in their pale tabby silks, with their toy bridge and their toy dogs and their five-course dinners. They curse, and see in their minds' eyes rose petals and roast meats and sweet-flavoured jellies that glow from within. Their hungry mouths water round their bitter curses. When the law allowed the Seigneur to slay two – only two – serfs on his ride back from the hunt, and to cool his feet in the blood that ran from their opened bellies, at least this brutality was honest. Swift and summary. At least you knew where you stood with your betters when you bled for them.

The harvest is so bad that the older children are deemed to be no longer children, and are sent away to the city. Ten sous or twenty sous or whatever can be spared is pressed into their hands with ceremony, reverence. Misspelled prayers for the blessing of Saint Cristophe, who carries the blessed on his shoulders, are pinned to their jackets and shawls. Mothers and fathers monitor this deracination, watch as their young ones dwindle propitiously in the fog of the horizon, and hope that something sticks, that they don't return in the spring, the boys lamed or drunk or boxed up in unvarnished board caskets. The girls pregnant by who knows who from Adam, all their crisp country beauty chewed on and spat out. That they might send a little of their wages home is too great a thing to hope. That they might find someone who would pay them wages in the first place is just about conceivable. Tarare watches them go as well, and he is jealous, because he knows that they will see – perhaps even befriend – the giant wooden spiders in the city, those 'looms' that the meneur spoke of.

And then it is winter, which means, for most, *hunger*. Which means for all the heavy snow covering over the rooftops, with its sculptural silence, and the roads hidden away, and the horizon folded up in white. A hard winter in the valleys is mortal in the hills, and indigents pass through the village in joyless processional, with skinny goats and with tambourines tied to their belts. The dead lie in the hedgerows, rosaries clenched in their embrittled fists, and you say a Pater when you pass one by. Maybe even take the boots off their feet if the boots look good enough to sell or to have for yourself. No one likes it. It's just how things are.

In the little cottage Tarare shares with his mother, three babies are crying all the time. Then, one bright morning in early November, when the frost branches in renewed mycelial splendour across the puddles in the road, just two babies are crying.

Tarare's mother lifts the dead one from its bed of straw. Her face is pale. The baby's face is paler. Stiff as a board, she mutters, her breath clouding even inside the cottage. Tarare stirs the embers in the grate. Must have died in the night, she says. From the cold.

Is it my sister? Tarare asks.

Tarare's mother is digging about in the linen chest, and does not answer.

Is it my sister who is dead? he repeats.

Get the fire going, she non-answers.

Tarare does as he is told, feeling the chill bite of tears at the bottom of his eyes as the embers jump and catch. Death had been there among them in the night, and the dog hadn't barked, and no one had noticed death and told it to go away. He imagines death gliding silently in through the door. Death stroking his mother's yellow hair, death prising up the loose floorboard in the corner to examine his treasures, his rusted ladies' shoe buckle, the rumpled picture of Monsieur Americain, Benjamin Franklin, that the vintner had given him, clipped from an old gazette (in the picture, Monsieur Americain wears a kind smile and a periwig on his head, fluffy and silver as rain cloud).

It is so easy if you're death.

Tarare's mother wraps the stiff little body up. An apron for a shroud. She is pretending she doesn't care now. She can even pretend she planned it, if she chooses. Well, she says. Gone to Jesus and Mary. She drops her smock from her shoulder and finds another mouth for her chapped nipple. Tonight, Tarare – she says, as the baby suckles – you'll wait until it's dark and then carry her up the wood. Cover her over with leaves and snow. A bit of luck and the foxes will find her before anyone else does. Do you hear me, Tarare?

Tarare crouches by the grate with his arms tight around his knees. Is it my sister – he asks, one last time – that died?

You do not have a sister, Tarare, his mother answers. You never had a sister. There are two little ones come from the city, and two little ones will go back. Do you understand me, Tarare?

Tarare understands. Tarare never had a sister. He nods.

(And the little body that Tarare obediently carries up to the wood by night, and duly covers over with slimy dead leaves and hard-packed snow, is not, in point of fact, the body of his sister at all. But when Tarare's mother speaks Tarare listens: he does not have a sister. Ergo his sister has died, ergo this little body covered over with slimy dead leaves and hard-packed snow is his sister. He weeps over her, tears blazing on his cheeks as he crouches in the cold winter wood. This error – this misbereavement – will follow him for all his life, even as his true sister, his blood sister, flourishes, unknown to him, elsewhere.)

And far away to the north, a prince is born. He is born in a room where pale sun falls on ashes-of-rose panels, where plumes and compressed bosoms quiver in the powder-scented air. They raise their croziers and crack their painted fans over Louis Joseph Xavier François, the child of France. They lay over his tiny gurgling body the sapphire sash of the Holy Ghost.

And though the nights are cold and dark, there is rejoicing in Tarare's village too. A great fire is lit again, and the last of the cider drunk, and they eat sheep's tongue with black pudding and soft yellow apples. Tarare sits by the fire with his mother and listens to the old women telling their stories about clever hares, and a giant in a dress of heavy iron chains, and a little once-upon-a-time girl who had a little once-upon-a-time doll that shat lumps of gold.

And the fire burns until All Saints', and the braver boys jump over the embers, calling Long Live the King Long Live the Dauphin curse the millers curse the taxmen.

*

The patient's brow creases, and he turns his head toward the wall, where he stares for a long time, as though there were a window set into the stone. He looks sad. It is the first time that Sister Perpetué has seen him host to an emotion, she thinks. A real one.

You will like the next part, he says, eventually. I find God, after a fashion.

That is good, answers Sister Perpetué. The Lord is the greatest comfort to a troubled soul.

He looks at her again, an insolent gleam in his eyes. But I don't suppose, Sister, he says, that you have ever sampled the alternatives? And so you cannot say with any authority that *the Lord is the greatest comfort to a troubled soul*. Greater than food, or fucking, or jumping over fires? Even fighting. Peasants like to fight, like to raise a little hell, because it is exciting. Because it makes them feel real, for a moment. It makes them feel real when they are doing it, cracking bones and making blood flow.

She cringes. He notices this.

I know what you have heard said about me, and it isn't true, he says. Never did I drink human blood, except my own. And never have I eaten a fucking – a fucking – here he pauses to gasp for breath, dropping his free hand on to his breast, over his heart – I swear. By the Lady. I am no danger to anyone.

Then why, she asks, have they chained you to the bed?

Because I'm going to die, he says, with a rueful smile, and when I do, they're going to cut me open so they can see how my insides work. They wanted to before, when I was a soldier, but I ran away before they could. So this time they are making sure I can't run away.

Who wants to cut you open? No one here wishes you harm. I assure you—

The doctors, he answers. Your Citizen-Doctor Tissier.

But you came here of your own volition, she says. You came to the hospital.

Shit, he says. I was going to die either way. I thought, I should try to die in comfort – here he flicks his eyes toward the laudanum, grins – I should try to die – here he opens out his arms as far as he is able, with a little wince of pain – among friends. Perhaps, he muses, bringing his hands to rub at his trunk, they will keep some of my parts. Like a saint.

The idea of this seems to amuse him.

Don't be foolish, she says. The Citizen-Doctor is making every effort to ensure your recovery. (She says this, but she knows there is a cellar in the hospital where swollen glands float in a sterile fluid like weird lunar fruits, and where a baby that was born with two heads is kept, with a deep red scar around his – their? – conjoint necks.)

And why would he do that? the patient asks. I am a peasant. Hundreds like me die every day in the bread lines, in the ditch, and no one stirs to save them. Have you been to Paris? They say Englishmen faint from the stench of the streets. Peasants. Citizens of the Republic. Whatever name you give them, they are dead. No, he sighs, tenting his fingers over his chest – I am for Hell. All that remains is to make my confession. Perhaps a few good satisfying shits. He chuckles weakly.

You say you found God?

He looks at her, confused.

The next part, she says. You said you found God, after a fashion.

Ah, he says. Yes. I felt I had a secret, you see, after my sister died and I hid her in the wood. In the winter we went to church, went to mass, because we had nothing better to do with the ground frozen up. You should have seen it – the services a dumbshow, everyone standing up and sitting down at the wrong times. In the pew beside my mother. Wrap my hand in her shawl – he closes one hand around the other as he speaks – I remember the smell of her shawl. Like sheep after rain. The incense, too, so rich. And the abbé said his words and they struck at me, this time. Of God's infinite mercy and the Passion. I listened. How the sin of the village was attendant upon our great poverty. Poverty of the body, poverty of the soul. It made me feel sicker and sicker with my secret, but also like a man, you see? To have a secret that burned in me with such low fire only the saints could see. I went around the village very seriously, clinging at my rosary. People laughed at me. *There goes Tarare, the little bastard. He'll be a big bastard soon, eh? Just like his father, God rest the fool. Remember Jean-Louis, huh, with the big feet? Remember when Armand slammed his dick in the wine shop door? Better times.* Because it was a rotten winter, really rotten. They said it was because the King made love to the Protestants. And I had never seen a Protestant at that time, and I did not rightly know what a Protestant was, and I remember that I imagined a Protestant was a man who pulled a little snow-cloud behind him on an iron chain like a dog. The patient chuckles inwardly. Then he winces, then he pauses. All this was before Nollet, he says.

Nollet?

Nollet, the patient repeats, massaging his chest. Nollet Nollet. I will get to that. I will get to him. He came after that winter broke. And all the people and their pigs came out of their houses and set to their ploughing. We made the abbé sprinkle holy water on the furrows that spring, though he said it was base superstition he ought not to indulge. And things grew, although not enough things – never enough things—

1782

The stream runs through the hills at the top of the village, fringed by alder trees. The children go to play there, spreading their lousy clothes on the scree and poking at the toads with sharpened sticks. Tarare goes to the stream as well when he has finished his work early. He strips his trousers from his backside and wades into the cool water with a wild shout. It feels so good to him, to lie back in the torpid flow and feel the grime slough from his body. To stand and wheel his skinny arms in circles, tickling at the water's soft skin.

The other children do not want to play with Tarare, never want to play with Tarare. Their mothers tell them not to play with him because his own mother is/was a whore, but the children ignore their mothers and decide not to play with Tarare on their own terms, because Tarare is weird on his own terms. He is, to begin with, too tall – at ten years old, he outstrips most of his peers by a good head.

His height might have endeared him to the older boys, who liked to stand waist-deep in the water comparing things for size – feet, muscles, cocks – if it was not for the mildness of his character, strung along on every timid shift of his bony lineaments, bared in the fallow of his eyes. Tarare does not mind. Tarare's joy in the world is huge and autogamous. Soaking his skinny legs in the stream, he watches the other children cheerfully – the little girls piling stones on the bank, the boys wading mid-stream to kick sudden rainbows into the sunshine, all their bodies variously hollowed by winter and purpled by fathers' fists – and feels no real desire to wed his joy to theirs. It is enough. He is enough.

When the sun sinks and a chill begins to tint the air, red-cheeked Tarare gathers up his clothes and walks back through the village, where the doves are suckling in the eaves. There are men asleep in their chairs outside the wineshop with their hats pulled down low over their eyes. The bees are awake now, and have come to browse among the raggedy flowers. He sees the biggest cat in the village – who is therefore the *best* cat in the village – hunting the miniature filaments of spring, the pollens and motes that spread themselves across the meadows this time of year. The hunt is like a dance. Tarare watches as the cat bounds from beneath a cart, rears on his haunches, rakes the air with his paws. Then the cat goes low, and his white fur rises in a kinetic bristle.

From the top of the hill Tarare looks down to the cottage and sees his mother's crimson headwrap catch in the sun as she bends at the garden gate, sweeping an infant up into her arms. She is all red and white, broad shoulders shaking as she laughs. She is speaking to – and laughing with – a man. A man in a long, dirty coat with a tricorn hat.

Nollet is not Tarare's real father. This he understands. His real father, Tarare knows, is not only dead, but would be shamed by the many instances of Tarare's disobedience and wickedness, had he been alive to see them. So his mother says. But what is Nollet? Nollet is a man of intentionally indeterminate origin – accent Gascon, patois Auvergnat – and no small vanity about his brandy-coloured hair, tied with ribbon in a shiny tail at the back of his thick neck. He is a man who leaves 'on business' in the evening, after dinner and his post-prandial pipe, and returns in the watered glow of the morning, dead leaves crusting his gaiters, a tune on his pouting lips and the musk of bandits' hillside fires under his armpits. He knows bird calls and legerdemain, and that women like his foxy close-lipped smile and the thick brown curls that thatch his knotted flesh from yellow neckerchief to thick waist. He looks like a farm boy for two days after he shaves, and like a devil when he neglects to.

A light comes from Nollet's person, and it is the light of self-possession. His eyes reflect a world to be despoiled, or, at best, dishonestly participated in.

The first thing Nollet says to Tarare, at the garden gate on that fine April evening, as Tarare clings to his mother's skirt and tilts his doleful blue eyes up at this stranger, is: Jesus, this valley has good soil for the growing of a boy, eh? A fine fellow. Hello, little Tarare. Hello, not-so-little Tarare.

Tarare says nothing, until his mother taps her thumb against his cheek. Don't be rude, poucet, she says. This is Monsieur Nollet. He is from the city.

Monsieur Nollet lowers on to his haunches. *Hey*, he says, and his hand shoots out toward Tarare. When he withdraws it there is a liard between his forefinger and thumb. He presents the coin to Tarare with a genial laugh. There is dirt under his fingernails.

Tarare balks and clings more mutely to his mother's sleeve until she buffets him again, hisses *take the coin, Tarare* – Tarare has observed how money, however insignificant the amount, makes the people in his village strange and shrill, abrupt. Tarare takes the coin and squeezes it tight in his fist, and he wonders, what is this man-in-a-yellow-neckerchief come to his village, and for what does he bend and scrape at the garden gate, and talk to his mama? His mama who is pink-cheeked and tucking a wisp of hair behind her ear.

Nollet comes and Nollet does not leave. Then he does leave, and returns again a week later, after nightfall, in a cart, accompanied by a lazy-eyed man in an equally dirty overcoat. The new man has a black beard and a protuberant lump in his throat, like he has swallowed a shoe last. Nollet and the lazy-eyed man come into the house and, by the light of a single candle, begin to lift the floorboards. Then they bring from the cart two dozen wrapped packets about the size and shape of bricks, which they stow beneath the floorboards before nailing them down again. They keep close watch on the door while this is done.

Tarare watches this mysterious procedure from the bed, tucked between the belching infants.

The boy sees, says Lazy-Eye to Nollet. The boy knows not to tell?

Easy, Nollet replies. The boy's a half-wit, a goose. Doesn't know what he's seeing to tell of. Has as many thoughts in his head as a toad does feathers on his back.

Little jugs have big ears, says the lazy-eyed stranger. He meets Tarare's gaze, grins, and raises a finger to his lips: *ssh*. Then he gives Tarare's mother a purse and an appreciative nod of the head, tucks his collar up around his face, and leaves through the back door.

Tarare closes his eyes and pretends to fall asleep again, listening to the quiet voices of Nollet and his mother over the tickling sound of shifting, piling coins.

There are fifty sous here, Vincent, whispers his mother.

I know, says Nollet. There will be more.

Fifty sous, Vincent!

Buy yourself a hat.

Their talk stops and Tarare hears chair legs squeal against the floorboards. Grunting, and the fumbling of a belt buckle.

Tarare half-opens his eyes. Nollet is sat at the kitchen table, his head thrown back and his expression supine in the candle-light, a twist of smoke rising from his pipe. He groans. Tarare's mother is bent between Nollet's skewed knees. Her head moves hungrily. Nollet's hand is twisted into her pale hair.

And now there are five of them living in the little cottage. Five of them, plus dog plus pig. Tarare loves pig, with her mild, intelligent brown eyes. He loves dog, with his bottle-brush tail and beard of mange. But he cannot love Nollet, who comes and goes as he pleases with his dirty greatcoat and his walking stick and his yellow neckerchief and his satchel at his hip. Always with his blackguard grin, always with his quips.

The babies reach the age where they will put everything that they can grasp with their hands in their mouths. Spiders and dirt, fistfuls of grass – the whole world a festival of innocent mastication. They toddle, they blurp, they pull at the dog's tail, they coocoo in their uncommitted sleep. Tarare's mother sighs with relief and massages her ulcerated nipples, which have done their duty by the Children of France. Soon the infants will be sent back to the city, and Tarare will be happy to see the back of them. More Mama for him! he thinks – but then, there is Nollet.

And then, too, there is a scorch of famine in the wind, and the crows skating low over the meadows. Tarare's head is so full of worries that not even looking at the picture cut from the gazette of the good Monsieur Americain, Benjamin Franklin, with his kind smile, will reassure him.

Once a week, Nollet strips to the waist and takes a sharp

knife and a little shimmer of broken mirror and he sits in front of the fire to shave. Tarare will watch, if he can. He sees that Nollet's chest is covered in thick curly hair. He sees that Nollet has thick, sinewy arms. It makes something nameless move in him. Something roll down his front like a shiver, to see Nollet like this. It is how he knows that Nollet has a scar, raised and white on his shoulder, and shaped like a word (Tarare knows what words are, though he is certain they are not, and will never be, for him). The signification of this word-scar preoccupies him. He takes a stick and scratches it in the dust by the onion patch from memory. He takes a piece of dry charcoal from the hearth and draws it on a scrap of cotton:

GAL

A broken horseshoe, a short house with a pointed roof, a scythe resting against a wall. Tarare needs time to consider this, to turn these mysterious objects over in his mind. Perhaps string them along a story that might account for Nollet. Or rather, for all the Nollets. There is the Nollet who ruffles Tarare's hair and gives him liards, who comes in the evening and catches his mother by her waist and kisses and kisses her neck until she bats him away, blushing – and there is another Nollet, whose name Tarare does not know, half-fused with the sullenness of the big bad of the night he slinks in from three days later than he said he would, with livid rings underneath his eyes. He needs the bed, needs to rest, he will say. And will tolerate no disturbance. And then you walk so lightly, as if on a bed of glass. A door is closed too loudly, a dog barks at a goose or a drunk cackles in the street, and out of the house will come Nollet, shiny hair in disarray and red cock swinging loose beneath his nightshirt, looking for a throat to grasp or a face to spit in. Sometimes Tarare's throat, sometimes Tarare's face.

Nollet does not like to be woken up and Nollet does not like to be proven wrong. When he is woken up he will use his fists, but when he is proven wrong he will simply stew, cultivating a petulant and pointed silence that fills whatever corner of the room he occupies like a stink. This is Nollet. Then there is the Nollet who teaches Tarare how to hit with a closed fist, how to draw a daisy in the snow with a stream of hot piss. This is also Nollet. All these different things are Nollet. He puts Tarare in mind of a Harlequin in a tricolour suit, red and white and black by turns. Bells jingling above a blood-coloured mouth.

*

What was it that they hid under the floorboards? she asks.

Salt, says the killer. Pounds and pounds of the stuff.

Sister Perpetué's tired eyes meet the killer's, bloodshot, and they both laugh. They laugh together for a spell, remembering there was a time when people smuggled salt. That was just a thing that people did, that happened in the old days, when the country had a different name. When men with jewelled swords and white perruques drove the peasants to smuggle salt, as though it were cantharides or gunpowder. The killer brings a hand to wipe at the corner of his eye, still grinning. No, he says, no. It's not funny. Well, it is – *white gold*, Nollet called it.

There was so much profit in it?

Oh, he says. Very much. They would buy across the border, over the mountains. Then through the forest, down the water-ways by night, north and south – he traces a hangnail through the air as though marking a route on a map – packed into their boots, sewn into the hems of their jackets, in apple barrels and

onion sacks. It was going on everywhere. They'd pay little girls
to line their skirts with it.

Everyone needs salt, I suppose.

Everyone needs salt, the killer agrees. Life is miserable without salt. It's miserable with salt – but maybe more bearably so.
That was why it was clever, because everyone needs salt. And
because even though you sold it at a higher price than you
bought it for, the higher price was still lower than the lawful
price, so people felt you were doing them a favour – though
you might profit by it, they profit too.

Because you bear the risk on their behalf, she says.

How old are you?

Nineteen.

Then you would be too young to remember, he says. Yes.
Caught once and you were fined, but a second time – hanging.
Breaking on the wheel if they found a weapon on you. He
grimaces. I used to have bad dreams about that. Bad dreams,
red dreams. Mama and Nollet lashed down and spinning like
tops, big birds with spindles for beaks. He rubs his neck. So
that was life then. Nollet, and a firelock in the kitchen cupboard. The tumbrils coming and going, floorboards prised up
and nailed down, Mama always with an eye on the door. I had
bad dreams. I had everything else I wanted. What we wanted,
Nollet bought us. Meat. Stockings.

And your appetite, Sister Perpetué begins – how ought she
to put it? How can it even be phrased? . . . And you ate—?

The killer kisses his teeth and swivels his blue glooming eyes
toward her. Everyone is a part-animal, of course. She thought
The Great Tarare would be a wolf, but what he is, she thinks, is
largely fish – silvered belly upturned, limp and pathetic beyond
his natural element. Gasping bottom-feeder. I ate, he says, no

more or less than a growing boy ought. I liked eggs, and I liked cream, and biscuits with sugar.

Then, then how is it that—

The manacle grinds against the bed frame as the killer moves his body. You wish me, he wheezes, to account for myself? To tell you why I am what I am? In the old days they would have said – some still would, perhaps – that there was a curse put on me. His mouth trembles as he looks at her. But I can't. I can't tell you why, I can only tell you how. I don't know the word for what I am. Is there a word for what I am? Is it written somewhere? Did they tell it to you, the word, before they sent you to attend to me? I – I – don't—

—and his speech dissolves in a tearful cringe. He presses the back of his manacled hand against his eyes and turns away from her on to his side, where he tries, with a whine of pain, to draw his knees up against his chest, to curl into himself, like a child. His smock rides up at the back and Sister Perpetué, who has never made anyone cry before, sees where his vertebrae press against the freckled skin of his back, like the seam of a bean.

She is moved to pity – or at least part-way. She reaches out a hand to touch his shoulder. He is mewling gently, the chained man, chained creature. With a sniff, he shifts, turns back toward her. His eyes, that are themselves like sources of a dim pelagic light, are glazed. Here – he says, peremptorily – and, taking her hand in his, he draws it up toward the back of his head. With surprising strength he compels her, until her hand is cradled around the back of his skull, as though she were raising it, like the good Samaritan did the denuded traveller's, to enable him to take a drink of water. Her body is leant fully out of the chair by the bedside and across his own. *Feel*, he says.

And she feels. At first, the texture of his light, stringy hair, and the cool sweat of his patchy scalp, which disgusts her. Then, at the back of his head, a lump, a smooth raised pleat, a suture that the hair grows around. She works her fingers along its length, from the base of his neck to the highest point of his skull. A scar, broad and deep and long, at the soft root of the brain.

The killer releases her hand. There, he says. That is your short answer. You feel it?

Oh yes, she feels it. How? she asks.

A gift from Papa Nollet, he says.

She can smell his acetose breath, feel the sickly heat of his expiration below her. And then his tongue, and then his teeth. With a cry she shambles backward, away from the bed, beyond the range of his chained wrist. The killer is laughing, laughing uproariously, yipping like a bandog, his face creased around a Devil-grin. She touches a hand to her face, to the edge of her jaw, moistened with spittle, to confirm she didn't imagine it. He actually *bit* her.

The killer catches his breath. Only a nibble, he gulps. How many men can say they have bitten a nun? – and he begins to laugh again.

He could have sunk his teeth into her and ripped a chunk of flesh away. Easily. He did not. Nonetheless, she is rattled by her carelessness, shaking with indignation. Literally shaking – she feels her body hum with fright in her stiff black habit as she plants her hands on her hips. She sets her face as she watches the killer laugh, waiting for his convulsions to subside. And when they do, she says: You have abused my trust and have taken a wretched liberty. I see now why you are chained. In view of your behaviour, I will recommend to the Citizen-Doctor that your restraints be increased.

The killer wipes a finger at the tail of his eye and forms his face into an expression of perplexed indignation. Oh, come off it, he says. It was a joke. I thought we were friends now. Can we not joke with each other, as friends do?

I am not your friend, Sister Perpetué replies, and I did not find it amusing. In fact, I have not found any of your jokes, nor your careless blasphemies, amusing. You are telling me these stories so that I will pity you, so that I will think you hard done by, and I do not believe you. You are not a victim. You are a vile, unpleasant man.

He rolls his blue doleful eyes toward her. Can I not, asks The Great Tarare, be both?

*

You have known Tarare now for some years, and what you have begun to suspect ought to be confirmed: that from Tarare, you will have no unexpected acts of heroism, nor observations of startling genius. Nor was he built for love. Yes, he will fuck – in the shades of a dovecote near Croissy, smeared with blood and feathers, casually gathered against a wall in Paris while Foulon swings from the fateful lamp-iron, his mouth stuffed with straw – but that is all.

To say something good of Tarare, it is perhaps enough to note that he was curious about the world and all within it, and that this curiosity engendered a kind of love. It is perhaps enough to say that there was no true cruelty in his character.

If history is a stone lion, Tarare is the ivy that fills its mouth.

1788

Lady Day

Seasons roll on the gusts, with their Saints' Days, with their various toils. The worms rise through the earth after the rains. The hawks and kites circle over the watermeadows in sleepy lingering shapes, as though they love themselves, and love to watch their reflections dip and soar in the smooth water. The price of bread rises.

Tarare grows and Tarare fills out, an overripe fruit. A sparse gingerish stubble prickles on his chin. In the summer months he spends his nights alone in the garden, wrapped in a blanket and overspread with stars, where he falls asleep imagining that girls are touching him, and that boys are touching him too. He wakes up, his face wet from morning dew, with a dry mouth and a hard cock. There is that smell to him that some boys have on the threshold of manhood – sweating crotch, foaming horse, a dairy in July.

His regular lustrations in the stream running through the hills at the top of the village – where the other boys and girls strip off their dirty clothes and strew them on the pebbles – are enlivened by a fresh signification, a newly discovered responsiveness to the bare and white and bruised and tender meat of it all, before beheld in innocence. He stands waist-deep in the flow as before, circling his arms around his body, and below the cool skin of the water he tingles and stiffens, tingles and stiffens for Hervé, for Hélène, for Gaston, for Louise, the milfoil clutching at his skinny ankles in possessive-caressing loops. That the world around him could change – in a trembling moment, tint itself with devastating lushness, reconfigure in an arrangement of almost frightening beauty – is something that Tarare has known for as long as he has known anything. But that Tarare's inner world would deepen and complicate, delivering him into states of shuddering pleasure so close to pain, was something no one ever bothered to tell him. It filled him with joy and excitation for the future. If, by fifteen, his soul had matured to an understanding of pleasure, then perhaps by twenty he could finally understand God, as the old black bird-women of the veilleé doubtless did, fondling their rosaries, creaking so intimately with Saintes Isidore and Agathe.

But his visits to the stream, where he reaches for the face of God, are rare now, because he is big and robust enough to join the real business of the village. The lifting and carrying, the ploughing the planting the hammering. For a sou, Tarare is anyone's for the afternoon – *takes after his mother, eh?* – so he is there to put his eye to the nostril-size cavity of the swallows' nest the thatcher finds in the eaves of the slaughterman's cottage, and he is there in the top field when Charton's plough hits a human skull worn clean of flesh, so old it glows like varnished ebony. He wonders aloud who this skull belonged to, and what colour the eyes were in the empty sockets where the farmer's boy now presses his stubby thumbs. He is there when a red gelding kicks the blacksmith so hard in the throat that the blacksmith never speaks again, and everyone laughs and says it is a vast improvement, and that the business of the village is done far more efficiently now that the blacksmith spends more time shoeing and less time chatting with whomever has brought his horse to be shod, and that God has answered their prayers through the ornery red gelding. And after a week, the blacksmith laughs as well when they say this – or smiles, at least, and makes whatever sound is nearest to laughing that he is now capable of. Easy come, easy go – none knew it better than Tarare's people, there in Tarare's village. Life has a way of cutting you down to size.

And when the work of thatcher or farmer or blacksmith is done, they pay Tarare his due and invite him to sit a while with them. They drink a little cider and eat a little hard cheese while the sky mellows mauve, and at last freckles all over with dainty particoloured asterisms. Then Tarare goes home to his mother, to whom he imparts whatever gossip he has learned that is worth the telling, and sleeps well and long and deep as a princess in a song.

Tarare pulls his weight, says Nollet. That is all very well. But a boy needs a trade, needs to get out of his mother's house.

Why do I need to get out of the house? Tarare asks.

To make room for another one, says Nollet. Isn't that right, Agnès?

And Tarare looks at his mother where she sits stirring the cauldron, and Tarare's mother looks at Tarare, then shrugs, then nods.

I thought you were too old to have babies, says Tarare.

Tarare, she sighs, bringing the spoon to her lips to taste the stew, I am thirty-two.

Another Nollet coming, eh? says the original, who is in a cheerful mood this evening. Just what the world needs.

Although – he adds, with a low chuckle – the taxmen might disagree.

Tarare clears his throat. What about salt? he says. For my trade.

Nollet and his mother exchange a look. It's too dangerous, says Tarare's mother.

You're too stupid, Tarare, says Nollet. He rubs his beard, draws on his pipe. I have business in the city next week, he says. I will find work for you there, good honest work. You will find much to entertain yourself with. I envy you, even! To be a young man in the city!

But you have said – Tarare says – why do honest work when you can be ruined by a spurt of the taxman's pen? You said, honest work is only called honest because it keeps the poor man poor, says Tarare. And he is right, Nollet has said all this within his hearing, and without his hearing, Nollet has said more. He has said that Cartouche and Ponchon and Grand Nez and all the errant bandits who laired in the shades of the forest, picking their teeth with landlords' bones, had the right idea of how to go about things. He has said the peasant is taxed of his arse and taxed of his elbow by the ink-shitters of the customhouses. His flesh is served up like a dish of petit fours: seigneur, curé, King – they all take their little savouring bites of him. He has said only a fool would toil for a pittance to, what – to buy a goat? To drink sour goats' milk, and sell smelly goats' cheese to his neighbours, and pity every baby his poor skinny wife presses into his arms because they will have nothing but goats' milk and stinking goats' cheese as well? It would be funny if it wasn't so sad, Nollet has said.

Nollet's shoulders stiffen because he has been contradict-ed, which precipitates an instinctive stiffening on the part of

Tarare and his mother. Listen to what I say *now*, Tarare, says Nollet. I will go to the city and I will find you work in the city. Things are different in the city. A man can make himself there, distinguish himself.

Where will I sleep in the city? asks Tarare.

I don't fucking know, do I? says Nollet. As it stands, you sleep quite happily in the fucking garden, next to the fucking onion patch, like a mutt, Tarare, so you will forgive me for not thinking it necessary to arrange rooms at the hôtel.

Language, Vincent, mutters Tarare's mother. Nollet says nothing more and they are silent for a while, listening to the fire crackle and the *chouette chouette* of the happy mouse-eaters over the meadow outside.

Eventually, Tarare speaks. What will you call the new baby? he asks. He knows it is stupid and silly, but the upsetting thought has occurred to him that he might leave for the city and then they would give his name to the new one. Same Mama, same Nollet, a Tarare so fresh and exciting. Tarare may be a nonsense and mean nothing, but it is his nonsense, and he doesn't want anyone else to have it.

Don't know yet, says Nollet, scratching at his groin. Nothing, until we are certain he is hale, until after the winter has passed.

Tarare's remembers the baby he buried in the forest, under the bracken, when he ought not to have. Tarare imagines the baby is now just weatherworn bones, scattered about by a length of mildewed rag. He feels sad then, so he stands up and pretends to yawn, and says he is going to sleep.

I didn't wait to name you, Tarare, his mother says as he opens the back door. I named you right then and there, as soon as I saw you.

His mother is pointing her spoon toward the mattress in the corner, to the exact place where he was born. It had never occurred to him before that he was born there, on that very bed, but of course he was. Where else would he have been born? There is a look in her eyes as she gestures, a gleam, which we might all wish Tarare would recognise as the gleam of a total, unconditional love. He does not.

Why? asks Tarare.

Because the neighbour-woman said you were too small and you would die, says Tarare's mother, returning her spoon to the pot. So I knew you wouldn't, because she's a slut and wrong about everything. And anyway, I was very young. And stupid.

As the name *Tarare* itself attests, interjects Nollet.

That night is mellow. Tarare lies in his makeshift bed in the garden and laces his hands behind his head and thinks about what it means for a man to distinguish himself. What he would have to do. He inventories in his head all the men he knows, trying to determine which of them is the most distinguished. He supposes that if it isn't obvious, then none are particularly distinguished. As he drifts toward sleep he decides that it's Nollet. It's not the miller, though he is the richest. Nor the smith, who has the strongest arms. Neither the miller nor the blacksmith would ever wear a yellow neckerchief, as Nollet does every day. The audacity of that yellow scrap of cloth is what it is, is all it is.

The next day is Lady Day. The day that an angel, many years ago, so sweet-faced and neither boy nor girl, and with hair white and soft like lambs' floss, had come to the Holy Virgin Mother and told her she was having a baby and that the baby would not be her baby but God's.

Tarare tries to picture the scene as he dresses – the angel, in heavenly garniture, with the voice of a thousand four-string fiddles, searing the door off its hinges. The dust dancing on the floor. The cowering girl, shielding her eyes against the light of divinity. How does God get a baby in a woman's belly? How does anyone? It makes no sense to Tarare, how that happens. He has seen the parts, the parts of a man and the parts of a woman, and he knows they fit together in some way that is compelling to all parties. But how does this joining go on to make a body? To make blood, and pump it up into a little red heart? Do the bones and nails coagulate like ice crystals in the belly at the angel's very bidding? And does it hurt? It terrifies him sometimes, how much there is to know that he does not. But he knows that these mysteries are God's and that they ought not to frighten him, but humble him.

He dresses carefully for Lady Day. The fête will be held in the customary meadow between Tarare's village and the next over. There will be dancing, and tripe sausage, and beribboned ponies. And because he is a man now, Tarare is going to the fête alone.

He scrubs the smut from himself. He puts on his breeches and a clean shirt. He puts on his jacket of grey woollen check, which is cut short in the Italian style and has brass buttons which please Tarare very much, as they shine and are each embossed with a five-pointed star. He wets his hair with spit and smooths it down and ties it in a tail at the base of his neck. Then his tricorn, then his black boots, which are Nollet's old boots, laced tight to his shins. He remembers about distinguishing himself, and looks around for an appropriate accessory – he can find nothing yellow, but he comes across his mother's crimson headwrap. He ties it loosely at his throat and admires the effect of his reflection in the water pail.

Outside, Tarare feels the afternoon sun on his spotless face. Standing at the stoop, he sets his hands on his hips and glances up the little road toward the church and down it toward the wineshop, closed for the day in deference to the Virgin. The village is at its prettiest, tinct with the verdigris of summer, the water pepper and fiddle dock. Mottled pigeons make their unfussed progress about the square. He finds his mother by the back door shelling broad beans, her skirts rolled up around her knees. She smiles at him from the shade of her faded bonnet. My little gentleman, she says. Well, not so little now. Is that my scarf, poucet?

Tarare nods, and fingers the knot of his neckerchief. I'm going now, Mama.

Her smile falters. A bean plops into the bucket between her knees. Don't start any trouble, Tarare, she says. And if anyone wants to start any trouble with you, you just walk away, you hear me? Everyone will be drinking cider, too much cider, and they will want to start trouble if they are given the excuse.

Tarare nods again. Tarare doesn't want trouble. He wants to look at things and listen to things and enjoy them, in his own quiet way. That is all he ever wants.

And don't talk to anyone about our business, you hear? Our business is our business.

Tarare nods again.

No wickedness.

A third nod. She is thick now with the baby, in a lovely way. Shoulders and arms soft like white bread. She hasn't gone hungry in years, Tarare knows. She hasn't gone hungry because of Nollet, and for this, at least, Tarare is grateful to him. You worry too much, he says. Mama?

What?

I love you very much, he says, and I want to always take care of you, as Nollet does.

Well, go out and earn some money then, she tuts. But Tarare sees how her cheeks redden with pleasure. Tarare sees how, after he has tipped his hat and turned to leave, she wipes a tear from the tail of her eye.

The light is blue over the fields, and the air pregnant with the scent of early blossom, and Tarare can hear the keen of the fiddle and the rasp of the tambourine before he sees the great fire and the smaller lights set in the trees among paper streamers. Anticipation squeezes round his heart like a fist. The people are gathered in groups around the fire, or else are sitting on their haunches in the dry grass. Most of them Tarare recognises, some he does not. A plaster Virgin presides. The girls in their dirty sprigged dresses, who are dancing now, in pairs together, hand in hand, have left her flowers with their prayers; she wears a wreath of browning roses slung around her plaster shoulders.

He finds Hervé and Louiset, the farmer's boys, sitting with the miller and the slaughterman. They are propped on their elbows in the grass. Ponderously, they watch the girls dance.

Hervé breaks his reverie to dip his chin in greeting. Tarare.

Hervé.

Here, have some cider, says Hervé.

Tarare has some cider, and it is cloying in his throat. He hands the mug back to Hervé, who offers it to the miller, on his other side.

The miller demurs. Cider turns your skin yellow, he tells them.

And what have you been drinking, miller, to turn your cheeks so red? asks Hervé. The blood of honest labouring men?

And Hervé and Louiset and the slaughterman all laugh,

because the miller is thickset and ruddy, and also not as poor as they are, so it is a good joke at the expense of someone who can afford it. Even the miller laughs, although the joke is more against him (everyone hates the miller because he is the miller, and the miller owns the mill, which is the best thing you could own, after the land itself).

Tarare sits quietly, listening to their low and manly talk, and inside he marvels at his apparent acceptance among them. He looks at Hervé and wonders if he sees one of his possible futures in the farm boy's loucheness, his lightly worn insolence. They are both young – there are maybe only three or four years between them – but already Hervé's body is different, more robust, so unignorably *there*. The nose, broken and healed crooked. The tanned forearms where the cords of the muscles press thick against the skin.

How's your mother, Tarare? asks the miller.

Yes, Tarare, how's your mother? How's our sweet Agnès? The slaughterman's face slices open in a ribald grin.

She's well, says Tarare, rubbing his thumbs against the thin cotton of his trousers.

Come on, says Hervé, clicking his tongue, leave the boy alone. What about you, Tarare? Have you settled on a trade? Or – he inclines his head toward Tarare, with a meaningful eye-flick in the direction of the twirling love knot of white-gowned girls – found a sweetheart, eh?

No, says Tarare, no sweetheart. But Nollet is finding me work in the city. I don't know what kind of work, but he says good work. I don't know what it is people do in the city.

The slaughterman and the miller exchange another look.

And where is Monsieur Nollet this evening? asks Hervé. I had thought—

You will dance with me, Hervé! Elise, the vintner's daughter, has broken from her clique and approached, red-cheeked and gasping. Come on, she says, and bends down to pull at his arm. She is extremely pretty, with a gasping, enlivened heat on her skin. Hervé laughs and allows himself to be tugged from the grass with a show of feigned annoyance. He is following her into the crowd, toward the light of the fire, when he stops, turns, and says, Someone must dance with Tarare, too. And faces are pulled and fuss is made, but eventually a candidate is found, and red-haired Annette, who is tall and a little cock-eyed, pulls Tarare up beside Hervé.

Tarare has never danced before, but he soon realises that this is no impediment. The fiddlers play, and he wheels and skips with the others, feels himself slung against shoulders and spun wildly toward the fire. It is as if nothing exists beyond the sawing of the fiddles, the stars held up like a monstrance on the shoulders of the trees, the sweat beneath his clothes. He loves it, twisting this grace out of himself and throwing it up at the darkening sky, the vernal moon, like *here heaven, here Virgin, have me*, and the fire-brightened faces and the laughing faces in parts, lace, wrists, ankles and stockings slipping and the crushed flowers trembling down from the loosened hair. And now Hervé has clapped his shoulder and pressed a mug of cider into his hand, and now Hervé is hugging him, flattening him to his chest that smells of nicest darkest dirt, before they dance again, and again, until he feels himself topple sideways—

Fucking – son of a bitch—

Tarare? And Hervé is beside him, Hervé's hand rests on his back. The blow from his reeling shoulder was dealt to a man Tarare does not recognise, which means he is a man from the next village over, which Tarare realises with a sudden rush of tipsy indignation is the village whose men killed his father, and this – this man, with his ugly glower, in his ugly jacket, shaking spilled cider from his bottle-green waistcoat – is one of those men of that village.

Pardon me, *friend*, says Tarare, only he says it as though he does not mean it, perhaps because he is a little drunk, perhaps because he feels Hervé's hand on his back and he wants Hervé to know that he is actual as well, that he is just as undeniably *there* as Hervé is.

Do you have a problem? the man is saying. Do you want a problem, *friend*?

Hervé says, Come on, come away Tarare—

Tarare? The man grins. I've heard that name – the whoreson, is it? Whoreson, are you?

Big man, snarls Hervé, Big man, you think yourself? To look around on the day belonging to the Holy Virgin and decide to start trouble on a fatherless child?

Child? Hardly a child, is he? The stranger rolls his reddened eyes up and down Tarare. Their voices are raised now and people are watching.

Hervé pretends to lunge toward the interlocutor, makes as if he will punch him, and the man cowers, crumples backward on himself, and Hervé laughs a big laugh that confirms he is himself a big man, the real kind, and grabs Tarare by the wrist, saying quietly, Come on, let's get out of here before he finds his friends—

So they do. They leave the fête behind and reel across the top field, laughing, then stumble down the hill to the stream that flows between the alders, pricked out by the white needles of the moon. Hervé has a flask of wine that they pass between themselves. Tarare wonders if they will take off their clothes and swim, and perhaps – but Hervé sighs heavily, and sits down on the stony bank, slapping a midge from his brown neck.

Tarare settles beside him, catching his breath.

What was it happened to your papa? asks Hervé.

He was beaten, says Tarare, my mama says. Killed.

Mine too, says Hervé. Hanged. For poaching, on the Seigneur's estate, see? You have to be a real idiot to get caught doing that twice. And then my mama died having my brother, and then Charton took me in. He takes a deep gulp of wine, swallows, then spits on the stones. I fucking hate the aristocrats.

The farmer is a good man, says Tarare.

He's all right, Hervé shrugs. He smiles conspiratorially. Tell you what I do like – I like *his wife*.

She's kind to you?

Hervé throws his head back and laughs again. No, Tarare, you sweet fool, he says. Because I'm tupping her.

Tarare thinks about the farmer's wife, whom he knows by sight from the village, from church. But she is old, Tarare thinks – doesn't just think, but *objects*. Her mint-striped parasol, the blowsy way her flesh hangs from her bones, trimmed with cheap lace, rotsweet in attar of roses. Oh, he says. What is it like?

Nice, I suppose, says Hervé. He rubs his finger around a hole in the knee of his trousers as he speaks – It's a bit like – you know when you are hungry? But you push the hunger down and pretend that you aren't, and then just one bite of food baits the feeling back up from inside you, like a wriggling fish from your belly, and your mouth waters and you feel dizzy? It's a bit like that. I didn't care that much for it at first, but now that's what it's like. When I hear her skirts rustling on the staircase, when I smell her perfume. I get hungry and I can't stop.

Tarare thinks, that doesn't sound very nice at all.

It's another reason I want to get out, you see. She won't leave me alone, and if Charton catches us at it he'll kill me, string me up. The farm's going to his son someday anyway, Hervé says, lifting his eyes to the sky, and I don't want to work for that arse-hole. No. I need to get far away, do something else – he looks at Tarare. Your Monsieur Nollet. Do you think he would – do you think he wants help in his ... his business?

Tarare is not surprised that Hervé knows. It is an open secret in the village that Nollet is a salt smuggler – half of them buy from him, and the other half only demur because they are frightened that if they are caught with his salt in their houses they will be taken for salt smugglers themselves, and fined. So they buy at lawful prices, or eat their stew plain and savourless. I don't know, says Tarare. Mama says it's dangerous.

I can handle myself, says Hervé. Maybe I can talk to him – is he at your mama's house tonight?

No, says Tarare. He is in the city tonight, I think, but Hervé—

What? says Hervé, and turns his dark, petulant face toward Tarare. Tarare takes in the blunt nose and the shorn curls, the dim sad hollows of his eyes, and whatever *it* is, his flesh is hum-ming with it, and so he leans forward and he touches his lips to Hervé's mouth. He feels where their lips touch as sharply as the slash of a knife. Hervé's breath is hot and sour with cheap wine. It is entheogen, filling Tarare and making him feel like a dream where he is falling, until Hervé presses his hand against his chest and pushes him away, not ungently. And it is done. A night-blooming rose among the thorns of his small life.

Tarare – says Hervé, in a tone of soft reproach, and Tarare is astonished at himself but he is not frightened. He decides that whatever happens next, it was worth it, for that feeling of being in a falling dream, by the side of the water pricked out by the white needles of the moon. He decides that whatever happens next, that part was perfect.

Hervé laughs softly. Can't hold your drink yet, can you, Tarare?

Tarare shakes his head. Hervé's hand is still at his chest, enforcing distance. He clicks his tongue and lifts the hand to Tarare's head, ruffling his hair. Brotherly. I think you should go home to your mama, Tarare, he says. Get some rest.

So Tarare does. Head full up with bells and roses.

*

A condition of unease: to be woken in the middle of the night certain that what has woken you was a noise, a loud noise. To lie awake, suddenly very wide awake, in the avid night silence, anticipating – and dreading – a repetition of The Noise so that it can be identified, so that the gravity of whatever situation precipitated The Noise can be properly assessed.

So it is that Tarare lies awake now.

He knows it is early because the grass beneath him is wet with dew and the moon is very low in the sky, barely cresting the trees at the foot of the meadow, where the day yet to come cringes in wait. He had been dreaming something, he is sure. Something soft and sweet, before the noise. He rolls on to his side, tucking his blanket close around him, and decides that he will hold his breath for as long as he can, and if, whatever the noise had been, it does not recur in that time, he will go back to sleep and search out that soft, sweet dream. He has been holding his breath for about twenty seconds when the serenity of the night is pierced, again, by a scream. The scream comes from inside the house. Tarare is scrambling to his feet when he is grabbed at by the throat and hauled backward on to his knees. He grasps ineffectually at a thick arm wound around his neck, and feels breath hot against his ear, and the voice of a man, a voice he does not recognise, says, There now, behave yourself, lad. The breath is sweet, like aniseed. The man hauls Tarare backward into the cottage, holding him tightly, doubled over. Inside, Tarare sees a lamplit flash of his mother's white and startled face. She is sat up in bed, bare-shouldered, clinging the coverlet to her naked breast. There are two men besides he who holds Tarare by his throat. He sees the dog, dashing between the intruders, wagging her tail and scrabbling amicably at their knees.

I found the boy in the garden, says the one who has Tarare in a chokehold, says Hot Breath.

Is that all of them? Shit – cover yourself, woman – says the pair of black boots closest to the bedside, and Tarare hears his mother whimper, and the rustle of fabric, and Black Boots and Hot Breath and the third man all laugh, and Tarare knows the third man's laugh. It is a laugh he has heard before.

Mother Mary, look at her tits.

That's all of them, says the third man, the man whose voice and laugh Tarare knows. The smuggler's away for the night, don't know when he'll be back, or who with. And Tarare listens and Tarare knows that the third man is not the Third Man at all. The Third Man is Hervé.

Shit, says Black Boots. Best do it quickly, then. The dog gets up on her hind legs and nuzzles at Black Boots. Black Boots kicks the dog. Let's just get the stuff, he says. Where is it, sow?

Tarare's mother snivels. He can see her bare feet, pressed together, squirming, and her white hands in her lap, pressed together, squirming. She says nothing. Black Boots twitches and there is a slapping noise. She cries out.

Where is it, sow? The salt.

Tarare claws in a breath. Floorboards, he says. By the hearth.

His mother whimpers his name. Black Boots strikes her again. Sit on the lad, he says to Hot Breath. And you – help me with the boards – he says to Hervé, who is peering at the back door, keeping watch.

Hot Breath forces Tarare down to the floor on his belly and lowers his weight on to his back. Tarare can feel the rough boards under his cheek. Hot Breath puts the tread of his boot against his jaw. Tarare does not feel especially frightened at this moment, although he knows he ought to. Tarare is not frightened, but he wishes he could go to his mother, who is whimpering quietly in the bed. He wishes he could go to his mother and put his arms around her. The men produce a crowbar and begin to work at the boards. Tarare twists his head so that he can see them. They work by their meagre lamplight, their shadows thrown up across the walls. He sees they have covered their faces with soot. Hervé's eyes flicker upward to meet Tarare's, briefly, briefly, and then the boards come up with a squeal and Black Boots reaches down into the cavity beneath. He brings out the bricks of salt, wrapped in their waxed paper. He leans back on his knees. He scratches at his ear.

Is that it? he says.

I never promised you the world, says Hervé.

That's it, that's all, says Tarare's mother. Take it, please. Take them.

Get up, says Black Boots, and he gets to his feet himself and grabs Tarare's mother by the arm to wrench her from the bed, and when she sees the blade she screams, loud and piercing, and Hervé makes a noise as well and grabs at Black Boots—

Body of Christ, says Hot Breath from on top of Tarare.

Quickly, says Black Boots, look in the cupboards. I don't know. Anywhere. And he sinks the knife not into Tarare's mother but into the mattress where she was sat. The blade snicks through cloth, opening it up like a belly and releasing a cloud of dust so that Black Boots starts coughing and wheezing as he shoves his hands into the stale straw of the mattress. Hervé begins to throw open cupboard and chest, trailing petticoats and flowered linens and bright ribbons all over the floor, knocking over chairs, saying fucksakefucksake. They make an unmerry havoc in their search, porringers and dishes clattering down from the sideboard, jugs smashed and ground under boot heel.

Fox, says Hot Breath, jabbing his boot harder against Tarare's jaw, Fox – we have to go. Too much noise. We have to go. Take what there is and go.

Fuck. Black Boots (also known as Fox) pauses with a clump of mattress straw in one hand and Nollet's best jacket in the other. Hardly worth getting out of bed for. You found some money?

Tarare hears the clinking of coins from where Hervé stands. Yes, says Hervé quietly.

See, the mattress never comes to anything, says Hot Breath, chuckling. I think you just like waving a knife around.

Come on, says Hervé, agitated. Let's go.

Tarare is relieved of Hot Breath's weight on top of him. And one more for luck, Hot Breath says, and kicks Tarare, hard, in the middle of his chest. Then they are gone, spilling into the night with their prizes. The door creaks loose on its hinges, and the room is plunged back into darkness. The dog chases the men out over the starlit meadow, though seemingly for the simple joie de vivre of doing so, rather than out of any belated sense of duty.

Neither Tarare nor his mother moves for a long while. Tarare remains where his assailant left him, gulping in air, twisted in an awkward pile on the floor. Eventually he moves to press a hand to his chest. The flesh is tender. He can already feel the bruise forming. He feels his limbs out from the middle, his arms and legs that are so long, that he had felt so proud of before the fête, that had so quickly bent into submission. He is a fool, a weakling, a *boy*.

He hears his mother rise from the bed at last. A little candle flame lights the lunatic vista of the floor, catching at the scattered hay and the slivers of broken pottery.

What a mess, she says. Get up, poucet, for God's sake.

He does.

Are you all right? she asks.

He hit you—

Tarare's mother cringes and touches a hand to her purpling cheek. Not very hard. Cowards.

Where is Nollet? Tarare asks. Will he come back soon?

She gazes around the room. I don't know. Probably. She laughs ruefully. He left his tobacco, after all.

Tarare rights a chair and sets it back at the table. Everything is so quiet now, the early-morning chirruping benign beyond the open door.

You have been talking, she says, haven't you?

It was Hervé, he says. One of them was Hervé, from the farm. I – I said to Hervé about Nollet – about Nollet being gone... There is no sense in lying. Tarare has never lied even once to his mother, anyway. He's not sure he would know how.

Oh, *Tarare*. She lowers her head to her hands. You told him Nollet was away?

I didn't think— Tarare begins. We were friendly, and—

That's your problem, Tarare. You think everything is what it says it is. Foolish, foolish. His mother continues her invective, sinking back on to the remains of the mattress, while he stoops to gather the pieces of a broken jug from the floor. No man is above enriching himself if he can, you see? she tells him. They will be counting him out his cut as I say these words now, and they will be laughing at you, laughing at stupid who thought he had a friend among them. Lucky it wasn't the law, lucky it wasn't the taxmen, or there would be a fine on us, or worse – fines for all we have or more. We'd have to sell the cottage, sell the land. Oh Tarare. Idiot, idiot. They took the money. They took all of the money. And who do you expect will do anything about it? It's not as if we can go to the law, no. So Nollet will have to do it, won't he, if it is to be done? Will have to go over with his gun and try to get it back, and he could die, Tarare – DIE – and if you think you're going to the city now—

Tarare makes no attempt to argue for himself. She is right. He is an embarrassment, a liability. *One must howl with the wolves.* Had the abbé not told him so, all those years ago? Years ago, and yet he has remembered it, because it struck him, the image, even if he did not comprehend its meaning until now. He stands mute by the table pushing the fragments of the jug uselessly around his hand. It was painted, the jug, with small blue birds and sweet william. His mother had had all these lovely things, and now, now *look.*

I'm sorry, he says.

You might be, she says back. Oh, you *might well* be.

It is still just about dark when Nollet returns. He stands at the kitchen door in his dirty overcoat, a glaze of sweat on his brow, and looks in at the disordered scene with an expression of long-anticipated desolation. He takes a breath. Who? is all he says at first.

Tarare's mother begins to speak, to tell Nollet that they had not found so very much, not much is gone, about thirty sous, and no more than – and Nollet raises his palm for silence, and says again, very quietly, *Who*? Who was it?

One of them was Hervé, the boy from Charton's farm, says Tarare's mother. The rest, I don't know. I didn't know their faces, Vincent.

Nollet rights a chair and sits down at the kitchen table. He fingers the broken stem of a clay pipe. He rolls his eyes around the room, then leans forward to take off his boots. Then he seems to think better of it, and sits straight again, boots on. *Hervé*, he says. Friend of yours, Tarare?

Tarare looks once over his shoulder at Nollet. Tarare says nothing. His mother brings a fresh shirt. Not much in for breakfast, she says. Let me see, now—

Nollet stares at Tarare.

How much was it, under the boards? asks Tarare's mother loudly, fussing with the bread knife.

I don't know, says Nollet. About forty, fifty sous' worth. It's warm, he adds, shaking off his coat. Why is it so warm in here?

Fifty sous, as much as that? Virgin mother – she whistles – Those men seemed to think that it wasn't very much, that it was hardly worth the bother for it.

It isn't very much, says Nollet.

Fifty sous, Vincent. I don't know, I – we have no recourse—

It *isn't very much*, Nollet repeats. Stop going on about it. Just *leave it alone*, for Christ's sake, Agnès, he says. There is a warning edge to his voice.

As you say. She gazes about listlessly now she is done slicing and buttering the bread. Tarare looks toward the open door. The birds have begun to make their motets in the treetops and in the long grass at the edges of the fields. Everything, except for the little cottage, except for the three of them, is ordinary. An ordinary pale blue pale yellow morning.

I screamed, says Tarare's mother. But not a soul came, none of the neighbours.

You ought not to have, says Nollet to Tarare's mother. Screaming. You think anyone wants to be a hero for you? No one wants to be a hero for anyone. Not for a felon, and especially not for a felon's woman, but not for anyone else either. No one wants to be a hero unless it's easy to be one. Another lesson for Tarare, eh?

Tarare is still when Nollet says his name.

Come on, boy, says Nollet, hefting himself up from the table. Let's fetch some firewood, leave your mother to tidy up.

There's wood on the pile still, says Tarare's mother.

Nollet ignores her. Come on, Tarare, he says. And he is smiling now.

Tarare finds his clogs, puts them on.

Vincent, breathes Tarare's mother—

Tarare follows Nollet out through the back door. Nollet stands in the yard and weaves his hands above his head in a languid stretch, the sun warming his pale belly. Then he takes the axe from the woodpile, shifts it in his hands, and looks expectantly at Tarare.

Vincent, please—

Tarare looks over to where his mother stands, but she is silent now. She stands trembling at the doorway. As Tarare follows Nollet down toward the wood, he looks back over his shoulder and sees that she still stands there trembling in the doorway. Now she has raised her hands to cover her eyes, left and right, like a child trying to make herself invisible. Although he does not know it, this is the last seeing-of-her Tarare will do, this her-not-seeing-of-him. Except, of course, in dreams.

They cross the meadow and follow the path alongside the stream for a little while. The darkish, wet-skinned hour is peaceful and cool. The birds are still tuning their throats, committing no more than an experimental warble – a weird spear of sweetness – to the clammy shade-bound wood. Nollet and Tarare walk single file. It is four, maybe five o'clock in the morning. A timorous rain begins to fall, tip tipping at the canopy, lithering down slow through the density of leaves.

Nollet sighs deeply. I think there can be nothing better, more soothing to a man's soul, he says, than the noise of rain when it isn't falling on you. Well, he laughs, maybe one thing. But you are too young for that, eh, Tarare?

Nollet walks purposefully, with his chin raised and the axe propped up on his shoulder. The raindrops spot the thin cloth of his shirt, making it cling to his skin, making the ghost of his brand visible through the fabric. G-A-L.

You mean fucking? Tarare asks.

I mean fucking, laughs Nollet. Then again, maybe not too young. I was fourteen when I had my first. Hélène. No, Ninon. On Sundays the housegirls in town would have their mornings to do with as they pleased – they were meant to go to church, I suppose – but they would pin little flowers of woven silk to their breasts and come down to the quay to look at us, instead.

Cool their swollen ankles in the river. He laughs again. Half of them were fat with their new masters' bastards not two months after arriving. And what to do about it? It is a cruel world, Tarare. And it gets crueller every day. My brother told me what to do.

You had a brother?

I had three. We were always fighting, always. I tell you one thing, Tarare – Nollet looks over his shoulder – women want it just as much as men do. Women want everything just as much as men do. Some things they even want more. It has served me well in my life, remembering that, he says.

Their footsteps are soft in the velveteen mulch of the forest floor.

You mean like my mother? asks Tarare. What does she want?

Nollet whistles through his teeth. Your mother? Your mother wants someone to tell her what to do. She wants someone to show her what to do. And she wants you, Tarare, to be happy.

They walk a while in silence after that. The wood reveals its depths through sloping fern-stroked passages around them. Now his blood has cooled from the fright of the burglary, Tarare feels a deep tiredness in his bones, a tiredness that dulls all other feeling, smooths the edge off thought. It is almost all he can do to continue putting one clogged foot in front of the other. To make a meagre response to Nollet when he says something that ought to be responded to. Where are they going, and why? It is a pertinent question, but Tarare cannot make it matter to him, cannot hold it at the centre of his mind. No, it isn't to fetch firewood that they are here. The detritus of the forest floor is too wet for lighting.

Eventually, Nollet stops in his tracks and turns on the spot, with a nod of satisfaction. Here will do, he says, and sets his feet on the ground, making a few test swings of the axe. His shirt rises to flash the wiry hairs on his belly.

It is the clearing where an old oak fell during a storm, a whole six summers ago, which humbler flora – winders and creepers and clingers – have since surged over to claim. Tarare knows they have not come to gather wood, but nonetheless, he goes through the motions. The sun has risen now and the rain abated, making a fine white mist.

Jesus Christ, Nollet mutters, chewing on a twig, I wish I had my pipe. You should start smoking, you know, Tarare. It's good for you. Soothes the soul, like praying. And – his hand twitches on the shaft of the axe – it would give you something else to do with your mouth, besides run it off to people you ought not.

You're talking a lot, says Tarare, for so early in the morning. Aren't you tired?

Perhaps I talk to keep from weeping, says Nollet, because my livelihood is lost.

You talk a lot to fool people, says Tarare. When they're listening they aren't thinking, and then you can do what you like.

Nollet laughs, and crouches over a tangle of branches. Is it working? he asks.

You need not bother, says Tarare. We didn't bring anything to carry firewood in.

Tarare, look here – spider eggs—

Tarare crouches down beside Nollet. A long gash in a fallen branch is covered over with a second silver skin, a lovely trace-work cradle. You have to squint to see the eggs there, sugaring the fissure. As white and perfectly round as moons, clustered there in the splintering wood. Tarare bends lower. And when the side of the axe-blade smacks hard against the base of his skull, he thinks, *well, there we go. There we have it.*

Tarare keels forward, maybe sideways, maybe backward? – he isn't sure – as Nollet rains down the blows on his shoulders his head his belly, until his eyes fill with a blackness, and his mouth with vomit, and he can't see, only hear and feel. Feel the everywhere pain of it, which was expected. Hear, between blows, Nollet's choked breaths, Nollet's sobbing and whimpering, which was not expected. Nollet uses only the flat of the axe, its blunt sides, because to tear into the boy, to open his meat with the blade, would be too much even now, he knows. Tarare wants to open his mouth because he wants to say, *stop. If it is causing you pain to do this, to kill me, then don't. Let me go and slither away and I will slither wishing you well, and never come back. Or let me come back and I will never speak, never open my mouth again, this will be the last time I open my mouth, to say this, to beg you, I will sleep curled in the corner with the dog and like a dog.* And he isn't sure if he has said these words, or just thought them, because, at last, Nollet stops.

There is a flat ringing sound in Tarare's blood-filled ears. Beneath it, he hears Nollet shift on his feet and gasp for breath. He hears Nollet say a Pater, and then he hears no more, because Nollet wipes his brow on his shirt sleeve, tosses the axe into the undergrowth, and leaves.

The sky is whitening. The birds begin their fractal chorus, delicate in its thousand component parts. A grass-coloured woodpecker, a lovely blackbird. It would do no good to describe Tarare's pain, which is enormous and in every part of his body, because in pain we are all alone, latched into the flesh, where the blood whistles and cells knit and unknit themselves. To tell you that the pain fills him like a heavy fire all over his young body would be feeble, and perhaps ultimately deceitful. To tell you he tries to open his eyes and finds they will not open would be to pick your pockets of a truth you are likely already in possession of, and perhaps wish to forget: that in our suffering, we are all of us totally, irrevocably alone. To describe the vignettes that play out behind his swollen eyes – the screeching of hideous marionettes illuminated by a flat red glare (his mother weeping by the hearth, the robbers counting up their money with frilled whores in their laps) – a mere sideshow. Tarare lies there in the wood, entirely alone with his suffering, for a very long time. The only real thought he has to cleave to, the only certainty that sustains him, is the certainty that everyone who knows or cares that he had been alive now thinks that he is dead.

But Tarare is not dead. As he lies on the cool, loamy forest floor and watches the morning light sparkle blurrily through the canopy, the pain slowly dulls until he finds himself able to think again – or to reflect, at least. A mottled slug comes from the leaf mould and anklets him in silver. The mist rises around him in lovely swirls.

He considers what it means, to be alive but thought dead by everyone who matters. He realises that in quite a crucial sense, he no longer exists. Nollet had said a Pater, so it is possible that even God is now labouring under the misapprehension that he, Tarare, is dead. He has also shat himself, and with the slow dulling of the pain, the more routine discomforts of lying on a forest floor in your own wet shit begin to reassert themselves. More than anything, he finds that he is hungry. Eventually, he gets up, and takes the measure of himself. His shirt is heavy with gore and the damp of morning, and it clings uncomfortably to his skin, so he takes it off. One clog is on his foot – he pauses to vomit into a patch of nettles – and the other lying a short way off, by the track. Also lying by the track is the axe, with his own red blood drying on its iron beak.

He takes the axe and he sets to limping, deeper into the wood, toward its heart. He knows that beyond the darkness is a world that he does not know. It will not welcome him, but he can probably take something from it.

II

L'homme sans fond

[The Bottomless Man]

If I go into a butcher's shop I always think it's surprising that I wasn't there instead of the animal.

—*Francis Bacon*

1788

Tarare is hungry. And aching, and tired.

He finds himself in a pasture when his clogged feet, sticky with dried blood, give way beneath him. The shaft of the axe slips from his benumbed fingertips. He has made his way into another morning, more or less. A haze is rising from the tuffets of grass. There is cool moisture on his chin, and on his tongue. He decides to lie a while, and rest. His eyes are half-open to the pale gloaming. Something has happened to Tarare. Something has been done to him, he knows – the work of a fair devil. Inside he feels his mind scabbing, hardening around the sore places. His thoughts, torpid as they are, running new channels, shaping new inlets at the edge of his wounded soul.

It is slowly, slowly that he becomes aware of them. Their red-brown clouded hides, shifting their sour hefts around him in the long grass. A rough warm tongue licking the blood from his hands. She muzzles his chest, then lowers herself into the grass a few feet away. Her sigh, redolent of sugars and rhizomes, warms his face.

Tarare opens his eyes.

Cow, cow. She is beautiful. Crowned in a dither of midges, silver-edged in the morning sun. A baldachin of pure and pale blue sky. She looks at him. Her eyes are deep and thoughtful.

Hello cow, says Tarare.

Hello Tarare, says the cow.

Can I stay in your field for a while? I have nowhere else to go.

No, the cow answers, through a mouthful of cud. The farmer will come before too long, with his dogs and his boys, and chase you away.

The farmer can try, says Tarare, but I'm not sure I could move if I wanted to. He tries to flex his shoulders, but even this slight movement revives the totalising pain in his body.

Then his dogs will tear you apart and eat you.

So be it, says Tarare. Will you watch over me while I rest?

I can watch, says the cow, but I can do nothing to keep the dogs from you. Time has worn my teeth flat as pegs and stripped the muscle from my haunches, says the cow. She raises her head to gaze across the steaming pasture. Our ancestors were mighty, she says. They had thick fur a person could sink their arm in to the elbow, and long tipped horns that cradled the new moon. And they gathered in great herds to eat the best grasses, that grew by the meltwater, and they were strong, and called the aurochs; and men like you, like the farmer and his boys, took fright to see them, and were proud when they killed them.

All this the cow says with her deep, thoughtful eyes.

I'm sorry, says Tarare.

The cow lowers her head to nibble at a frill of mallow, but says no more.

Tarare sleeps then.

*

By noon the sun burns all softness and mellow sweetness away. Long gold grasses, tranced by the warmth. Tarare rolls over in his sleep and throws his arm outward, sending the riled flies in helices around him. Then Tarare wakes, sticky-eyed and sour-throated. He listens to the little bugs and crickets crooning extravagantly by his ears and in his bloodied hair. Harlequin-coloured bodies. Earthworms and weevils and tender grubs and little rabbits. France. Here he is, living. Clinging to this warm breast, France. He thinks of his mother and for a moment he feels sad. But then the sadness is drowned in a breaker of pain.

Tarare cannot even properly remember the event that he is trying to determine how much time has passed since. Lying in a meadow, among meadow flowers. Fine, very nice, but *how*? He does remember his name. He does remember his home. He does remember the iron beak of an axe. He reaches a hand, cautiously, to the back of his head. It hurts. He can feel a fissure, a cleft, between the plates of bone. There is also a novel cavity in his mouth, a sucking gap between a sharp tooth and a flat. He presses his tongue there, which also hurts. Tastes salty. Rolling his achy head in the grass, he takes the measure of the place. No buildings nor beasts. One flounce of cloud skirting at the edge of the sun. The brow of the woodland wavers at the bottom of a field beyond a field. And beyond that wood is where he, Tarare, lives. Lived.

It is then that Tarare hears a voice. A man's voice, and it is raised loud. I SAID, the voice says – do you play the fiddle?

Tarare turns on to his ear and looks away from the forest, down the slope, toward the other end of the meadow. There, leaning on the palings at the field's end, a good thirty yards away from where he lies, is a man in a feathered hat. To Tarare's dazzled eyes, his shape is trembling in the thick heat of the afternoon.

Ah! exclaims the man in the feathered hat. You are awake! I asked, do you play the fiddle?

Tarare now sees that in one hand the man is holding a fiddle and in the other a bow. The man hoists the fiddle to his shoulder and strikes the bow across it, demonstratively, releasing a tuneless and trenchant wail.

Tarare winces.

Like so, says the man in the feathered hat, lowering the bow. The fiddle – can you play it?

Tarare tries to moisten his lips. He opens his mouth to respond, but his parched throat will produce no voice. Instead he shakes his aching head, slowly and emphatically.

The man understands. I see, he calls. I only ask because I found this fiddle in the meadow, and then I found you in the meadow. I thought the two discoveries to be, perhaps, felicitously linked. The man pauses to scratch at his head with his bow hand, then shrugs. A fiddle is nevertheless a fine thing to find. Good day to you! And abruptly, the man turns away from the palings, and makes to leave.

Wait, calls Tarare, weakly. Wait.

The man must hear, because he does wait, squinting back across the gilded field.

Monsieur. Please – do you have any water?

Yes, he calls back, after a small hesitation. Yes, I have water.

With a vigour born of desperation, Tarare clambers to his feet and lollops over to the fence, clutching at his side. The man in the feathered hat sets down bow and fiddle and offers Tarare a flask from his jacket. The water inside is blood-warm and earthy tasting. Tarare feels the scratch washed from his throat, and the world densifies before his dry, fuddled eyes. He gulps and gulps until he has drunk almost the entire flask. Splashes the rest over his head and face.

The man in the feathered hat watches him carefully while he

does all of this. When Tarare is finished he hands the flask back to the man. He moves to wipe his mouth on his shirtsleeve, which is when he realises he has no shirtsleeve, because he wears no shirt. His body, his body that a shirt is meant to cover, is ripe with congealing bruises. And this is when he becomes aware of the careful scrutiny of the man in the feathered hat, propped on the low palings, who whistles through his teeth. What kind of half-finished job are you, my boy? he asks. You, I see before me? Poor shit-rat, you look. Must hurt. Must be hungry as you are thirsty.

Tarare *is* hungry, now that it is mentioned. Famishingly so. He gulps down the glot of saliva that fills his mouth at the thought of food. Yes, Monsieur, he says. Very hungry.

If the man intends to feed Tarare, then he appears in no hurry to do so. He leans back from the fence to sweep Tarare's sorry shape up and down with his eyes. I won't ask who it was that went and did you up like that, he says. And you ought not to tell me if you think you ought not to tell me who did, he adds, gnomically. And I won't ask what it was you did to deserve it, if deserve it you did. But I will say it is some kind of miracle you survived.

My father did it, says Tarare. Which is more or less true.

The man's expression clouds momentarily. Yes, he says. I know how that can be. Where's your father now, boy?

Tarare looks over his shoulder, swaying on the spot. Sunshine. The grass fizzing with flies. No other soul can be seen besides the man in a feathered hat.

I don't know, says Tarare. There is a village, beyond the forest – but – please Monsieur. I'm very hungry, if you have—

Oh! the man interrupts. Thought he killed you, did he? Thought he'd finished you off?

Tarare nods. He said a Pater over me, he says.

That's a laugh, says the man, pushing his hat back off his burnished brow. That's a funny thing. It is then that Tarare realises the man stood leaning on the fence is unlike any man he has seen before. Despite the heat of the afternoon, he is wearing a coat of rusted black velvet, open at the neck and trimmed with pale blue ribbon. At his throat is a froth of white lace, and tucked into the band of his hat are cockerel plumes, glossy and green-black. The brim of this hat casts a shadow over a pointed, congenial face. A thin beard covers his brown cheeks, and above his lips his black moustache is waxed up at the tips in a style that appears, to Tarare, antique. The man is tall – taller even than beanpole Tarare – and skinny under his marvel of clothes, but he holds himself with the winning complacency of a man who knows how to fight, or to spend his money well. Despite the obvious attention that has been paid to the details of his striking ensemble, the approximation of magnificence, the man is very dirty. The dust of the road whitens the hem of his coat. The lace of his cuffs and jabot is jaundiced with stale sweat. This very dirty somewhat lord-like man extends a gloved hand across the palings. On the middle finger of the proffered hand, over the glove – an innovation Tarare has never previously conceived of, the wearing of a ring over a glove of leather – glows a lozenge-shaped turquoise. Pleasure, says the man. Lozeau. Jules Lozeau.

Tarare, says Tarare.

Pardon? says the man.

Tarare. That's my name.

How wonderful, says the man. How singular. And how old are you, Tarare?

Sixteen years. What day is it?

The seventh day of June Year of Grace seventeen eighty-eight – the man spreads his arms and lofts them toward the virgin blue of the sky – a Saturday.

Tarare frowns. It was Lady Day, when I last remember being.

Being what?

Just . . . being.

Lady Day was many weeks ago. Lozeau waves a hand diffidently, as though to lose many weeks of one's life is not so unusual an occurrence. Today is the seventh day of June Year of Grace seventeen eighty-eight.

Seventeen years then, says Tarare.

Too many sevens to be ignored.

What?

Did not the walls of Jericho fall on the seventh day? says the man.

Is it a test, an impromptu catechism? Tarare remembers nothing about what or whom Jericho is. Yes? he ventures.

And seven pillars of the House of Wisdom? Seven years of famine in the Pharaoh's dream?

Tarare reels on the spot. His head pounds. His belly growls. Sins? he offers, meekly.

The man reaches a hand over to clap Tarare on the shoulder. Good! he says. And what is it you do, Tarare?

Do?

Yes. Seventeen is old enough for a profession. Do you have any especial talents? Skills?

Tarare thinks for a moment. My mother says I'm funny, he says.

Monsieur Lozeau throws back his head and laughs, long and loud. That's cute, he says. Very cute. Come, now. He drops his hand to Tarare's arm and draws him toward the fence. My friends are camped near here. You can be fed and you can be washed and – here, the man cocks his head cockerel-like beneath his shiny cockerel plumes – we can find you some more respectable attire. How does that sound?

Tarare allows Lozeau to help him over the fence. Are you a Protestant? he asks.

Oh, says Lozeau. Certainly I am not that. That's a thing I'm not.

Are you a gypsy?

I'm Lozeau, says Lozeau. Jules Lozeau.

*

In a culvert where meadow meets wood, two men, Lozeau's so-called friends, squat by a fire scorching bacon in a blackened skillet. Their appearance is not pleasing, but the smell of the bacon is. The first man is very large and his bald pate shines in the sun. He shifts on his monoceros haunches at their approach.

Here he is, the Wizard of Marmaros, he calls. Did you find any eggs?

I found a boy, says Lozeau, with a flourishing gesture toward Tarare.

Does he propose we truss and roast the boy for breakfast, like the savages of Aldabar? says the big man, looking sceptically at Tarare. This man is called Severin Vidal. He has hands like spades, a spotted blue cloth knotted around his bullock neck. He is the kind of man who likes to drink and talk too loudly and then start fights with the other men he notices noticing him talk too loudly. His skin is weathered brown and he wears gold rings in his ears. His eyes are too small for his big head, but very canny. A whitish keloid scar runs from the crown of his skull to the root of his nose. This scar makes his face look like it has been at some point in the past prised apart, then stuck together again inexpertly. This is Severin Vidal.

The smaller man speaks next. A boy? he says, narrowing his eyes over the spitting pan. And look, the meat of him already tenderised. This man is Jacques Bonfils. When Bonfils speaks, which is often and at great length, he cultivates an appearance of education because he may not appear educated but, in fact, is. Bonfils can read and write. Bonfils used to set type at a printing house in Montpellier, his fingers black with ferrous sulphate. Now he just drinks. His hair is a crazy nest of red-brown curls like the end of a tobacco plug. He wears a pair of dirty round eyeglasses. The smell of his mildewed suit of clothes is so thick as to seem almost sophisticated: something like elderflower over cat piss. A bottle of brandy sloshes in his jacket pocket, above his heart. This is Jacques Bonfils.

Give the boy something to eat, Jacques.

Bonfils shimmies bacon on to a tin plate, sucking the grease from his fingers. Sit, he says, sit. Eat, dirty beaten boy.

Tarare sits on his haunches by the fire and Tarare eats. Bacon and the heel of a loaf. He eats this very fast and it is good, and when he is done he wants more to eat. But Lozeau and his friends are talking among themselves and he isn't sure how he should ask, or whether a further demand on their hospitality might sour the situation. With food in his belly, he feels a little more clear-headed. A little more rational.

The one called Bonfils is holding the fiddle that Lozeau found under his chin and is plucking at the strings experimentally. I tell you, he says, I could outplay the Devil.

Do it then, says Vidal.

A little music, why not? says Lozeau.

Give me the bow and I will.

Lozeau gives Bonfils the bow and they watch as he rises from his crossed legs and strides to a raised tuffet a short way off, flouncing the tails of his patched coat. He saws from the strings a manic little jig of aeriform delicacy, his narrow hips swaying, his fingers buoyant on the fiddle's neck. When he is done, Bonfils bends at the waist in a flourishing bow, and Vidal and Lozeau hoot and applaud.

Tarare applauds as well, until he feels Vidal's eyes narrowed on him. Vidal chews on a piece of grass and looks at Tarare askance, his small eyes screwed up even smaller, and says, What's your story then, waif?

Let the poor boy settle himself first, Lozeau sighs. He takes off his magnificent hat and uses it to fan himself. I will vouch for him in the meantime. He is called Tarare and he is seventeen years old. I found him asleep in the meadow, among the buttercups. Will that suffice?

In the meadow, among the buttercups? repeats Vidal, with a shade of disdain in his voice, as though to be found in such a place automatically compromises Tarare's integrity. But he does not press the question further.

Is he joining us? asks Bonfils brightly, resuming his seat and settling the fiddle across his knees. Has he talent?

Vidal wrinkles his nose. Smelling like the Devil's crack.

That's not a talent, says Bonfils.

Try sitting closer to him. Smells pretty talented from here.

We're going to Paris, says Bonfils.

Vidal scratches at his belly and sneers. I still think this is a cock-eyed kind of plan.

Because everyone in Paris remembers the time you got so

drunk you shat yourself on the steps of the Saint-Gervais and the abbé wept.

Slander! says Vidal. That was my friend, Georges—

I realised a long time ago that when you talk about something happening to one of your friends you are talking about something happening to yourself. You have no friends, Vidal. You are a flea, a tick.

Your mother was a whore.

No, she wasn't, pouts Bonfils. My mama made hats. Stupid little hats for rich women, priced inversely to their size.

My mother was a whore, says Tarare, wishing to involve himself. For a little while.

This information appears to sweeten Vidal's disposition to him. He grins and smacks Tarare on the back, just hard enough for the blow to smart. There! he says. See, it's good we can admit to it. It's just facts after all. No one should look down on us for having whores for mothers, eh? Perhaps *everyone's* mama is a whore really, eh? Selling her tits to the whelping merveilleux, or her little white hands to the factories?

Why stop there? adds Bonfils. Perhaps everyone's papa is a whore, too? Selling the sinews of his back to the landlord, his arms to the miller?

I know you are mocking me, Jacques, but where is the lie? Everyone is a whore! Vidal declares with perfect good cheer.

Paris, interposes Lozeau. There to pursue sweet-faced *Fortuna*. Gold, jewels – he gestures with a waft of his black hat – or good bread, at least.

In Paris, a man can eat good bread (Bonfils).

In Paris, a man can maybe eat, anyway (Vidal).

Are there jobs to be had in Paris? asks Tarare.

Bonfils winces. *Jobs.*

Jobs? Vidal loops his thumb into his neckerchief and tugs it up behind his chin like a noose, crossing his eyes and lolling his coated tongue.

With jobs come taxes (Bonfils).

With jobs come bosses (Vidal).

In Paris, we will do the same thing we do wherever else we find ourselves, chuckles Lozeau, putting his hat back on his head. You can join us if you want, Tarare.

I have none of the proper papers for travelling, says Tarare (says Tarare who has no shirt, no coat, no hat, no money, no food. One shoe, which is more or less the same as having no shoes. Tarare has only Tarare, his person, on his person.)

They laugh as one would laugh at a child. Papers is nothing, says Lozeau. Bonfils can make you some papers.

Bonfils is a curé? Tarare asks, looking uncertainly at the angular little man, with his patched jacket and concave chest, who has taken himself away from the cooking fire to lie on his back in the grass between fiddle and bow, seeming to cloud gaze, seeming to be drunk even before he has performed the little offices of the *sexta hora*.

Lozeau laughs again. Your whore-mother was right, he says. You are funny, Tarare.

*

The men find clothes for Tarare and send him down to the river to wash. An undershirt of faded brown cotton, a pair of drawers, culottes in a red stripe (patched at the knees) and a waistcoat to match. He carries them, along with a cake of Castile soap, to the river. He does so with a limping reverence, as though he is an ambassador taking a moonstone to a queen, which, in reality, would only be slightly stranger than the truth of what he is: dead boy, still-very-much-alive boy. *Too many sevens to ignore. The House of Wisdom.* Alive, but enormously hungry. Still hungry after bread and bacon, which is a richer breakfast than he ever had at home. Home? Well, *no more.* He wonders if his mother weeps for him. He feels light-headed as he tramps down to the water. Sweat prickling behind his ears.

Behind the ridge at his back he hears Bonfils strike up at his fiddling again, and the pendant sounds of merriment. Was this luck? These dirty, Egyptian-seeming people, with their bad skin and black velvets, who had fed him and were now clothing him – were they what luck looked like? Tarare considers that perhaps he is dead after all. He thinks back to the tales told by the black-cloak crows at the veillée, and to the stories the abbé read from the book, which had spirits, which were different but not so different from ghosts. Holy spirits. Could it be that he, Tarare, had died – died to the earthly world at Nollet's hand, lost in the sloping fern-stroked passages of the wood, to wake in the relucent domain of limbo, where there are no kings, and the merry – too merry by far for Heaven – dance, the unbaptised watching from the trees like tiny sacerdotal birds? With an addled feeling, not unlike vertigo, Tarare holds his new clothes to his chest and bends forward to press his palm into the warm grass. He feels the breathing carpet of it prickle at his palm, and the cool solidity of the earth beneath. Still bent over, he withdraws his hand and sees that it has left a mark there in the grass. Flattened stems. Evidence of his being. Evidence enough? He should have listened harder in church.

Did you find a coin, stranger?

Tarare looks up and sees that the person who asked this, with laughter in his voice, is standing right in front of him. A young man – a boy, really – of a beauty so exceptional it does little to dissuade Tarare of his growing conviction in his own post-mortem condition. The boy is naked to the waist and stands with his hands on his hips, a red jacket draped over his shoulder. His tanned skin glisters with moisture all across his hairless chest and down to his taut belly. The boy is buttoning his trousers. His hair is wet. His body is like the body of a hunting dog, all lineaments refined to a single purpose. His body is like the body of a saint, dripping gold droplets and set up high to catch Heaven's light all over. Tarare sees how the beautiful boy catches the light all over.

You can see me? asks Tarare, bent slack-jawed in his metaphysical stoop.

I can see you, says the beautiful boy, shaking out the shirt that hangs over his arm. Smell you, too, he adds, pulling the shirt over his head.

Tarare rises to his feet. He rises too quickly, and sways, while shapes like white roses float dazzling behind his eyes. Lozeau, he remembers to say. I'm with Jules Lozeau.

The boy laughs. Me too. From the cradle, near enough. Antoine, he says, holding out his hand. The brother.

Antoine. The brother. Both Lozeaux have the same dark eyes and the same wide brow. Tarare wonders if the elder, beneath all his frip, might have some of the younger's beauty – but he doubts it. Antoine Lozeau's face is a rare phenomenon. Its features, taken singly, would not be particularly striking, nor even necessarily pleasant (his nose is sharp and crooked, a scar splits his left eyebrow through the centre). But together, and enlivened by a happy arrogance, they sing. Tarare can look neither directly at nor away from this boy. So he looks at his golden-brown throat. He watches his Adam's apple bob as he speaks.

Mother Mary, you really do smell like a corpse.

Everyone is saying that today.

Can you not smell yourself? asks the boy.

I suppose I'm used to it.

Antoine laughs. That's nice for you, he says, but I don't want to be. His eyes dart to the suit of clothes, the cake of soap. Get along to the water, he says. You shouldn't take too much time with it, though – we'll be moving along soon.

And the boy strides away, wringing the drips from his hair.

Tarare follows along the bank of the overhung stream until he finds a spot where the water is deep enough for him to sink in up to his shoulders. The water flows around his naked body, cloudy and sun-warmed. He sets to work with the soap on his dirt-streaked legs, his swollen feet, his crusty hair. His wounds sting preciously. Once he is satisfied with the approximation of cleanliness achieved he lifts his hips in the water to float on his back, cock sticking up in the air in a way that amuses him. Like the mast of a ship. How wild his own body seems to him, and how rogue its longings. (Tarare has never seen a ship, except in pictures, where long-nosed dolphins nosed at the ocean rain.)

And there on his back in the water he composes/prays: oh, cover me over. you sunshine

Founts of strange colour speckle on the inside of his eyes when he closes them. But the water soothes the aching of his body, and he feels more or less good. Still hungry, but good. A tree by the stream has fruit which must be sweet to pigeons, because four wood pigeons are perched in it, weighting its branches with their grey dowager heft. As though the pigeons themselves are the tree's proper fruit. Tarare smiles to see them clustered there. Pigeon-tree.

Like a boy, he smiles, and like a man, he plans.

They soon decamp, Tarare and his new friends, and head north along the Mâcon way, right sides hot in the declining afternoon sun, shadows lengthening on their left. The fields empty around them, green and green, then blonde, then stubbled. Loose formation, strapped up and hung with stuff – cooking pots and water cans and billhooks and rolled canvas tents, gaiters white from the dust of the road and backs clammy with sweat. They walk on, until the clouds above their heads begin to fructify with the glow of dusk.

Bonfils talks the most.

Those sedan chairs, he says. As are common in the cities—

Antoine sighs. Not this again.

But do you not *see*? Bonfils insists. The practice of having oneself carried by other men is a great abuse. It contradicts nature. These canons, these bishops, these magistrates, these *fops*, anyone who wants to cut a figure – shut up in a box and carried on the shoulders of other men, who stagger through water, mud, snow and shit, crushed if they make a false step. Could they not employ their strength more usefully in cultivating the fields – here he flings his arms out to the sides, indicating the velvet latifundia around them – rather than carrying around other men perfectly capable of walking with their own two legs? He pauses to take a breath. And then a gulp of brandy. His face is red.

There is no Sunday for your tongue, is there Jacques? says Vidal.

Quick, says Antoine. Someone fetch Bonfils a box to preach from.

(Tarare watches Antoine where he walks up ahead. He sees how he wears his crimson jacket short above his hips, in the Italian way. He sees how he walks with a swagger. Tarare sees a lot of things, watching Antoine walk up ahead, and he finds he wants to touch them all.)

Preachers, spits Bonfils. That's another thing. If preachers were to speak out about this abuse instead of declaiming on metaphysical points of doctrine – if the churchmen excommunicated these men who carry and these men who are carried, instead of witches, who do not exist, or, or fucking *caterpillars*, who do much harm, it is true, but who fear the sparrows and the blackbirds more than they fear excommunication—

Of course witches exist, chimes Vidal.

Oh? Lozeau peers backward, his interest piqued. How can you be so sure?

Because, says Vidal, licking his sweaty upper lip, I fucked one.

This was in Mâcon, was it?

No, says Vidal. In Dampierre, when I was young. She had one supernumerary nipple, pink as a strawberry – he raises a finger – here. He jabs the finger into the side of his torso.

I see. Lozeau smiles. And how is it that Bonfils knows that excommunication holds no terror for caterpillars? Are they not also God's creatures, Jacques?

Bonfils opens his mouth to answer but Antoine answers for him: because Jacques was fucking the caterpillar while Severin was fucking the witch.

Fucking a caterpillar, sighs Bonfils. How such a thing—

They look at your little dick and get confused. They take it for a friend, a playmate.

I swear, all you think about is—

Antoine is still laughing at his own joke when two women appear on the road ahead. Lozeau hails them. Though their shapes are indistinct in the heat haze, Tarare can tell these women are whores: their heads are uncovered, and their wide campanulate skirts are hiked up to display their sunburnt calves. One raises her hand to wave back at Lozeau.

The cocottes are outfitted with pastel abandon. One older, one younger – and the younger, Tarare thinks, little older than fifteen. She wears a filthy pale yellow frock over a crimson petticoat and her hair falls in a matted tangle to her breast, like the Magdalene in the wilderness. She has no front teeth. The teeth she does have are small and white in her sun-browned face. She is called Pierette. The older wears a mauve cretonne with chartreuse ruffles, cut to halfway down her breasts. She is called Lalie. Stopping to adjust her stays, she fans herself with the flowered bonnet looped around her arm. Lozeau introduces Tarare and they look at him once, with indifference, and then begin to talk to Lozeau, prodigiously, over and across one another, passing sentences backward and forward to be extended or discarded, like so: they have dogs though four dogs big nasty things! Oh the family will go to mass tomorrow yes a chicken-house an old mule in the back and good clean apparel – did you see what she was wearing? Yes rude, wouldn't let us in the house but brought us out some milk – the wedding – yes! The wedding! We asked eggs of the grocer but—

A farmer, about an hour's walk from here, says Pierette.

Not the farmer, his daughter, adds Lalie.

They're raising the chapiteau.

Hanging streamers from the trees.

They have a lot of food, and drink—

Cider? asks Vidal, who is squatted on the roadside wiping his shiny face on his sleeve.

Cider.

Lozeau looks from the women to the men, brow perched querulously. What do we think? he asks. Are we clean and bright and ready to don our finery, my friends?

All right, says Vidal, cocking his head at the glowing sky. It's a fine evening for it.

Yes, says Antoine. If you all behave yourselves.

I can play my fiddle! peeps Bonfils, bouncing on his feet.

We're going to a wedding? says Tarare. I don't understand.

Antoine pats him on the shoulder. You will soon, my friend.

*

The dark has thickened by the time they reach the house. Not a fine house, but a good house, set back from the road in well-tended fields belonging all to itself, lights shining yellow in the windows. The creepers on the stonework are sere from the heat of the day, and the subtle fragrance of trampled grass flavours the evening air. They hear music from the chapiteau, and laughter, and the screeching of many children practising their little savageries together in one place. Tarare's stomach growls when he smells the roast pig, the meat pies.

It is not difficult to gain admittance to a wedding feast, explains Lozeau (it's not difficult to gain admittance to anything, if you know the right words – cunt, feast, poorhouse, theatre). But wedding feasts are a special favourite. Everyone is drunk, everyone is merry, and the occasion encourages the disbursement of largesse. Even toward men who look like convicts. Because that is what the farmer, who greets them at the door of the house in a chestnut periwig and too-small velvet suit, says – having cast a sceptical look around the dusty murder of vagrants gathered in his yard, having listened to Lozeau's spiel, his glazed eyes lingering on Vidal – *that one looks like a convict*, he says.

Lozeau stands before the stoop, his plumed hat pressed to his chest in supplication. What, Vidal? A convict? *No!* he says. Vidal is the strongest man in France. He can walk on his hands like they're feet. I tell you – put a plank on his shoulders, and then three girls at each end of it, and he'll heft them up as dainty as a dairymaid does pails. You have never seen the like, monsieur.

I have seen the like, and worse, says the farmer. Hand-walkers and gypsies. At fête.

Here Lozeau tilts his head toward Pierette and Lalie and lowers his voice, and says, Well then. In that case – perhaps you have never seen the like of *these* – and Lalie smiles and strokes a hand across her sunburnt décolleté, and Pierette crosses her eyes and swats at a gnat (and Tarare thinks this a strange gambit on Lozeau's part, given that even he, Tarare, green Tarare, has seen such things as Pierette and Lalie before, cocottes cheerful and pliant, dolls with crooked faces). Our Eulalie and our Pierette. They are very obliging, both.

But it works. The farmer in the doorway chuckles warmly and rubs a hand over his thigh. He glances backward into the house, then says, Yes, all right then. But none of you are to go into the house, you understand? You can sleep in the barn but by morning you must be gone. You hear me?

Loud and clear, monsieur. Loud and clear. Tonight you will enjoy the finest entertainments in France, and awake in the morning to find us – Lozeau splays his fingers in a starburst – melted away with the dew.

You talk very prettily for a vagrant, the farmer mutters.

Lozeau smiles and bows so low that his cockerel plumes brush the ground. Perhaps I talk so prettily *because* I am a vagrant, monsieur.

You'd think a man who could talk so prettily would be able to find a job, says the farmer.

Perhaps I learned to talk so prettily in the leisure my vagrancy affords me, monsieur.

The farmer snorts and takes hold of Lozeau's shoulder. Remember: if I catch you in the house, I'll break your legs. And the women – he moistens his lips – there's an outhouse round the back with a blue-painted door. Take the women there, eh?

So it is that they join the wedding party in the chapiteau. The air is tint blue-white with smoke and dense with the warmth of many drunk bodies. When Tarare looks around, he finds that these bodies are somewhat like the bodies he has known before, the bodies of home. There are the old women sleepily dignified in black widows' weeds, and there are the laughing girls in their ill-fitting dresses of homespun chalk-white chalk-pink, permitted a dab for the evening of Mother's rouge and lavender water. Brown men buffed to a shine by weather, happy men with the faces of pigs smoking pipes. Heady sweet farts. Broken teeth, good teeth. Lace-on-goitre, and little dogs root-ling for morsels in the dirty straw. And there is dancing – to a tambourine and fife. Tarare follows Lozeau and Vidal and Bonfils through the morass, and Vidal finds the cider barrel and taps them all drinks, and they stand for a while around the barrel considering their prospects, taking measure of the space, and Vidal nods along to the music and says it is good, good. It's good, no? Good pickings? (because Vidal, for all his size and apparent self-possession, likes to have his opinions ratified by those he suspects may be his more worldly peers).

It's good, agrees Bonfils, his little red eyes – growing redder from the smoke – darting side to side. I want to play though. These people are amateurs. He gestures at the fife player.

Go and play then, says Lozeau. My God.

And Tarare peers silently into his cider cup, and he feels hungry, and he realises why it is that men like to drink – because when you are drinking, you are not doing nothing. You are doing just a little bit more than nothing. Tarare shifts the cloudy liquor in his cup. Tarare hesitates. Tarare drains it.

The night drops, mortcloth black over the bright chapiteau, and the moths swarm inside and around the lights that twinkle in the apple trees, dusty and flirtatious: Forester, Nettle-tap and fat grey goat. The people in the chapiteau become tireder and wilder, and the people in the chapiteau are drunk, and Tarare is drunk now too, and when his fifth drink is drunk he finds himself stumbling back to the barrel, nearly doubled over, and wrapping his hand around the tap to steady himself.

All that comes next has the mad and fugitive quality of a dream.

He sees Vidal. He sees Vidal on hands and knees, roaring and rearing like a beast, and two little children on his back riding him like a beast, slapping their little hands on his bald head, and more children surrounding him, clucking with laughter and poking him with sticks they have fetched from the orchard and shouting BEAR BEAR DANCE BEAR. And Tarare sees Bonfils, who stands with one foot propped on a box in the middle of the tent, sawing a carmagnole from his fiddle, and all around him a swirling mass of red and blue and mottle and striped skirts, and faces broken down in the flickering light to their constituent parts, a shining sweaty wreckage. And last he sees Lozeau, who stands at the table where the bride and groom sit, playing at thimblerig: he shows them three brass cups lined up, a marble of red glass. With crisp, economical movements he hides the marble and swaps the cups around, twice, three times, four, while his audience watch keenly. The bride sets her lacy finger on the middle cup. To a roar of mock outrage Lozeau lifts the middle cup to reveal – nothing – and then the left cup, and the right. All empty. While the bride and groom laugh in childish disbelief, Lozeau holds up his hand, crosses his eyes, and knocks a fist against his chest. He coughs, and there it is – the red marble rolls from his mouth and clatters on to the table and into the bride's lap. Again! she shouts, handing him the marble, and Lozeau obeys, setting the cups on the table, exchanging them with a flounce, and opening out his hands to say, *choose*. This time the bride is ready, and cries *your mouth!* And Lozeau grins, showing all his teeth, and throws back his head. He puffs out his cheeks. From his mouth crawls a single red admiral butterfly, flickering its scarlet rags. There are cries of wonder, real surprise from all observers. With an ever-so-delicate touch, Lozeau gathers the butterfly on his finger and presents it to the astonished bride. They are laughing, they are shaking their heads in tipsy wonderment as the bride takes the butterfly into her cupped hands and says, It's real – it's really alive – and the father of the bride, the farmer in the chestnut wig, takes a purse from his belt and shakes his head and gives Lozeau money, coins, a whole handful.

As Lozeau turns away, counting the coins, Tarare stumbles slack-mouthed up to him, his new friend, his new father, and Tarare says – and Tarare means it – Monsieur, I have never seen anything so beautiful in my whole life as what you did then, with the butterfly.

Lozeau looks at Tarare. He smiles benevolently. You are drunk, he says.

Yes, I think so, says Tarare.

Enjoying yourself?

How do you do it, with the butterfly?

I put a butterfly in my mouth and then I take it out again at the proper moment, he replies, with cryptic simplicity.

But I didn't see you put it in your mouth.

No one ever does. No one ever will, unless they know the trick beforehand. See?

It's like a miracle, says Tarare.

Not like a miracle, says Lozeau. It's like people sleep – all their lives. They go about their days asleep, and they see nothing.

And on the boards the butterfly, now forgotten, hauls herself convulsively through a reservoir of spilled brandy, weighted under her clammy wings, and the night broadens and it deepens, until the children have fallen asleep in the corners draped in their mothers' shawls and the old men have fallen asleep hunched over their walking sticks, their pipes still lit, and the virgins dance and run giddy in their little perfumed packs, rouge smeared around their mouths as though they have been eating raw flesh in the purple shadows of the orchard, and no one cares that there is mass tomorrow. A wedding. A wedding. Tarare dances with Vidal. Tarare dances with a pretty fat girl who kisses his bruised jaw so hard he yelps. The butterfly is crushed ignominiously under the heel of a saddler's boot (having brought, in its ephemeral life, much joy). Then there is a darkening and a rumbling among the men and the dancing stops because someone has brought with him a rumour from the south which he heard from a man in Crémieu which he heard from a rider come in from Saint-Hilaire-de-Brens who stopped off at an inn with a crab on its sign at Domarin where there was a meneur in a cat-fur hat who had just come from Nivolas-Vermelle who had it on good authority from a girl he saw in Les Éparres with a wen by her eye whose mother in

Doissin had a cousin in Rives that a man came on a big steaming black horse through the river valley of Voreppe, his voice quivering with emotion, saying that he had heard from a porter in Saint-Égrève whose brother in La Tronche had seen with his own eyes that there are soldiers shooting at people in the streets of Grenoble on the orders of some marquis or other, some duke or what-have-you, some cardinal, when he's at home. That there are people dead and dying in Grenoble. Good people, common people, armed with no more than sticks and hayforks and the tools of their trade. And these people had come to Grenoble because they were hungry and could not buy bread, and now the King's or the Duke's or the Marquis' soldiers are shooting them in the streets. The porter's brother in La Tronche has seen men hauled through the square, their jaws hanging loose from sabre cuts, heart's blood printing roses on their shirt fronts. All this had happened, had been happening, as they lifted the chapiteau in the meadow behind the house, and strung the apple trees with streamers, and danced. And now, knowing this, because the people inside the chapiteau are good people, broadly speaking, they feel some small and itching shame that they had lifted the chapiteau under which they now sit listening to this news of horror, and strung the apple trees with streamers, and danced.

There is talk among some of the men that they will ride their horses, still apparelled for the wedding in red ribbon and honeysuckle, over to the town hall, there to make their feelings known on the infamy done to their brothers in Grenoble. The father of the bride has a face like a thunderhead. An uncle stabs his knife into the table. They gather around to make this plan. When it is resolved upon, they drink to it. Then they drink to it again – Take up swords! Down with the aristocrats! – and once they have drunk to this plan a third time, it is forgotten almost entirely.

Tarare, Lozeau, Vidal and Bonfils are seated on a bench silently observing these new developments when Antoine enters the chapiteau. The elder Lozeau hails the younger with a lazy tip of the hat. Business good? he asks.

It was, until about an hour ago. Antoine glances over to the long table where the men are gathered, then slumps down beside Bonfils. Ah. Here is where all the tricks have got to.

Trouble in Grenoble, says Bonfils.

I don't see the use in making bother here over something that's happening in Grenoble, says Vidal. He tents his hands over his stomach and splays his legs out in the straw. I don't see what difference it will make. Say – he turns to Antoine – if it's quiet, can I have a go? With Lalie?

No.

Vidal pouts. Come on, Antoine.

I said no. There are plenty of girls here, if you are wanting to dip your little wick.

Don't be unfair, chimes Bonfils. You know as well as I do he looks like a bollock.

It's true.

A bollock? Vidal glares.

Antoine snakes a hand under his shirt to rub at his chest, saying in a careless sing-song: Looks like a bollock, smells like a bullock. And its name was Vidal. I'm getting a drink.

The father of the bride rises at last from the table and looks around the chapiteau, bellowing that they will have music, where is the red-headed one? Bonfils gets to his feet, flexing his bow hand. He begins a jig but the farmer says No, no – something slow, something sombre—

Dawn is close, stroking a supple line of crimson on the horizon. The chapiteau reeks of stale pipe smoke and bad wine. Tarare feels saliva flood his mouth, and a nausea build in the upper parts of his belly like a fist is pressed there. Surrounded by drunks on the wrong side of morning. Fiddle music, sleepy disquisition: there is so much. There is too much. He stumbles to his feet and makes for the mouth of the tent. He has just reached the fringe of the orchard when he falls on his knees and vomits up a thin syrup against the bole of a tree. He spits, spits again, wipes his mouth on the sleeve of his jacket. He feels better, almost clear-headed for it – the quiet and the new-day dark of outside a balm to his warm sugared brain. He smells the washed perfume of dog rose, the mild tang of the ordure spread in the fields that lie in darkness all around. Behind him he hears snatches of laughter from the chapiteau, the muffled music of the wedding party. A dog barks from somewhere in the yard and is answered by its brother near the outhouse. The warbling of a nightingale. Or does he dream the nightingale?

No one has followed him, Tarare, from the chapiteau. No one has come to see if he is well.

He slackens his arms and allows himself to roll on to his back in the dewy grass. He thinks, I have made it, made it back to life. There is no question. He could just get up and leave, he thinks, in his suit of new clothes. Go – where? Wherever it is that he would like, alone. The last stars shimmer above him like nitre on the black. He could go, but he doesn't. Now his belly is emptied of drink, hunger strikes him anew. He feels emptied, famished – flensed, even. Practically concave. The fumes that propelled him through the last vivid hours are exhausted. He is so hungry that it hurts, and hot tears prick at his eyes. Though Tarare has known hunger, never before has it caused him to

cry. He must eat. Whatever he does, he must eat. He will eat,
or he will die – that is the imperative. Already, he feels, lying
on the ground, as if the processes of decay have begun to act
on his body. The mollescence of the flesh, fluids curdling under
his skin. He is revenant. He is *starving*. A corpse with a will.
Shambling dry-tongued, he finds his feet. He lurches toward
the dark, squat shape of the farmhouse and tries the first door
he comes to. It is unlocked.

Inside the cool back kitchen his senses are rarefied by the
insistence of need. An acid savour in the air leads him to a
bucket of the browning apple peel kept aside for the pigs. He
crouches down and plunges his hands into the slimy curls of
matter, bringing whole fistfuls to his mouth. He chews. The
zesty bitterness of it is good, so good – God – he eats and eats
and scrapes at the bottom of the bucket with his nails until
every scrap is gone, then he raises the bucket to his face and
licks the sap from its sides. It is good but it is not enough. He,
Tarare, needs more. The low fire that burns in the grate slicks
the shapes of cooking pots and porringers in tarnished gold.
Scraps of pasty uncooked dough, and sweet jams: strawberry,
gooseberry. He lifts lids and throws cupboards open. A pot
smashes on the flagstones. He flops on his belly and laps up
whatever was inside it – bitter, too, and spicy – mustard? – and
he licks and licks and doesn't stop, shards of broken pottery digging into his cheeks, and now it is a mania, an ecstasy of want,
and there are doors – doors to cold stores, pantries? He throws
open the first and what he finds in the scullery is not food.
It is bodies. It is buttocks, white and sculpted, limned in the
meagre light of the cookhouse fire, the swell of a gartered thigh,
the seethe of lacy underskirts, upraised. A little blue-ribboned
shoe. Antoine turns his head toward the opened door and their

eyes meet and Tarare sees Antoine's face and sees him grin, a pale hand twisted into his black curls, and the bride says Shit, shit! and Antoine says *hush, hush* and thrusts into her again. *It's only one of ours. It's only Tara—*

Only Tarare closes the door and backs away. He feels compelled to move further from this spectacle, this tableau of infidelity. A bride! On her wedding night! He gropes his way to the far wall, feeling a quickening, an unbidden rush of blood to his cock. Gropes hard and stun-blind across the stonework until his sticky fingers grasp at the handle of another door, and this he opens, goes through (being alive, feeling in the darkness, he takes himself out of his trousers with a shudder of mad pleasure) and the dawnlight comes into this cool still room through a small window, and falls on stores and pickles and jams and mustards and loaves left to cool under damp white cloth and pale soft-moon cheeses and the boy, the boy Tarare, who quivers in delight and terror of himself and his so alive life and his vast, enormous appetite—

*

In his dream, Tarare eats the whole of France. His face looms over the rooftops of thatch and red tile as the sun will loom on the Day of Judgement, laurelled in cirrus. He scoops the glassy lakes up in his hands and brings them to his mouth to drink. He prises up the wheatfields with his nails and they spiral into fuzzy ribbons, like apple peel. He sees his mother then, so far below him. She comes out of their house and lifts her face upward, and the sweet waters of the Gaude and the Bourget trickle from between his fingers and fall on to her cheeks as a life-giving rain. He grasps at the sides of a mountain and wrenches it from the earth. Holding it to his ear he hears the screams of the little people in their gaily painted houses. Skinny goats roll down the scree like crumbs, unfooted, and the geese take flight. A white swan with its wings outspread passes as a glitter across the vast darkness of his pupil.

And when he is full, he sleeps, with his spine curled against the Pyrenees.

*

It is the charwoman who finds him. A pale, hazy dayspring. The sun comes in sideways, glancing pinkly at the stretched silks of the hedgerow and along the low, damp branches of the apple trees. The house is, for the most part, breathing softly through the draff of sleep. The house is, for the most part, hungover.

The charwoman has woken early. She goes down to the cookhouse to stir the fire, and finds the place in a state of high disorder. Buckets overturned, smears and bootprints on the flagstones. Then she opens the pantry door, and what she sees is this: a filthy-faced boy she does not recognise, curled on his side with his trousers around his ankles and his hand outstretched toward an empty pie dish. His hair and his too-large suit of clothes are whitened with flour. Over the waistband of his striped drawers his belly protrudes, plump and round as a glutted baby's. Swollen to unnatural size on his juvenile body.

The floor is covered with the detritus of a feast: crumbling pastry, puddles of milk, apple cores and coffee grounds, broken china. And everything – a summer's worth of cooks' labour – is gone. The pickles and the tapenades, the creams and the curds and the cured meats, the speckled pears and the veiny cheeses. Even the tripe, even the pigs' hooves for the master's dogs to eat. The boy is breathing, slow and deep and even. The boy is sleeping, gorged.

The admirable charwoman retains her composure. Quietly,

she closes the door. Quickly, she goes upstairs to find her master and tell him what has happened. Or what she thinks has happened, for surely, she says, as the farmer listens, clutching his throbbing temple and steadying himself in the doorway, not less than five men could have wrought the havoc she has seen in the cookhouse.

What her master does is fetch his musket. What her master does is wake his sons. And what Tarare feels first thing in the morning of the eighth day of June Year of Grace seventeen eighty-eight is a boot to his belly. What Tarare knows is running.

A hew and cry tears the gauze of morning, and the wedding guests, who slept where they fell, are yanked from their stupor by shouting, and banging, and the bawling of their host, who is chasing the varlets from his barn, pursuing them through the orchard and across the meadow toward the wood. He waves his musket. The hounds dance around his feet.

And the vagrants are running. Lozeau is running like he was born to it, plumed hat jammed under his arm and coat-tails flapping out behind him. Antoine is running like a wayward schoolboy, running and laughing, tearing at fistfuls of long grass as he goes. Bonfils is running, holding his eyeglasses against the bridge of his nose. Vidal is running, bare-chested, the straw he slept on still imprinted on the naked flesh of his back like raw whip stripes in the meat of a felon, clutching at his knapsack, and Lalie and Pierette are running, with their slippers in their hands and their dirty skirts bundled up in their arms. And last of all runs he, Tarare, the mounting sun blazing hard in his face, the bile lurching sour in his bulbous stomach, and running like he is afraid to die but he isn't really, not any more.

When the barking of the dogs at their backs has quietened, they slow. On the edge of the yellow wood, they stop. They catch their breath. Vidal squats down and clutches at his stitch. Alright then, he says – what the fuck was that?

I don't know, says Lozeau. And usually I do know. Usually I know very well indeed.

They peer at one another. Well, says Vidal. One of you did something.

To effect our abrupt ejection, adds Bonfils.

It was Tarare, says Antoine, massaging the toe of his boot.

Everyone looks at Tarare and Tarare looks back.

What did you do? Shit in his groats? asks Vidal.

Broke into the pantry, says Antoine, matter-of-factly. Heard the Big Man saying it to his sons. The place was stripped, ceiling to floor.

It's not possible, says Lozeau. Look at him, a stick. A boy.

Antoine shrugs, gets to his feet, and picks his way further in among the trees. I don't know what's possible and what's not possible, he calls over his shoulder. I am not the arbiter of that. I'm just saying what I heard the man say.

Tarare – Tarare knows it is possible because he knows that he did it. He knows that his clothes are covered in flour and his mouth is red with jam and his belly is swollen to a prodigious, unnatural size and that soon they will all see this. And soon they do. Pierette lets out a weird high-pitched laugh. Bonfils shakes his head.

Lozeau snorts. You broke into the pantry? he asks. Ate the stores? All of it?

Tarare sits in the grass with his knees pressed together. He nods. Shamefaced.

Not on your own, says Lozeau. Surely. Someone must have helped him. Vidal?

Don't look at me, boss. I'd sleep through angels' white

trumpets on a belly that full. Or so I assume, having never had a belly so full. He reaches out a thick finger and prods Tarare's pendulous gut.

Tarare groans and encloses himself protectively in arms and knees.

I think it's funny, says Pierette. The man was an ass.

I'm relieved, says Antoine, coming back through the trees with his hands on his hips. I thought it was my fault. I thought the chit had gone to her father.

Explain, says Lozeau.

Antoine takes something shiny from his pocket. It is a blue cameo brooch edged in chased silver. He brushes it against the lapel of his jacket, vauntingly.

Let me see, says Bonfils.

Antoine tosses it over and Bonfils turns the bauble in his hands. It's nice, he says. Agate. I'll bet it belonged to her mother. I'll bet that poor young flower you picked it off has a poor rotting dead mother in the ground, and that this belonged to her. I expect she'll weep when she finds it's gone.

Are you writing a ballad, Jacques? interjects Lalie. Heedless of male company, she draws a cloth from her bodice and reaches under her skirts to rub it at her sore parts. Anyway, the dirty beaten boy is making trouble for us, and for what? I say we leave him here.

Bonfils tosses the brooch back. You're a real motherfucker, Antoine. You know that?

Antoine laughs. Motherfucker? I'm an everythingfucker.

As you wish.

We'll take a vote, declares Lozeau.

On what? asks Vidal.

Lalie clicks her tongue. On the boy, Vidal! Do you stop up

your ears when I speak, pig? Do you not hear me? Do we take him with us, or leave him here? She takes the rag from under her skirts and tosses it at Vidal, who presses it to his nose, inhaling the fresh pudendal musk with a theatrical relish.

Little Pierette crackles with lewd giggling, throwing up her heels.

Bonfils, an enthusiastic democrat, moistens his wine-stained lips. Very well. A vote! All those *against* Tarare's continued membership of our esteemed company – raise your hands.

Lalie raises her white arm high. Vidal follows, with a grunt.

They look to Bonfils. He huffs inwardly and pushes his eyeglasses up his nose. In view of the boy's intemperate disposition, as has been proven to be – one could almost say, *Saturnalian*—

Vidal throws back his head and groans. For Christ's sake, Jacques – declare yourself!

Bonfils offers a simpering smile to Tarare. With regret, my friend – he sighs, raises his hand.

Lozeau, leaning against an oak and chewing the inside of his cheek, looks long and hard at Tarare. Tarare looks down at his own clogged feet, silent and unsure. Three against, he says at last. And those *for* the lad?

Lozeau's gloved hand is first in the air. Antoine's follows, and then Pierette's, who pokes her tongue out at Lalie. Why ought we not to keep him? she says. I think he's sweet. Besides, I'm bored of all the rest of you. You're *old*. Practically dead, in some cases.

Bonfils whistles. Deadlock!

Except it isn't, Lozeau says. Because my vote counts as two.

Since when? Vidal is indignant.

Since I say it does, says Lozeau.

Bonfils narrows his eyes. But why should your vote count twice?

Lozeau sniffs the air like a limbering hare and smiles. Because, my friends, he says – have I not led you wisely, led you well, through these months of drought? These months lean and cloudless? Has not my wisdom served our collective? He gathers up his sack and his frying pan and turns on his heel, striding off between the trees as he speaks. Have I not led you to lucre, and plenty? he calls out loudly, walking with mysterious purpose through the coppice. And cushioned you from the buffets of these cruel times, when the sun burns our backs raw? The milk – he shouts now, clambering over a bank of bracken – of my kindness is yours to drink, my friends. Only follow!

Where is he going? murmurs Pierette.

Madman, says Vidal, with admiration, shaking his head.

They all get up, gathering their meagre possessions, and begin to follow Lozeau, their Pharos in a plumed hat. Tarare remains where he sits, cradling his belly, until Antoine touches his shoulder and smiles his perfect diabolical smile down at him.

Tarare, Antoine says. Aren't you coming?

IV Vendémiaire an VII

Very well, says Sister Perpetué, fingering at her sleeve. But this Jules Lozeau. Who *was* he?

The patient gazes at her blandly for a time, his mouth slack. Then he wrinkles his nose and shrugs before speaking: Who *was* he? She asks – who *was* he? What would the little nun like to know of Jules Lozeau?

Sister Perpetué considers. Well, she says. For instance, was he a *Christian* man?

The patient snorts.

Was he . . . a gypsy, then?

The patient says nothing.

She lowers her voice to the pitch almost of a whisper: Was he a *Jew*?

The patient puffs his cheeks and laughs derisively. Good to know, he says, that our sweet Mother Church can be relied upon to give succour to the old hatreds. It would be a shame if our traditions were to be lost. Heretic this, Christ-killer that—

Sister Perpetué colours. I didn't *say* that, did I—

Monsieur Jules Lozeau had many gods, the patient sighs. Fortuna foremost among them.

Fortuna?

Fortune. Coin. It was a woman to him. That is what he said. A woman, Fortuna, to be chased, wooed. Possessed for a night and given up by dawnlight with lingering looks and a promise to follow . . . Christ. The patient rolls his dilated eyes toward the laudanum bottle. What do they put in this stuff? It's making a poet of me. How shameful.

Sister Perpetué grows frustrated. But his . . . his origins, his parentage—

The nun's frustration butts up against the patient's own. He groans, balling the bedclothes in his fists by his sides. He was a souteneur. Does that satisfy you? A maquereau. A ponce. A pimp. He won starved flesh to himself and rented it back out. Do you understand?

Oh. Sister Perpetué purses her lips. Oh. So, you . . . so—

The patient closes his eyes and chuckles. Don't worry your pretty head, Sister, he sighs. No one was wanting my shitty arse. More's the pity, I say. There were other things they wanted. Other things I could do. You will see.

They are silent for a little while. The candle puts small deep shadows on the bed linen, like a flame-spirit setting out its mourning clothes.

How long did you remain in his company? Sister Perpetué asks at last.

The patient works a hand down over his distended belly. One summer, he sighs. He opens his eyes, frowns a little. The best summer of my life. He opens his eyes wide and feels them flooded by the hard brasslike morning light—

*

Hard brasslike morning light. As they tramp from village to village along the Mâcon way, Tarare is never not hungry. His stomach gorged and his legs weak and shaking between his leaden entrails and the dirt road. Tarare is a peasant; he has known hunger. He has known hunger all his life, long and well. Hunger lived at every slumping house in the village he was born in. Hunger slunk to the wineshop, and leant against the garden wall to gossip, hunger played at skull-and-bones in the narrow dirt road. Hunger, mother-of-nothing. He knew hunger before he knew there was a word for it, that peculiar tightening, that hollow. But this hunger is new. He feels it running through his bones like marrow. What he might eat – and where he will find it – is the first thought he has upon waking, and the last he has as he curls on the roadside (or in a hayloft, or on a softer bed of early-shed leaves, jacket pillowed under his head, the bodies of his friends around him in the grass) to sleep. When they come by a stream, Tarare fills his cupped hands with water, again and again, gulps down so much he feels he should burst – but it does nothing to ease the empty ache of his belly. He chews dandelions, bitterroot and bark from the trees. In his worst moments, he wonders if a man can eat the meat off his own body. He is sure it must have happened somehow, somewhere. A man must have been desperate enough to try taking a bite of the fat and marbled flesh of his very own arm.

The boy, Tarare, is literally insatiable. Day by day his wounds heal and his strength returns. Something desperate, something feral, shines from deep in the sweet blue water of his eyes.

Lozeau sees all this. On a June night, oppressively hot, they have come to rest in a copse. Crouched by the low cooking fire, Lozeau thumbs the cork from a bottle of brandy and rolls it across the ground toward Tarare. Here, he says. Tarare, eat.

Tarare picks up the cork. He purses his lips and blows the dust from it, girlishly. And then he swallows it whole. His mouth opens wide when he does this. His jaw unhinges in a ghastly way like a snake's. It is quite a thing to see, thinks Lozeau.

In the mornings they walk for as long as they can before

it gets too hot for them to walk any further. Sun cooking the dust, frying the napes of their necks. Sun inexhaustible. They walk toward Paris. There are people on the roads. So many of them it is like half of France has stood up from her empty pot and strode out into the scorch. Peasants in felt caps and patched tunics and flowered bonnets, dragging bony mules behind them. Knife sharpeners, organ grinders. Men blind and lamed. Soldiers – or what were soldiers – the fringed epaulettes torn from their coats. Everyone has something to sell or to trade: cheese, horsehair, cunt, bonesetting, babies. They see Spaniards, and mulâtres with golden teeth. They see a rat-catcher in a long black greatcoat, striding the ridge behind his pack of tame red-eyed ferrets who fill the road before him like a bank of snow. He talks to his ferrets in a mysterious patois. He tips his hat and grins like a King of all Ratcatchers.

In Moulins, Lozeau takes Tarare into the town proper. It is Sunday, early, and the church bell is ringing. A few ragged dogs have been let out to wander the cobbled streets. Red-headed flowers nod at the mild sunshine. They pass a boarded-up inn, an empty schoolhouse. At the door of the butcher's shop stands the butcher.

Do you have any offal, monsieur? asks Lozeau. Any waste?

The butcher frowns and gazes over the dark plumes of Lozeau's hat into a little crosshatching of cloud in the sky behind him. Offal's not waste, he replies. I can sell offal.

Then here, says Lozeau, is a buyer.

The butcher leads them through his shop to the yard out back, where honeysuckle clings incongruously to the blood-flecked stone and flayed carcasses hang spreadeagled to the sun. He gestures to a long, deep trough that runs against the far wall, filled to the lip with gut. There's offal, he says.

I'll buy, says Lozeau.

All of it? the butcher asks, in a tone of respectful disbelief.

Lozeau looks at the trough, scratching his beard. Raw sheeps' lung and viscera, pearled with melting fat. A collagenous duct of flesh, amorphous and swarmed about with jubilant blue-bottles. How long has it been here? he asks. Is it turned?

The butcher shrugs. You'll be wanting it all? he asks again. Is it for dogs? It's good for dogs.

Lozeau's mind wanders then, as his mind is prone to do. It wanders to the tales of antiquity, to Father Time cracking the heads of his children open like eggs. Lowering wriggling naked godlets into his vast paternal maw. To the shy giants who were said to live in the mountains, Og and Gibborim and Ferragut, stirring their green bubbling pots with the long bones of war-horses. The ghouls of the churchyard whose faces are made from the mist of All Hallows'. Tarare, Tartarus. Is it a good or a bad thing to feed this boy? Lozeau cares to know what is good from what is bad, even if he chooses, in the end, the bad. The boy needs to eat, he knows. The boy *wants* to eat, he reasons.

Monsieur? says the butcher.

It's not for dogs, says Lozeau. Tarare?

The stench of the rotting flesh is powerful. Tarare's hunger is more powerful. So he eats. He eats all of what would be good for dogs. Gorges on it. Lozeau and the butcher watch Tarare eat, until the trough is empty and the blood baked dry. He never gags. He never stops, even, it seems, to breathe. When he is done he turns from the trough to look at Lozeau, his chin slimy. And he blushes, actually blushes. As though he has been caught in a lie. The real lie, thinks Lozeau, is every moment Tarare spends upright and empty-mouthed. Every pleasantry Tarare exchanges, every polite smile Tarare bestows, with this

dog, this wolf, this Gibborim under his skin, slavering and famished all the while. Now Lozeau has seen Tarare. Now he has
seen what Tarare is. It is quite a thing to see.

Mother of God, says the butcher.

I know, says Lozeau.

*

They walk back through the fields near to dusk. Clouds have
crowded in above, and a light rain falls. The fields exhale the
fragrant spice of this rain. After the butcher's shop, Lozeau had
taken Tarare to a buvette on the street corner and bought him
sausages and dumplings and café au lait. He ate like a starving
man, even having gorged himself on offal.

Did you like the dumplings? asks Lozeau.

Yes, says Tarare. Very much. Thank you, monsieur.

You deserved them.

Tarare says nothing, but looks sidelong at him, curious, his
cheeks flushed pale pink.

How do you feel, Tarare, when you eat? asks Lozeau.

Feel, monsieur?

Yes.

Tarare thinks for a moment. Hungry, he says.

You feel hungry when you eat?

Tarare nods.

How many words, thinks Lozeau, does a boy like Tarare even
possess to describe how he feels? Hungry, angry, happy, sad.
Itchy. They continue in silence through the field for a little
while, until they see the barn where the others have holed up
for the night, a dark smudge on the lightly misted horizon.
Lozeau is planning, in his mind.

Did you like the offal? asks Lozeau. Smell didn't put you off?

I couldn't smell it, monsieur.

I wish I knew how you worked, Tarare, says Lozeau. He puts his hand on the boy's shoulder. Tell me your life.

There's nothing to tell, monsieur.

We'll have to make something up then, says Lozeau. Tarare. I feel it is time to impart to you a lesson.

I don't have my letters, monsieur.

Lozeau smiles indulgently at the boy. Not that kind of lesson, he says. A lesson in the ethics of our non-profession.

Here follows what Tarare learns:

All that is left in carelessness within easy reach may be taken, for man should not lay up for himself the treasures of the earth where moth and dust doth corrupt: the smalls left to dry in the hedgerow, the pies cooling on a windowsill, the satin purse attached to a waistband by the meagrest of threads. Lift nothing that is difficult to lift. Upholsterers will pay a good price for horsehair, and a man ought always to carry a pair of shears for the snipping of tails from unattended geldings – but hazards abound at the tail end of a horse. The henhouse is to be avoided. Many fine vagabonds have met their end face down in the dander, arses wedged in a narrow wooden hutch. Dogs are the enemy. Cats are, in all things, indifferent (and the finer specimens can in point of fact be sold to furriers. Though it is to be remembered that to skin a cat, even indirectly, is a very inauspicious thing.) Milk straight from the udder may be sweet, but a man is never more vulnerable than when he lies on his back like a baby. People enjoy a leper, because they know them from the Bible. A little blood and egg white smeared on the skin will create the likeness of embarrassing and transmittable affliction – apply the decoction generously on the neck and forearms, leave to dry, then head to the nearest church and grasp desperately at the glittering hands of fine women, who will pay you generously to breathe elsewhere than on them. Said fine women, and often their servants, go to church on Sundays. This means their houses are empty. If you pick a dandelion you will piss yourself. Check for pox before you put your dick anywhere. Honey is better than bile. Always carry a little Saint Christophe somewhere about your person. If you are being chased, you must cross a river. If you are being beaten, you must curl in a ball to shield your softer parts and wait for it to stop. Which it will, eventually, in one way or another.

And so forth and in these ways, young Tarare, you will live well all your earthly days and find Heaven thereafter.

*

It is early on market day when they arrive at Saint-Flour. Lozeau says the town was made when a good bishop came to be among the heathens of the wood, who had lived in that place since Creation, painting their faces blue, and having never heard the name of their creator or thought about how they had come to be there at all. And the bishop struck his staff against the mountainside, and water had tumbled from the gash he made in the rock, and this water became the river that they cross now by the narrow stone bridge. Tarare sees brown trout swaying in the shadow of the bridge, luxuriously open-mouthed in the even flow. Lozeau says for this reason Saint-Flour is an auspicious town, cleaving as it does to an auspicious river. Vidal says not everything has to be a story. Lozeau says yes, my friend, everything does. Everything is.

The cobbles of the town square glisten with the last night's rain, but the sky is clear now, and shell-coloured. Lozeau sets Tarare on a bench in front of the shuttered wineshop. You wait here, Tarare, he says. We have things to do. Preparations to make.

Tarare nods obediently.

Lozeau turns to leave, then hesitates. He looks at Tarare again. You will be all right here, on your own? (What he means is: you will not run away, will you, now that I have discovered how I might profit by you?)

Yes, says Tarare.

Pierette, says Lozeau. Stay with Tarare. Keep him company.

So Pierette settles on the bench beside Tarare and the others leave. Pierette and Tarare sit for a long while in silence. The sun creeps down across the walls until it bleaches the square, and Tarare feels their silence to be at least companionable, and is pleased of the room it makes for his thoughts, which he has had no opportunity to be alone with in so many weeks. In his mind, he tries to turn his thoughts as though they are stuck on a spit: warming them evenly on every side. His first thought is of Lozeau and himself, and their relation to one another. On the one side he understands that what Lozeau and his band offer is protection, and that it is good and easy to belong to such a person, who knows the world – and how to move smoothly between its maws and pratfalls – well. On the other, he knows a real man is meant to belong to no one but himself. So Nollet said. So Nollet told him often, like a credo. On the one hand, he is part of a band now. Brothers, Lozeau calls them, sometimes. On the other, when he lays his head down to sleep he feels a desperate and terrifying loneliness, and even terror, as though the bodies of Vidal and Antoine and the rest of them prone around him in the darkness were the shadows of vast nocturnal birds that eat flesh and have no language. 'Brother' is, after all, just a word. On the one hand, he feels blessed. On the other, cursed. But he is too small to contend with what God, presumably, has made him. And he is too weak to move from where God, presumably, has placed him. And should he take solace in that? The workings of God, the ineluctability of fate, cradling him like a silvered net? Tarare is thinking these things, or trying to, when he remembers that he is hungry. So hungry. And then his great hunger becomes all that he can hold in his mind and he can no longer think of anything else. It has been this way since the hunger began. Since Nollet left him for dead in the green belly of the forest. If he wants to have thoughts at all, he must first expend his energy in hefting the enormous hunger aside. Hunger is the air Tarare breathes, and the espadrilles on his feet, and the hair that sprouts on his arms. Sometimes he worries that hunger is all he is. He thought it would go away. That with time it would diminish. But it hasn't. It is in this moment, with the delicate cruciform shadow of the church's weathervane grazing at the toe of his shoe, that Tarare realises he faces down an existence of unrelenting, insatiable want. Of eternal suffering. That a void opened up underneath him when it opened up within him. So now what? It is in this moment that Pierette, tucking her hair behind her ears, turns to him and says – What is your favourite colour?

This is something Tarare knows and has always known. Green, he says. Like the grass. But I like all of them.

Oh, she says. Yellow?

Yes, says Tarare. Yellow meadow-flowers.

How old are you?

Seventeen.

She laughs. Why meadow-flowers, then? People will think you're soft.

Tarare closes his eyes and rests his head against the brickwork. The day is beginning now. The square is filling with people, and the sounds of market day are familiar to him, and sweet: the saw of wagon wheels, shod hooves on compacted dirt. Farmers, the quiet chatter of men who prefer speaking to dogs than to other men, the scents of cabbage and old leather. I think everyone is soft, says Tarare. Some are just better at hiding it.

Lalie says we can get new dresses soon, Pierette continues, as though Tarare has said nothing at all about the ubiquitous softness of men. I saw a girl in Moulins in a very pale blue, and I liked that. But maybe green? A light green. I don't know what the fashions are in Paris and Lalie says she does, and that the fashion is for pale colours, but she doesn't really. Do you think green would become me?

Tarare opens his eyes to look at Pierette. She looks back at him, expectant. She is wearing powder today and it sits on her small face like a dust. Her gown gapes on her flat body. Yes, says Tarare. (He doesn't know if it would or not, but he thinks it would please her to hear it.)

If it does please her, she shows no sign of it. Are you from Lyon? she asks.

No. A village near to Lyon.

I'm from Lyon, she says. Lalie and me. A convent. We slept in the attic with six other girls and it got so cold in the winter, and sometimes the other girls would put your hand in a pail of cold water when you were sleeping so you pissed the bed, and then the Sisters would beat you with a strap. They were meant to teach us to read and write, but they didn't bother. They taught us to sew, so we made purses, and they sold the purses at market. So whenever I see a woman take her purse from her reticule I wonder if it is a purse I made. Foundlings, you see. I didn't know my mother or my father. So when we go with men I try to look very hard into their faces to see if they could be my father or even my brother, because they wouldn't know and I wouldn't know, but God would know, wouldn't he? That we were committing an incest. God would know it and condemn us. She scratches at the side of her hand, where the skin is dry and flaking. But I think I would know my father if I met him, she concludes.

It would be an honest mistake, says Tarare. God wouldn't condemn you for an honest mistake, says Tarare. But he is not very sure of this.

Maybe you could be my brother, says Pierette. She says this and then she leans in very close to Tarare, their noses almost touching. So close that he can see her yellow dress is printed with a pattern faded through wear and the bleach of the sun: ghostly flowers in her skirts, tiny triplicated buds. She looks deep into his eyes with her eyes, which are a mottled brown. He can smell her polysaccharide breath (milk, black bread). He thinks for a moment that she is going to kiss him, Tarare, and is trying to decide if he wants her to or not, when she shakes her head sadly and says, no, no. Not you. She draws away.

I had a sister, says Tarare. But she died. We didn't tell the abbé like we were supposed to. We took her to the forest and covered her over with branches and leaves. This was in winter, and her hands and her eyes were so small, and you could see through them to the veins, like she was made of clouded glass.

As Tarare tells Pierette this, he realises he has never told anyone before. And he feels a large and long-held weight shift like a stone from his throat.

Pierette looks at him thoughtfully. You don't need to tell people things like that, she says. It's too sad. You are Tarare but you can be anyone now. You can be soft and seem hard. If you want, you can pretend that nothing sad has ever happened in your life. People will like you more that way.

I don't care if people like me or not, Tarare lies.

Are you ready? asks Pierette. Without waiting for his answer, she extends a finger and pokes him in the swollen gut with a moderate violence. Where does it all go, anyway? She giggles. Aside from this little pouch, you're skinny as a rake.

Tarare flinches and wraps his arms around himself protectively. Don't touch me, he whines.

Don't touch me, don't touch me, he asks! You're older than I am. You ought to know by now that *asking* doesn't get, she sneers. She takes her vicious little finger and prods him again and again, this time in the shoulder, this time in the arm drawn over his body, until Tarare, flustered and anxious, begins to whimper and swat at her.

They cuff and slap at each other in this way for a short while, Pierette laughing wickedly and Tarare growing increasingly rattled until tears begin to burn in his eyes. With one last whimper, Tarare pushes Pierette away from him, draws his knees up to his chest and lowers his head to hide his face away from her. His shoulders wobble.

Are you crying? Jesus Christ.

Tarare, drawn up into himself, does not answer.

Why are you crying? Pierette asks. Her voice softens. She leans in close.

Because I'm hungry.

You're crying because you're hungry?

Tarare peers up at her. She tries to speak gently but there is an edge of disdain in her voice as she repeats: You're crying because you're hungry?

He groans. And I'm afraid. You wouldn't understand.

Of Monsieur Lozeau? Because sometimes—

I'm afraid the hunger will never go away.

Pierette considers him, then sighs, settling back into the bench. Tarare lowers his face into his sleeve again with a dry, guttural sob. He was right – she didn't understand, and no one will, ever. His hunger cannot be told. The hunger is all he is and it cannot be told and the whole world and everything in it, the things that should make Tarare happy – a sunset, a kitten, a psalm remembered – make him hungry instead.

He is thinking this with a deep aching when he feels Pierette push her small hand into his and squeeze his fingers. Then she begins to sing. She sings *Oh! Shall I tell you, Mama* – and Tarare knows this song, which is a song his own mother would sing.

Papa wants me to be all grown up—
Yet I say that bonbons—
Are better than reason—

*

Pierette and Lalie hold a drape between Tarare and the crowd. The sun comes around the sides and above, but behind the drape he stands in shadow. Tarare can hear the people who have assembled, but cannot see them – yet. Instead he looks up at the sky and sees there are gulls wheeling there, above his head. They drop and soar in such a way as to sometimes become invisible against the flat blue of the sky – mere slivers – before seeming to regain their bodily shape as they resume their heavenward arc. The gulls, Tarare thinks, know just as well as everyone else when market day occurs. They fly north, the silt sparkling on their feathers, for the carrion of commerce.

It has become another day of almost unbearable heat. Tarare staunches the sweat of his upper lip on his sleeve.

On the other side of the drapery, Tarare hears the beating of drums. He hears Lozeau. His voice is raised high against the babble of the market-goers.

Words, cries Lozeau, fail me in this enterprise. They are too small, too dainty in their construction to hold fast around the horror I would contain within them. My friends – what I can give you is his name. His name is Tarare – here he pauses in a momentous silence. And that strange and memorable name, my friends, has been often preceded by 'Great', and often by 'Terrible'. But I want to ask you, the good people of Saint-Flour – who do you think it was that gave him this name? Was it an ogress, perhaps, dandling her newborn on a couch of bone? Or perhaps it was a god? For some would say Tarare is like unto the sons the gods fathered on the maidens of old, before time and reason tidied their rusted spears of thunder away. Tarare is a Hercules of the gullet. An Ajax – of the arsehole (here he pauses to wait out a ripple of laughter from the gathered crowd). For those who have witnessed true wonders in this world – and modestly, *modestly*, I will say that I stand among their number – will tell you that to see wonders is not to walk away from them with smug and clear-eyed satisfaction that nature's genius has found its ultimate expression. At Rouergue I saw the wild boy wrested from the forest, covered all over with fur, who walked on his hands like a dog and spoke in howls. In the hills near Avignon I met men who summoned angels into their presence, bright shapes that caused the furniture to quake and tremble, to come apart at the joints. To see wonders is to be filled with questions. To see wonders is to set the mind aflame. But what begat it? you will ask. Under what black horoscope was he born? And what further wonders will this, will he, beget? But enough. I am no learned man. I can give you only theories. Mine is this: that it was the Devil himself who named him Tarare. It was the Devil himself who, needing a quicker route home from the Palace of Versailles (a little more laughter, here), took a boy, and by some strange magic, or else with a locksmith's toolbox of burnt irons, put a door in his throat – a portal to the sulphurous and unfathomable depths of Tophet. Mesdames and Messieurs, I give you The Great Tarare – The Glutton – The Bottomless Man!

The drape falls and there Lozeau stands. His arms outspread in the massive sunshine, his head thrown back. Like a burning effigy.

Tarare blinks purblinded into the faces of the strangers arrayed before him – not so many, but enough that Tarare, for a moment, seems to feel his gullet knot and close itself off, to be looked at, to be seen in this way. Bonfils and Vidal beat furiously on upturned buckets, and when their improvised tattoo is done, there is silence.

Then there is laughter, an uneasy tittering. Then the heckles begin.

It's a skinny boy? calls out a man in a dirty coat and tricorn. Thank you, monsieur, but we have those in Saint-Flour.

Can you do the angels instead? cries a woman.

Lozeau smiles benevolently and wheels on the spot. Pearls of sweat stand out on his brow. But my friends, he counters. My good people. The Great Tarare needs something to eat!

He's hungry, eh? shouts a farmer. And that's the wonder? Then perhaps you should put *me* behind a velvet drape on market day, Egyptian.

What we have to eat we will eat for ourselves! cries a woman cradling a baby at her breast. She screws her mouth small and spits, spits over her baby at Lozeau's feet. Some of the laughter turns to jeering.

Here, calls a brindled herb merchant with a striped feather in his hat. The boy can have a liard and get himself something to eat with that, for I pity him. He thumbs around in his pockets and a brown coin tickles across the cobbles.

Here! shouts a boy from the middle of the crowd – your *Bottomless Man* can eat my dick! And a something, a something large and dun-coloured, is thrown over the heads of the assembled, and lands at Tarare's feet. And Tarare looks down and sees a dead rat. Grey-furred and stiff with mortis, its grain-swollen belly turned up toward the sky and its lips curled back from sharp brown teeth. The rat's fingers are clutched at its own downy breast, frozen in an attitude of strangely human-seeming panic. He can see no marks on the body, no blood. As though it died of a nightmare in its bed of rag and tiny cottons. An old-man-of-rat. Of what, Tarare thinks, do rats dream? Of cheese and malt, and bacon rind, and the beckoning warmth of tallow light. Tarare lifts his eyes from the rat and finds, in the now-silent crowd, the face of the boy who threw it. He stands in the third row back. Tarare can see that the boy's face, partly obscured by an artful mask of streaked dirt, is Antoine's face. When their eyes meet Antoine's pretty mouth bends into a smile, and he dips his chin into the barest perceptible gesture of encouragement, the barest perceptible nod. It was planned.

The elder Lozeau murmurs his name so that only he can hear it. *Tarare.*

Everyone is looking at him. All of them are waiting to see what Tarare will do. So Tarare stoops low, takes the rat by its stiffened tail. He holds the rat high in the air, and he throws back his head. He opens his mouth as wide as it will go. He unhooks his jaw like an adder.

It is quite a thing to see.

*

Reader, see now through the dry peppercorn eyes of a dead rat. Your hands are lifeless. Sliding down the gullet, you have had your death. The rest – as they say – is silence. But this isn't. You hear the beating of a giant's heart, and the sounds below, as of a river running through the dark. We are inside Tarare. He constricts around us, breathes. All pink and craquelure.

We will go no further.

Our Tarare is not flesh.

Think what you wish to, when he unhooks his jaw. Take as benison this reticence – magic will be left alive. The dark work done in him is yours to digest. Look inside. Perhaps you see a red devil throned in a cavern, priapic, his erection slung across his knees. Laughing. Perhaps you see a body of water, so deep and luminous with the wrigglings of lanternfish and blindworms gorged on scribbles of meat.

Perhaps he is empty metaphor. Perhaps.

Before the end, Tarare will be opened up. The mystery of him held up naked to the light. And at that time we will cleave to our wonder, and agree to look away.

IV Vendémiaire an VII

Sister Perpetué's face is pale. Even the thought of it raises the bile in her throat, prompts a nausea that is almost overwhelming. The odorous, bristling fur. The small and shard-like bones sticking in the throat. The crunch, the tear, the rancid squirting of the small organs. She holds her hand over her mouth.

The killer chuckles and moistens his lips with his tongue, watching her. It is interesting to me how women – milliner, duchess, nun, whichever women you like – will put their dainty little hands up to their mouths when they want to show how they are appalled.

Sister Perpetué swallows, composing herself. It is instinct, she says. Not affectation.

Instinct or otherwise, answers Tarare, a little hand over the mouth won't stop your fancy getting in. I want more syrup of poppy.

You can't have it, yet. How did you do it?

The rat?

A nod.

Easy. The same way anyone eats anything, Sister. The teeth, the tongue. You see, little novice, I have theories of my own. It is the mind that leads us to eat certain things and reject others with disgust. And if you *want* to eat anything, the mind is the only obstacle to be overcome.

But. *Why?*

Tarare sighs, as though he finds her questions tiresome. Why *not*, little novice? When you are young you want to please everybody. When you are a man, you want to make a name. If there is a proscription against the eating of dead rats among the laws of God or man, then I am yet to be told of it. Please – he holds his hands out toward her in a gesture of supplication – if I am wrong, dear Sister, then educate me.

It is wrong, she says, because *we feel it to be wrong*. Because the sound mind reels from it in disgust. And it is in the workings of the mind and the body, given to us by God, as well as in the Holy Book, that we might best apprehend how it is He wishes us to use them.

Men of *sound mind* would wake before dawn and walk twenty miles through the ground fog to see me eat. Tarare smiles with pleasure. His blue eyes are dilated.

They should have looked upon you as a creature to be pitied.

I have never wanted anyone's pity. His mouth twists downward.

Besides, she continues, the proscription against eating rats and corks, and golden forks, and whatever other nonsense you have willingly put in your body ought to be taken as included within the proscription against self-slaughter.

No one has ever wanted to die less than I do, Sister.

Yet here you lie dying. A man of—

Tarare's brow furrows as he reels the years taut in his mind. It is the process of thirty, forty seconds. Year of the Talking Cow, Year of the Severed Head, Year of Tears for Mirabeau, Year of Tears for People's-friend Marat, bathed in scarlet. Rainbows of news-sheets and proclamations pasted to the stonework. Heavy weather. Voltaire's skull on a pillow of oleanders. Cannon, grapeshot. It felt like one hundred years in ten, to live it. Twenty-seven, he says. A man of twenty-seven. Then, more quietly, almost to himself – (ah, poor Pierette. A child. She might have children of her own, by now).

So here you lie dying, a man of twenty-seven.

This is why I don't like religious people, he sneers. You think everyone should think the same way that you do and browbeat them when they don't. This is why no one likes religious people any more, and why they drive you out on to the roads from your convents and holy houses and throw stones in the street—

They are not driving us from the hospitals.

What?

They are not driving us from the hospitals, for all their cant against our orders. For all their altars to reason. Sister Perpetué sits composed as she says this. Do you know why? Because there are no others who will do as we do. The work of mother and charwoman together, caring for the sickened and the needy. Dressing their wounds and wiping the sweat and the shit from their bodies and holding their hands when they cry out in pain. We do not all do it well, and we do not all do it with grace (she thinks of Mother Superior's dolomite eye). But we do it. We do it for the love of God.

The killer lets out a laboured chuckle. You're chatting shit again, Sister. Mother and char? Is there a single woman of the Third Estate who is not both of these and more? Save for those that starve before they breed. Mothers, charwomen – some even found time to mount cannon outside the Tuileries, calling for bread and soap. What you are describing is not a nun, it is a woman. He stretches his legs out beneath his ragged blanket. I've met some cunty nuns in my time. Then he softens his voice slightly, almost apologetically. Not you, though, he adds. You seem all right.

Thank you, she says, smoothing her kirtle.

In that dark cell a silence settles between them. The killer resumes his watchfulness. Sister Perpetué sees the candlelight play on his puzzling face: at once gaunt and piggy, placid and calculating. So, she says. Was it at this time you ate the fork?

Are you a fool? he says. An idiot? Do you think the peasants of the Moulins and the Saint-Flours of this world have gold-plated forks to hand to be throwing at vagrants in dirty suits? No. He takes a rattling breath. That was after. After the time of my true glory.

Glory?

Yes, he says, with a wistful smile. And you can hold your tongue because that was what it felt like. Glory. That is what I have now, all I have. And that is what I choose to call it. Glory.

*

At the Lion d'Or in Saint-Flour everyone wants to buy drinks for the Rat Boy. That is what they are calling him. He ate other things, but the rat is what they remembered. *Didn't you see? He took a dead rat, long as my forearm, fat as your wife, and bit into it like a fucking pork sausage. Horrible stuff. Vile. Brilliant. Bonaventure was sick all over his new shoes, haha.* The stinking snuffing men who say these things press around the bar and around the little tables, just as they do after every market, except this time their conversation is enhanced by the novelty of their day's experience. *Yeah, he's still here. That one over there, the blond one. He'll eat your cork for a sou, your belt for five. If you want to see.*

Tarare eats six corks and two belts and drinks four mugs of cider, gratis, from the innkeeper. Whenever he eats anything everyone cheers. Two beltless men shuffle drunkenly through

A. K. BLAKEMORE

the straw on the floorboards, their trousers sagging at their ankles, their bare arses merrily slapped by their friends, crying out, Look what he did to me, the Rat Boy! The Great Tarare! in pitchy tones of mock hysteria.

Glory.

As the evening wanes and the mood settles, Tarare is sitting with Lozeau and Bonfils and Vidal at a table overburdened by the offerings of these strangers, who are delighted with him: meat pies and red wine and roasted chicken thighs, the juicy flesh falling from the bone. His heart is light.

What I don't understand, says Vidal, shaking his head with a joyful bafflement, is why any man would want his belt eaten. Let alone pay five sous for the pleasure? But you know, gift horses. Mouths.

Five sous is a pound of good bread, says Bonfils. Or is it, even, these days?

Lozeau leans back in his chair, tracing the stem of his pipe around his whiskers, and sets his heels on the table. It's the patina of celebrity, he says.

That's something you know about, is it? (Vidal).

In my time.

And when was that? interjects Bonfils. The time of Charlemagne?

Lozeau chuckles. I'm not over the hill, he says. I'm under it. Dancing where the mandrake roots grow white.

You do chat a lot of shit, says Vidal.

You know he colours his hair, Tarare? Like an old whore? Bonfils leans across the table to pluck at Lozeau's black ringlets, and Lozeau brushes his hand away with a laugh.

And will continue to do so. Do you know how much money we made today? By Fortuna—

144

How much money *Tarare* made. It is Lalie who says this. She has cut through the crowd and rests her hands on the sanded board of the table, fixing Lozeau with a cold look. A curl of her messily dressed hair has fallen loose from its pinnings and sticks to her temple.

Speaking of old whores. You look like you're spoiling for a fight, Lalie, says Vidal. I like it. Come, have a glass of anisette.

It's how she's drawn on her eyebrows that makes her look like that, says Bonfils.

A conciliatory smile from Lozeau. Lalie, my dear, he says. These are academic distinctions. What money we make through our conjoint enterprise, we share.

I don't see you doing any of the conjoining, Jules. Pierette is upstairs. Crying.

Why would she be crying?

I don't know. Yet she is. She is crying all the fucking time and Antoine is no help with her.

Vidal laughs.

What is this fat prick making? she says, waving her wrist at Vidal with a clatter of paste-gemmed bangles. What does this swine contribute to our *conjoint* fortunes?

Lozeau's mouth flattens into a curt line. You were pleased enough with him when that bastard tried to drown you in the trough in Neuilly.

I should say, adds Vidal, snaking his hand down under his belly and squeezing his parts for Lalie to see. *Very grateful.* I hope some other bastard tries to drown you soon, I really do.

Lalie throws her body across the table and slaps Vidal hard. The two wrangle, Lalie scratching and shrieking. Vidal pushes his splayed palm on to her face and across her mouth, but she gets his finger between her teeth and bites down hard, drawing blood. Vidal roars. The men crowded at the bar turn to watch, hooting, laughing. Lozeau moves spider-fast. He winds his gloved hand into Lalie's neckerchief, hauling her across the boards. Her belly is turned upward. Tarare sees her lacings strain with each guttural breath, her cheap satins soiled with grease and spilled wine. Lozeau winds the neckerchief tighter so that it bites her flesh. He lifts her face up to his own. A nerve jumps in his jaw. As he holds her there, gasping, Lalie's eyes roll like a trapped rabbit's, from right to left. Her teeth are pinked with Vidal's blood. She has tried as best she can to cover the flaking sore at the corner of her mouth with a cosmetic paste.

Quite an advertisement you are making of yourself, sweet Eulalie, Lozeau says, his beard almost brushing the cocotte's rouged cheek. He raises his head, considering her. His gaze is cold and thoughtful. Then he releases her back against the tabletop. Why are you dressing yourself like a gâteau these days, Lalie? he says, resuming his seat. All these bijoux. He reaches out to pluck a paper flower pinned in her hair. He closes his fist around this scrap of colour.

Lalie slides from the table and gets to her feet, rearranging her neckerchief. Her hands shake. We'll leave, she says. Pierette and me.

What's that? asks Lozeau, groping around the wreckage of their meal for his pipe.

We'll leave.

Oh, says Lozeau, lighting up, kissing a billow of blue smoke toward the low, clouded rafters. Where will you go, my dear?

To Paris.

That's convenient, says Lozeau. We're going to Paris, too – perhaps we could travel together? The roads north are dangerous these days. Especially for a woman, no? A beautiful woman?

Lalie looks around hopelessly. At Bonfils, then at Tarare. Tarare and Bonfils look into their cups. She turns and shoulders her way back through the watching crowd. The men simmer with mirth. When she is gone they turn back to their drinks, as if nothing has happened. As if no woman had happened since Eve in the garden.

Do you want me to follow her? asks Vidal, sucking his bitten finger.

Absolutely not, says Lozeau.

That was a nasty thing you said (Bonfils screws his courage to the sticking place). You deserved every slap and bite she gave you.

Vidal squeezes his face into an ugly porcine nublet and repeats Bonfils' words in a pitchy whine. *You deserved every slap and bite she gave you.* Whoreson. Thinking you are better than everyone else because you can read.

I don't *think*, says Bonfils, cautiously fingering the rim of his mug. I *know*.

We are rich enough tonight, Lozeau sighs. Perhaps we can enjoy it without all this row? Food, wine, a little song? Can we simply delight in these, our small blessings?

Aye, says Vidal.

Fine, says Bonfils. *Our small blessings.*

(Both without conviction.)

What of you, Tarare? says Lozeau, with a false brightness. Enjoying the wine?

Tarare takes another gulp. A black sediment around his lips. It tastes like sweat smells, he thinks. I like the way it makes me feel, he says.

Vidal smacks him between the shoulder blades, approvingly. Laughs from the belly. Says, Perhaps next time we make him look a little scarier, eh? A little blood around his mouth? Perhaps we black his face with polish? What do you think, Jules?

Tarare feels he is going to be sick. Could be the wine, could be the corks. He closes his eyes, light-headed, and when he opens them again the low-ceilinged room seems not to be filled with smoke but with a tinctured water, and everything he hears – the low chatter of men, the crackling of the fire – is as through a pane of glass. The beat of his blood through the delicate innerwork of his ears. Nausea. A lurching in his stomach. (So many people, pressing in on one another, each a great depth cased in skin. Frayed cuffs and withered stars of honeysuckle pinned in hatbands.) His lips are sticky. He opens them, says he needs some air. The bile rises in his throat. Standing, he staggers for the door.

Outside the inn, where the houses meet the fields, all is bathed in quietude. The sun settles, mixing its fire with the milk of the summer evening. Outside the stables a black cat rusts slit-eyed in the lateral glow. In the distance, beyond a wide meadow, the auspicious river twists away, mirroring the sky, a bloody scar. Tarare squats on his haunches to be sick.

Whenever I see you, you're staring at the floor, says Antoine.

Tarare gulps the sour bile down and straightens. I thought I was going to be sick, he says.

And you went outside to do it? How polite. Antoine laughs. You know places like this keep a pail in the corner for vomit? And piss and shit. In case of rain.

Antoine leans against an outbuilding, thumbs thrust into his belt. The expiring sun blazes lovingly against the V of skin between his neckerchief and his unbuttoned shirt front. He has cleaned the dirt from his face. He is smiling. He arrives, implike: holding his body at a slant, trailing the musk of another world on the poor clothes he wears so pretty. Antoine's beauty is not incidental. Antoine's beauty is the crucible of his dilatory, amoral character. Antoine Lozeau knows there will always be someone else in the world who will say *yes* to him.

Antoine takes a little box from his jacket pocket. Do you want some snuff? he asks.

What does it do?

Makes you kind of dizzy?

I'm all right.

Antoine takes a pinch. Snorts deeply. Puts the box back in his jacket pocket and throws back his hair with a twist of the chin, his expression beatific. You're a queen, aren't you?

What?

A queen, Antoine repeats. You like kissing other boys, fuck-ing other boys.

Tarare's cheeks flush.

You didn't know you could do that? Antoine grins.

Tarare is silent while the wheels turn. Men don't have that part, obviously. But they have others. They have mouths. Antoine has a mouth (silk-mouth cloud's-mouth, way inside). He feels again the unbidden frisson of arousal twitch under his belt buckle, shifts so he is standing with his legs pressed close together. He hates cocks, he decides, which cannot keep their secrets.

Don't look at me, says Antoine. I'm too expensive, even for the Rat Boy of Saint-Flour. And anyway, I don't shit where I eat. Unlike most.

More wheels in Tarare, more silence from Tarare.

I suppose you didn't know boys could do that, either? Antoine's lip curls. What a day of discovery it has been for young Tarare. Anyway, he says, tugging at the gold ring in his

ear – I wanted to say. The rat. It wasn't my idea. It was my
brother's. I thought it was a mean trick, not telling you first.
Just throwing it at your feet like that.

Making it so I didn't have a choice. But you still did it, is what
Tarare thinks. What Tarare does is shrug. What Tarare says is:
Lozeau is truly your brother? He is so—

Much older than me? Yes, he is. Same bastard father, different
mothers. We travelled in—

Their talk is truncated by an echoing crack from the direction of the town. It sounds singly, then lingers on the mellow
of the evening like an aggressively posed question. Antoine
squints in the direction of the clustered rooftops and lifts a
hand to shade his eyes against the sun. Sounded like musket
fire, he says.

Tarare follows his gaze toward the bend of the river. Tidy
housefronts, the regular heave of the mill wheel, the sprouting
of ephemerals. All appears calm, except for the birds. The noise
has shaken them loose and scatty from the eaves and treetops.
They fill the sky all around, like a powder, whirling in erratic
murmuration between the thatch and the rosy firmament. For
a time, their distress causes them to forget their order: starling
flocks with pigeon, swallow with dove. A hundred hundred
pinhead hearts circling over their heads. If there is further
report from the town, the birds' wail drowns it out.

I don't know what that sounds like, says Tarare.

Never heard musket fire? Christ. You really did grow up in
a shoebox. You should get used to it though, no? My brother
says there will be civil war.

War?

Antoine murmurs confirmation. He is looking upward now,
into the pretty chaos of birds. The red sunlight fills the hollows

of his face. You know what else he says? He says that if you watch birds and listen to them too, for a long time, you learn why it is they sing and what they sing about, and that they aren't singing at all, but screaming. They're screaming at the top of their lungs, *this is my oak tree, my larch* and *my crust* and *my eggs* and *I'll kill you for them, if I have to, peck your fucking eyes out*. He says that they are not God's little choir, that they're nasty motherfuckers, simple greedy motherfuckers, rascals, like the rest of us. Only worse. And if God in a strange caprice made them men for a day and they came tumbling naked from the trees, spitting feathers from their mouths, they would sow such chaos in France as has never been seen. He says that there is no beauty in their song. No divinity in it. They rain down their poison and we smile like fools.

The colours of the clouds and the sun are so bright and clear that they seem poisonous as well. Their poisonous clarity fills every hollow of Antoine's face.

*

Lozeau wakes them early, and soon they are back on the road, trailing through the wan groundmist. Nursing hangovers and embittered sentiments, some love-bitten. It is outside Mâcon they first see the parade of the floating. Men and women bowed under the weight of all they have ever owned – cookware, moth-frissed linens, tools, wheels, leatherwork – heading north to Paris, or west to the coast. Some come from places, they claim, where there has been no rain since Lent. They travelled from, and through, wastelands – wide red planes stamped with crack, dry as ache. Dead animals bleaching and leathering in the fields where they fell, swollen tongues and eyeballs glittering solidly with flies. Debt and default, beds of brittle hay.

Streams and rivers thinned to a meagre shimmer in the mud. They trudge onward as one body, one great eyeless slow worm. Dirty children dangle their naked feet over the end-boards, eyes shrunk with marasmus, clutching mouldy scraps of bread. A nun – or a woman apparelled as a nun – stands on a barrel and harangues the itinerant processional, stabbing at the cloudless sky with her black crucifix. She implores them to pray, for God has passed his judgement upon them, and all that has put down roots south of the Loire, every blade of grass and every luscious grapevine, will dry up and die. Famine is only the first of the riders: you all know those who gallop after.

It is the hottest part of the day. The band look down from the ridge on to this mass. They can be smelled from far away, like a tannery. Sweat, curdled and layered. Dirty fleece, sopping diaper-rag, gleets. Lozeau lights his pipe. A melancholy sight, no? he says.

Tarare cannot conceive of how many of them there are. The way that the longer you look, the more there appear to be. Each dirty and huddled shape multiplies, becomes three souls, becomes four: a mother slung with a baby on her breast and another on her back, a youth with an old white-haired woman on his shoulders, a precious late lamb folded tight in his arms. Tarare says this.

Souls? says Antoine. Where?

What happened? asks Pierette.

It didn't rain, says Bonfils. Or, it rained too hard.

Lozeau squats in the grass and tears up a stringy handful. That one there, he says – indicating a sallow man in a dirty red waistcoat who limps along with a stick – borrowed money from his neighbour to lease a field so that he might grow grapes, as his father did in the old days. And grow grapes he did. But when they ripened the Seigneur called him to help lay a road through the hills between his hunting grounds, and the grapes rotted on the vine. When he could not pay his debt, this neighbour sent his sons to beat him. Now his back is crooked and his legs wrong, and he can't kneel from the pain of it to tamp the soil, or fix a trellis, or plant anything at all. Or that one – a man ruddy, well-muscled, pushing a barrow – was a stonemason. Blessed with a strong body and a fertile wife. They had four children, and could put a little money by every week, until they had six children. Then the guild fees went up and a seventh child came and he pawned his tools, and did so blithely, because his wife was a weaver and weavers could earn twenty sous a day. They would get through. They did, for a time.

Until? Pierette listens, her eyes shiny.

Lozeau smiles. *India cotton*. English cotton. Slave-picked, spun by steam. Washed white. Cheap. The weavers' wages fall to fifteen sous, then ten. And the price of bread rises. And now you see him here, with his sad fertile wife and seven whelps, standing in the world that is an entirety with its blue back bared for the whip of the man who owns the jennies, harnesses the steam, charters the ships. It is commerce. Free trade happened to them.

Pierette gazes at the stream of indigents. You can tell all that by looking at them?

Vidal grunts. I could've told you most of it, he says.

And those ones there, those boys – Lozeau inclines his head toward a group of dirty youths who walk more upright, more clear-eyed – are a likely sort. The clever wolves. They will follow the train until nightfall, and like wolves they will watch to see where the weak ones lay their heads down to rest. Then they will take whatever of value they have left. Plate and lace, any little bijoux hidden under their rags. Lambs, mules, if they have them. Perhaps have a go on a girl if they find one clean enough for their liking. That is what those boys will do. And what one boy does, two boys do – all boys, then, can do.

*

Tarare's new suit is blood red and white striped, with wide lapels faced in mulberry velvet, a scarlet sash around his waist. Pig's blood is smeared on his chin and his cheeks and his skinny throat, where he wears a necklace of dog teeth strung on a yellow thread.

There he stands, Antoine and Pierette his only mirror, seventeen years old and of defiled appearance. Scarlet stockings. Burrs stuck in his backcombed hair, a cautious smile on his thin sanguinated lips.

Well?

Tarare the Terrible. Antoine nods approvingly. You must practise your grimaces and growls. Bursting a rat won't cut it, they've seen that. It's old hat. You must *perform*.

Tarare touches his hair. I would like a hat, he says. Like Monsieur Lozeau's.

Don't be greedy. Tell me: do you feel like Tarare-not-Tarare? Are you the monster now? The ravenous beast?

Yes.

You're lying, says Antoine. Look at your shit-eating grin. Because you want to please us. You are the same Tarare who wants to please everyone. Who spends his days among the crawling creatures of the grass, and the grass-eaters. A boylet. But Tarare doesn't eat grass. Tarare eats flesh. Tarare drinks blood.

Antoine comes toward him and takes his face between his

hands. Antoine's eyes look into Tarare's eyes. Aren't you hungry? he says.

Yes.

Still lying. Louder.

Yes! I'm hungry!

More! You are The Great Tarare! Tophet seethes in your belly! I can smell your breath – he tightens his grip on Tarare's face and presses their brows together until Tarare can feel the blood beating in his ears and under his skin, a latent charge – I can smell your breath and it smells like slaughter, like an open grave, like an unwashed cunt – blood beating like a drum in Tarare's ears and now he can't breathe either, the bile constricting his throat because it hurts. It hurts to throw off the past like a coat. When it comes away it takes a layer of skin, leaves you raw and red where it used to touch the flesh, unprotected. Antoine's hands become the hands of Hervé, of Nollet, become maternal, become evil, become fungal, become fire and all the red-black yesterday rising in him and choking up his throat and covering his tongue like a scum until for the first time in his life he raises his fists and swings and beats away, beats away Hervé beats away Nollet beats away Tarare. Beats the past away and feels the release, the lightness, hears the laughter not of Hervé or Nollet but of Antoine, who sits sprawled in the grass, rubbing at his jaw. There are trees again, green trees. And there is blue sky again. And *There*, says Antoine. *There he is.*

So it is Tarare-not-Tarare who stands in the next market square, and the next, in scarlet stockings and a spot of untarnished sun; Cluny, Péronne, Beaubery. In front of churches of smoked glass and travertine Virgin (serene countenance gnawed half away by milk-green lichen). Tarare-not-Tarare growls and gurns. The children climb over each other to get as close as they can to him, howling with horrified delight to feel their faces flecked with mesentery and the vinegar of rotten apples. Screaming, squirting. Gizzards smack on the dusty cobbles. The abbé on the church steps shakes his grey head, but watches just the same. Meat in Tarare's hands, living and dead. Meat sliding down his throat. Blood slicking Tarare's hairless chest. They have come to see him, as Lozeau said they would. They have come to see the thing that is quite a thing to see.

Because you have heard the news! Lozeau calls out. You have heard the news of this prodigy risen from the thirsty south, this herald of chaos. It was in a meadow that I found him; but could you call it a meadow? A dark miasma hung over that place like a cloak, but I screwed my courage together, and on I marched. In the heart of that wasteland I found The Great Tarare, who, having slaked his thirst on the blood of rabbit and of lamb, had lain down to rest like the Lion of Judah. Be not afraid, mesdames – though his appearance may be alarming, he will do you no harm. Mesdames and messieurs, I give you the strangest of all creatures sublunary – The Great Tarare – The Glutton –The Bottomless Man!

In this time Tarare swallows rusty nails and dry bones and rotten cabbage and dead things and things living, squirming, frightened. Trotters and snouts, sod and corks, snakes and rats, mice white and brown and throbbing in mute terror as they are dangled by their tails above the mouth, scrabbling their tiny person-like hands uselessly. And Tarare sees that the crowd that gathers wherever they go indulges this theatre of horror with screams and shouts and wild widened eyes. Tarare sees that what he gives them is a kind of pleasure, and that the more appalling the thing he does is, the more pleasure he brings them. He lifts his shining face from a meal of raw meat and sees all the smiles in the world. Broad and half-toothed and yellowed and rouged, pretty and ugly, gashsmiles, whip-tail smiles. Shrieking their skin hymns. Bubbling faces through the summer haze. Grinning sinners through the summer haze. Why would this be? Chitterlings and gizzards sticky on the cobbles. He feels it is good to bring pleasure – no matter how one does it.

At the end comes a new part of the act, when Lozeau, who reels and mummers around the crowd, shepherd of their delight, finds a woman holding a baby, and, encouraged by laughter and cajoling, plucks the infant from the woman's arms and brings it to Tarare. He dandles it close to Tarare's terrible mouth, which he will open wide to show his remorseless teeth, and to a chorus of screams he will make as though to bite at the baby's linty frill-capped head. At the last moment, however – at the very last moment – Tarare purses up his lips and kisses the baby instead, leaving a greasy bloodied mark on the feather-fine hair, a grisly anointing. How they laugh. How they howl at that part. And they leave, comforted, knowing there is a line left uncrossed (at least here, at least today). Morality – taxonomy – reasserted.

They get into their beds with the wonder the joke the question in their minds: is he, this Tarare, a person? Could they see, beneath the scarlet tatters, the body of a boy? Of what does a man who has seen The Great Tarare dream? Of an ouroboros, of an O-men. Of the end of all. Of a thing crouched and nimble, biting at its own pink-dipped delicious heart.

*

It is the first morning of June, Year of Grace seventeen eighty-eight, and Tarare's body contains five news-sheets, a hat, three thimbles, twenty pigs' trotters, two candles and a blind puppy.

He wakes to find the sky is yellow, chalked with haze around the phantom imprint of the tiny declining moon. Already so hot. The sky is a squalorous yellow – and the smell of his sweat has changed. His body is slick with sweat under his clothes, but it does not smell like his own. This seems an important thing.

Tarare gets to his feet and picks his way between the shapes of the sleeping – Vidal snuffles and turns over, a knife clenched loosely in his fist – to the edge of the stubble field where they had made their bed. There, he buries his nose in the fust of his sleep: his armpits, one then the other, the damp cotton of his undershirt.

Tarare always liked the smell of his sweat. It was luscious and wholesome to him, mingled in the mornings with the mellow sweetness of earth and dew. He lived in it, like a good animal. A ripe fruit. Now the odour of his body is unfamiliar, over-poweringly strong and lipid. Like wax or curdled milk. Wrong. Tarare panics. Tarare works his hands over his belly, but he feels no pain where little organs and teeth combust. He imagines ascarids, seething through his entrails like a tangled ball of rib-bon. He pulls his soaking shirt up over his head and stuffs it in his mouth to try to taste his own wrong smell—

Tarare?

Lozeau peers at him through crusted eyes. What's the matter now, child?

Tarare spits his shirt into his lap. I smell wrong, he says.

Wrong?

I don't smell how I used to smell. My sweat.

Lozeau takes Tarare's undershirt. He lifts it to his nose and inhales deeply, without hesitation. He frowns.

See? says Tarare. Wrong.

Smells ordinary enough to me. But I'm no physician. Is your health otherwise well?

My health?

You're shitting every morning? Regular?

In the evening.

No pain? No blood in your shit?

Tarare shakes his head.

(And what if there was? thinks Lozeau. Blood in his shit, pain in his belly? Seventeen. What would I do then? Leave him at the tall gates of a hospital with a note pinned to his jacket? Wave goodbye and God bless you, boy? If I was good, that is the best I could do by him.) Lozeau says none of this. Lozeau asks: and do you dream?

This question has never been asked of Tarare before. I dream I'm giant, he says. Or – *a* giant. I eat the trees and the fields. There are clouds around my shoulders like a fur mantle.

Tarare touches his hand to his shoulder as though he wears this mantle of clouds even now, in the waking world. Lozeau finds this unconscious gesture moving. He smiles. Of course you do, he says.

And I dream of my mother.

You are very dear to me, Tarare, says Lozeau. He squats on his haunches in front of him and places his hand on Tarare's overlarge head as though offering a benediction. Very dear, he repeats. It is important to me that you are contented with us, and want for nothing. What do you want for, Tarare? What do you want for that we might give you? Put your ear to the shell of your soul, my boy.

Lozeau means a seashell, in which the insistent whisperings of the ocean are heard long after it has been plucked from the surf. Tarare, who has never been near the ocean, pictures the shell of a snail, mottled and deep brown, coiling into itself in ever-smaller, tighter circles. He pictures raising a snail shell to his body and the snail shell coiling into his heart in ever-tighter circles. He thinks into the magic of it. A shell? he says, timorous.

Lozeau does not answer, simply smiles his indulgent smile.

Tarare ponders. Tarare can think of nothing a person might want for, besides food, and a safe place to sleep at night. Food he has now, in horrifying abundance. And safe enough is what he feels, laying his head beside Vidal with his granitic face and fists, and Lozeau, with his netherworld guile. This is what he tells Lozeau. *What else is there that a man might want for?* This is not flattery. This is not a sop to Lozeau's avuncular generosity. This is a real question from a boy who grew up in a shoebox.

Well, says Lozeau, scratching at his eyebrow. You might want a wife. A kind, smiling face for yourself. You might want to see something of the world that you have not yet seen. Like a shell, which is an exceedingly pretty thing that comes from the sea, and that the creatures of the sea wear like a coat. These are things a person might want.

See something of the world? Tarare gazes around himself. At the sunburnt bocage, the unpromising dust, the withered daisy heads. Everywhere they have been so far looks like somewhere they have been before. The same pock-faced people, the same bad dogs, the same filthy hay on the wineshop floor. Brown dirt and bone rosary. Perhaps, Tarare thinks, he lacks the refinement to appreciate the textures and the shades that would give these things signification to his soul.

Lozeau reads these thoughts in Tarare's face. What if I told you, he says, that you could see the most beautiful thing you had ever seen in your life every day of your life?

Tarare would believe it if Lozeau told him so. But not here?

asks Tarare. The field is almost alight with morning, the east-erly sun dousing the white ruin of the tiny moon in renewed brightness. Like they are at the centre of all things, the fulcrum of the turning spheres, as they sit in this stubble field stinking of sweat. It is a beautiful thing, Tarare supposes. But not *the most beautiful.*

No, says Lozeau. Not here. Perhaps at Versailles?

Where the King and Queen live?

Yes, says Lozeau. But anyone is allowed to go there, however humble. A long, wide road runs for twelve miles south-west of Paris, and every mile is lit with lamps, all day and night. In the menagerie at Versailles they keep a clever beast called a quagga, that is like a horse but with a red tongue as long as a man's arm, and they have taught it to speak French. When I was last there, they sent a black cockerel and a ewe up high into the sky in a painted balloon. And the music – he pauses, putting his hand over his heart. The flutes, the virginals. Would you like to go to these places, Tarare? Would you like to see and to hear these things?

Tarare nods eagerly. A cockerel and a ewe – high into the sky.

Lozeau stands, the rising sun bisecting him at the waist. It is settled, he says. After Paris, I will take you to Versailles. No more dallying. If that is what Tarare wants. He smiles down at his young charge, full, apparently, of affection. You know, Tarare, he says, they will love you there. The jaded eyes of the Parisian so rarely alight on a thing of true novelty.

Lozeau shapes the long fingers of his right hand into an arrow, a firelock, points them down at Tarare's bulging middle. He grins. Your belly changes everything, Tarare.

*

They walk north for five nights and five days. Where rain has more lately fallen, the country unscrolls green and with a luminosity startling to their eyes. The fields and the meadows and the vineyards are like a beautiful brocade. One evening, they pass through an orchard of pears that are small and hard and have such bright yellow skin they seem to glow in the vespers light, like lanterns strung on the damp black boughs. They fill their pockets with these faerie pears. They feast. Nobody stops them. It is the most beautiful thing Tarare has ever seen in his life.

On the outskirts of a village they pass a little house where the laundry has been laid out to bleach in the sunshine of the lawn. Pink-ribboned smalls and petticoats of printed India cotton. With cautious looks, Pierette and Lalie climb the fence and skim the garments indiscriminately from the grass. All afternoon they laugh and drape themselves in this stolen finery with a mock-hauteur. They look like lady pilgrims, like rouged white-robed virgins. It is the most beautiful thing Tarare has ever seen in his life.

They go by the small ways, through the green mesh of forests and winding hill roads, leered over by the ophidian eyes of white geese. Stone rolls under blankets of lavender, and hogweed grows along the lane-side in dense banks of white.

I saw a man cut the head off a goose and fuck the neck stump once, says Vidal. In Poisson. This is the most hideous thing Tarare has ever heard in his life.

*

On the seventh day of their journey northward, at around noon, they crest a hilltop. Lalie, pausing, says – Do you hear that?

What Lalie hears is music on the breeze. Charivari music, with the whistle of fifes weaving through the clang of beaten metal, pots and pans. Soon the rest of them hear it, too, and come to a stop, dropping their baggage, glancing between themselves uncertainly, because the charivari music is menacing, as charivari music is intended to be, and because the racket of it is coming toward them, growing louder.

The head of a stag rears sudden over them. His antlers are strung with bells. He quivers, huge and gory like the head of a dire forest king, a ghost sigil, and appears to stare at them, through imperturbable death, above the rising music. Blood is running from his nostrils and muzzle and eyes. His velvet hangs flayed from his bone crown. Pierette screams. The charivari music falters, and the stag head rises and rises, lofted into the air on a pike. The man carrying the pike crests the hilltop, himself a sight only mildly less alarming than the bloody effigy he bears: he is huge, with a dense red beard, and wears a gown of a shocking pink satin, his bulging pectorals ensconced in white lace as he hefts his bloodied offering into the sky like he is trying to puncture holes in the perfect blue of it. Blood has dripped from the stag's severed neck, speckling the cheeks and the vivid pink gown of this man, who at last sees them standing in the road before him, paralysed in shock and awe – Lozeau and Antoine and Vidal and Bonfils and Pierette and Lalie and Tarare – he sees them standing there before him, open-mouthed and trembling, and he throws back his head and laughs.

Soon he is followed by other men. Some are large and some small, and some are in fact women, bareheaded, their dirty hair streaming wild around their shoulders like the hair of maenads: twenty or thirty of them in all, faces and hands glotted with blood, throats and wrists glotted with lace, done up like merveilleux with coral beads and powdered wigs and rigid glittering ladies' riding hats perched skew and feathered on their heads like tiny perching equatorial birds. They carry pots and pans to bang together, and they carry weapons: spiked boards, rusty sabres, truncheons, shanks, muskets. Above this androgyne processional floats a strange herd, impaled. More deer, sawn in half, viscera tangling from their gaping bellies, tongues lolled and blackening; banded pheasants and pheasant hens and ducks hanging by their necks; great fat river trout swaying like church bells, their scales already blistered matt by the brightness of the sun. A hawk is nailed to a crossbar, her copper wings outstretched in a raptorine parody of martyrdom.

The gamey stink is rich in the noonday summer sun.

The man in pink stops at the head of this sanguinary parade. He takes his grisly effigy in both hands to wave it like a standard as he hails them, silks straining over his bruiser's body, ruffled hem rising to disclose mud-caked boots. Tarare has never seen anything like this man, wearing a woman's dress as though it is nothing. As casually as if he was standing naked in front of a person who loves him.

Travellers! the man calls. Good day to you!

And to you! Lozeau replies (if he is frightened by their anarchic spectacle, their shanks and muskets, he does not show it). A pause. Been out hunting?

Hunting? repeats the red-bearded man. He throws back his head and laughs, and the laugh simmers backward through the crowd, banging its pots and pans together again. When the laughter and charivari are done, the red-bearded man says Hunting, yes. The Seigneur said the forest and everything in it belonged to him. Well. Who does it belong to now? He raises his voice above the broken music to answer himself: IT

BELONGS, he cries, to François, and Maxim, and Beak! This prompts cheering, and more clangour, and louder cheering from François and Maxim and Beak (the small one who is called Maxim wears a scarlet riding jacket with a gold twisted braiding, but upside down, with his legs thrust through the armholes).

Vidal crosses his arms to have his right hand on the blade he keeps in his inside pocket.

The Seigneur is not at home, then? Lozeau asks, his voice primly modulated.

In Paris, says the red-bearded man. There to hear doleance from all corners of France as to the state of the poor man and woman, and how they live. We give him our own doleance here today! We say: this is how we live!

Quite a feast you will make of all of this, says Lozeau, lifting his eyes to the airborne game.

Feast? The red-bearded man shakes his head and laughs again. We will not be eating these. If we eat them then the Seigneur will say we did what we did from hunger. But we did what we did from anger (more cheering from his compatriots, closer to jeering now).

Seems a waste of good venison, mutters Vidal.

Lozeau gives Vidal a warning look before turning back to the red-bearded man. Hunger can lead to anger, my friend, he says. You should eat them, or else find yourself hungry, then angry again, and with nothing left to kill for it.

My *friend*, answers the red-bearded man. Until the fainting of the Wormwood star, there will always be more things to kill.

Lozeau smiles warily. I suppose there will, he concedes. Since by your law of possession this road now also belongs to François and Maxim and Beak, I would ask their permission to make our way by it?

Of course, says the man, lifting the corner of his skirt with a delicate, ironical flourish, as though granting his hand for a quadrille. Make your way in peace, stranger. On one condition.

Speak it.

The red-bearded man fastens his hands around the pike. Down with the aristocrats! he shouts. His companions answer him until the whole hillside rings with the words. The red-bearded man fixes Lozeau with a challenging look: Say it, he demands. You must say it, each of you, and then you may go on your way.

Down with the aristocrats! shouts Lozeau, without hesitation. So do Vidal and Bonfils and Pierette and Lalie, following his lead. So does Tarare, because they are just words and no one is here to listen to them except those who approve their sentiment, and the baggage is heavy, and the sun is scalding at their necks, and sure, the aristocrats seem like cunts and look like cunts, so why not? Down with them, down. Down where? To the worm-ridden dirt the ferment the shitty hay of the shitty wineshop floor the turnip bed the empty cellar, down to the dust the skin flakes. The boring, banal squalor of it.

All of them say it, except for Antoine, who has lit his pipe and draws on it complacently, squatting at the side of the road.

The red-bearded man's hooded eyes fall on Antoine, so squatted and complacent. And you, friend?

Antoine blows a smoke ring. No, I don't think I'll be doing that, he says.

Antoine. Lozeau through gritted teeth.

The man's face puckers underneath his red beard. Why not, friend? he says. Why not? A tone of brittle jollity willing itself to crack.

Antoine rises from his crouch, shrugs. Because *I like* the

aristocrats, he answers. God set rulers above us. He made men wiser than me so I wouldn't need to worry my pretty little head with polity, and statecraft, and ugly men's business. So I can spend my little time drinking, and fucking, and enjoying myself, see? Antoine smiles. He smiles, and waves his arm at the red-bearded man. And then you have stupid cunts like this – he continues – stupid cunts like this. He's so stupid he's letting louis' worth of good venison turn in the sun, and he thinks *he* can solve the problems of this world? Feed the many starving? Dick the fucking English off? He thinks *he*—

The stag's enormous head topples into the road, gory prongs narrowly avoiding Bonfils, as the red-bearded man rushes forward and takes Antoine by the neck. Lalie screams. The red-bearded man is speaking into Antoine's face and shaking him against his lacy breast. A glint of metal is at Antoine's belly, the glint of a blade. Tarare cannot hear what the man is saying over the jeering of the crowd, the clanging of their iron pans, the stench of their rancid meat. Tarare sees the shimmer of metal between their bodies and all falls silent except his mind, which repeats as refrain: *it's done it's done how sad how sad*. How sad for beauty to have its blood drained and its eyes closed and to find its end like this, on a dirty white road under a sky of enormous and indifferent blue. Tarare looks away at the trees, indifferent, and the shadows that pool under the trees, indifferent. How sad how blue how arbitrary how indifferent, that there will be no more Antoine, because Antoine said the wrong thing to the wrong man come by chance to the end of a dirty white road. His beautiful face and his beautiful hands will purple and peel away from his bones and turn to grass the cows will eat and shit out, and all the while shadows pooling indifferently under the beautiful full-blooming trees—

Tarare is thinking all this, is blanketed and bound by this refrain, when the red-bearded man shouts A spy! An Austrian spy, perhaps? and Antoine wriggles from his grasp and spits in his red beard, stumbling back on his knees to the dirt of the road, holding up a hand between himself and his assailant – I'm not a fucking spy, man. I just don't like hypocrites—

Wait! cries Lozeau. His face is leached of colour as he fumbles in his jacket. A contribution – he says – a contribution to your cause, monsieur. He produces a purse from his jacket, rattles it urgently at the red-bearded man.

The red-bearded man swirls his head like a bandog scenting blood. He loosens his grip on the prone Antoine and takes the purse from Lozeau, weighing it in his free hand. He shoves Antoine back to the ground, answers the hock of spittle to his chin in kind, and straightens to his full height. Satisfied with the transaction.

Pierette is sobbing into Lalie's breast. Antoine sits on his elbows, massaging his bruised throat. The company begins to move, in its grumble of looted silks. The red-bearded man hefts up his stag head with a roar, and soon the processional is gone, vanishing over the side of the hill. Their charivari resumes, now quieter, quieter, and soon the birds can be heard again over that strange, disjointed music.

They wait in silence for some time. Bonfils speaks first, edging to Lozeau's shoulder. How much was in that purse?

Lozeau closes his eyes. Don't ask, he says. My own brother trying to ruin me. When Lozeau's face goes hard like this his whiskers become severe as ink strokes on his weathered skin. He turns to Antoine, strides over to where he lies in the dust, and kicks him roughly in the ribs.

Antoine lets out a spluttering laugh, clutching at his side.

Coquillard, spits Lozeau. Sick little boy. Spouting lies he doesn't even believe because he knows it will cause problems for me. I know your game. It is an old game, a lifelong game.

Antoine smiles. It passes the time, he says, rubbing at his bruised side.

You are earning that money back. All of it. *Brother*.

No trouble at all, *brother*.

The others watch this fraternal wrangling, until Lozeau turns away from Antoine and stoops to fetch his pipe, and Antoine calls over Hey – Papa would be proud of you, Jules – and Lozeau tosses his pipe aside and advances again on the prone Antoine, specks of fire in his eyes. Vidal steps in and takes hold of Lozeau's shoulders, murmuring in his ear Hey, hey – leave him, boss. Leave it.

And Tarare, who is standing close to Lalie, who is holding Pierette in her arms, hears Lalie say quietly: *Men*. Cunting men. She says this squeezing Pierette tightly in her arms, and she says it with a pitying and pitiful little laugh.

Vidal holds Lozeau by the shoulder and Lozeau is shaking with anger. Paris, says Vidal. Cajolingly, soothingly. Come on, boss. We've a lot of walking to do.

All right, says Lozeau.

I'll let you go now.

Lozeau nods. Vidal releases him.

Lozeau fetches his pipe from the dirt. In three deepest drags' time his body is slackened. You know what I think we should do, he says. I think we should call on Monseigneur. Have a look at this estate, no?

Won't be anything left worth the taking, says Bonfils.

Looking, says Lozeau, is a flavour of taking.

*

On the seventh day of June Year of Grace seventeen eighty-eight, a fine house stands at the green fold where a forest meets a river. By seventeen ninety-eight, the house will be gone, obliterated. Shucked from the earth. The forest thinned, the river banked. For now, here is the house, sitting like a thing carved from moon behind rosebushes and delicate sheaths of geometric topiary – the natural conclusion of a wide avenue of beech trees. A thin black finger of smoke unspools from somewhere behind this beautiful house, climbing high into the radiant summer sky. The crows have seen the smoke and come to strut like bailiffs along the buttresses, to hold court from the shoulders of lissom stone nymphs.

They walk through the gardens toward the house. Fountains stilled. The conical breasts of a sphinx emptied of their clear milk. Squares-on-squares, greenery regimented into spike and orb. Tarare touches one of these strange growths. Perfectly round, like the bottom of an egg. How could a person cultivate such a thing? The only way Tarare can conceive of that a plant might be coaxed into these alien, harmonic shapes is if one was able to speak to them, to tell them what they ought to do. Perhaps this is possible. Who knows what kinds of magic money might give you access to? Not Tarare.

A flight of broad steps leads to the great door, swinging open on its hinges. They come to a hall of wonderful coolness; gleaming floors of blond parquet and bone-yellow walls, a high ceiling purled with drifts of plaster cherubim. In the centre of this elegant room, above an overturned table, hangs a crystal chandelier, and from the chandelier hangs a grey dog, twisting at the end of a rope. Above their heads curves a stairway. The walls of the stairway are daubed with words tall as a man, in what there can be no doubt is shit, still-warm human shit, by the smell:

A BAS LES ARISTOCRATS
[DOWN WITH THE ARISTOCRATS]

and clustered around these words are the smeared impressions of rouged lips and bloodied hands. Of breasts and buttocks, even. Kiss kiss. Tarare may not be able to read the man-tall words written there, but he understands their spirit. They are saying, *here is my body. You have seen my body labour, now see what else it can do.*

Lozeau lets out a low whistle. A real number they've done here.

Pierette tugs at his sleeve. We shouldn't be here, she says quietly. We'll get in trouble again. The gendarmerie will come and – or the servants—

And what? says Antoine. The *gendarmerie* is probably one old man called Thierry.

And the servants probably among the looters, adds Lozeau. He rubs his lip. Good for them.

A suit of armour shines dully at the bottom of the stairs. Antoine knocks his fist against the dark and hollow metal, as though to confirm its deadness. Then he fumbles out his cock and begins to piss on it.

I thought you liked the aristocrats, Antoine, says Bonfils.

I like pissing on whatever this is more.

Their voices seem larger here, overheard by the minor divinities of the cornicework. Antoine groans with the pleasure of release. The dog spins slowly and limply at the end of the rope, turning her clouded eye on each of them, one after the other, hunt-hardened body rigid beneath blood-stained fur, thick gums exposed in a petrified snarl. Pierette shudders.

I'm going to cut that thing down, says Vidal.

Leave it, says Lozeau.

Why?

Out of respect for the gesture.

Do you think there are any gowns left? Lalie wonders aloud.

Let's have a look around, says Bonfils.

They separate in the fine house. Tarare passes with guarded curiosity through chambers as silent, glaring white, picturesque and absent of meaning to him as a Lapland. Parlours, libraries, sitting rooms where wounded chintz bleeds horsehair stuffing and books lie open and piled on the floor, their marbled end papers soaked in urine. Things. All these many Things. Brass things, tortoiseshell things, porcelain things, luminous crystal things. Things painted with roses, things painted with bridges, things painted with pretty red-cheeked washerwomen under a sky filled with plaintive little birds. Things painted with armies, things painted with lovers meeting beneath a willow, things painted with Romans poised at the edge of noble self-slaughter, things painted with sinewy youthful gods hard at work on their raping. There are silk panels, there are inlaid lacquers. Everything is grand and still in the expensive shade. Everything is overlain with a tint of pinkness, as though the house existed in perpetual sundown. In a parlour, he passes by a long mirror set into a niche. The flicker of movement at the edge of his vision makes his heart quicken, and then he sees. Himself, top to toe. He is not the most beautiful thing he has seen in his life; a gaunt ash-haired boy, with big hands and big feet, waistcoat and culottes filthy with dust. He bobs his head before his own face. A warp in the chased silver distends his brow, swells his features, until a pane of light flows like mercury between his red-ringed eyes, breaking him in two. He decides that to look at oneself every day is not a good thing, and wonders why the rich insist upon it, why they incorporate their own image so unrelentingly into their glowing habitat. For there are many such looking glasses set in many such niches around the great house.

Tarare is hot. Tarare is hungry. Finding a bedchamber, he settles himself on the creamy satin lip of a chaise that has avoided the onslaught of the rioters. He seats himself to better set his mind to work through the hunger. He goes about thinking life into these rooms, these bright chambers, which have none. He looks at the unmade bed, with its tasselled damascene curtains, and tries to summon his mother to it. In her floppy nightcap, with her summer-day freckles. He imagines and imagines persistently, until the counterpane rises before his eyes over the shape of her sleeping body, and her pale hair creeps over the goose-down pillow. Then he says, come to me, Mama. It's me, it's Tarare. Tell me how you slept. She shifts slowly in the wide soft bed, but when he blinks she is gone, and Tarare is alone in the elegant empty room with a sense of thwarted magic.

Then he sets himself to the answering of a question. The question is: do I wish to destroy or take for myself any of these many Things I find before me, at my fingertips, in this fine house? He looks around the room. The drapes are beautiful, embroidered with songbirds whistling from a dense web of jacquard foliage. A statuette of a rearing horse sits on the bureau. This is also beautiful. Tarare is a boy who feels the allure of the beautiful with a special keenness, but here everything is so beautiful that its beauty seems meaningless to him, paltry. Perhaps a precondition of true beauty is surprise, he thinks: real beauty must seem as though it has fallen abruptly from the sky, or else come from deep inside the earth – some place where it had shone secretly and unseen, until you came along and saw it. These nominally beautiful things are not like that at all. They have been arranged just so. They are luxurious, certainly – but luxury is the opposite of surprise. Tarare realises that the rich might suffer, too, in the pearl-glazed worlds they make with their money. It brings Tarare no comfort to understand this. He experiments with destruction instead: he draws his dirty hand over the satin of the chaise, where it leaves an oily mark. It is satisfying, he concedes, but the satisfaction is fleeting. He hears the voices of his friends coming from elsewhere in the house. He hears their laughter echoing through galleries and chambers and passageways. The sterility of this loveliness; the declining sunshine caught in broken glass, the complicated arabesques of imported wallpaper. He finds a tallow candle to eat, and proceeds to the gardens, chewing it like a carrot.

The breathing warmth of the day is pleasing after the grave coolness of the rich man's house. Down tree-lined avenues and past dried-up fountains he wanders for a while, happy in his solitude. At the end of the gardens' severe geometry a sparse, tamed woodland speaks in summer greens. At the edge of the trees, a dovecote stands picturesquely overcreeped in a gap between the boughs. The dovecote has a door. When Tarare opens it – more from curiosity than with real purpose – a ripe stink hits his face like a slapstick.

The dirt floor is steeped with reddened down, a lake of feathers. Here and there the swell of a twisted white throat, the distended aeriform of a wing. Doves, and the sweet lukewarm noise of them. Some already collared in firebead trails of ants, working their way under the pinfeathers to the cooling flesh. Dead.

Tarare steps into this shadowy catafalque. The light is grained with dander where it stirs in the shafts from the narrow arched windows. Dead birds. He counts dead birds on dead birds until he forgets what dead birds he has already counted, a dozen and a second dozen. He knows that it is this, of all the things he has seen this day, that will remain unblotted in his memory. The comprehensiveness of what has been done. The slaying of doves. Of every last dove. Necks wrung with methodical and sober dedication. Tarare finds himself quietly horrified. This horror metastasises in him swiftly – until he fears he sees, in the shady corners of that stone cote, the spasmodic jerking of dove-ghosts, rising into the foul air like broken puppets on invisible strings to fix their polished black eyes on him. When a shadow falls across the doorway at his back, Tarare screams.

It's only me, says Pierette.

At first Tarare does not recognise her. She stands at the dove-cote door in a voluminous gown of peach-coloured satin, a bandeau of pale silk flowers stitched across the bodice. A powdered wig frames her small face, a single artificial curl trembling over her clavicle. She touches at this self-consciously. Poor little birdies, she says. On top of the powdered wig is a dainty straw hat, overburdened with more silk blossoms and tied under her chin in a bow. Do you like it? she asks, taking a short step back and dipping into a curtsey. The gown, like the world, is too big for her.

You look very pretty, he says.

She smiles, showing her absence of teeth. Tarare realises that Pierette is the sort of thing a man is meant to protect. To shield from such horrors as firebead ants feasting on the flesh of doves, and charivari music. That Pierette presumes him to be a man himself, and therefore wishes him to be the one to do the shielding, is not yet a facet of his discovery.

Did you see something in there? she asks, leaning on tiptoe to look past his shoulder – but Tarare says nothing, and turns to draw the door behind him.

You screamed, she insists.

I thought I saw a ghost.

You *are* strange, Tarare.

It will be dark soon. We should go back to the house, find the others.

I came out here to find you.

Why? Tarare asks.

Pierette steps toward him, fingering the pale lock of hair at her shoulder, and tilts her eyes imploringly into his face. She steps forward and Tarare steps back, and again, and again, until his shoulders are pressed to the dovecote door, and he feels her breath on his chin, and hears her throat form a gulp, and smells the stale floral perfume of her stolen clothes.

I thought today, she says – so close to his face – that Antoine was going to die. It made me sad, but I wasn't surprised. I wasn't surprised because I have known for a long time that any one of us could be taken to the Virgin, Tarare. There is no knowing when it might happen or stopping it from happening. Even if you are careful. There was this Sister at the house, this old Sister, Odile—

You won't die, Pierette. You are young, and we have Lozeau, and Vidal—

She died right at the table. Said her grace and then her eyes went funny, like thickened glass, and she fell. Her face went right in her bowl, and at first we laughed—

Pierette, please—

I still sometimes laugh to think about it now, but then I feel cruel. Because however funny it was, I saw she was just

THE GLUTTON

a little sad old woman, Bride of Christ or not, and when she
died she had nobody to love her – and now Pierette's fingers
are fumbling at Tarare's belt buckle – nobody was really sad she
had gone—

Pierette—

She takes his part in her hand and Tarare is made mute
by the sensation emanating from the small of his back, the
shudder of this shiny new pleasure. To be touched. Wanted.
He goes hard in her grasp, despite himself, and his protest-
ations crumple into a moan of pleasure. Pierette leans firmly up
against him, rubbing at him, and Tarare is half-conscious of his
breeches sliding down his thighs. Her mouth finds his mouth,
tongue his tongue—

(through the feeling, raw and warm and animal, Tarare's
mind flickers, tosses itself into dark corners of want, until there
is no longer a Pierette, or even really a Tarare. The golden-hour
light, the puling of the birds-yet-living from the beech trees,
the abject sweetness of stale perfume on silk – all is swallowed
under the rush of sensation, as abruptly as if a fissure had
opened in the earth and gulped him down whole. He floats
in a charged darkness, and in that charged darkness, he sees
things. He sees cords of muscle shimmer, flex, under white lace
cased in satin. A stag rears his silvered antlers in the black –
the black of – a pantry – Antoine. Antoine nailing the bride
against a shelf of neatly labelled jars. Conserves, moon-white
cornichons, capers, jams pink as the inside of a mouth, the
curve of her uncovered thigh, hips bucking two three, blue-
gartered bare white skin – *it's only Tarare* – hips in his hands,
his hips under Antoine's hands, no, mouthpink where shoulder meets throat. Antoine. He feels himself inside, where doves
clatter on the night)

—your breath smells like shit, says Pierette. She turns her face away. Takes away the warmth of her mouth, and at that moment, Tarare comes. Surfaces into the glare of the sun on the afternoon of the seventh day of June, Year of Grace seventeen eighty-eight. Gasping. A warmth and a wetness on his thighs. Pierette takes her hand off him. I – she looks down. Her mouth makes a ring. Already? I thought—

Tarare says nothing. Breathes dry-mouthed against the dovecote door, cock going limp in the golden-hour light of the afternoon.

Pierette steps back. Tarare watches as she considers her sticky hand for some moments, then wipes it on the lustrous skirt of her gown. Her wide, faun-like face inscrutable.

Tarare can think of nothing to say. She looks at him. He sees her see he is not what she wanted. Or thought she wanted. Sees the fraying of a fancy in her deep brown eyes. It hurts him, just a little. What should he say? Thank you, is what he says in the end. Then: I don't have anything to pay you with.

Pierette's blank expression sharpens into a glare. Oh my God, Tarare, she says. Oh, my God. And he sees by the golden-hour light of the afternoon that her eyes are glistening with tears, before she turns away from him and runs back toward the house, between the sharp shadows of the topiary, her stiff skirts billowing out behind her in the sunshine.

Though he could not tell you why, Tarare understands that without either of them meaning to, she has hurt him and he has hurt her back, and that means they are no longer a girl and a boy, but a man and a woman instead. The realisation prompts a feeling of quiet desolation. He pulls up his trousers and buckles his belt.

It is late in the day. The topiary casts ectomorph shadow

across the grass. The birds-yet-living live on, in their minuscule scribbling way. The seed that came out of him is drying on a rich woman's silk dress. These are the mysteries of God, and they ought not to frighten him, but humble him.

IV Vendémiaire an VII

The patient has fallen asleep, at last. He rests his hands on the sides of his sunken chest, as though he is holding the two branches of his ribcage together. Keeping himself whole for as long as he might. His breath rasps in his throat, slow and uneven. It is both difficult and not difficult, Sister Perpetué thinks, to picture him as a boy. She imagines his nailbeds bleeding and bitten – a foul habit, biting one's nails – his blank eyes furtive and artless by turns.

She sits beside him as he sleeps, and she ponders. How strange, she thinks, for God to arrange things so each soul has just one earthly body to contain it.

Tarare, the thing called Tarare, has worn this body all his life. Here it is, in repose before her. The body that has done – or had done to it – all of the things he has spoken of. The skull that met the hard blow of the stepfather's axe. The lips that sought the timid press of another boy's lips on Lady Day. The fists that closed around warm, corded entrails.

She thinks of her own body, housed in its straight habit of black serge. How strange that she will never see herself laid out before her eyes as she sees Tarare. As she has seen many bodies laid out, poor and broken, living and dead. Strange, she thinks, perhaps even perverse, that we are denied the measure of ourselves that we may take of others. Sister Perpetué knows her own body only in parts. The seam her palms make when she joins her hands in prayer. The swollen flesh of her feet after a night walking the wards.

As Sister Perpetué watches the sleeping man, it occurs to her she is frightened of death.

Or sometimes she is frightened of death. Albeit He is the resurrection and the life. She fears it – Him – anyway. She fears that her death will be violent, when it comes. And that the violence will neither purify nor transfigure her. Only *hurt*. Her fear is not ridiculous. The Sisters have all heard tell of the sixteen Carmelites who rode the tumbril to the scaffold in full habit. Who held hands in a ring like little girls, and chanted the *Salve Regina* and *Laudate Dominum* over the pale whine of the guillotine. Until their heads – grey-haired and yellow-haired and red-haired and black-haired beneath their veils – were weighting a sack. Seventeen ninety-four. Just a tenday later the spectacled heretic Robespierre himself was sent to his death, and they rejoiced, Perpetué and her still-living Sisters, in their quiet way.

When the Terror was at its height, when the doors of the holy houses were kicked down, and the plate and cantatoria gathered up, no one knew if they would come, or when: but at least if you were a real person, at least if you lived in the world, you knew who *they* were, and how they might be bargained with. Sister Perpetué knows she is not a real person. Or rather, she knows she is part of one larger person. In the dormitory with her Sisters she looks around and sees the same thin face, the same tired eyes, the same mousy braid unwound twenty-fold by the same lye-reddened hands, and she feels this, the synonymity of their persons, to be a comfort. To be wedded to Christ is to exist in unison. Not so much the safety of a pack, as the blur of the murmur. That they exist together means that she, Sister Perpetué, exists less, and would therefore be harder to kill with violence (to run through with a spike, to slice the breasts off, to swing from the lamp-iron, her mouth filled with mucky straw). She saw pictures of what they did, during the worst years. Women were not spared, not even holy women. What bodies did to other bodies, she has seen pictured. The pictures of it are sometimes enough to keep her awake at night.

Versailles is what she sees when she looks out the window. It was a palace for one hundred years, she knows. Before a king came along and made it a palace, it was a village like many others, with a watermill and rough wooden cottages, where people sang and slept and swatted flies and drank eau-de-vie. Before that it was forest, she supposes, like everything else. Dark and dripping. It isn't a palace any more, because King and Queen and Duke are dead or banished, so what is it? They sent in men to efface every curlicued cypher – every gold crown and white lily – from the walls. As though the ghosts of a place live in the plasterwork. As though ghosts dwell so shallow. Everyone knows a spirit will burrow in deep.

There were fountains at Versailles. Enormous planes of water coaxed to entire mirror-like stillness. Fountains that danced, sprawled, streamed voluptuous over the heads of the most important people in the world. Two steps removed from God, they thought themselves, under those diamond-green streams. Fountains that trailed like fingers through satin. Glistening streams from the pretty bronze mouth and pretty bronze dick of the boy-Apollo, wetting the backs of brazen dolphins. Grottoes laced with sword fern. There was a huge pit of glittering ice, like a mineshaft, so the ladies could have their sugar syrups in July. Powdered incests. Horsemen so accomplished they used only threads of blue silk for reins. And all of this, and all of this.

She wants to ask Tarare why this was the place he came to; that he chose to die in. She wants to ask him why he came, most likely from Paris – along the wide twelve-mile road, and in such pain – to be here. To un-be here.

Tarare chose this place, she thinks, because he likes stories. And because he likes stories, he knows how it is that they are meant to end.

1788

They arrive in the village of Bercy by wagon, on the eve of the Nativity of Saint Jean-Baptiste. They pass by the fire lit in the scrub before a calvary, which stands great and white in the wide field, seeming to lean in toward the licking flame. The trees are drawing their secrets to themselves in the dark, but there is commotion in the village. Clamour. Laughter and drinking, the narrow cobbled streets like a rocked cradle. A joyful unease can almost be tasted the second Tarare slips from the end-boards of the tumbril: it sets a smoulder on the dusk. Dangerous and savoury.

Lozeau pays the roadman.

Tarare can tell that Antoine, standing beside him, tastes the smoulder too. His body is stiffening. His eyes glisten. It's going to be a good night, he says. I declare it now.

Lalie brushes hay from her skirts as she speaks. We'll need to find somewhere to get cleaned up if you want us to work, Jules.

We'll find a hostelry, decrees Lozeau.

Pierette steps down from the wagon. Her gaze catches on Tarare's. Her face seems older, drawn into the middle. Her eyes are pillowy and large as though she has recently wept. At her throat is a band of peach satin, raw-edged, already fraying. The yellow colour of her gown is putrid in the vividness of fire. She fixes Tarare with a look of eloquent hatred before she takes Lalie's arm and turns away. Tarare watches the back of her matted head shrinking in the darkness. Although he does not know it, this is the last seeing-of-her Tarare will do, this her-not-seeing-of-him. Except, of course, in dreams.

Bonfils, his fiddle at his hip, presses his eyeglasses to the top of his nose. It's always big fires, he says. A dauphin is born? The peasants light a big fire. Midsummer? Big fire. Saint's day? Night before a saint's day? – oh, let's set a big fire going, why not?

Spark of the gods, says Lozeau, hooking his thumbs into his lapels. Small wonder at the edge of flint, since first Prometheus came down from the mountain with blazing flambeau in hand.

Look, you've set him off now. (Vidal)

Who the fuck is Prometheus? (Antoine)

He is Eve, says Lozeau. As though this answers everything, or anything.

They walk through the cobbled streets, between hovels of daub and mildewed thatch, windows brightened by votive flame. Air sharp with ash and cider. They follow the throng to the centre of the village, where the pink-black finger of a church spire indicates, peremptorily, the ethereal throne. People all around. Drunk and happy, weather-worn faces transfigured into receptive holes and aggressive peaks by the incipient darkness, ubiquitous firelight. The discordant music of pipe and hurdy-gurdy.

You may not think you remember a time before fire, Lozeau continues, grasping Bonfils' shoulder as they walk. But your soul does. Children, raw and unreformed, innocents, remember it better. This is why they squall when they are left alone in darkness. Think about it, he says. Men huddled in the cold and the black of the cave mouth, while monsters snarled on the plain and the sun hid away for whole seasons. Your bones remember it. Or, the stuff your bones are made from remembers it.

Why must you always spoil the mood, brother? Antoine is practically bouncing on his heels to be released to his element, like a waterdog scenting fowl. Eating everything with his eyes: the girls in their tissuey white gowns and the sotted, vaunting farm boys, the old beaked women with their claws for hands (who are the same here in Bercy as they are everywhere, who are the same here as they will be until the Day of Judgement, when they will huddle short-boned under the hooves of Pestilence and wonder at the colours in the sky). I want a drink, he says.

Of course you do, says Lozeau. We drink to forget the harrow of the night.

Be quiet, old man! laughs Antoine, before he slips into the crowd, shouting a God bless the Holy Virgin God bless Saint Jean!

They find a hostelry on the edge of the village with two vacant rooms. By the time they have set their miscellaneous burdens down and made themselves presentable, the music has died in the village. Tarare steps into the streets and finds them seeming near-deserted, save for a few knots of the reeling super-annuated, some happy drunks overspreading the stone steps of the church. The cobbles are slippery with sour wine and crushed flowers.

Tarare walks alone through the dark streets, with the vague idea of looking for Antoine. Past butcher's shop, carriage house, along the back wall of the church. He scrubs his fingers along the cool, mossy stone, and tries to remember what it is he knows of Saint Jean, who baptised the Lord Jesus in the fast-flowing waters of the river Jordan. Tarare sees him as a tall man with long, dark hair and a serious face. Glossy fish sway around his ankles, and his white robes cling to his attenuated body. He wants him. Is it wrong, he wonders, is it blasphemy, to want a saint like that? Their bodies – spread, pierced, apportioned like nutcake – are the sites of their allure. But when you look on them, what are you meant to feel? Pity? Glory? Not lust, probably. Perverse, perverse. Tarare chuckles aloud to himself. Behind the church are figures clustered in the darkness, making muffled sounds. Boys, girls – Tarare can see the whites of their half-opened eyes, patches of their naked flushed skin – pressed into the shadow, into adoration, their fingers variously in each other. He wants to stop and watch, but he doesn't. The charge of them is enough, the fumes of their quiet profanity thickening the night. Tarare himself begins to feel pleased, and a little profane. Tarare himself begins to want a drink.

He turns the corner. Now he hears footsteps, shouting – and then an unearthly screech. A small flaming object streaks across the street like a meteor, dripping sparks. The thing has four legs. The thing has fur, just about. The thing is a cat, aflame. It flashes down a side street. It is pursued by a throng of men. The men are laughing and tipping over one another as they race after the burning cat. The faster, the soberer, try to break ahead, but are pulled back by their wrists and waists. Men tumble, men roll. The street is filled with them, haunch to haunch, like the Gadarene swine. Spark of the gods. Tarare wonders how long it takes for a cat to burn through. Not very long, surely? But until then it will run terror-bound, its ears full of the men's mocking laughter, mouth choked with the smokes of its own sizzling body, flesh searing with pain scarcely imaginable. Tarare does not resent the men their midsummer sport, but the thought of the cat fills him with horror. This is the worst end he can conceive of for any creature. This is how the demons would race after the damned souls of Hell. Tarare himself begins to run.

He takes the next street down from the throng of men, left, then right, to the rear of the grocer's shop – to what? Catch the cat himself – and then? Hide it? Douse it in water, drown it – any end better than the burning. Burning is a traitor's death. He can hear the men in the next street over, howling with laughter, hissing *puss puss*. Rounding into an alleyway on his right hand he sees the cat, the fireball. It has slowed – almost – to a halt. Flames lick through the shambling shape of it. It stops, begins to crumble into a nothing, whiskerless cheek laid to the cobbles. Tarare drops down on his knees beside the nerveless beast. Its skin spits. He wants to touch it, to comfort it, to show it that there was good in the world it leaves behind. But its body seethes with fire and leaks a dark liquor. The denuded tail, barely more than a cord of bone, thrashes and twitches wildly. All Tarare can say is I'm sorry, I'm sorry. Tears are pricking at his eyes as he gropes around for a stone, a loose brick, something to bring down on the beast's blackened un-eyed head, a way to end it, all this death—

and in his groping and crying Tarare finds himself swept up from behind by many arms and lifted high in the air by many hands. He caught it! He caught the cat! someone cries out. In the name of Saint Jean-Baptiste! He caught the cat! They are carrying Tarare on their shoulders, the crowd of men, with laughter and delighted faces, and they cannot see through the darkness that there are tears on his cheeks as they heft him starward. He finds himself borne along, swilled back through the streets to the church square, where they deposit him on his feet with vivats and singing and delirious kisses all over his cheeks. Pitchers of wine are pressed on him, and his back is slapped, and soon his dry sobs have turned into hiccupping laughter, a sense of warmth and fellow feeling for these men of Bercy who have made him their champion, the cynosure of their revels. They ask him his name and he tells them, and soon they are bellowing it up at the spire-pricked moon, TARARE, THE GREAT TARARE, FAST AS LIGHTNING—

Antoine squeezes through the press and grasps at his arm. There you are—

Here I am! Tarare grins like a cabbage. His eyes are red and tear-smeared, but he grins.

Are you *drunk*, Tarare?

No, *you're* drunk.

Tarare is right. Antoine is drunk. He sways in his boots. A fat shiner glows on his cheekbone, new. Tarare wonders from whose knuckles he collected it. Antoine flickers his eyes around the crowd. He says: Tarare is drunk with love, more like. You have a gift for making friends, don't you? You caught the cat?

Tarare lowers his head mulishly. I was trying to help it.

Antoine smiles and rolls his eyes. Of course you were. He takes Tarare's head in his hands and kisses his liquored mouth to his browbone, and the crowd press in around them, oblivious, drawing a dark knot firm around their intimacy. Holding their bodies close together. At the centre of the crush, Tarare feels absolutely alone with Antoine. Asway in warm water. His forehead prickles where he is kissed, as though all the longing in Tarare's young body is rushed like blood into his head and concentrated in that one galvanic point. The jostling of a shoulder at his back brings them closer together until Tarare is stumbled from his feet—

Woah, woah – easy—

Antoine holds Tarare tightly by the upper arm, and they

extricate themselves from the crowd. Beyond the throng, Tarare is sorry the intimacy has passed, but the cool night air on his face is good.

Vidal and Bonfils are near, haunting the shadow at the doorway of a shuttered cooper's.

Antoine crams conspiratorially into the stoop, his back to the street. His eyes are pricks of light. *Look what I found*, he breathes, and produces from beneath his jacket a firelock. A pistol. It gleams darkly, the handle cased in mother-of-pearl. Antoine moistens his lips, fitting his hands around the weapon with a laugh.

Sacred blood, hisses Vidal.

What you *stole*, you mean, clucks Bonfils.

Is it loaded?

Don't know. It doesn't need to be, does it?

Doesn't need to be, Bonfils repeats, incredulously. What do you mean? For what?

It's beautiful, says Tarare. (And it is. Luxury and violence in its gleam, alloyed in its heft.)

I knew a man in Marnes who was shot by his own dog. God knows how, but he swore to it. Shot by his own dog. With his own musket by his own dog, in the shoulder while he slept. Can I hold it? asks Vidal.

Fucking *no*. Where is my brother? Antoine is reeling. One side of his face weighted lower than the other with liquor. He slides the firelock back into his deep jacket pocket, spits in between their feet. *My bro-ther*. Cunt. I think I will break with him in Paris, you know. I'm sick of his mincing and his using.

Antoine steps down and begins to walk across the square. The other three follow, Bonfils slinging his fiddle on to his back. Shit. Where are you going, Antoine? he calls.

To find my brother!

Vidal looks darkly at Bonfils. Jesus, come back here, Antoine!

Ha ha, says Antoine. Cain and Abel. Ha.

The sky of midnight is schist-black. The streets are peopled now with the loudest talkers, the belly-laughers. Fire, fire in the dark. They hear the hollow shriek of a woman somewhere having something done to her. Barking dogs. A window cracked open. Saint Jean-Baptiste was born of Elizabeth, cousin of the Holy Virgin. Tarare remembers this. The Virgin went to visit with Elizabeth when they were both with child and, greeting one another with a kiss, they felt their swollen bellies quiver with the miracles that the Lord had planted in each of them. Saint Jean knew the Lord was close, even then, the saviour of mankind curled blind as a bean in amniotic broth, beneath the skin and fat of a virgin girl. It makes Tarare feel uneasy in his body. Could the Lord put a baby in a boy, if he wanted to? It must be the story that is making him feel this rising nausea, this rush in his head, because he hasn't had that much to drink. Or has he? He finds it hard to keep track. He speeds, falls into step beside Antoine.

We are friends, aren't we, Tarare? says Antoine, keeping his pace, eyes fixed resolutely ahead. He is very much going, but appears to have no idea where. They are at the edge of the village already, passing meagre lightless huts, scorched little gardens. The night swells around them, the clean lively smell of grass. Ahead, Tarare sees only the open figureless black of the countryside.

Yes, says Tarare. Good friends.

I think you should come with me in Paris. You and me, Tarare. We'd make a good pair, no? On the Pont Neuf. You do what you do and I can pick their pockets. Full pockets, in Paris.

Rich men. Split the takings. What do you say? Find a – he searches for the words – a boarding house. A hostelry. To live at. Just (he slurs) us.

Is Paris where we are going now? asks Tarare. Gently.

Yes.

I'm not sure this is the right road for Paris, Antoine. Tarare looks over his shoulder. He can just make out the shapes of Vidal and Bonfils following, although those collections of shadow could be anyone. Following them into the wide, watchful night. He begins to feel frightened. He can hear the giggle of a stream flowing somewhere near.

Paris is huge, snaps Antoine. You have no idea, Tarare. North, south. Twenty miles, thirty. We will find it, eventually.

Why not wait for daylight?

I spit on daylight, Antoine declares, meaninglessly. Just walk.

There is a rumble in the sky. Antoine pauses momentarily, clutches his hat tighter to his head, then continues on. Faster than before. Tarare's breath catches in his throat from the effort of keeping up with him.

I have the pox, says Antoine. He says this suddenly, casually. Did you know that? They say it drives you mad. Your cock falls off and then it drives you mad. He laughs.

I don't care, says Tarare. And he doesn't. *I would be driven mad for you, Antoine*, he wants to say. *It would be worth it to hold you lovingly*. Perhaps it would even be nice, Tarare thinks. Antoine and Tarare, rendered down together into a shared world of menacing indeterminate shapes, laughing wildly at the pale blue face of the moon, hairy palms conjoint. Pressing their cockless bodies together in the dark, forever and always, amen. Tarare doesn't say this. He says, You aren't mad, Antoine.

Yes, I am. He sneers, he gulps. I feel mad most of the time

– voice softer – I do things, say things, I can make no other account of. Not even—

You are drunk, Antoine! Drunk, not mad! Tarare gets in front of him and tries to grasp at his shoulders, compel him back toward Bercy. Antoine shakes him off.

The rain begins to fall. Lightly at first, in fits and starts. Shoals of raindrops. They hear the hiss of it swallowed in the black empty around them where it hits the ground, as though the ground were red-hot. Micromovements of thirsty worms in the thirsty soil. Then it falls heavier. For a moment they are still. Clinched together in the dark, they raise their faces to greet the novelty of precipitation. Like children. Raindrops big and warm.

Let's go back, Antoine, says Tarare. If you want to go on to Paris, just us, we can do that. I swear it. But tomorrow. We can talk about it and we can go, perhaps – but *tomorrow*. Tarare knows how to speak to drunk men. Softly, gently. As an ostler speaks to a horse chafing at the bridle. While Tarare is speaking he realises he can see Antoine's face. A pale light suffuses his brow and the hollow of his bruised cheek. Lunulae of gold widening on his black eyes; Antoine is looking past Tarare, through him, toward the approaching source of this light.

Tarare looks over his shoulder. Twenty or thirty yards away, at a fork in the road, a carriage approaches, rain sparking star-like around its lantern-blazing bulk. Two white horses, mud streaking their legs. Things happen fast. Antoine pushes Tarare away from him, hard, so that he falls on to his side into the mud of the road. Antoine takes the firelock from beneath his jacket and holds it raised at chest height in front of his body as he advances toward the carriage. The carriage rolls to a stop with a heavy creak. The rain falls, falls. Tarare tries to get to his feet, but his clothes are sodden, lead-heavy. Already the meagre roadway is a reservoir of black mud. Antoine says something – shouts something. Tarare half-hears as though through water. Footsteps, the muffled plash of boots around him in the dark. A hand fastens round his collar. Bonfils pulls him to his knees. The ghostly fingers of steam rising from the horses, their blink-ered heads twitching uneasily from side to side. He can see Antoine, a narrow shape thrown long in the carriage-lamps. Rain stitching the blackness together. The pistol now levelled at a coachman in a scarlet livery. Tarare sees the coachman has a pistol of his own, levelled back at Antoine. The coachman's mouth is moving. The window of the carriage opens and a lace-gloved hand reaches out into the night. Everything too bright and gilded to seem real. Vidal is there too, waving his shank in the coachman's face. A scream splits the ringing in Tarare's ears. A woman, panniered in a cumulus of cream satin, tumbles from the carriage door and into Vidal's arms.

Now Tarare can hear. The rain falls, falls.

Her jewels, Antoine is saying. Shouting. Her jewels, Vidal. Antoine spits in the dirt. Stand down, man, he barks at the liveried carriage driver. Stand down or I'll shoot. Stand down or it will be the worse for you.

You said my name, Vidal shouts back. Now he is holding the scrabbling lady down in the mud, twisting a thread of seed pearls from her blue-veined neck. You said my name. Rain streams down his face. Rain streams down all their faces.

I'll shoot. I'll shoot you. Antoine cocks the pistol. His hands, his voice, all shaking.

Tarare sees they are doing an ugly and a dirty thing, and they are doing it badly. Blind panic in the hammering rain. The woman writhes beneath Vidal, scratches at him until he bends her arms back over her head and she screams in pain. He tugs the rings from her fingers. Tarare tries to move, to do something, but Bonfils is holding him firm. He hears his shallow breathing. Mercy, cries Bonfils. Antoine—

A shot is fired, rings out over the figureless dark of the empty country. Tarare feels Bonfils pushing him down. Feels his whole weight on top of him now. Dead weight. A warmth begins to soak the back of his shirt. A body warmth.

Jacques!

Suddenly Vidal is above him. He lifts the weight – the dead weight – from Tarare. Rolls Bonfils on to his back in the mud. By the carriage light they see that the front of his head is blown out like a rose. That is what it looks like: petals of flesh, opening from the point of impact. Behind his cracked spectacles his eyes are open. The neck of his fiddle has snapped under the weight of his body, the strange dead weight, dead meat. Vidal kneels over him, shaking his shoulder. Jacques, Jacques. Bonfils is motionless. Rain and red blood darkening his paler red hair.

He's dead, says Tarare – because that is one thing Tarare can do. Say what he sees. What he sees is a thing he has never seen before. Friend, dead. Shot in the head. Eyes wide open and bloodshot behind eyeglasses, a small fragment of naked bone gleaming at the temple like eggshell. Already the rain washing into the bloody hole in his head.

Vidal's face folds in. He lets out a strangely dignified sound of plangency. An oh, an o-h.

A second shot. The coachman lifts his hand to his chest, where blood pools across his starched shirt. Fist-wide, then liver-shaped, then seeping down to his navel, the blood. His expression is of disbelief – almost of affront – and then he topples soundlessly to the mud. The woman screeches again.

The boxes, says Antoine. Coldly now, shadow ravelled long. Get the bandboxes at the back. You see? Vidal!

Crouched over Bonfils – the remains of Bonfils – Tarare watches them work. The horses are streaming, stamping their feet. Of what do coach horses dream? wonders Tarare. Of two horizons simultaneous, one green one gold. Hippocampi with velvet hides and the shapely breasts of women. Antoine mounts the rear of the carriage and begins to tumble luggage down. Bandboxes, hatboxes, painted chests. Lucre studding the mud all around. Believe his greenness, his innocence – it is the first time that Tarare sees that these, his supposed friends, are frightening men. Also complacent. Also inept. He can feel Nollet behind him, arms folded, chewing a stem of grass, in the same casually adjudicative attitude he would adopt when he stopped to catch a thatcher at work, or the blacksmith lifting the dainty hind leg of a colt. *Getting this all wrong, aren't they,* poucet? says Nollet. *She knows your names. You should kill her, too,* he says, inclining his head toward the lady, who has clawed her way under the carriage like a spooked cat. *But then you're in a spot, aren't you? Killing a rich woman. Mind you, you're in a spot anyway. God's blood. A mess. A real sow's ear. What to do,* poucet?

Reams of petal-bright silk, fox furs, beads, coin, tortoiseshell combs, gilded plates and golden cake forks with pretty campanulate stems. Antoine and Vidal are stuffing their pockets. Bonfils is dead. A silver watch, a string of pearls, inlaid snuffboxes, silver toothpicks, lace-edged chemise—

Get over here, Tarare.

No.

What's a name, anyway. Names can be changed, papers. You can run away. Leave all this nastiness behind you, and be well.

Take something, Tarare. Come on.

Why?

Fucking *why*? Antoine pauses over an open chest, a gut-fat chain of gold in his fist. I don't know, Tarare. Why do you eat rats, and nails, and corks? If I asked you *why*, what—

Hush. Vidal stops his rummaging, suddenly alert.

You killed a man, Tarare says. Sobs. Bonfils is dead and you killed—

Shut the fuck up. Antoine also stiffens, raises his head. His hackles.

Out on the night there is the greeling of a horse. Hoofbeats. Not far from where they stand, and coming closer, a torch glints in the streaked dark. A voice. In the name of the King—

Fuck—

Militia? What are the chances – an escort?

Come, come. Run.

Antoine grabs Tarare by his arm, but Vidal lingers in the circle of the carriage-lamps. The woman, he says, gesticulating wildly. The woman—

No time, spits Antoine.

They run. Not by the road, but across the fields, gold things flying from their pockets like clockwork birds, rain beating at their backs, the sound of their churning feet erased by the downpour. Until the downpour is all poured down, and they stand blinking in the washed-empty and blackly shining streets of Bercy. The rain turning cold on their skins.

Antoine hustles them into an alleyway. His eyes are holes of panic. Vidal bends at the waist, vomits. Wipes his mouth summarily. We should find Lozeau, he says.

The three of them gasping like landed fish in the narrow alleyway.

Tarare, says Antoine. You're covered in – you're all – (he wants to say *blood* but he can't say it) – here. He pulls off his sodden jacket, hands it to Tarare. Shivering. They're all shivering.

Tarare puts the jacket on. Feels around the hefty pockets. Produces a watch on a chain, a ring, a little golden cake fork. Such meagre spoils. He holds them out to Antoine, like an offering. He doesn't want them. He knows he mustn't have them on him. He knows that much.

Antoine makes a noise in his throat. Blows his nose into his clenched fist. We need to get rid of it, he says. Hide it all.

Vidal empties his own pockets. More rings, pearls – still warm, he says, rolling the luminous string through his fingers. Yes, he says. Hide.

Where? asks Tarare.

Vidal and Antoine look at him.

No, says Tarare.

Yes, says Antoine.

Vidal sighs, as though impelled to a bothersome task. He lifts his free hand to Tarare's throat and urges him firmly to the wall. Come now, he says. Tarare. Boy. These jewels are either in you or they are on you. Do you see? And you are either with us or you are here alone when the gendarmerie come. He squeezes the base of Tarare's neck like he is testing a fruit for ripeness. I can make it so you are still. Believe me. I can make it so you are still until the gendarmerie come and put you in irons, boy.

Why him? The large childish part of Tarare repudiates the injustice, even as the rational sees their reasoning. He is their hiding place, their portable pocket, stitched in flesh. None-theless. Then I'll tell them what you did, Tarare says.

Vidal laughs. His face, the seeming stone of it, transfigured. He has that switch, that bell pull, some men have. Two suits of soul. This the darker. Clubs shuffled with diamonds. Of course you will, he says. And they will listen, and they will pat the peasant boy on his little head, of course. And they will apologise for the misunderstanding, and set him on his way. Of course. Then again. Perhaps it is good to die with friends, eh? A martyr and two thieves on the hillside. Like in the Bible.

No one need die, mutters Antoine, his eyes flicking between each end of the alleyway.

No one need die! Vidal releases Tarare and rubs his hand idly across his pate, as though Tarare's throat was merely a convenient resting place for it at that time, and now he has found another.

So Tarare swallows the silver watch on the chain. Tarare swallows the rings. Tarare swallows the golden fork. Tarare swallows the pearls, still warm. Feels them coiling in his gullet, behind his heart. He looks at Antoine, who paces at the mouth of the alley, gaunt and sobered. The enchantment has loosened its hold. He no longer wants to kiss him. He no longer wants to hold him lovingly. He no longer wants to make of him a bluebird to cradle in his hands.

We should find Lozeau, urges Vidal.

Antoine hisses through his teeth.

He'll know what to—

It is then the tocsin sounds, loud over the clustered rooftops. A window opens, an unintelligible shout drifts from the square. Vidal looks imploringly at Antoine. Antoine looks at Vidal, and while they are looking at one another, our Tarare bolts. Too late, Vidal realises – he grasps for the hem of his jacket, but by a weird revolution of his hips Tarare frees himself, and runs. Without hesitation, Tarare runs, unfathering himself again to the night.

He runs and hears his name called after him, quieter and quieter:

Tarare!

they chase but they aren't fast enough

Tarare!

alone again

in the dark he thinks of Antoine's black curls, the black curls on his head thick and loose that made it look, sometimes, like his face emerged from a cloud of smoke, as a devil's might, in a good or bad dream.

*

Tarare runs, and then he walks. Having nothing left but a road to walk on. The rising sun is at his back, shellacking the low cloud in carcinomic pinks and tentative oranges. All around him the trees droop, fettered with the late rain, and the hedgerows fill with lively music. Crickets, calling birds. He walks up little hills and by the side of streams. Past hovels with goats picketed in their scrubby gardens. He sees the monumental nests of swans, white-masked waterbirds sunning their long yellow legs. He is alone again, but this time with a strange lightness in his heart: the world seems washed clean. As though this dawning day was the very first, when God sat back in his bright chair and looked at the waterbirds and the sloping hills and smiled, wiping a cloud over his pearled brow. As though this dawning day was the very first, before any man had done anything in or on the world.

Morning comes humid. A sparkling fog where the moisture burns off the meadows and flats. Tarare stops in the shade of a copse. He removes his bloodied shirt and hangs it from a branch. Puts his – Antoine's – red jacket back on over his bare shoulders. He walks a while longer until he finds his sodden boots are pinching, so he takes those off as well, and hangs them in the hedgerow, and continues barefoot. Feels himself to be a Franciscan, a pilgrim, naked and holyglowing in meagre jacket and culottes. Alone under the smiling cloudless sky. He walks on and on, chewing damp bark to dull the pangs of his hunger. He finds a box of browning apples by the roadside, thrown or fallen, no doubt, from a cart bound for Paris. They are waterlogged, and sprouting maggots, but he eats them anyway. A little further along he finds a deep puddle in a wheel-rut and sees how it is shimmering with life: a frog passing in the night has taken it for a pond and laid her eggs there. Crows and rooks have gathered to peck at the rich jelly. This makes Tarare unaccountably sad, when he thinks of the frog, sleeping in a damp hole somewhere, flush with a new mother's pride. Unaware of her negligence. Of what do frogs dream? Tarare wonders. Of gentle cool-blooded love, and still black water. Of the holograph appendages of dragonflies.

By noon he has reached the great grain-whitened fields that stretch to the walls of Montmartre. He sees Paris. There is no mistaking it, and he finds he feels no particular way about it. Paris, all right. Paris dreamed of. Paris feared. The air darker around and above, the moons-of-domes and spires casting their punctilious shadows over the red and grey and dun rooftops. The smell. He walks. His feet are bleeding. He is shoulder to shoulder with the day labourers who trudge from the suburbs to the Place de Grève, stinking of armpit and eau-de-vie, through the gates, through other gates, beneath the raining mettle of hawkers' shouts. The rancid mud of the city cooling his bare and bleeding toes. Tall white houses. Wide junky rivers. Flags and laundry – big-flowered and crimson-striped calicos and cottons – strung across the streets in rainbows. People. More of them than he has seen in his life. Not a single one of them looks at Tarare for more than a moment. Not a single one of them marks Tarare, this filthy big bleeding-footed boy. His eyes are heavy in his head. His head is heavy on his neck. He walks and walks, until, on a wide bridge, he stops. Oranges are piled on the bridge in pyramids, glowing through their pored skins in the sunshine. There is a man made of metal, riding a metal horse, his sword unsheathed to the sky.

Tarare stops at last, and stands still, and the city moves around him. Shifts, in dizzying noise and verbiage. The gulls move in the air above him and the dirty grey water of the river banquets on itself below him and hearts beat all around him, in the high white many-windowed houses, along the quays, in the gilded carriages. He can feel it all, everything everything. A great namelessness pressing down on him from above, like a thumb from the lidless blue. His feet are bleeding. He has a bellyful of pearls and thwarted love. It is here he falls, on the Pont Neuf. Falls forward on his belly, in accidental genuflection to a long-dead king.

*

And wherewith, let him fade again into dimness—

IV Vendémiaire an VII

Sister Perpetué moves down a seemingly endless corridor. Does not *move* – is compelled. She glides, her feet an inch above the flagstones. She is compelled faster and faster in this way, the little lights ensconced in the walls blurring to a blazing stripe at the periphery of her vision. What draws her, she does not know. God? Love? The two being one and the same, of course. She is light like a ghost. Faster and faster down the empty corridors, until she comes to an abrupt stop. There is a door-way. The door is ajar. She takes a candle from its niche in the wall.

Inside the cell it is almost unbearably warm and the floor feels sticky beneath her feet. She plucks at the neck of her habit. She breathes. Someone else breathes too. The breath is all around her, heard and felt, flush against her cheeks and breast. She sees the washstand, the chair, the unstoppered laudanum bottle. She sees the narrow iron bedstead. It is empty. The thin coverlet pushed back, the pillow bearing the shallow impression of the patient's absent head. Panic rises through her spine. He was her responsibility. *He is to be watched at all times.* Feebly she stirs at the bedclothes, as though she will find him there, shrunk down sou-sized: a spider, a three-spotted ladybird, a white mouse. Her mouth is dry with fear. The darkness that drowns the far wall is a red darkness. She was set to watch over him, and now he is gone, lost. Perhaps he is playing a trick on her, she thinks. A game, yes. Perhaps he is there, standing just beyond the circumference of her little light, and laughing, laughing.

So she leaves the bedside and moves into the darkness.

Ten paces, twenty. Thirty. Deeper still. She finds no far wall, but those on either side of her begin to narrow. A passageway. A gullet. She reaches out a hand to touch the walls and finds that they are soft and moist. Walls not of stone, but of flesh. They shine, veined and marbled. Above her, vaults of cartilage. She can hear him, his laboured breathing, putrid and hot. So close it disturbs the folds of her habit. Sister Perpetué must find him, wherever he hides.

The throat slopes downward and she follows, shielding the little flame with her hand. The rancid smell intensifies, stinging at her eyes. When she calls out his name, a noise comes from the deepness. Then she understands: she is inside him. Swallowed. Her terror grows. In desperation, she lifts the hem of her habit and turns to run, back toward the doorway, the passage, the light. She runs, she slides, she falls to her knees – the candle rolls across the floor, dripping scalding wax over her splayed hands, flame guttering to a cinder. She must force herself to breathe as the darkness wads close in around her. She gropes for the candle across a gristly softness, as of a tongue. She finds it and lifts it high. The little light pricks at shapes: the faces of rats. Hundreds, perhaps thousands. Brute and rascal and flooding down the throat toward her. A carpet of them, a squealing river. As rats run from the flooded places when rain fills the storm drains, as rats run from the holds of sinking ships, yellow teeth bared in desperation, scaly tails upraised, bodies stiff with instinct and infection. She screams as the swarm reaches her feet. And then she wakes.

She is sitting in her chair at the patient's side, slumped forward over the bedstead. Her arms laid over his body. A thread of light falls through the open door. Morning light, grey matins-light. The patient is still. Sister Perpetué remembers her purity, and sits up to arrange her kirtle and cornette. A night terror. She is not superstitious of these. She understands that they emanate from a deep thing that will not show itself naked to scrutiny: a thing that opens out – that flowers – only in the darkness. She understands her dream was the dream of the cosseted. The rats were not rats but people. Stiff with instinct and infection. Swarming.

The patient lies still before her. His head is turned away toward the wall, his wrist twisting upward to the bite of the shackle, veins showing blue like faded ink on the underside. Very still. Too still. Sister Perpetué's breath catches in her body. She takes his wrist in her fingertips and finds the flesh is cold.

Citizen? she says quietly. Then again. Citizen?

Tarare? Tarare

Tarare

Tarare no more.

III

Drapeau rouge

[Red Flag]

No-one can hear our lesions of laughter as we hang onto the omphalos, decorating the plaque of the world. Tendrils still, when the pick comes what a basket we shall be carried in forewords the aspic falter of calfdom.

Lucy Mercer, Emblem (2022)

September 1792

The Argonne

You are here because you have been – here, the aide-de-camp in his beautiful scarlet-braided coat pauses, and looks down at his notes – stealing. Is this true?

The soldier nods.

Stealing – the aide-de-camp refers to his notes again – food. Rations.

I was hungry, monsieur.

The aide-de-camp looks at the soldier and the soldier looks back at him with the jaded pale eyes of a vegetal cat. He is ragged and narrow-hipped, with an unmagnificent growth of beard on his cheeks. Twenty-one years old, the aide-de-camp's notes tell him. But the boy sitting in front of him could be older, could be younger. That is how it goes with peasants. They either look fifty by fifteen and remain that way forever, or live out their short mean lives cased in the milk-skin of youth, starved down to slats. This boy, this particular peasant, is somehow doing both at once. His jacket is ripped at the shoulder, show-ing his undershirt. His horny toenails poke through his frayed espadrilles. Big, watery debaser's eyes. Not a man of quality, far from. But then, so few of the volunteers are. Checked for little more than four intact limbs then sent slack-jawed to the front, with their bad teeth and bawdy little songs. They don't know how to handle bayonets. Most of them barely know how to wipe their own arses. The Ministry may as well be sending them cartfuls of dressmakers' dummies, for all the good these boys do. (They're good in a tight spot though, some of them. Dirty fighters. Hair-pullers. Entirely unsqueamish when it comes to blood and mud and shit, their own or anyone else's. At Verdun the aide-de-camp had seen a peasant boy glance down at his own shin bone poking through the meat of his leg. No wailing, no tears. He just said 'oh', as though his maiming was a tedious inevitability, then cadged a smoke from the field surgeon come to hack off the limb.)

The boy looks right back at the aide-de-camp. He has his own thoughts. I will never be as clean as this man, he thinks. I could spend all day every day bathing, slicking myself with oils, and I would never look as clean as this man does, in his scarlet-braided coat, with his plumed tricorn. Smelling of orris root powder.

Rain tickers on the canvas above their heads. A northern rain, bone-rattling. Briny.

You were hungry, repeats the aide-de-camp. Do you not receive daily rations, citizen? As your brothers in arms do? A pound and three-quarters of bread, three ounces of meat, daily?

We do not receive this, monsieur. They give us beans instead of meat. Dried beans. I have never seen any meat, monsieur.

The aide-de-camp frowns. He opens his hand on the table, clears his throat, and says, *regardless*. Your brothers in arms do not feel the need to supplement their ration through thievery, do they?

Some of them do, the soldier insists. And some of them gave me their ration and then said afterwards that I stole it. You see, so it isn't fair.

Why would they give you their rations? the aide-de-camp counters. If they are so meagre, as you say.

The soldier, the boy, looks down into his lap. In return for favours.

Favours?

The soldier says no more. He nods, his eyes still tilted downward.

But some you stole, yes?

Yes. Some I stole.

Cock-sucking, then, the aide-de-camp surmises. Although why anyone would want his cock sucked by this nasty streak of piss sitting in front of him, the aide-de-camp cannot imagine. There is a pungency to him, a sour emanation entirely unprecedented in his now not inconsiderable experience of the lower social orders. Riper and more aggressive. Even separated by the wide tabletop, the aide-de-camp can smell it. And then there is the matter of the horse, the aide-de-camp says.

The soldier's cheeks flush crimson as the aide-de-camp consults his notes. An artillery horse, the aide-de-camp says, that fell on the road outside Lunéville. Mestre Descremps says that when he and a party of others returned in the evening to clear it from the road, they found you there. Eating its flesh. The aide-de-camp screws his nose small. Raw, he adds.

The horse was dead. The soldier moistens his lips, stammering. It was of no further use to anyone. Besides, people eat horse, monsieur. They eat horse where I come from.

Raw? The aide-de-camp lifts his eyebrows. They eat raw horse in – note-check – *Lyon*, do they? You surprise me. I have visited Lyon, and I remember the tripe, and the schnitzel. But never once did anyone try to serve me *raw horse*.

The soldier looks down into his lap again. No, monsieur. Not raw.

The aide-de-camp sighs. The point is that your behaviour is – was – most disturbing. People were fond of that horse, the mestre tells me. He looks at the soldier again. He has pretty eyelashes, the aide-de-camp notices. Not suck-my-cock pretty, but still. Thick and gilt-coloured, like a china doll's. You are ashamed you did this? the aide-de-camp asks.

Yes, says the soldier. (He was himself fond of that particular horse, with the white star between her brandy-mellow eyes. He was sad – and sorry – when she died, groaning in the hitch, dropping on to her bloodied knees like a puppet when its strings slacken.)

The aide-de-camp leans back in his chair. He likes to play a game he calls anywhere-but-here-anything-but-this, in which he allows his mind, for the barest moment, to drift from the task at hand through the blue voile of memory, to revisit moments in his life that were in all ways preferable to sitting in a tent in a military encampment on a rainy September evening wrangling with the abjection of the Third Estate. The first time he read *La Nouvelle Héloïse*, for instance, on a lawn washed with sunlight – *should I live for centuries, the sweet period of my youth would not be reborn, nor effaced from my memory* – and he had looked up from the page after reading those words, overcome by the sweetest sadness, and smelled honeysuckle, and heard the birds singing with a renewed bell-like clarity. Or else on the Loire in a white boat – Marguerite, her lovely little hand trailing in the water like a flower, the lace of her hem frothing over his foot *o Mathieu, Mathieu*. The music of his name when it was she who said it, when it was her lips that gave it life – but no. Sawdust and latrine pits. Here he sits, not with Marguerite, nor even Rousseau, but with a peasant boy who will suck a cock for a fistful of dried beans. He sighs again. So, you have come here from Lyon, he says—

Not Lyon, Monsieur, says the soldier. A village near to Lyon.

And you are a volunteer. So you have come here – the aide-de-camp widens his arms to indicate the conceptual dimensions of his 'here' – from a village near to Lyon because you believe in liberty, and in honour, and will proudly shed blood for the patrie?

Liberty, the soldier thinks, and honour. Liberty, Tarare thinks. And honour. Perhaps there was some blaze in these words when he was first given them, along with his blue coat and boots, before the boots were stolen while he slept, before the cannonade at Valmy, when he saw how the guns opened boys out from the middle like curtains. They won at Valmy, without really seeming to do very much, beating back the Prussians so that Paris was saved. The old and secretive forests of the Argonne had conspired with them, the sons of France, in growing the hard and sour green apples that had made the Prussians sick. Tarare's side had seen them growing on the low boughs, swelling like teardrops, and had known not to eat them somehow. As though the breath of the pines, the groundmist, had seeped a warning in their bones while they slept on the cold ground. But the Prussians had eaten the apples, so that by the time the guns were positioned in the valley and the creaking windmill razed, by the time they were squatting in bushes with their hearts in their mouths and rusted bayonets in their hands, none of it had really seemed necessary. The Prussians were shitting themselves to death. Brunswick tearing his white perruque in frustration. Nonetheless, they had opened out some Prussian boys from the middle with their guns. Fed the roots on Prussian blood, *schlecht schlecht* the sound of molten bowels fanning on the grass from the sons of Brandenburg. Green hills maned in smoke. And the day after this glorious cannonade the new Republic had been declared in France. There was a clear biblical resonance to all this. They, the volunteers, had no guns, no regulation billhooks or gravy pots, and meagre rations. But their spirits were high, thinking themselves Maccabees. God on their side. God of the forest – god of Vercingetorix, older than the god of the Maccabees – on their side. The Warriors of Liberty. All the piss and vinegar. As if at any moment General Dumouriez might ride out on his charger, gilded epaulettes shining, and, raising a white-gloved hand, stun the sun into stillness in its oblique passage across the sky. Stranger things have happened, after all, than a conspiracy of trees. Stranger things have happened in the past three years, to any man among the Army of the Rhine you would care to stop and ask, as he is digging a latrine pit or polishing a cannon or budding tobacco between his fog-numbed fingertips: oaths sworn on tennis courts, armies of fishwives in Versailles, feasts on the meat of roasted giraffes. Unaccountable and violent things. Financiers stripped naked and lynched in the streets. The noblesse leaching the ancient sapphire from their veins and taking the common names of colporteurs and valets. And in the middle of it all this boy, yes, Tarare. Now with added chest pain and a brand on his shoulder. Thief. Yes, perhaps, Tarare thinks – when he rolls his fingers over the raised white scar beneath his shirt – a thief, but a good one. A brand provides no context. A brand doesn't give you your due. In Paris, he had stolen everything there was to steal. He stole until it became a nature.

Lord of legerdemain, rattling his stump-toothed mouth in the grocers' shops on the Street of Five Diamonds and the Street of the Lombards with fine-day pleasantries while he pocketed buns and cheese and cherries. Sliding into wineshops and picking bones off the plates of eloquent drunks (one of these drunks was the angel-faced Camille Desmoulins, although he did not know it, and one of them was jaundiced People's Friend Marat, and he did. *You are Marat*, Tarare had said. *Yes*, Marat had answered, *I am. Well done.* Before turning away with an abruptness Tarare had thought was not very People's-Friend of him.) Tarare was almost invisible. Sylph of quay and refuse heap. Lurking by the shopfronts with the wasted dogs in the jonquil-gold of morning to collect the fetid offal. All it took to be a good thief was *not caring*. All it took was to die twice and leave your shame behind in the old body, the short bones, the child grave. He couldn't read the newspapers because he couldn't read, but sometimes he had listened to the eloquent drunks with their barside rhetoric, their gentlemen's debates, and from this he learned other things. He learned that France has a parasite with its mouthparts buried deep in her armpit. He learned that he is one of *the twenty-five million* (a million being a thousand thousand, a thousand being a hundred hundred) who starve and die and reproduce themselves with a doomed mayfly abandon, railing at the empty sky. He learned that the pain and starvation of the twenty-five million is *contingent*. Not ordained by God, at least, but by men. This was news. This was meat for thinking. All the suffering and all the pain simply *need not happen*. And Tarare thought and Tarare saw that this was also, in his case, untrue. He was the one man among the twenty thousand thousand hundred hundred who was abject head to foot, to his very bone. No revolution could reform his hunger, which had grown all-consuming. He never thinks of his mother any more. He has forgotten her face. He would not have known her if she had passed him on the Pont au Change. He sometimes thinks of Pierette, or of Antoine (one already dead, the other soon to be, although he does not know it). What he thinks of mostly is hunger. Morning hunger evening hunger hunger that wakes him in the night hunger that he trips over like a loose cobblestone hunger he carries heavy on his shoulders like a litter hunger bitter hunger sweet hunger like a beggar-child with its arms wrapped round his middle hunger red-eyed pigeon hobbling on beshitted stumps hunger darkness hunger light hunger water hunger fire. How to tame it, if he cannot sate it? How to meet it like a creature? No revolution will reform Tarare. Topple kings and queens right into his open mouth, even, and watch him ask for more.

Citizen? says the aide-de-camp. Do you believe in liberty? Why are you – that conceptual flap of the arms again – here? War is uncomfortable. War is painful. Why have you come here, if not to suffer with honour? Why have you come here if not to bleed for the patrie?

I came, says the soldier, because I thought I would be fed.

You are fed. Have we not established, Citizen – he checks his notes – *Nollet*, that you are fed?

Still red-cheeked, the soldier mutters.

Speak up, boy.

I need to eat more than other men, monsieur.

This move toward individuation on the part of the soldier infuriates the aide-de-camp. What is a peasant doing with preferences, with appetites? With distinguishing characteristics? A peasant with preferences is a monkey with an orrery. A sheep with a china teapot. Do not mistake him: his politics are essentially liberal. He reads Rousseau. He has held Mirabeau in high esteem. But nonetheless. What business does a peasant, a serf, think he is about, when he says he needs to eat more than *other men*? *YOU* – the aide-de-camp wants to say, wants to shout – *YOU* are other men. You are all men. You will take what we give you. We will no longer require that you scrape, nor genuflect. But a smile, at least. A *thank you, monsieur*. Why? asks the aide-de-camp. Why is it that you would require more than your brothers in arms? You are not an especially large man. Nor do you appear – forgive me, citizen – especially vigorous.

The soldier's eyes begin to mist, until a tear rolls down his flushed cheek, cutting a track in his second skin of caked-on dirt. I do not know, monsieur. He weeps.

The aide-de-camp has Tarare whipped. Then he has him put on a wagon bound for the military hospital at Soultz-Haut-Rhin, where he will be somebody else's problem, some-body else's aggressively bad smell.

*

The cart rolls south away from camp, out of the sheltering breast of the blue-green forest, very early the next morning. The season has already turned and the sky is pink and grained with frost, like a sugar-dusted pastille. Tarare shivers in the harsh wind that blows over the plain. The fresh whip stripes burn in the flesh of his back. He is a southern boy with dope-warm blood and the juice of grapes running in his heart: this place is so cold. The lineaments of the countryside are alien to him, jagged and mean, grass like splinters. To him it seems a nordcountry, where great silver whales would sprawl their prehistoric bodies out on the sand, and the farmers who stop to mark the passage of the tumbril have German eyes and lantern jaws. It is so early a few tardy stars still blink in the upper reach of the sky. The vista brings Tarare little joy as it unfolds around him. But the packet of invalids who weight the tumbril along the muddy road are perhaps more promising. Their legs mingle under a heavy woollen blanket. They pass around a pipe between them. Tarare likes to smoke now, sometimes, finding it takes the edge off his hunger.

He avails himself of the pipe from a Breton whose hand has been crushed in a wheel of a cannon. There is also a glazier from Paris afflicted with profound tinnitus, as well as three giggling syphilitics and a boy with dark tousled hair whose face is three-quarters wrapped in bandages stiff with blood clotted nearly black. This rag-bound boy is watching him through his one uncovered eye. As Tarare hands the pipe to him, he reaches out a hand and touches Tarare's arm and says Here, you. You're Tarare, aren't you?

Tarare stiffens in his seat to be called that name again, a name he set aside in Paris out of caution. A name complicit, perhaps, in double murder. He looks at the boy with the bandaged face, who is smiling lopsidedly. Tarare asks, in his best left-bank hard-act voice: Who's asking?

It's me, says the boy, bringing his hand to his chest. It's Hervé. Remember me? Hervé, from Charton's farm. Remember?

Tarare stares. *The* Hervé, *his* Hervé, Hervé the farm boy, whose fault this all is, when you think about it. And Tarare has thought about it a lot. Hervé whose fault this all is, if you haul your way to the top of the clanking chain of cause and effect. To that balmy night, to that dance of Lady Day, to the fulcrum of Tarare's little life. This is Hervé, and Hervé does not look well. Yes, that is Hervé's overbite and eye, brown with gold speckles, like a snipe's egg. Those are Hervé's curls, matted with dried blood. Hervé's long arms and labour-thickened neck.

Hervé, says Tarare. He is stunned. What happened to your—

I knew it was you! Hervé laughs triumphantly, then cringes, raising a hand to the bandage whorled over his left eye. Shrapnel, he says. Lucky to still have the other. Must be the only Frenchman to have shed blood at Valmy. Isn't that a bitch? Maybe they'll give me a medal, ha ha.

Tarare shapes his lips to the words he wants to say and they come, eventually. My – my mother—

Yes, how is old Agnès? Did they find a place to settle?

Tarare looks dumbly at Hervé.

Hervé looks back, ingenuous. He frowns. You don't know? They went away, Nollet and your mother. Not long after you did. I don't know where. I don't think they told anyone. We thought they had followed after you, wherever you had gone.

This moment marks the deliquescence of a dream Tarare had not known he had. A dream of reunion. Tarare in his fine soldier's coat with the tails nattily pressed and a breast glistening with commendations. Returning to the village beyond the wood. This Tarare would find that village, where the poor wooden houses hutched around the white church spire. This Tarare has intuition, pluck. He would see his mother – see her there – standing at the garden gate in her red headwrap. A little older, a little greyer. Wet-eyed, she would take him in her arms and put so many kisses on his cheeks. Call him once again poucet, *Bibi*, her little warrior, her little champion. Doves would be suckling in the eaves, just as they used to. The imagined tenderness brings tears to his eyes. He wanted, he knows now, to go back. Someday. The notion that, as he had blundered forward, all behind him had remained the same

– burnished in the fine summers of the younger century – had lived in him. But of course it hadn't remained the same, because things don't do that. Things hate to remain. He sees a house shuttered and empty, an onion patch overgrown. He sees it so clearly, as only absence can be seen. Gone. Tarare feels a pain in his teeth, a rawness in his throat.

Hervé watches him. Ah, Tarare, he says. I'm sorry. I thought you knew. We all supposed that after you left—

The rawness in Tarare's throat is anger. He turns his head to fix the farm boy with his watery eyes. I didn't *leave*, he says. Nollet tried to kill me.

Hervé's mouth opens, then stays open, muted.

Yes, says Tarare. After what you did. After you came with your boys to the house. Don't you remember that? He took me to the woods, and he beat me mostly dead. So I ran away.

Hervé lifts his hand to his bandaged jaw. God's blood, he murmurs. I didn't mean for that—

Well. That's what happened, whether you meant it to or not. And now Tarare laughs, taking another puff on the pipe. Nollet tried to kill me, after you did what you did. So in a way, Hervé, he says – it's like you tried to kill me. (There, thinks Tarare. You and your beautiful right eye live with that, Hervé.)

Tarare turns away from Hervé to pass the pipe back to the Breton. The Breton grasps Tarare's wrist in his good hand. Pardon, says the Breton. I overheard – you are Tarare? The Great Tarare? Not waiting for an answer, he nudges one of the syphilitics with his foot. Hey, he says. Hey, Charles. This is Tarare!

The syphilitic leers at Tarare through rheumy, bloodshot eyes. The Great Tarare? Nah. I heard Tarare died. Heard he died in Neuilly.

Well this boy here says he's Tarare.

I heard he ate himself in Neuilly. At an inn in Neuilly, the Jeanne d'Arc. I've been there. I was told. The char went up to fetch the night soil and found the door locked from the inside and The Great Tarare's bones picked clean in the bed. He ate himself. Ate himself to death.

That doesn't even make sense, says the glazier, sucking his teeth.

The other syphilitics cackle. The Breton too.

I heard – adds the Breton – a surgeon cut him open. He ate a surgeon's pocket watch and the surgeon sliced him open from gooch to nostrils to get it back.

Tarare ate my sister! contributes the glazier. He started at the bottom – he taps his fingers in his lap suggestively – so she was enjoying it, at first.

More laughter.

Would you please *fuck off*, all of you? says Hervé, cringing and pressing at his brow. We were having a private conversation.

All right, friend-o. All right, cock-eye, says the syphilitic. Calm down.

We were just having a little fun, pouts the glazier.

It's a different Tarare, sighs Hervé. Clearly.

A *different* Tarare. Right, snorts the syphilitic. Because we all know a Tarare, don't we boys?

Yeah, says the Breton. They're everywhere.

Can't cross the road without brushing shoulders with a Tarare these days.

I named my son Tarare, says the glazier. We wanted something *traditional*.

After your father? suggests the Breton.

Yeah, after my father, *Tarare*. Of the esteemed line of Montrichard Tarares.

They chortle like waterbirds. Hervé sighs and cradles his aching brow in his hand.

I *also* overheard – says the Breton – Tarare over here saying that you tried to kill him, cock-eye. He flips a pointed index finger between Hervé and Tarare. Is that true? Did I hear correctly? Are you a rat, cock-eye? A mouchard?

Tell us the story, Tarare, says the syphilitic. He has folded his arms and furrowed his brow like a schoolmaster. Rat behaviour is no laughing matter. A mouchard isn't welcome among men.

Hervé raises his bandaged head. Fuck off and mind your own business, he snarls. All of you.

He doesn't deny it, see, says the Breton, rubbing his stubbled chin magisterially.

We must give him the opportunity to defend himself, counters the syphilitic. It's only proper. Tarare, did this mouchard try to have you killed? Did André hear that right?

Tarare hesitates. Then nods. Yes, he says. He did.

Go and fuck your mothers, says Hervé. My head is killing me. Can we not have some peace? Tarare, what the fuck are you doing?

Hervé gazes imploringly at Tarare. Tarare looks straight back, nonplussed. In his mind's eye stands the shuttered house, the overgrown onion patch. The gaping absence, the pain of his first half-death. Tarare shrugs. I'm telling the truth, he says.

Well, says the syphilitic, clapping his rag-wrapped hands together. He's had his chance. Do we send the mouchard overboard now, boys?

Yes, the Breton concurs. He can walk to the hospital.

And the syphilitics rise up on their feet in the wagon bed and take hold of Hervé's shoulders while the Parisian grabs at his flailing feet. The Breton, handless, directs the operation. Hervé wriggles and throws his fists about uselessly, but he is over-whelmed. Out over the side of the wagon Hervé goes, falling head first to the roadside, rolling into the ditch with a whine. The driver glances over his shoulder at the commotion, then turns back to mutter steam-breathed at his trudging mules.

On the tumbril rolls. Tarare watches as Hervé rises to his feet, covered in black mud, shaking. It feels good. Hervé yells into the cold hard wind, which carries his words right back into his own face. The syphilitics and the Parisian and the Breton are laughing. Tarare laughs too, while Hervé the farm boy dwindles to a nothing against the bald white of the lightening sky. Is lost.

Tarare thinks to himself, apropos of nothing, *perhaps the world will end in the year eighteen hundred*. In eight years, that is. He had heard street preachers in Paris say as much, spittle flecking their reeky beards. He has heard it said and he feels it could very well be so. A nice round number. Eighteen is six and six and six. Eighteen hundred is God's head rising from a cloudy pillow, God's two empty eyes gazing down on his strange and perhaps misconceived creation.

*

The hospital at Soultz-Haut-Rhin gleams newly purpose-built among the undulant hills of the borderlands, where on the maps the -courts and the -villes of the Grand Republic begin to mingle hesitantly with the -kirchs and -heims of the Germans. This is the frontier, twenty miles west of the Rhine. The night of his arrival, Tarare reflects on his good fortune at having been sent here, away from the fighting, to this warm and dry and whitewashed and extremely sterilised place, where flesh is leached and knit and bled. Lying awake after lights-out, in the long dormitory, he screws his hunger up as small as he can while he listens to the snores of wounded soldiers and the tap of rain on the zinc roof, and he swears to God on his mother that he will try to be good now. The dormitory full of soft beds, like a flight of fluffy grey clouds, carrying their wounded human freight. Tarare has never laid himself down on anything so soft. So he will try to be good. He will try to be abstemious. He will try to *control himself,* even though it hurts, even though he has never before come anywhere close to success in bridling his desperate, inhuman hunger with reason.

The little routines of the place augment these monastic aspirations.

6:00: red-cheeked ward sister sits you up in bed fluffs your pillow changes bandages drains off the pus sweet morning on the clean-scrubbed tiles like a mirror

7:00: breakfast (bread, warm milk, groats)

8:00–11:00: bed and chatter battered news-sheets ha those poor fucks in Paris poor fucks at the front take the air in the courtyard whitewashed little sparrows peeping from a single unhappy-looking cherry tree already names have been scratched with a nail or knife into the stuccoed wall ANDRE BIJARD PICRDY SEBASTIEN LUC BEAUCHAMP TARARE TARARE you pace and sigh names and of course cocks and cunts scratched into the stuccoed wall just in outline or squirting thick and veined slit of winking eye source of all life? GOD <3s BOYS OF MARSEILLE JEAN + JEAN FOREVER

11:00: lunch of green underseasoned beans and boiled mutton

12:00 leeches applied to the supple skin of the underarm

13:00: ANDREW BIJARD PICARDY or whoever else is carried away for surgery haha poor fuck his screaming shakes

the lead in the windows those doctors very upright and educated men

15:00: supper of underseasoned beans and boiled mutton
bread to sop the juices up

16:00: Vincent Nollet, twenty-one years, APPETITE
GREAT is all his referral says well what does that mean what
are we to do with you greeting us every morning when the
blinds are lifted with such a wide and unbruised smile like a
little boy trying on gentlemanly manners never seems to answer
to his name like he forgets it simple-minded green nowhere on
him cut or needing cutting by all accounts robust and cheerful.
appetite, great? we must ask the citizendoctor we must ask the
surgeon Courville what it means why he's here what it is we're
supposed to do with him

18:00: last repast (bread and warm milk, groats)

19:00: lights out tapping of rain on the zinc roof screwing
hunger up in his breast on a belly full of warm milk in this
dry and whitewashed place God by my mother I will be good
abstemious control myself even though it hurts. do you know
where it hurts, God? Am I a part of you? Leashed on your thin
silver hairs of moonlight can't sleep can't

And on the fourth such night after the fourth such day,
Tarare lies awake feeling out the cramp in his throat. He listens
to his stomach, how it gurgles and drips like a cave mouth.
A mutton chop and a crust of bread is not very much after
all, is it? Porridge with thinned milk? His mind is borne back
in a half-dream to the streets of Paris, so velvet blue by starlight, little glass lamps illuminating the windows of restaurants
and cafés, the brightly painted fascias of buvettes. The smells,
the delicacies. Mussels in white wine sauce, flecked with pars-
ley. Tenderest roast goose. Hot onion tarts embellished with

divaricate flowers. Bread and butter pudding, crusted with sugar. Spicy sausages with oily fried potatoes. Brandied plums rolling tipsy in crystal-cut tumblers. Bitter-sweet choucroute. He stirs in his bed, he chomps. His teeth close around nothing but the stale medicinal air. In the darkness behind his eyes stellar formations of spun sugar float and merge and dance like thistle seeds. He could catch them on his tongue. It is like there are two hands fixed around different parts of his prone body. One pressing his chest down against the bed peremptorily. The other stroking softly at his chin and beckoning, beckoning him into the black. *Tarare, Tarare.*

Tarare rises from his bed.

The corridors are narrow, winding and entirely empty. He feels so weak in his body that he walks with his shoulder pressed to the wall. Hobbles, like a crippled man. He tries each door he comes across. The first two are locked. What is it that Tarare is looking for? What is it that Tarare imagines he will find, if he only opens the right door, in the military hospital at Soultz-Haut-Rhin? A restaurant? An eatery? Yes, to visit a restaurant is perhaps what he is half-dreaming of as he stumbles along the corridor, the cold of the flagstones biting at his bare toes. He can almost see it: the door will open on a chamber illuminated with the lilac flames of thermolampes. Tables and chairs of carved rosewood. Spotless white tablecloths. A handsome maître d'hôtel with a pencil moustache in a pearl-grey waistcoat will usher him toward a seat, with the utmost ceremony. His feet will sink into a carpet of crimson plush. There will be music all around him: a tall silver cage of parakeets singing a barcarolle as the maître lays a cloth over his bony knees. *Will Monsieur have any wine today* – lords and ladies picking at lobster tail and sweetbreads. And there is Tarare, in his dirty nightshirt—

The third door opens on a storeroom. There is a herbal savour here. As his eyes acclimatise to the darkness, Tarare picks out the hefty shapes of glass jars, bottles. Folded bandages, reams of gauze. Tarare starts with these. Packing his mouth with dry cotton, swallowing it down, tearing it into strips with his teeth and hands. Filling himself. Pills and ointments and poultices and syrups that burn his throat. The tastes and sensations are eclectic. Some liquids are viscous and sour like turned wine. Others sweet. He moves faster as the frenzy overtakes him, knocking vials and dishes aside with his hands, looking for more, more. Alcohols and acids sizzling on the floor and abrading his nose and eyes with their chemical sharpness. He closes his fist around a murder of gorged leeches. They stretch like jerky between his teeth and when they burst release a metal flavour, an imbrued juice of diseased blood, on to his tongue, dripping down his chin, the mouthparts crunchy—

Good God, says the doctor.

Tarare's nightshirt catches at his throat where the doctor grabs hold of him. He cringes and cowers like an animal, raising his hands to shield his face from the inevitable blow.

Hey, says the doctor. Hey, calm down now. He releases Tarare's collar.

Tarare presses himself small into a corner. The doctor stoops down beside him, so that they are face to face, the light from his taper reflected in broken glass and pooled iodine. He is a young man, youngish man in his face. A young doctor. In his shirtsleeves, with dark circles under his wondering eyes as he surveys the ruin of his storeroom. Listen to me – says the doctor – what's your name? There is no anger in his tone. Just surprise, curiosity.

Tarare, whines Tarare.

Tarare, repeats the doctor. No pique, no flicker of recognition. Listen to me, Tarare – it is very important that I know what you have eaten. There are things kept here that could hurt you, could poison you, if you've eaten them. Do you understand me? The doctor speaks slowly, in a voice so soft. Then he stands and raises up his taper to move the flame across the plundered storeroom shelves: vegetal syrups, Faynard's powder, tobacco pills, camphorated lotions. All emptied out, scattered.

Tarare is silent, shivering with adrenaline. An acetose bile begins to flood the back of his mouth. His stomach sways like a coracle.

You're not sure? volunteers the doctor.

Tarare squeezes his own throat in his hand. Leech – *leeches* – is all he manages before he doubles over and begins to vomit. Pills and ointments and syrups that burn his throat as they rise back up it again, chemical sour like turned wine. Vomit flecked with blood and chalk and gobbets of black worm-meat. Even he is disgusted by the sight of it, the smell of it.

And Citizen-Doctor Jean-Pierre Dupuis stoops down again and places his hand on Tarare's back and gently rubs there and says, Good, good. I know it doesn't feel good, Tarare, but it is good. You need to get it all out. All out. Good.

*

Citizen-Doctor Jean-Pierre Dupuis' office is small, untidy and lighted by rushes. The doctor sits Tarare down on a leather-topped examination table. I'm going to fetch warm water, he says. No point waking the Sisters. You'll be all right here on your own for a few minutes, Tarare?

Tarare nods, swinging his ankles and looking around.

Doctor Dupuis leaves. Doctor Dupuis has a high domed

forehead and grey hangdog eyes. Doctor Dupuis is *a gentleman in the truest sense*, Tarare decides. It is a descriptor he has heard others use: *gentleman in the truest sense*. But never before has he met someone to whom it could be applied. Doctor Dupuis has gentle manly grey hangdog eyes and gentle manly long pliant hands and Tarare likes how the doctor bolts his name on to the front or back of everything he says, every order he gives. *Tarare, I will do this now – can you do this now, Tarare*. It makes Tarare feel solid. It makes Tarare feel extant.

In the doctor's absence, Tarare examines the office. A bookcase, a washstand, a little window that overlooks the darkness of the courtyard, where Tarare knows that a single cherry tree grows. A desk is pushed against the far wall, upon which rests an open notebook, scribbled over in the doctor's own cramped shorthand. An enamelware mug browned with coffee dregs. A jolt of alarm runs through Tarare when he sees he is not alone: he is observed, from the shadowed corner furthest from the window. Two dark circles in a gaunt, grinning face. Hello? he says.

No answer comes. The face is still, the dark holes unblinking, the smile hard as rock.

Cautiously, Tarare rises from the examination table. Closer, he sees that the dark circles are not eyes, but hollows, and the gaunt face is not a face but a skull. A skeleton hangs there, naked bone held erect by a wire, a metal frame. Breathless fleshless white. Tarare stands before the skeleton, face to skull. It is frightening – the stasis of the slackened jaw, the blind caves-of-eyes – but he finds it beautiful, too. The way the dipping, shapely ribs are drawn together in the centre. The harmonious flexure of the slender armbones, kissing top and tail. A thin layer of dust has settled in the molars, velvets the collar.

He holds out a hand and runs his fingers along the fattest rib. Smooth and cold to the touch.

Making friends with Marie Antoinette? the doctor chuckles, setting a steaming basin down on the examination table.

Tarare withdraws his hand. Blushes.

It's all right, says the doctor. Touch all you want.

Is it real? asks Tarare. Is it a man or a woman?

The doctor laughs again, sopping a cloth in the warm water, wringing it out in his lovely long hands. No, no. Just moulded plaster. I bought her at a bar in Paris, if you can believe it. I was exceedingly drunk. Some toothless type in a catskin hat had her in a chest under the table. I think he must have stolen her. Cramped down in there, like he'd pulled a coffin out of the ground of the Calvaire. I felt sorry for her. Come here now, Tarare. Doctor Dupuis patpats the examination table.

Tarare resumes his seat and the doctor begins to wipe the vomit and sour sweat from his face. But she is *a she*? he asks.

I don't know. The doctor shrugs, dipping and wringing the cloth again. I call her *she*. But it is hard to tell from bones alone. He smiles. I think it is a good thing for a physician to be reminded of – that every man or woman is more or less the same underneath the skin, the meat. Just a frame of bones. Shorter or longer bones. That's it, in the end.

As a man of peasant meat, this observation strikes Tarare as asinine. The meat, it matters. The colour of it, where it swells or suntans, where it bruises and who bruises it. The uses it is put to, by choice or compulsion (or compulsion made to appear choice). The nourishment that sustains it, or does not. There are no hearts beating in the cold ground of the Calvaire to be warmed, after all, by this notional post-mortem equitability. But Tarare can see the doctor is kind. Tarare can see the doctor means well. Tarare can see he sees more than the doctor does, when it comes to many things. You call her Marie Antoinette? he says.

Just a little joke, Dupuis says, biting boyishly at his lip. Most doctors are secret goliards at heart. Take your nightshirt off for me, Tarare.

Tarare does as he is bidden, shivering in his drawers while the doctor sets the basin aside. Are you a Republican, monsieur? he asks.

The doctor turns and looks at Tarare askance. He blinks his tired hangdog eyes. Why, yes, he says. Aren't you? Most soldiers I meet are Republicans. Lie down for me, Tarare. Arms by your sides, please. Committed Republicans.

I don't know, says Tarare. I don't really know what it means, besides that you hate the King and the Queen.

The doctor smiles indulgently as Tarare lowers himself on to the table. It's complicated, Tarare, he says. I neither *hate* nor wish harm on any. But a Republican believes that king and queen have no God-given right to rule. He believes that the people who are the patrie – here, the doctor motions with his hand between their two bodies, one laid out, one upright – should be able to *choose* who it is that leads them. You see? Choose the best man for the job.

But what if you don't know the best man for the job? Not every man knows every man. What if the best man for the job lives in Normandy, but you live in Lyon?

The doctor laughs at that. A Republican also believes that men should take their place in society according to their merit, not their wealth or name, Tarare. That way, the best men might be known to all. Do you see?

Tarare does not see, but demurs from further discussion of

polity. I saw the Queen once, he says. (He had indeed, through a crowd of rioters outside the Hôtel-Dieu. They rode in a fine carriage, the royal couple, with gilded eagles at each corner that spread their wings over the press of filthy bodies all around. Their faces were just pale smudges at the window. A woman with a tricolore rosette pinned to her breast reached down under her skirts and drew a bloodied rag from between her thighs, smearing menses warm from her body across the glass of the window, beneath the Queen's nose, sticky clots of it. *Bread*, the crowd were shouting, and *Soap*. He remembered the woman. He had wondered if she had planned to do what she did, or if it had only occurred to her in the heat of the riot. The gesture struck Tarare, so he remembered it best of all the things he had seen that day. A demand: look at my body, apprehend the humanity of it. This he does not tell the doctor. All he tells the doctor is that he saw the Queen once.)

I'm not surprised, says the doctor. They'd be locking the whole House of Bourbon up in a cage like albino monkeys for the people to poke at them with sticks if they thought the Austrians would let them get away with it. The doctor laughs, and gently begins to palpate Tarare's trunk, before moving his hands down to his belly, where the skin is taut and swollen like a drum. Doctor Dupuis frowns. Tell me, Tarare – are you eating three meals daily?

Here, says Tarare, yes.

And before?

I ate what I could find to eat.

Like gauze, the doctor smiles, and poultices? He shakes his head. That's no good Tarare. That's no good. Tilt your head back for me, will you? The doctor fetches a rushlight from the desk and looks into Tarare's gullet. Sniffs at his breath. Say ahh.

Lift your tongue for me. That's good. Good. Tarare can smell the doctor's hair. Tobacco smoke, the lingering aroma of lavender wig powder. I'm going to listen to your heartbeat now, Tarare.

The doctor presses his naked ear to Tarare's pigeon chest, his face angled downward. Tarare can feel the doctor's own breath against his midriff. The doctor listens. The doctor taps his index finger against the ribcage, before moving his ear lower, to the stomach. Tarare feels the doctor's breath and the light scratch of evening stubble against his bare skin. The doctor mumbles something and presses the flat of his hand against the lower curve of Tarare's abdomen. Tarare cannot remember the last time he was touched like this, with care. Was it ever touched with care, his body? Maybe by his mother. Maybe. He is overcome with the urge to raise his arms and cradle the doctor's head. To hold it against his body. To pet the doctor's thinning hair like the silky fur of a cat.

But the doctor stands up. Do you have pains, Tarare? In your chest, or your stomach?

Sometimes.

The doctor fetches his notebook and takes a pencil stub from his rolled sleeve. Chest, belly or bowels? he asks.

All three.

The doctor frowns. Jots. And do you know how old you are, Tarare?

Twenty-one.

The doctor's pencil stops its scratching and his eyes flicker from the notebook to Tarare's prone body. And your appetite – he asks – how often do you find yourself hungry enough to produce this state of – of – mania? You can put your nightshirt back on.

Always, answers Tarare. I am always hungry, monsieur. (This answer, though true, seems insufficient. He wants to say: hunger is all I am and all my life is. Hunger runs through my veins like blood, branches through me like a fungus, swelling and renewing itself daily. I am lost on a sea of hunger, blue and black and heaving and full five fathoms deep below and rarely, rarely do I feel anything besides *hungry*, rarely, rarely does a jolt of feeling or emotion pierce the hide of my hunger, and never, never have I been able to live the life God presumably gave me to live, to dance and think and remember and kiss, no, all my life I have stood at the threshold of my life waiting to be let in because of this hunger, no living for Tarare. And he hears Lozeau again, his booming voice in the market square under searing sunshine among the carts of cabbages and casks of wine and vinegar, vying with the rap of cobblers' hammers, Tarare abject, Tarare debased, Tarare *the strangest of all things sublunary*—)

The doctor's brow furrows. Always?

Tarare nods. Tarare says: I am the strangest of all things sublunary.

The doctor's gaze is questioning. His eyes are tired but searching and soft. Tarare wants to give him something in return for the care of his touch. So Tarare gives him his story, from beginning to end. He gives him the clouds and swarms and Nollet and Monsieur Americain Franklin, the neighbour-woman and Lady Day, the Lozeaux and the cocottes, the bad blood, the seed drying, the black cats tarnishing in the hard dry summer.

The doctor listens.

*

The next morning, Tarare is woken by two voices insinuating themselves into the wedge end of his wide and dreamless sleep in his little white feather bed on the convalescents' ward.

Is he a lunatic? asks Voice the First.

No, I don't think so, says the second. But. There is a lassitude to him. An intense – what is the word? – *apathy*. He doesn't appear to *care* about anything. Himself least of all.

Sounds like a lunatic to me.

Perhaps.

What do you think?

If I were to guess – *Tænia saginata*. Tapeworms. See how skinny he is. He isn't feeding himself, with this gorging. He's feeding a parasite. All that raw meat.

And the greyness of the complexion.

Indeed.

So – purgatives, mercurial clysters? (laughter) – a gudgeon on the navel?

Gudgeon? Christ, Laurent. You sound like my grandmother.

What is the surgeon if not the voice of tradition?

(More laughter, a short silence.)

It will cause the poor boy misery.

Sounds like he's exceedingly miserable already.

He's lived a sorry sort of life. If it could even be called that.

Tarare opens his eyes. Light, brittle and white-edged with the early November frost outside, floods the quiet ward through the tall windows. Sitting at his bedside are Doctor Dupuis, now clean-shaven and perruqued, though with the same weary eyes, and a second man. Tarare smiles to see Doctor Dupuis, whom he thinks of, already, as his friend. The second man is florid and casually handsome, with a black beard framing his thin, cautious mouth. Good morning, Tarare, says Doctor Dupuis.

I hope you are well rested. I would like to introduce you to my colleague, Citizen Courville, Surgeon General of the Ninth Hussars.

The florid man inclines his head and smiles compactly.

We would like to discuss a course of treatment for you, Tarare.

And tests, adds Doctor Courville.

Tests? repeats Tarare dubiously. Tarare resents any challenge to his person, any game not carried out on his own terms. In truth, the word 'tests' puts him in mind of God, demanding filicides of sandy-bearded patriarchs, sending thirsty angels to their doors in bleached linen. These are stories he remembers, barely. Abraham was tested. Lot was tested. The various saints. Tests that Tarare has long suspected his callow self-centredness would cause him to fail, establishing in fact his debased moral quality. Test means pain means judgement, and Tarare wants none of either.

Dupuis smiles encouragingly. Only to learn more of your condition, Tarare. Nothing painful.

I am hungry all the time. That is my condition.

Dupuis closes his eyes and nods with scrupulous patience. Yes, he says. But there are many things that might be wrong with a man's body to cause him to eat all the time. That might enlarge his appetite beyond reason.

Or things *in* a man's body, adds Courville.

Tarare gazes at them blankly.

Doctor Dupuis opens the book he has cradled in his knees, holding it out for Tarare to see. The page is filled with drawings. Drawings of small creatures, like insects: bloated bodies with eyelash legs, earthworm bodies, sinuous ribbon bodies, bodies that are ugly as ticks, bodies that are beautiful and tremulous as lace. Dupuis turns the page. Here, a flask, filled with liquid. Within the liquid are more of the lacy creatures, undulating, extending probe-like antennae. You see, says Dupuis, there are these extraordinary little beasts. And they have been discovered to live on the food that we eat and even in the water that we drink. That way they enter our bodies. Most are benign – that means 'friendly', Tarare – but some are not. And within the body they can cause all kinds of mischief. They can poison our blood, even eat the food from our mouths.

Parasites, says Tarare.

Dupuis and Courville exchange a look. Yes, says Doctor Dupuis. That's right, Tarare. How do you—

They say France has a parasite.

Doctor Dupuis smiles faintly. Courville does not. Yes, says Dupuis. They do say that. And I think that you might have one too, Tarare.

This is something that Tarare had never considered, all the nights he lay awake on beds of damp newspaper or firecord or huddled in the doors of shuttered shops, made foetal by cramps and pangs, his eyes soldered with hot salty tears from the pain of it, wondering if it would not be better simply to throw himself from the Pont au Change down down into the dirty brown water of the Seine, where he would die and it would all be over and he would be a suicide which means that he would go to Hell, but could that really be any worse? Any worse than the cold and the pain and the stench of this? Could all available infernal genius really concoct a torture less tolerable than this hunger? Perhaps they would make it so he needed to piss all the time, too. Perhaps they would chase him with jagged knives and axes and swords of flame. So what? Child's play. But Tarare had never considered that it might not be *him* who was hungry, but something *in* him: a possession. One of these lacy, undulating fuckers making house in the warmth of his entrails, a year-round month of May. He makes a face and a body for it in his mind: a man, a six-armed man, his body swollen to horrifying immensity and cased in silks, his little legs waggling, an oily face staring out from an extravagant curled perruque. Floating and twirling like a plump putto through the rich juice of Tarare's innards. *Poisoning his blood.*

All right, says Tarare – adorably invigorated, made hopeful by this change in perspective. How do we get it out?

*

Tarare is weighed daily. On Doctor Dupuis' orders, his rations are doubled – he eats every morsel of his new, enlarged menu (bread, pickled cabbage, peas and a second chop at supper), and asks for more. His rations are tripled, and it is much the same. Tarare is now consuming daily the officially decreed allowance of three soldiers of the Grand Republic; and not a crumb, not an ounce of fat, adheres to his attenuated body. There he is, week in and week out, while the frosts glass the hills and a rose-red vixen picks through a thin dust of first snow in the hospital courtyard: Tarare, scarcely ninety pounds soaking wet, with the hollow eyes and tight distended belly of a street beggar. In it goes then out again, barely digested, on his salty belches, in his black and aromatic stools, which are carried down in a tin chamber pot for the physics to poke at with spatulas. Doctor Dupuis is at a loss. Surgeon Courville is incensed. Might as well be throwing good food down a well, says Courville. We should try purgatives. We should starve him out, see what happens.

Dupuis scratches his head. Boiled eggs, he suggests. Boiled eggs.

On the Feast of Saint Stephen, at the physics' request, the cooks hard-boil and peel exactly seventy-five brown hens' eggs. They boil them in a marmite large enough for a calf's head and pick the shell off until their hands cramp up. These eggs are placed, still steaming, before Tarare in Doctor Dupuis' office. The richly sulphurous odour fills the small room. Courville and Dupuis stand at Tarare's shoulders. Eat, Tarare, says Doctor Dupuis. As many as you can manage.

Tarare begins. Fast, but with no evidence of relish. His adder-jaw unhooking, his head tilted backward, he swallows them whole. At ten, the learned spectators exchange a glance. At thirty, they are mouthing *Oh, Mother of God* and *How?* Courville, with his notebook, counting them off (four lines and a fifth across to make a grille, a garden gate), at first finds it difficult to keep pace. Until, at the fortieth egg, Tarare pauses with a thoughtful look. He bends in his seat, with a hand pressed to his swelling stomach. Doctor Courville moves forward. Tarare? Are you – but Tarare raises a finger for silence. An elegant, contained gesture. Then once more he scoops his hand into the bottom of the marmite. Tarare is chewing now, his brow furrowed with determination. Two bites for each egg, separated by an interval of thoughtful mastication, through eggs forty-five to fifty. Tarare's cheeks are swollen and pouchy as a bandit's money bags, with eyes popping from his skull, glazed with a vegetable determination. Courville and Dupuis watch open-mouthed, even enchanted – the rhythmic grind of that imperturbable jaw, the nasal hiss of each considered exhalation, the colour rising in those sallow cheeks. Fifty-three, fifty-four. Tarare has *method*. Tarare demonstrates *technique*. Fifty-five. He pauses again. Shifts in his seat. Breaks wind, monumentally. Then begins eating again with a renewed fervour. Fifty-seven, sixty. Rocking back, knees wide, gullet bobbing, meldrops of saliva quivering on his chin.

Where? Quite simply, quite scientifically – where is it the eggs are *going*? The *matter*? The doctors watch in silence, aghast. Dupuis is blanched. A different kind of hunger ignites in Courville's eyes. It defies reason. It defies – sixty-two, sixty-three – all principle, scientific and medical. It simply cannot be. And yet it is. Here and now, in their *a posteriori* age of steam and bell jar and baby particle. Tarare scoops up the seventy-fifth egg, fixing the physics with a look of resolve, even of triumph. He pushes the egg on to his fuzzed tongue – the whole thing in his mouth – then gulps it down. Tarare smiles. Tarare fought God, and Tarare won.

That night, Dupuis and Courville sit up late drinking brandy, because why not. How many eggs, asks Dupuis, would you use to make an omelette, Laurent?

Three, Courville replies. Four, perhaps, if I'd had no lunch.

Doctor Dupuis splays his hands hopelessly. So that's nineteen omelettes, he says. *Nineteen.*

And he could have carried on.

What do we do?

We can't go on feeding him, says Courville. We'll bankrupt the nation.

Better men than us have tried.

Courville snorts. You know, he says, there are dilettantes who'd pay a fortune to cut him open. A singular abomination. *I* might, if I had a fortune. His value as a cadaver—

Laurent.

You say he used to eat live animals? Vermin?

He is weak-minded. He was made to. By some gypsy charlatan.

I should like to see that.

Dupuis frowns. We ought not to encourage the boy to debase himself, he says.

Courville purses his lips over his brandy. Do you speak from a medical standpoint?

A moral one. Moral and medical. God.

Courville smiles. Don't you want to see how deep the hole is? In all of France, perhaps all the world, there is no other Tarare. Come now. Aren't you curious?

No, snaps Dupuis.

Courville sighs. Then next, he says, comes purgation.

So it is that Tarare begins the Year of Grace seventeen hundred and ninety-three starved. Face down whimpering through a rag on the examination table while the surgeon Courville feeds a tube into his sphincter. Emetics, salt and vinegars, bloodless mineral stuff. Nil by mouth, save a thin broth thrice daily. Ice baths burning off his skin. He is taken from the convalescents' ward so that his cadaverous appearance will not discompose his wounded co-patriots. Bones glowing blue in the dark of his own private room. Meat may not adhere to his slippery bones, but it comes off them quickly enough, until his legs are sticks and his hips a narrow cradle. He cries and grasps at Courville's hand beseechingly, and Courville tells him: *it is the cure*. Tarare, he says, *must pass through the eye of the needle*. Then all will be well. So this is what Tarare dreams at night – of passing through the silver eye. Of being at great length purified, racked, his limbs and trunk thinning and extending like India rubber, until he is a mere thread, a worm. A needle gleaming on a mountainside like an argent tower. He knows he must climb it, but a cold wind numbs his fingers and makes him weak as a baby. He latches his arms around the slippery tower of silver, snow stinging at his cheeks, but halfway up he loses his grip, and he falls, and he wakes. When he wakes he hears that the bells are tolling, and that there are voices in the courtyard. Shouting in the courtyard.

It is still very early. The light from the window is powder-blue and frigid, leftover moonglow dusted in winter drizzle. Tarare hauls himself from the bed to the casement, his legs buckling under him. He looks down on the courtyard. He sees the hospital staff all clustered there: the cooks, braced against the January chill in their tattered roachy shawls; the thick-necked porters; the ward sisters; the big German orderlies; even the citizen-doctors, dragged from their beds without their elegant greatcoats, ungainly. Tarare sees milk-white feathers in the hat of an army courier. The courier is shouting LONG LIVE THE REPUBLIC, LONG LIVE THE REPUBLIC, and some of the gathered join him in his feverish vivats, while others stand stunned and blinking like just-born things. LONG LIVE THE REPUBLIC, bellows the messenger. LOUIS CAPET IS DEAD. THE CRIMINAL LOUIS CAPET IS DEAD. And there is some scattered applause, and there are quiet gasps, because they knew it would happen, it was planned to happen – scheduled – but would God let it? Would God allow His anointed-on-Earth to be toppled thusly? Some of the crowd, Tarare sees, raise their sleep-softened faces to the sky, as if searching for signs of the Lord's displeasure. One porter timorously removes his hat and presses it to his breast. The courier sees this. The courier strides over to the reverent orderly and backhands him hard around the face.

So it is that Tarare learns of this new epoch. And so it is that Tarare is borne back to the very earliest and most lovely flickerings of his consciousness, far away from the hospital at Soultz-Haut-Rhin, where he kneels weak and cold with inanition at the casement. To the village of his birth on a hot summer night, a great fire throbbing gold and red in the mistral, the legs of dancers combing round the flame. Milk sweet on his tongue, a breast against his cheek, for a new king had been crowned amid sunrays, washed with oils from the beak of a dove. And Tarare weeps. He has no shits to give for any Bourbon or Capet, but still he weeps. Because of time and all it has torn down and robbed from him. The gilt rubbed from the surface of the world. Because of time and all it has borne away, beyond his reach.

*

A week passes, and the criminal Louis Capet stays dead. Tarare has just finished supping unenthusiastically at his noontide broth when Citizen Courville enters the room. Tarare rolls his head slowly toward the surgeon. He hates Courville. He hates his florid face and his precisely trimmed beard. He hates his enemas and his salt-rubs. And now Courville is holding something beneath his jacket. Something that squirms and squeaks.

How do you fare today, Tarare? He smiles brightly, settling himself on the side of the bed.

Tarare gazes at him dully. I am hungry, he says. Monsieur, I'm so hungry. Please.

Courville purses his lips. We have declared war, he says. On the Dutch, and the English. And they say there is every possibility Spain will declare war on *us*.

Tarare can hardly bring himself to care. Tarare feels deadened, utterly. Still, he tries to moisten his lips. He asks, Why?

This is what happens when you kill a king, says Courville. The other kings don't like it. The Dutch – he rubs the side of his nose – we will fight to liberate them from the yoke of their oppressors. The English, well. He shrugs. It's always a bit of fun to be at war with the English, no?

And the Austrians? Tarare asks, in a tiny, starved scratch of a voice. The Prussians?

Oh, we're still at war with them as well. Courville shakes his head and smiles ironically. Liberty may yet be strangled in her birth cry! A lot of work for you soldier boys, eh?

Soldier boy. Tarare feels himself, correctly, to be mocked. He turns his head away on the pillow, gulps down a mouthful of sour bile. The emetics prescribed by Courville have done nothing but ruin utterly the last of Tarare's teeth. They burn to the nerve, fuzzy with melted enamel, loose in the gum. He worries they will fall out and condemn him forever to a diet of soups and broths. What kind of life is soups and broths? Never to tear, never to chew. His jaw aches with longing. Tarare sniffles. He asks to see Doctor Dupuis. Kindly, warm-hearted Doctor Dupuis.

Citizen-Doctor Dupuis is returned to Paris for the time being, says Courville. His smile fades. Then he produces a bundle from his jacket. A sack. He sets it down on the bedclothes, and Tarare sees, wriggling at the opening, a pored rose-pink nose. A kitten wriggles his way out – a flossy little black-and-white kitten, followed by a second, tortoiseshell. Brother and sister of five weeks, birthed to the kitchens' tiger-striped mouser. Bright-eyed, they paw their way around the bed with innocent curiosity, over Tarare's limp arms, on to Tarare's body. Having established the landscape, they mewl and gambol, tails erect, rubbing their soft faces against his neck, rolling joyfully in the hollow between his legs. They are warm-bodied and beautiful. They have known so little of the world, beyond the kitchen odours of grain and hot lard, their mother's rough tongue and enclosing limbs. And Tarare knows he will destroy them. Tarare knows that Courville intends for him to.

Courville watches impassively as the patient's face creases with pain. I concede, he says, that the course of treatment I initially proposed was, perhaps, misjudged.

Tarare closes his hands around the tortoiseshell kitten. He can feel her heart beating through her puny ribs as she squawls and wriggles. He dry-sobs.

I apologise, says Courville, for any unnecessary pain my palliatives have caused. I truly believed they would help you. He smiles. (Tarare's age as yet has no word for the sort of man Citizen Courville, Surgeon of the Ninth Hussars, is – the sort of man who derives pleasure of almost erotic dimensions from the infliction of physical and psychological torment. For Citizen [formerly Marquis de] Donatien Alphonse François Sade, though already a man of infamous reputation, serves at present on the National Convention, and is at this time better known for his panegyrics to liberty than for his sordid chronicles of rape on nail-beds.)

Tarare strokes a thumb across the kitten's velvet brow. He realises that it would be a good thing, a brilliant thing, to defy Courville. To repudiate his vicious gift, this blood-offering. But his stomach burns with emptiness. His heartbeat is a trace, a flutter. With immense regret, and tears rolling down his cheeks, Tarare squeezes until he feels the ribs crack in his fist.

It is the tenderest meat he has ever eaten.

*

New fronts open in the Low Countries, in places with names like the noise a child makes when he puckers his lips and blows air through a slit in a stem of grass: Neerwinden, Breda,

Maastricht. New fronts open on the coast, where English Pitt flexes his leviathan muscle over barnacled redoubts and fishermen's shacks. New fronts open even within the Grand Republic herself, where counter-revolutionaries have risen up behind traitor blue-bloods and the lily-white banners of Bourbon, in defiance of Paris (because there are still Bourbons left, yes: brothers and cousins, the once-was Dauphin, whom the Convention gave as a ward to a patriotic Paris cobbler, so his silky little hands might be put to a trade). These fronts must be fed on boys. The order is given that all able-bodied volunteers in convalescence are to return, immediately, to active duty. Tarare is, ostensibly, among these. But is he 'able-bodied'? Can an individual whose body is driven to such outrageousness by simple *hunger* be so described? He walks and he talks. He can kill, certainly.

On a bright March morning hazed with thaw, Doctor Dupuis returns from Paris to find the patient more vigorous – in fact, murderous – than ever. His cheeks glowing with the absorbed vitality of flesh miscellaneous. Citizen Courville is glowing too, with the success of his experiments. He has set Tarare on live hens, rats, eels, puppies and wriggling grass snakes. Allowing him to wander the grounds of the hospital at will, Courville has seen the patient consume a meal prepared for fifteen hardy day labourers – two meat pies almost the size of wagon wheels and four gallons of milk – in a single sitting. Moreover, the clever surgeon has devised a scheme whereby Tarare's unique oesophageal and digestive capabilities might be put to the use of his country.

He claps Doctor Dupuis on the shoulder, eyes alight. He says: I may have found a way that we can keep him, Jean. The *lusus naturae*, he says. The abomination.

From all parts of Northern France the officers come to par-
take of the demonstration. In the courtyard they drop from
their thoroughbreds like flakes of tinsel among their swarming valets and aides-de-camp, dress swords sparkling on their
hips; the raven-haired Citizen-General Alexandre de Beauharnais in a lilac coat and hat, with his extremely long face
and vermilion-painted mouth; the graceful Desaix, in a black
storm-cloak and plumed tricorn, nostrils flaring in time with
his charger's hoofbeats; the Corsican Bonaparte, who chews
at a hangnail with childish impatience while his frock coat is
brushed; the humble Pichegru, peasant-born, with pockmarked
cheeks; old wolf-eyed Kellermann and de Broglie; Alexandre
Dumas of Saint-Domingue, whose blackness and beauty raises
startled gasps from the giggling chars who have gathered in the
yard to bear witness to the arrival of these great and good, these
apogees of Republican masculinity, who stride about the yard
like glossy fighting cocks, kissing one another on the cheeks
and slapping one another on the shoulders, talking about how
they will save the world. In just three years' time, many of these
men, and their valets and their aides-de-camp, will be dead. Or
imprisoned, waiting to spit heart's blood in the executioner's
sack. In just ten, one will be the most powerful man in Europe.
(He does not know it – although already he strongly suspects it.)

Not since the birth of the Republic has such excitement been
known in the scrubbed white hallways and wards of the little
hospital. The stable is full of stomping horses. The cooks pre-
pare a grand dinner. The orderlies rush through the corridors
as though Judgement Day has come. They have come to see the
miracle, the abomination. Tarare.

Tarare himself is primped and polished. Bathed, brushed,
teased and perfumed, then dressed in white stockings and a

frock and waistcoat of moss-green velvet with a scarlet lining, silver-buckled slippers on his feet. He has that feast-day feeling. A nervous excitement fluttering against bone and in belly. There is no mirror for him to admire himself in, but he knows he looks good, perhaps even smells good. Like a gentleman. He knows this because at first sight Doctor Dupuis and Courville, themselves Sunday-bested, do not recognise the powdered dandy who stands before them.

What am I to do? asks Tarare. Is it a test?

Just be your fine self, Tarare, Courville answers. All will be clear.

Then they wait, Tarare and the citizen-doctors. They wait until well after nightfall, while the officers carouse in the upper chambers over a supper of goose and trout and pork shoulder, and talk more about saving the world. It is nine o'clock by the time the esteemed guests, hazed with Burgundy, can be reminded of the true purpose of their visit, and coaxed down again into the chill of the spring evening. The hospital courtyard is illuminated by flickering torchlight. They sway and gripe, smoking and stamping their buckled feet. They want the show to start. What they see is Courville and Dupuis. What they see, standing between the two, is a skinny boy in an outsize frock coat, standing before a pail of raw scarlet meat.

Citizen Courville bows low. Brother Citizens, he says – we have gathered you here to present to you Tarare. A patriot Lyonnais of unique and perplexing abilities. We believe these abilities may be put to effective use by our beloved Republic. A demonstration, if you will. Tarare—

Tarare, who is used to being introduced with greater pomp and circumstance, is taken aback by Courville's abruptness. But nonetheless, he does what is expected of him. Bunching his fancy frock coat at his waist and squatting down on his haunches, he scoops up a handful of flesh and begins to eat.

Courville throws out his hand. Within the pail – he calls out – are thirty pounds of raw bull's lung and liver. See how the patient eats, without hesitation or repulsion.

And the officers do see. A few chuckle uneasily. Tarare ruminates over fists' worth of the oily viscera, shifting his squat, his face puckering with concentration.

Thirty pounds? says Beauharnais. We'll be out here in the cold all night. Can the boy not go any faster?

The chuckles become outright laughter as Tarare wraps his hands around the pail and lifts it to his face, eating like a dog, scoffing down the chunked organs unmasticated. Beauharnais takes out his pocket watch with a genteel flourish.

What is this – sideshow? snarls the Corsican Bonaparte. Except for a waste of our time? A nonsense? Such things can be seen at any country fair. Wolf-boys and bottomless men. I suppose he walks on his hands as well? Perhaps you will shut him up in a box next, and stick swords into it?

I have never seen such a thing before, answers Beauharnais, still tittering.

Because you've never been to such a fair, snorts Desaix. Careful Alexandre, you expose yourself as a bourgeois.

I'm telling Robespierre, laughs Pichegru. Citizen Beauharnais fears to sully himself rubbing shoulders with the Third Estate!

Believe me, adds handsome Desaix, with a subtle smile, Robespierre already knows.

Robespierre knows everything. (de Broglie)

You give him too much credit. (Bonaparte)

Robespierre knows what your wife's cunt tastes like. (Pichegru)

Vulgar! (Desaix)

Who *doesn't* know what Madame Beauharnais' cunt tastes like? (Hoche)

While the officers chatter and rib, Tarare slops the last of the offal down his throat, belching bloodfully, wiping the juice from his chin. More pails are brought by the orderlies – pails of thick, creamy milk. While Tarare drinks it all down, he listens to the officers, and watches them, and finds himself disappointed. They are not so different from the breeds of men he has known his life entire. They have better skin, glossier hair. Change Beauharnais' silver-edged coat for a buckskin apron, wipe the rouge from his lips, and his face would appear authentic bent over a whetstone or anvil, sweat beading on his brow. Put Desaix in loose culottes and a stained shirt, whittle some of the fat from his cheeks, and he'd make a happy enough rascal boy-whore, propping up the bar in the worse Paris drink-holes, swilling rotgut. Strip Kellermann of sash and studded sword, transpose him to a half-ploughed field, and he might be any patrician farmer, gnarled as a root ball. All of them, apart from Dumas, Tarare concedes. The Saint-Dominguan stands apart from his peers, elegant and aloof, dark eyes trained on Tarare. Tarare has seen black men and women before, in Paris. Not many, but some. Mainly maids to the noisy Creole women who spill from the opera houses with their wrinkled cleavage pressed into poison-bright silk. Slivers of these bird-like girls seen through carriage windows, their curls teased away under roundlets of starched lace. And some freedmen too: cautious, watchful, well attired. But he has never before seen a black man like this Dumas. The general moves with a delicacy so absolute it will brook no questioning, a grace conformed as tightly to his long body as a suit of supple armour – because if a single misericorde of doubt or perplexity or mockery were to slip between the plates of this armour, Dumas, with his dark skin and dilute blood, would be done for. Tarare sees that a man like Dumas must exist infallibly if he is to exist at all. Tarare feels for him, even as the general wrinkles his nose in disgust at the sight of Tarare's bombastic swilling.

Tarare supposes it is true what the radicals say of the aristocracy – that all the sugared edifices of Old France were built on nothing but accidents, smoke and mirrors. Who feasts and who starves, entirely a matter of chance – chance then reified and made sacred, made other than it is, through God and debt and machines. And whips. A change is coming, they said – or perhaps, has already come. But Tarare cannot see it. They stand there, watching. He squats here, watched. These are not the words that Tarare uses to think about it, but this is what he thinks, seeing the officers laugh and fall about each other, watching them watch him. Beauharnais is now bent double in a fit of hilarity. And as Tarare drains off the second pail of milk and slumps on to his bottom, kicking it away with a thrash of his foot and breathing heavily through his nose, the Corsican, who alone among them appears immune to this absurd spectacle of engorgement, asks: Citizen Courville – assuming the demonstration has ended – perhaps you could bring us to the point?

Courville, silent until now, produces from his jacket pocket a tin capsule, about the length and circumference of his thumb. Brother Citizens – he says, and says it again, and again, while the officers right themselves and recover, gasping, from their bout of corporate hilarity – Citizens! Courville raises the capsule above his head. This tin casing was consumed by the patient yesterday, and was this morning recovered from his stool. Here—

Courville holds out the capsule for Beauharnais to inspect. Which he almost does, before withdrawing his hand delicately. His *stool*? he repeats.

I assure you, it has been thoroughly cleansed, replies Courville. Please, Citizen Beauharnais – open it.

Beauharnais puts on his gloves first. Then he takes the capsule and twists it in his hands, revealing a tightly spooled strip of paper within.

Read, urges Courville.

Beauharnais unscrolls the paper. He smiles. He waves it in the air. Long live the Republic! he calls out. That is what it says!

You see – continues Courville – the message has remained entirely legible in its passage through our Tarare. What I propose – he gestures between himself and Doctor Dupuis – what *we* propose – is that the patient's unique condition may suggest him for use in – in espionage. (The surgeon seems faintly dubious even as he offers this; but nonetheless, he perseveres.) He – he might eat any number of these capsules, and pass behind enemy lines to, ah, deliver them, with no risk of the messages he carries being discovered upon capture.

Beauharnais perks his eyebrow and thrums the paper against his hand. *Espionage*, he repeats. Intelligence? In this creature's belly?

Doctor Courville bows his head. Yes, he says.

The officers exchange glances.

The Prussians do hold Conté prisoner near Neustadt, Beauharnais ponders aloud. Not far from here.

He'll not get halfway to Neustadt before he's caught, Bonaparte scoffs. I'd put money on it.

How much? asks Beauharnais.

Fifty livres.

Make it one hundred and you've a wager, Citizen.

It is the first that Tarare, who sits heaving on the cobbles in milk-soaked shirt front, has heard of this plan. Espionage. He would be a spy. What a spy *does* is not readily apparent to him. But it sounds as though it would liberate him from Courville's grasp. Moreover, it sounds as though he would *matter*.

It's ridiculous, says the little Corsican. He jabs a finger at Tarare. The boy is clearly simple-minded, more animal than man. I wouldn't give him my riding boots to polish, and you want to give him, what? Orders, intelligence? On the movements of troops? You want to send him *behind enemy lines*?

Doctor Dupuis steps forward now. I assure you, Citizen Bonaparte – Tarare's wits are quite intact. Indeed, the circumstances of his life have imbued in him a certain cunning. A resourcefulness unusual in – in a man of his age, and of his class.

Now Pichegru raises his voice. He fixes Tarare with a speculative look and says, Stand up, lad.

Tarare gets to his feet, blushing. Brushing down his soiled jacket.

Stand up straight. Like a soldier.

Tarare attempts to pull his swollen belly in. Thoroughly gorged, he reels on the spot. His eyes swim between powdered faces, red plumes and gold braiding as the officers advance. They poke at him, squeeze at his stringy biceps, take handfuls of his soft, saturated flesh. He feels like a gelding at market.

A volunteer, shrugs an aide-de-camp. They are undisciplined.

Pichegru, standing in front of Tarare, takes hold of his shoulders, adjusting his stance, before he turns to answer the aide-de-camp: And they will remain so, he says, if we treat them as mere fodder. Give them nothing of consequence to do. And turning to Courville: I am not opposed to this plan of yours.

Nor I, says Desaix. Send him with some trifling missive. See if he gets through.

Yes, says Beauharnais, still chuckling. And if he doesn't, what is lost?

Well, says Pichegru, stroking his scored chin. The Prussians kill him.

Precisely, says Beauharnais. What is lost?

So everyone leaves the gathering at the military hospital of Soultz-Haut-Rhin content. Alexandre de Beauharnais is happy because he is Alexandre de Beauharnais, and Alexandre de Beauharnais is fabulous. The Corsican Bonaparte is happy because the monstrous little boy will be strung up like a dog by the Prussians and he will be vindicated, and vindication is perhaps the thing he likes best in all the world. It is manna from heaven to him. Surgeon Courville is happy because he feels he has successfully brought himself and his work to the attention of the men who presently wield power and influence, all while keeping one hand on Tarare, his beastly pet, his omnitrice.

And Tarare is happy because he thinks that he will at last be free of Courville and the military hospital at Soultz-Haut-Rhin, a person and a place that have caused him great misery, and because he will again be among trees and under sky, only this time with purpose greater than the fulfilment of his enormous personal appetite. He has never had purpose before, among trees or under sky or anywhere, and he is curious to know what it might feel like. He is happy because, worst case, the Prussians kill him. But that will not happen. Tarare knows this. Like all twenty-one-year-old men, he believes himself to be immortal, and with greater cause than most. Tarare can be brought low. Tarare can be starved and attenuated. Tarare can suffer, yes, naturally, and he does not like to. But killed? No, never.

The only man among them who is not happy is Doctor Dupuis. He is unhappy because deep in his heart, he wants Tarare gone, got rid of, and this causes him shame. He never wants to have to speak to Tarare or think about him or look at his vacuous blue eyes or swollen homunculus body again. The boy disturbs him on a reptile level. The boy, what he does and what he is, defies all medical precepts. Worse than this, he shakes to the foundations the moral edifice that the doctor has built to house his practice: the notion that all men are, at their core, of a kind. That they can be helped to help themselves. In Paris, Dupuis had sought out lecturers at the Sorbonne, poor doctors at the Hôtel-Dieu, even traded in remedies with the saffron-fingered apothecaries and quacks on the Pont au Change. The lecturers said *tobacco pills*. The poor doctors said *bleed him in the mornings, before he eats*. The quacks said *ah ha, born with Jupiter in the Crab*. Not a one of them could give him answers. Not a one of them could supply him with a precedent. Reason – to which Doctor Dupuis ministers as devoted acolyte – cannot live in the world of Tarare. So he chooses reason over Tarare. He chooses reason, silent mathematic grey-eyed Pallas with a lovely breast slipping from her pure white robe, over the shit and blood and screaming unaccountable opera viscera of it all, of Tarare. He was choosing reason when he spoke to vouch for Tarare's wits. He spoke to rid himself of that reason-less creature. Because the doctor knows that, set loose in the Rhineland wood, Tarare will be lost. He will wander from the moonlit path like the child in the tale (every child, every tale).

He will grope in nightmare darkness, the lone soldier, magic tinderbox in his ragged pocket, watched by black lions with ever-enlarging eyes.

The doctor knows that Tarare will never come back. And he is unhappy because he is happy he knows this. He is unhappy because he is happy that reason will, at last, live.

April 1793

The Palatinate Forest, near Wilgartswiesen

It is early in the morning. The air between the trees is the deep replete blue of smalt, and the scout urges his horse along the root-humped track cautiously, with whispered chucks. Prussians are close. Stealth and silence are of the utmost importance. But the scout's charge – the unpleasant-smelling boy who clings at his waist like a limpet – will not shut up.

It is so dark, the boy says. How will I see where is north to go north?

Did they not give you a compass?

Yes. (*pause* – the boy withdraws his arm from the scout's waist to rifle in his pocket.) But how will I see the compass in the dark? (The boy does not wish to admit to the scout that he doesn't know how to use a compass, much as he did not want to admit this to the spymaster who gave it to him in the first place – with the result that his own embarrassment has brought him to the thickest of forests before the breaking of dawn tasked with finding a specific location and with nothing but his instincts with which to do it. It is not an auspicious start, he feels, to his career. Why did nobody *ask me* if I knew how to use it? he thinks. You never need learn how to use a compass in Paris. You never need learn how to use a compass if you are the kind of person who never expects to leave their own village.)

Your eyes will get used to it. Now can you be quiet?

Yes, sorry. (*pause*) What side is the trees' moss meant to grow on? Is that the north?

Quiet.

Tarare's eyes aren't getting used to anything. The trees – thick fragrant pines and beech and durmast oak – throng tightly together. If the woods of his youth were renard-woods, where the rot was gold-dappled and blue forget-me-nots made chaplets for dead babies, then this is thoroughgoing witch-wood, wild and gnarled and black-blooded, standoffish when company calls. A boreal owl yawps from a distant crown. An overgrown waymark looms through the murk, and the scout reins the horse to a stop. Here you go, he says. Get down.

Tarare slides inexpertly from the horse.

Neustadt is north-east of here, whispers the scout. You'll want to start out through the trees – he raises his arm at an angle to the track, through the sinister press of the trees – that way.

Tarare demurs. Can I not just use the track? For a while further, at least?

The scout lowers his arm and looks his charge up and down. The boy is got up like a local rustic, in clogs and a little feathered cap, hose and apron of embroidered buckskin, a stippled pelt hung over his arm. But this costume is too clean to ring authentic, the scout thinks. Box-fresh. The boy looks like he's been plucked from the chorus of an opera, where he ought to be gambolling before a backdrop of garish painted clouds and aquamarine lakes, pressing flowers on some plump soprano with rouged cheeks and a braided wig of yellow horsehair. The image amuses him. Do you even speak German? the scout asks.

No?

The scout shakes his head in a way that signifies, *interesting, but not my problem*. Or in a way that signifies, *you're extremely fucked, kid*. It is too dark to tell.

The scout sighs. I thought the whole point of this was that you *don't* follow the track? He hisses. *Stealth*. (Stealth is a good word to hiss, and the scout tries to do so whenever he can.)

But it's so dark.

The scout takes hold of the reins, groaning, and turns the horse about. Honestly, he says. Do what you want, it's no skin off my balls. But the encampment is – he raises his arm diagonally to the track again – *that way*. Mother of God. What were they thinking when they came up with this one?

I think they were drunk, says Tarare, guilelessly.

The scout laughs and urges his horse on, back the way they came, leaving Tarare by the waymark at the side of the track before he can say another word. Before he can ask another question. Alone. The thrum of hoofbeats dwindles in the distance, subsumed at last into the thick mesh of forest sounds. Owl-call, owl-call-back. Breakers of wind shuddering over the treetops, as though wind can feel longing, and longs to be touched.

So Tarare begins. He presses his way through the overgrowth in the direction indicated by the scout. His wooden clogs make the going very slow. He stumbles over roots and fibrous brambles, torn on both sides of his body by bough and thorn, until thin little cuts sing all over his skin. He finds this sensation strangely invigorating. The sky, which he looks up to see in fragmentary shapes through the gaps in the treetops, begins to brighten. While he goes along, Tarare wonders if he *can* speak

German. He has heard German spoken before, and knew it for what it was, so perhaps he does after all. Ja. Nein. Gott im Himmel. So German goes. By the time he has reached the place where the trees thin out it is almost morning, mauve and misted, and Tarare has begun to feel quite good about himself. He adjusts his pelt and knapsack and walks on confidently, because there is a plan and he is a part of it. The central part. The key-stone. The plan is this: Tarare is to find the Prussian camp near Neustadt, where a captured colonel, Conté, is held. By virtue of his ensemble, he will blend with the local peasantry 'requisi-tioned' by the Prussians to clear the slops and muck the horses and feed the camp with lumber, and among these he will move unquestioned and unheeded, yes. He is to learn where Conté is kept, and at some point, before or after, shit out the missive he swallowed that very morning, and get it to him. Details fuzzy here. He will carry back a response, either verbal or written, if it is possible for him to do so. And when his task is complete he will slip from the camp, unquestioned and unheeded, and return the way he came. From Neustadt, through the forest, to the waymark on the track, where the scout will retrieve him, by cover of night. And then, who knows? Vivats and medals, perhaps. An audience at the Convention, Montagnards smiling down beneficent upon him, The Great Tarare, Tarare the Great. The Bottomless Man. Liberty's deepest pocket. The content of the missive presently sinking through his bowels in its tin cas-ing is a mystery to him. He did enquire, yes, but the spymaster looked at him askance and explained that it is vital Tarare *not know* the meat of the message: that way it cannot be extracted from him. Under torture. Torture! What has his life become? What torture could a Prussian visit on his body more strenuous than the being of Tarare, the insatiable, the ever-hungry? He laughs aloud to the trees. He is almost curious to know. Yes, *almost*. (Seldom have those dark trees heard laughter before. They will discuss it at length in the months to come.)

The forest parts at last to disclose a plain, warmed by the early-morning sun. The light is gorgeous, a toppling slant down beech-cloaked hills. The grass foams. Scrambling down a scarp at the skirt of the forest, Tarare finds a stream, shallow as a trail of silver coins, in which to bathe his nicks and cuts. Then he drinks. The water that runs there is the most delicious he has tasted in his life, cool and clear and sweet like pine needles. His belly rumbles audibly, but this is an eventuality he was prepared for: he shall picnic. He spreads his pelt out over the dewy ground and takes a loaf, a sausage and some hard cheese from his knapsack. A breeze ripples the grass and the wildflowers around him while he makes his repast, considering his next move. Now the sun is rising, he can find his way by that. It trembles on the eastern horizon, splashing colour at the underside of a single white cloud. To the north, beyond the shoulder of a thickly wooded hill, Tarare sees that the sky is hatched with thin pillars of smoke and vapour. That must be it, he thinks. The Prussians are lighting their breakfast fires. He feels pleased with himself, slicing bits off the sausage with his furrier's knife. The witch-wood at his back, the hardest part is over. He finishes half the sausage, and remains hungry – yet with a fierce exertion of discipline, he packs the remainder up in his knapsack, consults his compass (or pretends to, because he feels he should), and sets out again, toward the smoke.

Boldly, he takes the path northwards through a village: orderly kitchen gardens in their first tentative flourish, small two-room cottages. The cottages are wooden like the one he grew up in, but lovelier by far on their hillside perches, cared for. Eaves and shutters painted with cheerful stripes and petals of yellow, red and white, like gingerbread. He dips his head in greeting at a man chopping wood; he dips his head in greeting at a lady in an embroidered cap out hanging smalls on her veranda; he dips his head in greeting at the chunky geese and the woolly goats; he gives a wide berth to the wolf-like brown dog tethered to the picket of the little millhouse, resting her muzzle sulkily on her enormous paws. Tarare decides he likes it here, where the sky is wide and the water sweet like lavender honey. He thinks perhaps that he will come here to live, when the war is done and he is a hero and there are no more Prussians. He will live in a little wooden house, which he will paint himself with birds and dogs and daisies. Tarare has never painted anything before, but he thinks he would be good at it, given the opportunity. His shutters, he decides, will be yellow. For a moment he remembers Pierette, and wishes her well, wherever she might be (dead, though he does not know it).

Beyond the village the path divides. The wider route turns west, with a slimmer branch north, through the wooded foothills, toward Neustadt. Tarare takes the latter. Trees press in around him again on either side of the climbing path. He has not been walking long beneath the dappled shade of beech leaves when the sound of hoofbeats and the voices of men disturb his ambulant reverie. The voices of two men speaking. In German. Ja, nein – all the German words Tarare knows are there, wedged between many others he does not. Horses doubtless means soldiers, and, armed only with his furrier's knife, Tarare ducks swiftly from the path to avoid his Teutonic interlocutors. As they round the corner, he flops down to the ground on his belly behind the bole of a tree and holds his breath. He sees the riders but they do not see him. Prussians, yes: their blue coats crossed at the breast with bands of white, polished gold buttons, and bayonets glinting on their backs as they trot beneath the foliated patches of midday sunshine. They do not see him but Tarare sees them, with their long moustaches and their plumed hats, and because they are Prussians, he tries to make himself want them dead. He finds he cannot. Looking at them on their bay mares, with their lean, athletic physiques. Trotting along, enjoying the morning in manly innocence, cutting such noble upright figures. They have a look of something Other, these Prussians. Not angels, not those – but not men either. Something different and in-between, so easy and so sun-dappled. Something organless. They are beautiful, and once they have got a good way up along the path and out of sight, Tarare stirs. He decides, for safety's sake, to abandon the path and go on north through the cover of the trees.

Tarare gets up, spitting out a mouthful of leaves, and scrambles down to the gully on the right-hand side of the path. This is where Tarare puts his left foot directly between the serrated jaws of a rusty bear trap.

*

Tarare had presumed the soldiers would have heard his enormous belly-shriek, and would have doubled back, perhaps, with their sabres drawn. But he waited for five breaths, fifty breaths, and they didn't. So now it is almost sunset, and he lies propped on his elbows on the forest floor, his cheeks streaked with tears and his left clog full of lukewarm blood, flapping his hand weakly at the iridescent bluebottles roused and punchdrunk on the scent of his torn flesh, wanting to make love in his dripping wound. The trap hasn't bitten quite to the bone, but Tarare is stuck. The iron teeth of the trap dug deep in above the ankle. The pain is excruciating. Worse than hunger, actually, so he feels suitably chastened. Also faint from the loss of blood.

The ruby-red light of the sky flakes all over his prone body. It is an unseasonably warm April evening. He at last lies back, takes the rest of his sausage from his knapsack, gazes into the treetops, and prepares to die. A bear trap implies the existence of bears, after all. Let the flies lay their eggs where they want. He will be their substrate, their mother. Of what do maggots dream? Tarare wonders. Through spiracles wet-hot, of the bunched silk of entrails.

As Tarare raises the sausage to his mouth – a final supper – a midsize rust-coloured dog, who seems to come from nowhere, tail wagging, snatches it from his hand. The dog skips about him mockingly, raising a dazzle of jewel-backed flies, before settling in the leaf rot by his feet and gulping the sausage down in a single bite.

Bastard! shouts Tarare, and wags his good leg menacingly at the red dog. The red dog considers him cheerfully and sniffs at trap, wound and Tarare's mouth in turn. Then a whistle echoes from between the trees and the dog bounds away.

With a gurgle of pain Tarare props himself up on his elbows again and squints through the midge-speckled shade of the gully. Two figures approach. A man and a boy, moving at a jog toward him, led by the rust-coloured dog. The dog arrives before the others, stopping by Tarare and setting her feet apart with a proprietorial look, as though presenting Tarare for inspection. Tarare gropes over the ground for his knapsack, drawing it protectively over his belly.

The man and the boy look very alike. Father and son, Tarare decides. Eyes colourless and unyielding, like mountain rain. Their clothes are poor but well-kept: stained buckskin breeches, very much like those Tarare himself is wearing, woollen jackets, oily furred caps. The man stops at the edge of the clearing. He is older than Tarare – shortish and thickset, with red-blond eyebrows that meet in the middle over a snub nose. He is carrying a musket. A limp rabbit dangles at his shoulder. He looks down at Tarare, shifts the gun into his right hand and uses his left to push the boy back behind him, protectively. The man opens his mouth and says, with some alarm: Mein Gott.

Tarare's heart flips in his chest. German. Ja, he ventures, with what he hopes reads as a native flippancy. Gott im Himmel. He laughs nervously through teeth gritted with pain, and gestures toward the trap.

His words do read as a native flippancy, but with the undesired consequence that when the huntsman opens his mouth again he produces a lot more German, a crunching polysyllabic spate of German, so many words of German, none of which Tarare recognises, none of which Tarare can salvage from the outpour.

The huntsman looks at Tarare expectantly. Tarare stares back blankly. He forces a clement, embarrassed (and pained) smile.

The huntsman frowns. He speaks again. A very few words this time, ending with the upward inflection of a question. Tarare intuits he is being called upon to identify himself.

Tarare raises his hand to his chest, winces in pain, and says, *Helmut*. He will be Helmut now. Helmut hungry, Helmut stuck in a bear trap, Helmut bleeding out on the moss.

The boy peers around his father's bulk. The two of them exchange a look. Tarare's throat loosens as the huntsman laughs and speaks more German. Tarare doesn't understand the words, but he surmises the meaning of the enthusiastic gesturing well enough: the huntsman's son, by some mad stroke of felicity, is also named Helmut.

Ja? says Tarare.

Ja! replies the huntsman. Schatzi! He clicks his fingers and the dog eases from her professional posturing and trots over to nose at her master's hand. The huntsman stoops over Tarare's entrapped leg and motions for his son to assist him. It is a protracted and agonising process. Eventually, with a whimper of pain, Tarare is able to withdraw his leg, soiled buckskin trousers flapping loose around his knee.

The huntsman gently draws Tarare's leg across his lap, inspecting the wound. He winces in sympathy. He says a few more words of German, among which one prompts ominous recognition in Tarare: Soldaten. Soldiers. Tarare's body tightens up again. The huntsman, however, frowns as he speaks. He does not appear deeply enthused by whatever soldaten are under discussion. He takes a canteen out and rinses the crusted blood from the wound.

Soldaten, Tarare repeats. He pats his chest again. Nein soldaten.

The huntsman, now ripping a length of cloth, pauses. French? he asks, in French. Are you French?

Tarare hopes the panic does not show on his face (it does). He shakes his head. Nein, he says. Pats his chest, again. Nein – nein – French. (For the first time in his life, he hopes his inarticulacy will have him taken as a half-wit rather than a liar.)

The huntsman now returns to German. Another question. Tarare, presuming from the context that he is being asked where it is he is from, answers the only nearby place he knows the name of: Neustadt. It is then that he decides to relieve himself of the necessity of explanation by affecting a swoon. As the huntsman ties off his improvised bandage and gives Tarare a jocular slap on the thigh, Tarare lets out a sigh, rolls his eyes theatrically toward the treetops, and slackens his body to drop down on to his back.

Helmut? says the huntsman, shaking at his shoulder. Helmut? Agh.

Tarare keeps his eyes screwed tight shut as the huntsman and his son exchange words over his prone body. With the red glare of sundown shut behind his lids, the noises of the wood around him seem to grow louder: the crazed buzz of the flies, the rustle of wind in the treetops, Schatzi slapping her wet red chops at a cloud of newborn midges. Like a child, Tarare feels safe with his eyes shut tight. Insulated – as though a great hand has reached down from the sky and lifted his body on to a high shelf, out of the world's reach. He keeps them shut as the huntsman and his son take hold of his shoulders and heft him up to steady his wounded weight between them. He takes in their grainy, good smell. Woodsmoke and fresh sweat. Tarare's feet drag limply between them as they haul him onward – to where? A question for later, he tells himself. A question for the open-eyed Tarare.

On this occasion, as on a surprising number of previous occasions, his wilful ignorance is rewarded. The coolness of dusk is on his face by the time he feels his rescuers' pace slow and cracks his eyes open to dare a look: what he sees is a little wooden cabin set between the trees, the windows yellow with firelight. The cabin's shutters are painted with scarlet flowers, and a scrawl of smoke issues into the blue of the evening from a single squat chimney. The night is still warm. The door of the cabin is open, and Tarare smells onions fried in butter. Hears a child's laughter. Tarare is so happy, so relieved, that he could cry. That he could kiss the huntsman and little Helmut and greedy thieving Schatzi, who bounds eagerly ahead. He will be safe for tonight, at least. Not only safe, but, he ventures, comfortable. Unconsciously, he releases a groan of pleasure. His belly rumbles.

Helmut? says the huntsman. He asks something in German, that Tarare intuits to be either Are you awake? or Are you hungry?

Ja, slurs Tarare/Helmut in response to either proposition or both.

The huntsman and his son gently lower Tarare to the ground, bringing his back to rest against a trough in the little yard in front of the cabin. Tarare slumps his head to one side and gently paws at his leg – the pain is dulled and the bleeding slowed. A plum-red slash shows through the bandage, over the wound. The huntsman goes to the cabin and calls through the door. Little Helmut remains, standing close to Tarare, watching him with a casual curiosity, toeing the leaf rot with his boot. The two Helmuts, actual and nominal, consider each other. The boy has the tilted posture of a person who has grown faster than he expected himself to. The hair that sticks out in all directions from the front of his furred cap is a dirty blond. Like most wistful people, when Tarare looks at a child of even passing resemblance to himself, it is himself he sees. Standing there, ten or eleven years old, toeing the leaf rot with his boot (although Tarare had never owned boots at that age, just clogs – rope-soled or wooden, overlarge). He wonders what Nollet would have done if he had come across a wounded stranger in the forest. Probably robbed him, he thinks. And what would Tarare do if he came across a wounded stranger in the forest? Probably nothing, he inwardly concedes, with only the slightest sense of shame, because pain, manipulation and assorted abuses of his person have made of him a self-centred individual.

The boy Helmut looks into his face. Tarare raises his hands

and hooks his fingers into the corners of his already wide mouth, drawing it wider still, to truly gargoyle span. The boy gasps, and then a sly smile spreads over his face. He giggles. He pokes out his tongue. It is decided. They are friends now, Helmut/Helmut and Helmut/Tarare.

Now the cabin discloses other inhabitants: a tall woman in a pale blue dress with two girls at her heels. All three are scrupulously clean. All three wear white bonnets over their hair, buttoned under their chins. They have covered their golden hair because Tarare is a man and a stranger, he realises. He finds this quaint homespun modesty adorable. These are thoroughly *womenfolk*, and now they stand in a line while the huntsman moves to each, introducing them. Gerda, he says, pinching the rosy cheeks of the smallest girl, who titters prettily. Lotte, he says, patting the starched head of the older girl, almost a woman, who folds her arms and regards Tarare with a hostility he finds strangely arousing. Und meine Frau – he concludes with a flourish – Britta. He smiles proudly. Tarare sees that when the huntsman is not being a huntsman, he is a joker. A goof. Tarare decides he likes him immensely, and he thinks the huntsman likes him too, although he isn't sure why. Probably the huntsman likes everyone.

Frau Britta, wiping her hands on her apron, smiles in a strained way which suggests that unexpected and unpromising guests to the little cabin are not an unusual occurrence.

The huntsman winds an arm around his wife's waist and addresses Tarare again, at length, in German. Tarare smiles and gives no answer. Frau Britta gazes at her husband ominously. The huntsman whispers something in her ear. The corners of her mouth turn down and she shrugs, then the huntsman turns back to Tarare and says two words, loud and slow: Knödel, he says. Then, rubbing his hands over his belly and smacking his lips in an illustrative mummers' show – Mmm, lecker.

Oh! says Tarare. Ja, ja.

Helmut and the huntsman help Tarare into the cabin. The lower storey is a single rectangular room, with bed and wash-stand curtained away at the far end. There is a painted wooden hutch arrayed with shining copperware and enamel dishes, a cooking stove and a long table with six chairs. A narrow ladder on the right-hand wall leads to a loft above their heads. The huntsman sets Tarare at the table and the family busy them-selves about him, talking quietly. The home is as scrupulously clean as the homemaker; leaning back in his seat to inspect his surroundings, Tarare cannot find a single cobweb scribbled in the rafters, a single speck of grease on the table's sanded boards. Schatzi chews at her paw in a rag-bed near his feet. The huntsman and Helmut leave the cabin to wash themselves in a water-drum outside, while Frau Britta and the two girls work at the cookstove. It is warm and fragrant in the cabin, and Tarare begins to feel himself drifting off. A great weariness overcomes him, compounded by hunger and adrenaline. His poor heart, he thinks to himself, proudly, has laboured hard today. His poor feet, he thinks to himself, incorrectly, have carried him across borders, all the way to a strange and foreign land. As he wavers at the plush edge of sleep he feels a small hand fix itself to his shoulder. He opens his eyes and he sees the little girl, Gerda. She smiles bashfully at him. Frau Britta is setting the table for supper.

When they are all gathered there, the huntsman and little Helmut now glowing with the same wholesome cleanliness as their women, dinner begins. Black bread and a stew, savoury browned dumplings with fried onion and a thick, glossy gravy.

Tarare's mouth floods with saliva. As he reaches for his spoon, Helmut stops him with a gently reprimanding pat on the wrist. The huntsman rolls up his shirtsleeves and the family join hands around the table. Helmut and surly Lotte, on Tarare's left and right, extend their hands to him, so Tarare takes them, closing the circle. The huntsman smiles with satisfaction and lowers his head over his bowl of stew. Everyone closes their eyes and lowers their heads. Gott, the huntsman begins. Gott im Himmel – and Tarare understands no more of what he says, but knows he speaks a grace. A grace is a thing in which Tarare has never been involved before, and he finds it touching, and beautiful. As though a band of argent light has contracted around the table to enclose them there, softly and sweetly; he turns the word in his mind, twice, three times. Grace, grace, grace. He lowers his head with the others but he does not close his eyes – instead he considers his hosts, gathered around the table, one after the other. The huntsman, his expression beneficent under his thick red eyebrows as he prays, the rushlight sparkling in the receding thatch of his hair. Little Gerda, a dainty water-coloured miniature, her skin so pale it appears almost translucent. Nervous Helmut, shoulders hunched forward over the table as though he is unconsciously bracing himself against an indeterminate future. And finally Lotte and Frau Britta, with their high foreheads and queenly cheekbones, like matching bookends, ornaments of a virtuous simplicity. He finds them intensely attractive, but doesn't want to see them naked, ever. He doesn't even want them to have bodies under their clothes. He *does* want to see them churning butter under the rose-gold radiance of a harvest moon. He *does* want to hear them sing, their voices surely throaty and thick, like unstrained cream. Tarare thinks all this and he also thinks,

Fuck the Republic. Perhaps I'll stay right here. And he pictures himself nuzzling down into this family like a tick in dog flesh, comfortable and warm. Learning their strange cramped language. Becoming in time a brother, a son. Heading out into the leaf-dappled dawn with a musket in his hands and Schatzi at his heel, coming home to love and grace, and grace, and grace, while the first snows cover the world like eiderdown. And when the grace is done and the others open their eyes, Tarare flutters his own closed, as though they had been closed all along. His hands released, Tarare lifts his fingers to his brow to cross himself. Frau Britta gasps. The huntsman pauses with a spoonful of dumpling stew raised between bowl and mouth.

Slowly, in the sharp-edged silence of the moments that follow, Tarare realises that he has made a mistake of potentially geopolitical significance. Taking a spoonful of stew, he darts his eyes around the cabin, searching for the greasy candles, the laced prayer cards, the pinprick eyes of a tiny Madonna. Nothing. No crucifix nailed to the wall. No saints in rock-candy robes, no plaster martyrs, no dangling rosary beads, no pearl tears or spiked haloes glittering from a corner altar. Not a single minikin hand shedding a single bead of glazed minikin blood in the whole of the cabin. Tarare sees that he sits at the table of, under the roof of, a Protestant. And Tarare sees that the Protestant sees that he himself is not one.

The huntsman clears his throat and brings the spoon to his mouth. The tension is palpable, and little Gerda peers at her parents in innocent confusion. Lotte's lips are curled at the corners, as though she is suppressing laughter. Helmut stares at him with wounded disappointment. Heretic Tarare, able to do nothing else, lowers his eyes to his dish and fills his burning cheeks with stew. He waits for the blow, or for words of condemnation, but none come. The family finish their repast in mortuary silence. The moment Tarare is finished, Frau Britta plucks spoon and empty dish and beer mug from beneath his nose, as though they are contaminated things.

Tarare knows he should escape. He should make his excuses as best he can, and leave. He is very close to the Prussian camp now, he must be: he can blunder a few hours through the dark, even on a wounded leg, even so bone-tired as he is. Seeing the huntsman has begun to stuff his pipe, he senses an opportunity. He gestures amiably between the huntsman and himself with a weak smile, and points to the doorway. The huntsman looks at him askance, sadly shakes his head, and says, Non, *Helmut*. Then he turns to Lotte and speaks to her in German. She rises from the table and begins to make up the truckle bed in the corner. The huntsman exchanges words with Helmut, too, and the boy takes Tarare's knapsack from beside his chair and carries it away to the loft.

Tarare realises he is now a hostage. These yellow-haired people, this family, whom Tarare had idly contemplated loving as his own, are transfigured in his eyes. The huntsman takes on a vulpine aspect. Lotte and Frau Britta become as hard and unfeeling as pillars of stone as they move around the cabin, attending to their busywork. Even little Gerda and Helmut, rifling through his possessions in the loft, tread above his head malevolent and ghost-footed, too perfectly shaped for innocence to be true. Why did he not see it before? Trust was the real trap. Gaudy gingerbread cottages luring flies with their sugar-paint daisies. He feels despairing, and then he feels angry. They think he is a heretic, do they? And so? Perhaps *they* are the heretics. Denuding and drabbing his fabulous God, making a bumpkin of him. Letting beggars and women at their pulpits.

Things ought to be a certain way, Tarare thinks. Who are these Alsatian peasants to think themselves above gold and scarlet and smoke-of-balsam? Tarare couldn't tell you the Pope's name, but he knows he *matters*, in some oblique way. Tarare also knows that he must act, and he must act boldly, if he is to avoid disaster.

He rises from his seat to stand at the table, ignoring the jolt of pain in his leg. Abandoning all pretence, he addresses the huntsman, in French: Please, monsieur, he says. I beg of you. Don't go to the Prussians. They will kill me. And when he says it now it seems true, and his anger turns to fright, and desperation, and the desperation is in his voice as he speaks. Implores the huntsman.

The huntsman regards him charily, lighting his pipe from the reed on the table. He answers in French, crude but passionate: We don't like war, he says. We like to live our lives here, right with God. There has been war here, putting fire in the crops and carrying the goats away, for decades. My father saw war, I saw war. I don't like my son to see war. Soldiers.

No, says Tarare – placing his hands on the table and leaning toward the huntsman as though the minutely increased proximity of their heads might promote accord – I don't want that either. Please, monsieur. I just want to go on my way. In peace.

You are a French soldier, yes?

Yes.

A French spy?

Tarare hesitates. Only since this morning, he says.

The huntsman snorts. Yes, he says. You are a bad spy. Baby spy.

So let me go.

Frau Britta is standing at the sideboard, listening. Now she turns and speaks to her husband in German, her tone quietly urgent. The huntsman shakes his head, then nods it. Exhales a stream of pipe smoke and looks back at Tarare. My wife says if you are a spy, the Prussians will pay for you.

They won't, answers Tarare reflexively. I'm not important.

Frau Britta – who clearly understands French, if she will not speak it – laughs bitterly at that, and speaks to her husband again in German. A sour, sustained string of words. The huntsman shrugs, doleful eyes flickering between wife and prisoner. He sighs. They steal our food, he says to Tarare. And our firewood. Unless you are friendly with them. I must think of my family, he says.

Just let me go, repeats Tarare, his knuckles blanched white at the table's edge. I will go and they will never know I was here. He can see a way into the huntsman – a door left ajar. But Tarare doesn't know how to bargain, how to persuade. He has never learnt. He only knows how to take, and how to hide.

The huntsman drops his hand to rub at a knot in the wood. If the soldiers discover you were here and I allow you to be leaving, I think it goes very badly for us.

All Tarare can say is Please. Please, monsieur. I beg you. And then, though he does not know why, he says: I have a mother. I don't know where she is, but I have a mother. She is alive and I want to find her.

The huntsman rises from the table and puts on his fur-collared coat, unmoved. Everyone has a mother, he says, tamping down his pipe, lifting his musket from the corner. Enough now. I will walk, and I will decide. Schatzi.

The dog rises from her rag-bed, tail wagging, and follows her master over the threshold, into the night. The huntsman closes the door, and Tarare hears the bolt slid home. He slumps back into his seat. His leg throbs with pain, and his mouth is dry from panic. Frau Britta stands mutely by the sideboard, looking at him. Sniffing, she takes the covered beer jug and fills a beaker. Wordlessly, even apologetically, she places the beaker of bitter beer on the table in front of him. Then she turns and follows her children up the narrow ladder and into the loft. She pulls the ladder up behind her.

What follow are some of the strangest hours of a life that has encompassed many. Tarare sits alone in silence, listening to the shifting of his captors' bodies overhead. He drinks his beer, then pours himself another, and has many thoughts as he sits there, waiting for whatever doom. These thoughts range from the ungenerous (*I will raid the cupboards and eat all their food, every scrap, so they will go hungry*) to the nakedly murderous (*I will set a fire with this reed-light and burn the whole place to the ground and, yes, die – but take Frau Britta and Helmut and Lotte and little Gerda with me into the arms of God*). He sees in his mind's eye short bones, fluorescent in the murk. Fine yellow hair resolved to softest white ash. But Tarare has never been able to fully commit himself to spite, and as he turns in his mind the potential post-mortem satisfactions of mass murder through arson, the reed-light extinguishes itself, leaving him sitting at the table in total darkness. He listens to the children as they snort and snuffle in their sleep overhead. Of what do beloved, well-fed children dream? Tarare could not possibly imagine. Eventually he rises and gropes his way to a shuttered casement. Giving it a desultory shove, he finds it bolted. He could probably break through it if he wanted to, he thinks. If he really tried. Take a chair or an iron and beat it through, shatter the painted wood. But he is so tired, so hungry, so weak. He slumps to the floor and presses his ear to the slim gap at the edge of the shutter where the draught comes in, cooling his cheek and delivering the ambient noise of the forest to him, mysterious and fulsome with menace. Owls, and imperceptible predations, and the conversational rustle of the leaves. *I wish I was in you, forest*, he thinks. In the dark and at large. Silently, Tarare weeps.

And time passes. It is almost dawn by the time he wipes his eyes and crawls across the floor and into the truckle bed, cursing his weakness and his foolishness. He lies on his back, pulls the coverlet up over his head, and at last drifts off into a fitful sleep.

When he next opens his eyes, he finds himself gazing up into the face of a Prussian soldier, who has drawn the covers down from his chin with a gloved hand.

Oh, says Tarare.

The soldier wrinkles his nose against Tarare's sour bedbreath. His face is extremely ruddy, his neck thick and fleshly, his teeth somewhat protuberant and his eyebrows almost white-blond. He looks like a great large mole-rat stuffed into uniform. Everyone looks like something, Tarare thinks. Nobody looks like nothing. God loves to plagiarise himself. Pig, mole-rat, fox cub, peach stone. Sleepily, he wonders if this thought is heretical. Tarare tries to raise himself on his elbows, but the mole-rat shoves him back down on to the truckle and begins to bind his hands with a length of rope. Tarare allows him to do this without complaint or resistance. A second Prussian observes, bayonet brandished. Only two. They may even be the scouts he saw on the road the day before, so louche, so cheerful. He allows himself to be bundled from the bed and out of the front door, where their horses wait. They do not speak to him, nor to each other.

It is a cloudless spring morning, but too early yet to say which way the day will turn: the sky, seen through the treetops, is a pane of unblemished lavender. One bird calls louder than the others, two hard shrill tones that melt into a throaty jangle. As he is lifted on to a horse, Tarare wonders if it will be the last such morning he sees. Slumped pillion against his abductor's broad blue-coated shoulder, he looks back toward the cabin, shrinking behind him through the trees, and sees the pinched white faces of Helmut and little Gerda and Lotte all clustered at the door. And he sees the huntsman, his arms slack at his sides and his expression timorous. Schatzi paws around the hunts-man's feet, oblivious to the human drama of the moment.

Tarare watches the huntsman watch him being carried away. He cannot hate him, because what he did, he did for love. Love of his wife and his little yellow-haired children. Tarare believes this. Tarare feels a sudden glow of unexpected and even philosophical relief in believing this, as they dwindle down to dollsize. The key to life has been pressed into his hand, at last. Too late. Love. Love! It is love that makes the pain worth bear-ing, that gives existence, however abject, its purpose. Tarare wonders whom or what he might have time left to love before the Prussians string him up. Tarare wonders if things might have gone differently, if his strange peregrinations might have led him to a place of greater tenderness, had he understood this sooner. Love. Tarare wonders if death-near-at-hand precipitates thoughts of such serene inanity in all who face him, or just in Tarare. *Little birds in the treetops of indeterminate species*, thinks Tarare, *I love you. Bay mare under my body, carrying me dutifully toward violence*, thinks Tarare, *I love you. Life*, thinks Tarare, *I suppose I love you after all.*

*

It is three o'clock in the afternoon, and Citizen-Doctor Dupuis is bloodletting. An orderly appears at the door of the ward, cap pressed to his chest. Citizen-Doctor, the porter pants, like a dog. He has been running. Monsieur. You must come. At once. (They all do that, he has noticed, the porters and orderlies – take off their hats at the thresholds of the wards and sickrooms, as though they are entering a hallowed place, which, Doctor Dupuis supposes, with a certain degree of egoism, they are.)

I am quite busy, the doctor replies. He glances at his patient. A young man with a high forehead and a higher fever. His breathing is effortful, but controlled. The doctor gently arranges the boy's arm over a shallow dish and watches the blood pool beneath the limb from the fresh incision, the bright red of a half-ripe cherry. There is satisfaction in it – a feeling of purification even in the watching. What is it? the doctor asks.

You must come, repeats the porter. He wrings his felt cap in his hands. It's Tarare. Tarare is returned.

Tarare. Doctor Dupuis' scalp tingles when he hears that name, that nonsense. It has been four days since the boy left the hospital in his peasant's get-up, a perky scarlet feather in the band of his cap. Doctor Dupuis feels very much as he feels when he uncovers gangrene or a livid rash to find that the infection has spread. Something like hopelessness, but not quite. How could a creature so abject endure so stubbornly? With languorous delicacy, the doctor cleans his instruments and rises from the bedside.

Tarare had been taken straight to Doctor Dupuis' office. Inwardly, the doctor begrudges this implication of association, this assumption of responsibility. And straight away he sees Tarare is changed. He would go so far as to say, is broken. He looks truly terrible, sitting there on the examination table. Aged a decade in his face in the days since he left, demon-harrowed, pulped, cowed. They have wrapped him in a blanket, which he has bunched over his head like a beggarwoman. His big blue eyes — still glassy and sepulchral as a china doll's — stare out from beneath this woolly hood, bloodshot. His hand shakes as he lifts a beaker of warmed wine to his mouth, taking reticent little sips. The first thing Tarare says, seeing the doctor standing there, is: Did you know?

Tarare, says the doctor. Drawing up a chair, he forces as much compassion as he can muster into his voice. By God, man. What happened to you?

Did you know? Tarare repeats insistently — even resentfully. Did you know what it said? The message they gave me to carry?

The doctor takes Tarare's calf in his hands. It is ringed by a deep, clotted-over wound, like a bite mark, below the knee. All his visible flesh is mottled with bruises, swollen. His resentment of the creature is tempered by curiosity. What chewed him up so thoroughly and spat him out again? Surely not the Prussians. If the Prussians had laid their hands on him he would be dead. Surely. Your leg, Tarare — what happened?

Did you KNOW? Tarare says again, almost shouts, pulling himself free of the doctor's grasp like a petulant child.

Doctor Dupuis sighs and raises his head to look Tarare directly in his bruise-limned eyes. Of course I did not know, Tarare, he says. Meticulously gentle. I was not told.

They boy regards him doubtfully before releasing a grand, submissive sigh. It was all a joke, wasn't it? he says, trembling. A joke, a bet. He draws his split lip up against his teeth in an ugly, rueful grin. Dis-pos-able, he whispers.

The doctor goes to the cabinet and gathers clean cloths, rubbing alcohol. Tarare is right, and he will not contradict him.

What he wants to say is: it took you until now to see this, Tarare? That no one in the whole wide known world – not even me, and certainly not the likes of Alexandre François Marie, Viscount de Beauharnais – cares if you live or die? That you have made yourself picaresque, a curio, fit only for sport or mockery, to be cast aside like a battered plaything when the appetite for either is exhausted? That no one cares to hear of whatever dreams bloom like nepenthes in your sickly sleeping mind? It has taken you until now to have the measure of the self you were complicit in making, Tarare? What he wants to say is: it would be better if you had died. The world is changing and there is no place for you in it. It would be better if you had faded, become no more than a story, a whisper on sea foam, like the Cynocephali and the green-faced lotos-eaters. Wouldn't you prefer that, Tarare? To sleep, and be spoken of with laughter, perhaps even regret. What he says instead is: That wound will be needing stitches.

I'm hungry, Tarare says.

The doctor dabs at the wounded leg. I'll send for bread and milk, he says. Tell me what happened.

Tarare groans. I stood in a bear trap.

A bear trap? The doctor shakes his head. It is like something from a bad joke, he thinks. *A polyphage, a Prussian and a bear walk into a forest, etc.*

Then the man who the trap belonged to got me out of it. Then I saw he was a Protestant. And he sold me to the Prussians.

And you told them? You told them about the note?

Tarare pouts and narrows his eyes, as though he has honour and that honour has been questioned. They beat me first, he says. Twice.

What happened? Tell me, Tarare. From the beginning.

What Tarare tells the doctor is this:

At the edge of Neustadt his captors had taken him down off the horse and put a sack over his head. One took his bound wrists and the other prodded at his backside with a bayonet, compelling him up a steeply inclining path. They were speaking to each other all the time in German now, even laughing, cooing. Speaking to Tarare as well, in broken French. Things about dogs, things about Republican pigs, things about how tiny and shrivelled his cock was. At first Tarare had found his pseudo-blindness disorientating, but after a little while he began to find it novel as well. Specks of light, blue and white, pricked the loose weave of the hessian. Flashes of movement and colour. He thought he must be seeing the world as a fly sees it, through her faceted carbuncular eyes. This sense of solidarity with the small and rank things of the world was a strange comfort to him, as he stumbled over roots and clods of earth, up, up the hill, until the path evened out beneath his unsteady feet and, unable to see, he attentively listened, and he deeply inhaled:

gunpowder

latrines

dirty rope

adipocere

bare feet

tobacco smoke feat. morning dew

(ejaculate, sweet and rotten smelling, like flowers kept in water for too long)

hollering (German)

laughter (universal)

dry scrape, whetstone on metal

canvas straining in the wind

The sun had come out. He could feel its warmth on his

wrists and his bare, bleeding feet. Was he Christ? He felt somewhat Christlike. Walking his very own *Via Dolorosa*. Someone
took him by the shoulder, took him somewhere dark and cool,
where he was stripped down to his underthings. His drawers
and cotton shirt. He was searched all over. Held down. A finger
slipped into his anus, even. And when they found nothing of
significance on his person, he was beaten. The first time they
beat him the process felt perfunctory, mechanical and passion-
less. Tarare, still hooded, had curled into a ball and concentrated
on staying silent as the toes of boots caught him under the ribs,
on the chin, tra-la. He was not certain what this beating signi-
fied, besides a casual observance of the rituals of enmity. He is
French and they are Prussian, the French and Prussians are at
war. Why, though? He thinks to himself, as his neck is stamped
on, his belly pummelled. Why have these tall and light-eyed
men come from their homes to pummel me, Tarare? He understands why it is the Austrians have come. The Austrians have
come because the Queen is Austrian. But the Prussians? What
business do they have being here, beating him?

The Prussians have come because Republican sentiments
must be stifled, the doctor interjects, drawing a suture taut
across Tarare's wound. This thinking is a danger to every des-
pot. A true democracy cannot be seen to succeed. He smiles
grimly. Or else everyone will want one.

Oh, says Tarare. Do we have a true democracy now?

You have been gone only four days, Tarare, says the doctor.

What happened next, Tarare continued, was that he had
blinked in dazzlement and sat up as the sack was pulled roughly
from his head. Blood was coming in fat streams from his split
lip. He was in a large tent stacked with barrels and crates, sunshine blanching the canvas. The Prussians were standing in a

ring around him, an imposing henge of gold-tasselled jackets and fanciful moustaches. One clean-shaven soldier stooped down in front of Tarare and gave his shoulders a shake. Why, he had asked – in heavily accented French – have you come here?

Tarare asked for water and water was brought. He lifted the beaker to his lips and tasted the same sublime water he had the previous day, cool and pine-fresh, now tinged with the iron of his own blood. The taste of it, reminding him of the optimism of his recent past, his high blue yesterday in the beautiful valley, girded him with a strange and misplaced optimism for his future. I can still get out of this alive, Tarare had thought. If I play it right. There will be more high blues and valleys and springtimes for Tarare. He gulped three large mouthfuls of water and set the beaker down between his legs.

So? said the interrogator.

Why are you beating me? asked Tarare.

This question was unexpected. The interrogator cleared his throat and frowned, rifling through his vocabulaire. Because you are a Republican pig-dog, he answered at last.

Pig and dog, yes. These are two beasts with which Tarare has always felt a special affinity, it is true. Pig and dog, cow and bitch. He has also always wondered why it is a man invokes these very useful beasts when he wishes to insult another. The French do, and it would appear the Prussians do it as well. Why? When a pig is a profoundly intelligent creature, and a dog loyal and affectionate, and a cow sweet-smelling, with long, mystical eyelashes, tinted dark as though by the smoke of a ritual fire? Tarare gave voice to his confusion concerning this rhetorical gimmick, and the interrogator removed his glove and slapped Tarare hard around the face with the flat of his palm.

They beat him a second time, then. More ardently and with

real malice, because they thought he was being smart with them. Mocking them, somehow. When the sack was removed once more from Tarare's throbbing head, he spat a hock of blood on to the matted floor. His flesh was aflame. The interrogator repeated his question: Why have you come here? To report back on our movements? To count our guns? What information are you tasked with carrying to your pig-dog handlers? Good little pig-dog, are you? *Wau-wau*. We'll drown you like one. Drown you like a puppy in a sack. Hang your paws over a fire.

Tarare whimpered.

The interrogator said, We'll break your fingers, so. Willem?

A second soldier stooped down beside Tarare and took hold of his hand. He made a fist around Tarare's slender index finger and began to apply pressure to the joint. He was big, this Prussian, strong looking, his face masked with professional indifference. Tarare wondered if this was Willem's own special job, the finger-breaking. Tarare also howled and wriggled. While he can easily tolerate assaults on his meat, his flesh – bruises, cuts, beatings – the thought of his bones being broken, torn from their hinges, fills him with horror. Perhaps because the wheel, on which horse thieves and poachers were broken, torn limb from limb, occupied a special place in his imagination among all the carceral apparatus of the old regime. Perhaps because his bones have never yet betrayed him. There is a mineral truth to bone, a purity. Tarare is not the fault of Tarare's bones, he is certain of that. So he said, Please and No, and Mercy. And then he told the Prussians everything.

And when he was done telling them everything, the interrogator rose to his full height and regarded Tarare with a disdain so absolute, so acid, that it pierced through his battered hide. It scorched him. For the first time in his life Tarare saw himself through the eyes of another person. His pallid, pouchy flesh. His distended belly sagging over the waist of his drawers, a line of fine blond pubis dribbling from the navel where his under-shirt had come unbuttoned. His large, docile eyes. He, Tarare, was a patch of putrid white rot. And he, in his creature-feeling, deserved no mercy from these fine men.

Tarare, now in his bloodied underthings, was hauled around the camp from one tent to another, one official to the next, until he was at last presented to the general. The general looked nothing like Tarare expected a Prussian general might look. He was diminutive and whip-like and suntanned, his face deeply scored with wrinkles. Like a peach stone. Everyone looks like something, Tarare thought. Nobody looks like nothing. God loves to plagiarise himself. Pig, mole-rat, fox cub, peach stone. The general's accommodations were spartan in their arrange-ment. He was sitting at a broad mahogany desk, flanked on one side by a dummy in a jacket heavy with gilt medals and a brown perruque, and on the other by a small flag, the slanted eye of the black martial eagle glaring from the drape.

The general lifted his head from a plate of undercooked eggs and listened thoughtfully as the interrogator prattled to him in German. Then he motioned with his hand. Tarare was brought forward. The general pushed away his plate and arranged his perruque on his small head. Tarare wondered if he ought to bow. Tarare did bow.

The general cocked his head. Very nice, he said, in French. I am called General Zögli. And you are called?

Tarare, said Tarare.

Tarare, the general repeated. I have not heard that name before, ever, anywhere.

It is my name.

The general waves his hand. Maybe it is, maybe it isn't, he says. It doesn't matter particularly.

I want to go home, monsieur. Please. I promise I will never fight the Prussians again. I will swear to it, on – on—

Of course you want to go home, interrupted the general. So do I. So do we all. The daffodils will be sprouting on the Unter den Linden. They make me smile, so yellow. But I cannot. Von Hagen says you have a message for me?

I need to shit it out first, monsieur.

So I hear, said the general. He pursed his lips.

A long silence followed. The attendants and aides shifted on their feet and curled their lips – with mirth. The situation was, yes, ridiculous. They were all in a ridiculous situation together. The bonegrinder of war snagged on the bowels. Tarare noticed the collective unease and did laugh a little. Then General Zögli began to laugh as well, and soon everyone was laughing, until the general raised his hand for silence. It had been a pleasant moment, one they would all remember later, and smile to recall. But now it was over. The general disciplined his parched features. You are very accommodating, Tarare, he said.

I'm not a Republican, replied Tarare.

No?

No. I don't care if we have a King and Queen. It doesn't make any difference to me.

But you are a soldier. In the army of the French Republic.

I thought they would feed me, monsieur.

And they don't?

Not enough.

So you would reveal the secrets of your homeland to her enemies, the general said, raising his black eyebrows, because you are – he rubbed his flat little belly in circles – *hungry*?

Tarare's mouth hung slack. He had been caught. The question was a trick – any answer he could give was the wrong answer. He pawed at the floor a little, very aware of the general's eyes on his face. I have a wife, he said at last. He raised his head and straightened his shoulders in a posture of masculine sentimentality. I have a wife, he repeated. Her name is Pierette. And children. I only want to go home to my wife and children. (And when he said it he almost believed it – he felt, at least, it was not a real lie. It is a life he could have had, if someone had told him earlier about love.)

I see, said the general. What is your age, Tarare?

I am twenty-one, monsieur.

Well, said the general, shuffling some papers. You do breed young, you French. He motioned to an aide: Bring him a chamber pot and watch over him until he – he stirred his hand in the air – until he does his business.

Von Hagen and the mole-rat took Tarare to the rear of the general's tent, and a chamber pot was brought. They pulled down his trousers roughly – his hands were still bound – and bent him unceremoniously over its porcelain rim. Then they stood there, watching like nursemaids, as Tarare tried desperately to contain his now-molten bowels. A fly came to settle on his cheek. The sun climbed to its zenith in the sky. Tarare had not shat in a day and a half or more. He wanted to very badly. He felt like an iron ring was contracting round his middle. And yet he bunched his knees and pressed his buttocks tightly together.

Are you trying to stop yourself shitting, worm? asked Von Hagen.

Tarare said nothing.

Why? asked Von Hagen.

Tarare said nothing. He felt bloated, saturated. Filled to bursting. Was this the lowest point of his life? Yes, probably, Tarare thought to himself as he tried to knot his insides, as the eyes of the soldiers bored into his puckered face. So far. But there is always, always, a lower place.

If you don't shit it out, we'll cut your belly open, Von Hagen informed him.

Tarare said nothing. As he strained against the ineluctable loosening of his innards, he thought of bodies. He thought of war, and what even he, in his extremely limited experience, had seen it do to bodies: gathering them together, winnowing them small, flaying them open, bashing them against each other. He felt terrible. Tired, hungry, bruised – culled. He closed his eyes and allowed his mind to drift with the insidious clarity often experienced upon the chamber pot. A humble and animal understanding. It drifted laterally, to hills velveted with dwarf pine. It drifted up to the clement afternoon sky, threaded with vectors of slender cloud, where birds lived their small-time birdlives. It drifted down to settle in the grass, then dug in further, down down, to where good black dirt cradles the bones of other boys who went to war, and their mothers, and their pet dogs, and their beautiful horses (and the boys who killed them, too, and the kings they fought for, and their beautiful horses too). Dig a hole anywhere and find them grinning up at you indifferently. I am sick of this, Tarare thought. Let it end. With a groan of relief, he unclenched and allowed himself empty out at last, effluvium warm and plashing into the pot. When he was finished, the soldiers pounced, putting their hands in the muck, groping for *the message*, lust for pre-eminence overcoming any residual squeamishness. Tarare was thrown aside to lie face down in the soft grass, buttocks bared to the sky, and he breathed in deeply the sweetness of that grass and imagined he was drowning in flowers, like some dead hero on his way to the Panthéon. White oleanders, pale yellow roses. Always a lower place to go.

He was taken back to the general, who pawed at his thinning hair as he unrolled the missive and read it through. He read it through once, and then again, his eyebrows creeping upward. You are sure, said the general, you do not know what this message says? His mouth was set in a flinty line.

Tarare shook his head.

And would you like to know?

This question seemed like another trick, so Tarare remained silent, wobbling on his aching legs, until the one called Von Hagen stepped forward and grasped him by the collar, giving him a shake. Answer the general, worm, he said.

Yes, said Tarare. Because it was true. He did want to know the reason he had left his soft white bed in the hospital, and traversed witch-wood and wide valley, and stood in a bear trap, and been hauled up a hill with a sack over his head, and beaten, and betrayed, and shamed. It had better be good. Perhaps God had written on that little slip of paper that came from inside him, he thought. Perhaps it contained the secret of life. Or perhaps God had written *I loathe and abhor you, Tarare. I count you not among my creatures, and nor did I ever*. But he knows it was not God who wrote the note, but Alexandre de Beauharnais.

It says, said the general, moistening his lips, that my kinsmen and I – the Prussians – it says we should leave the lands of the Glorious Republic and go back home to do the things that we are best at. The things that we are best at, it suggests, are – here he dropped his eyes back to the note – 'eating under-seasoned dumplings and fucking our sisters'. He leant back in his chair and looked at Tarare. Then he laughed. He laughed long and raucously again, and his attendants and aides joined him. Von Hagen laughed, the mole-rat laughed, turning a more livid shade of puce. Everyone laughed. They shook their heads, they sighed with pleasure, they wiped tears from their eyes. He hadn't thought the Prussians were a people so disposed to jollity. Perhaps it was the water, Tarare thought. His eyes roved furtively from face to mirthful face, until the general raised his hand for silence again and took a deep breath. Hang him, the general said. Go on. Goodbye, Tarare, son of the Glorious Republic.

Seeing how the mirth of the aides and attendants was only intensified by this order, Tarare had at first thought it was a joke. Another funny joke – to hang a man, to kill him, for the conveyance of a schoolyard insult? A thing that might be scrawled on a latrine wall? But Von Hagen and the mole-rat took hold of him and began to compel him toward the mouth of the tent. The aides and attendants followed, jostling at Tarare, surging around him, slapping at his cheeks, tearing at the few garments left on his body. They lofted him up on to their shoulders and marched him out into the daylight again, out into the yellow afternoon, where Tarare could see the many tents of the Prussians spread out across the plateau, above and below, small and rumpled, like discarded handkerchiefs, like a flock of ungainly headless white birds. His captors began to shout and cheer triumphantly in German, and soldiers came out of their tents and left their knots around cooking fires to watch as Tarare was conveyed so helplessly along gangplank walkways, and through mud, to the very edge of the camp. The soldiers gathered and the soldiers followed, excited and raucous, shouting insults in their broken French, throwing dirt and shit.

The crowd had swollen to impressive numbers by the time Tarare had realised it was not a joke at all: there, in a wide clearing amid the tents, stood a scaffold, a gallows tall and primed and ready, the noose a hollow black teardrop against the balmy evening sky. They were going to hang him. Hang *him*, Tarare. As they set him on his feet before the steps of the scaffold, his body revolted. He would not mount it willingly. He wailed, he cried, he set his feet wide like a stubborn mule. This resistance revealed unforeseen reserves of strength in his battered body, but Von Hagen and the mole-rat were stronger. They tore the shirt fully from his back. They hauled him bodily on to the platform and braced his arms by his sides to present him to the baying crowd. They fell silent. Tarare stilled. Here he was, at the face of death. And the light breeze that carried the scent of bluebells and buttercups from the plain, the breath of death. And the blue eyes fixed on his body and face with undisguised curiosity, the eyes of death. And Von Hagen, declaiming loudly to the crowd in German, the voice of death. They positioned him in front of the noose. They had to hold him up because his legs were trembling, would no longer hold even his slight weight. And in the hands of death, where Tarare supposed himself, at last, to be, he felt no very great serenity. No – he felt anger. He felt thwarted. He wanted to bite and whimper. He wanted to look at the sea, which was a thing he had never done. And as the noose was secured around his throat, he screwed his eyes tight shut and willed his life to play out before them, as he had heard it might. His life, played in tall wigs, before creaking scenery. He saw he had only killed, never saved. There would be songs. There would be dogs and flies and doves and silver-leafed stars pinned to deep blue velvet. All the carcasses on all the butchers' hooks would drop to the ground and dance on their shin bones, waving their skinned limbs with hieratic grace in the spotlight. He waited for this to happen, for his life to roll like a flaming wheel before his eyes, but it didn't. That darkness was an empty one.

No last words, worm? said a voice by his ear.

Tarare wept.

Are you not going to tell them you are sorry?

I'm sorry, Tarare had whimpered. I'm very sorry.

Louder.

I'm sorry! Tarare had shouted.

And then there was laughter, cheering. A commotion all around him. He felt the tears hot on his cheeks. When he opened his eyes what he saw was an empty noose, and contained within its loop the tops of pine trees dark against a flushing red sky, twirls of smoke drifting up toward the untroubled sunset. He lifted his hands to his throat and found that it was bare. The soldiers were laughing at him, still. A cruel and delighted laughter. He felt a hand on the small of his back. That was all we wanted to hear, said Von Hagen. If you are truly sorry, little worm, then you are free to go. He smiled, showing his many robust white teeth.

Tarare felt the shadow of the noose between his face and the bloodied evening sun. He had stayed still, with his hands at his throat.

Go on, Von Hagen urged, still smiling. You are free to go. Scurry, small worm. Crawl away. He stepped aside and motioned toward the scaffold stairs.

Tarare swayed on the spot for a moment. Then he bolted. Down the stairs, through the soldiers, slipping in mud, tripping on tent lines. The soldiers followed, the soldiers chased at a distance, calling out at him, throwing crusts, laughing, laughing.

Tarare ran until the whiteness of the canvas and the red of the sun were smeared against the inside of his eyes. His bleeding feet carried him onward without the input of his mind, through the camp down an escarpment over grass, until the forest closed up over his head again, until night fell, soothing his body like a soft tongue. He supposes he slept, somewhere. He supposes he drank, something. And when the powdered fingers of dawn crept between the trees, the French scout, waiting by the way-mark at the edge of the wood, saw a horrid shape crawl from the darkness. It crawled on all fours, covered in a sticky bloody glaze, as though delivered fresh from the womb of a white devil or knot-witch. The scout went closer. He saw the most hideous miracle come from the wood, there. He saw Tarare.

*

Through late spring and early summer, Tarare convalesces in his old room at the top of the hospital. He is fortunate, the doctors tell him, his physical wounds merely superficial. But what happened to him in the forest was certainly not. It has whittled him out on the inside. He feels it in himself, in as much as a person can *feel* a void. It is like a tingling of his heart and mind where delight or care once were. A phantom soul.

Through the small high window that faces his bed, Tarare observes – with neither delight nor concern – many skies. Late April full of small fluffy black clouds, like the paws of spiders; May sparkling like a split geode, after rainstorms; June tidying away these aerial vapours and soaking the firmament in un-apologetic blue. The sun casts shadows around him. He eats, he shits. He stares at the wall. He reacts to nothing. The dummy, the ugly little doll.

Courville is pleased. He has had his way, entirely. The singular creature now submits to his exploratory proddings with vege-table docility, allows himself to be probed and starved and gorged in whatever manner is asked of him. Of what does the surgeon Courville dream? Of making an incision, a clean red grin just below the navel. Of reaching deep into Tarare's body, up to the elbow, and drawing a string of colour from behind the kidneys, endless, like a magician's knotted silks. Tarare is motionless, autolytic. Tarare is a bleached specimen, an insect run all through its insignificant – yet scientifically beguiling – body with a pin.

Of what does Tarare dream? Nothing.

Secretly, Doctor Dupuis thinks he ought to kill off the boy. It would be a mercy, he thinks, really. It would also be easy. Laudanum in milk. Ten drops, twenty. A gentle death. An uttermost floating.

At night, it is the hospital that dies. Sleep solemnises the wards and corridors. Tarare rises from his bed. He walks the halls, opens the doors, pads on bare white feet between the wounded bodies, the apportioned spaces of moonlight. Why does he do this? Something calls to him in darkness now. The warmth of blood. The life in flesh. Communion. With his mouth kissed to a wound he can taste what he has never seen: he likes the northerners best, with their savour of salt fish and breakers, blackened rock. Fresh amputations tender as veal. He is a connoisseur. Young blood is crisp and ardent, almost volatile. But old blood has its own particular delights: nutty layers of regret, tobacco, herbaceous notes of nostalgia (dances in meadows, slumber under the open skies). He can taste it all. It is easy. He makes no sound. He does it so quietly, so gently. They never wake up.

Soultz-Haut-Rhin, the soldiers say, is haunted. When the

ward sisters rise in the morning to tend their charges, they find them alert with confusion: something has been taken from them in the night, they are certain, though they can't say what. Bandages have been loosened. A grave-sweet odour, unplaceable, still hangs in the air. The lightest sleepers speak of a shape clothed in white with luminous, other-than-human eyes. It comes after the midnight bell, slit nostrils twitching, rubber-spined, drawn by the scent of pain. It never speaks. One attests he saw it change its shape. How it slithered on the floor like a viper, reared like a hound to smell the air, then settled to lap at a bleeding dish in the manner of a cat. They give this visitation names: ghoul, chalk-imp, upiór. Or else they say it is a thwarted soul. A girl's, most probably, from the rumoured tenderness of her suck, her gentle touch. When evening comes they set Madonnas at their bedsides, circumscribing their rest with her hallowed magic. And it works, after a fashion. As the days lengthen and summer reds the brick, the visitations become rarer, and eventually, they stop.

Glutted on stolen blood, Tarare heals. The person in him begins to stir. He turns his feelings in his mind like spindles. What is this? Regret! And this? Cynicism! Anger! Am I not a man like all these others? Am I lesser? Even a madman, he thinks – as he now suspects himself to be – is a man. How – considers Tarare – to live in this world? And how to love? He has no answers to these questions, and no one else he can ask.

On the eve of the Feast of Saint Lazare, which he knows to be his twenty-second birthday, it is time that preoccupies him. Now free to roam the grounds of the hospital at will, he sits beneath a tree in the kitchen garden and feels the sunshine on his face. It is the twenty-eighth day of July, Year of Grace seventeen hundred and ninety-three. The kitchen girls in their white kerchiefs are trimming pea shoots. A year seems to Tarare a horrible unwieldy thing, warped to cover the world entire, to draw a million million items and events – pea shoots, battles, grey horses, Cossacks, kidneys, fire ants, pearl buttons, plankton, constitutions – beneath its mantle. A year is really a kind of god. And I have lived, Tarare thinks, for a whole twenty-two of them. He smiles to himself. He even laughs aloud. He hears the hiss of rain in the grass around his feet. The kitchen girls raise their kerchiefed heads in the kitchen garden and fuss with their shawls. A sudden summer downpour threads the haze in rose gold.

That night Tarare dreams as he has not dreamed in many months. It is an old dream, given new dimension. The dream of giantism. Only this time, instead of opening his eyes to a vantage already cloud-like, he grows. His bones stretch and his flesh swells up and out until he feels his head grazing at the branches, his shoulders snapping through them as though they are twigs, up, up to the sky above, until the perfumes of summer are thinned by the cool of ozone, and fields of wheat tickle at the acreage of his feet. What can he see? Dense forests, lonely peaks, rivers and brooks sparkling like trails of broken glass. It is beautiful, but in this dream Tarare feels sad to be so large, so tall. He knows they will send armies against him, and he will feel the sputter of grapeshot at his ankles. He will look down to find his toes wreathed in smoke, red and yellow pennants small and bright as petals. With great sorrow, he will stamp these legions to the ground, flatten them, and then go – where? There is nowhere that a giant is wanted. There is nowhere that a giant is cherished. The Holy Land, perhaps. A pilgrimage. He will cradle the Saviour's mountain in his palm like Saint Agatha's white breast. He will raze whole orange groves. He will peel the roof off the Calvary and peer inside at the resting place of Christ. It will be good sport for a day or two. But he knows his great giant sadness has a source beyond loneliness. He knows this because of all the life and death he has tasted. It can't be got rid of and it can't be shat out. His insides are a grave-place, a charnel house. Giant Tarare understands this. He thinks of the kittens, the little kittens Courville had brought him. How he gulped them down, spat up fur and bone. Innocence! A salty megalodon tear swells at the corner of his eye, runs down the vast plain of his cheek, and crashes to the ground, flooding vineyards, washing little houses from the hillsides. What can he do? His existence is catastrophe. A hopeless anger boils from his belly. He sees, then. He sees he will only be safe, that he can only be good, when it is all gone. When he has eaten it all. So that is what the Giant Tarare does. He uproots old sweet forests, he crumbles ranges, he drains the seas. He packs his mouth with sand and snow. He bites through the crust of the earth, through life and death, through a billion years of sediment, scintillating with flecks of diamond, and obsidian, and anorthite. And when it is all gone Tarare floats, huge and alone, in the emptiness of space. All that remains is a little debris. A lot of silence. He picks at his teeth with his nail. He wakes, sucking the blood from his fingers. And then he sees what he has done.

Damp grass. Birthday present, on a plinth of starlight. Night

(Little bloodied ankle, little bloodied stocking. A lot of silence.)

*

At daybreak there is a hammering at Doctor Dupuis' door. Medical emergency, he thinks, splashing a palmful of water at his face and pulling his tailcoat on over his nightshirt: a fit, a choking, stitches come loose, spurting. He hears voices in the corridor, high and querulous. Weeping. A woman, weeping. Someone hammers at the door again.

The doctor calls out that he is coming, gathering his kit bag.

A muffled voice on the other side of the door. It's Manon, Citizen-Doctor. Little Manon.

Doctor Dupuis throws the door open. Gathered at the threshold are two porters and a labourer whom he knows only by sight, a gangly dark-haired man. Between the three of them they support a weeping girl, in white nightcap and knitted shawl. Their clogs and jackets, he sees, are damp with dew. *Who?* he asks, tired and testy.

Manon, the porter repeats. He gestures at the trembling girl. Her daughter.

She is unwell?

Gone, rasps the girl. She is gone.

Missing, the porter adds, gently squeezing at the girl's shoulder. Since late last night. Hélène put her down to sleep by the stove in the kitchens, as she always does, and then she was—

Gone, the girl sobs again. Hélène. Her cheeks are ripe and red like apples beneath her little nightcap. Such a healthy flush, the doctor cannot help but think. What constitutions these country girls have. I see, says the doctor (although he doesn't really – a missing child. What can he be expected to do about it?) And how old is the child? he asks.

Two and a half, monsieur. The girl sniffs, catches herself. Two and a half, *Citizen-Doctor*.

She can't have gone very far then, my dear. The doctor smiles weakly. Be reassured – the night was very clement. Probably she wandered in the grounds and lay down to sleep in the grass somewhere, warm as a kitten. She will be found.

The girl lifts her red-rimmed eyes to the doctor's face. Kitten? she repeats quietly. Then her simple features contort, and she lets out a howl, loud and horrid. It was the beast, the girl says. Screams. It was that monster that took her! Her body leers forward with the force of her convulsion and for a moment Doctor Dupuis thinks she will strike him, but the porters clutch her arms. In the face of this maternal outrage, he shrinks into the doorway. *His* mother never shrieked, in maternal outrage or otherwise. *His* mother was a mute confection in mauve damask and starched lace, dead now, of course. The beast? he repeats.

The labourer clears his throat. She means the patient, he says. The one called Tarare. The cook says she saw him, some years ago on a market day, near Mâcon. Says she saw him eat a – eat – he glances anxiously at the girl, lowers his voice – *a kitten*, there. Alive.

Preposterous, the doctor says reflexively. Ridiculous. Have you searched the grounds?

All night and all morning, says the porter.

Since the child was missed, adds the labourer. All of us.

She is – she is—

Nowhere! the girl howls. Rocking in the labourer's strong arms she begins a condemnation, a screed. Ghouls! she yells. Pimps. Do you think we don't know, do you think we are stupid? Who scrubs the blood and picks up the tiny bones? Keeping a creature like that a monster an unholy monster among civilised people – and why – like a rabid dog on your leash – it spelled disaster, it did – letting him walk around like a person letting him walk around among civilised – he has taken her he has taken her and eaten her my baby. It's your fault it's the doctor's fault – why – I saw him just yesterday smiling in the rain like a lizard a snake – her words are muffled as she turns her face to sob into the labourer's barrel chest.

There is a commotion at the end of the corridor. A door opens, and Doctor Dupuis sees Courville, clothed yet sleep-rumpled, advancing toward him through a knot of servants. More porters, more labourers. They are shouting at him. Surgeon Courville is shouting back. Gentlemen, gentlemen – good citizens – now by Dupuis' side at the doorway – I must speak with Citizen-Doctor Dupuis. We will both attend to you shortly. With that, he enters Dupuis' room, drawing the doctor behind him, and slams the door shut at his back. He takes a deep, composing breath and adjusts his drooping perruque.

Dupuis can hear the girl on the other side of the door, still wailing, still denouncing. What in God's name is this? he asks.

Children, says Courville. People get very upset once children are involved. We must do something.

Certainly. But all this about blood, bones? I don't understand it. Doctor Dupuis gropes around for his waistcoat. Kittens?

Courville looks at Dupuis significantly.

Laurent. Tell me you didn't?

I did, sighs Courville. I wanted to see if he would do it – how he did it. Only beasts, of course.

What do you mean, *of course*? I am meant to credit you for not gorging him on – what? Human flesh?

The idea did occur to me.

Citizen-Doctor Dupuis pauses, his buttons half-undone. He looks at Courville. They look at each other for a long time. Are you entirely godless, Laurent?

This is something I have considered for a long time, answers the young surgeon. And I think I may be. That there is some prime mover, some originating intelligence, perhaps, I will concede, but a providential divine— (Years ago, in Paris, during his training, Laurent Courville had gazed down into the deathly mesh under the skin of a convict, the waxy unpromising corpse of a hanged man, and he had been instantly disabused of faith. Blood vessels and nerves branching like a gorgeous coral under the skin. It was a machine, he saw. The body was a machine. A wondrously intricate machine. Was it any less perfect, any less mysterious, for that? In fact, he felt greater intimacy with the body removed from God. It was ours, not some divine lend-lease. Ours, *his*.)

The question was rhetorical, says Dupuis, hastily completing his toilette. Where is Tarare?

Courville winces. That's where I came from, he says. With those men. He plucks at his starched cuff. They're extremely angry, Jean.

Well?

Tarare is also unaccounted for. He's not there, Jean. He's not anywhere.

A chill runs down the front of Dupuis' body like water. Mother of God, he mutters.

Mere coincidence, says Courville. Certainly there is a mundane explanation. We will learn it.

Dupuis laughs wildly. How can you be so calm, Laurent? A child – I – Tarare was our responsibility. Our charge.

Courville clutches at Dupuis' shoulder. We will search for the child. She will be found, then all will be well.

And Tarare? And if we find the child – dead?

The hammering resumes at the door. Raised voices in the corridor. The atmosphere of distemper is growing. Courville sighs. If we find Tarare but not the child they will want blood, no doubt. But we haven't, yet. Spare yourself these grisly hypotheticals.

Don't you feel – don't you—

Hush. Let's go to them before they batter down the door.

Back in the corridor more servants have gathered. Men and women. The chars and cooks gesticulating urgently with their calloused hands, ward sisters in stark habits, even some of their more mobile patients, sallow-faced and dazed. The hall is packed, wall to wall. All turn their gaze expectantly to Dupuis and Courville at the threshold, in baited silence. Dupuis feels extremely hot, pricklingly hot in his body. With embarrassment, he supposes. Shame. He looks at the girl at the front of the crowd, the mother, balling a handkerchief to her tear-streaked face. She is right, he thinks. Whether Tarare took the child or not, she is right. He had looked at Tarare and felt his unwholesome desperation, his amorality, and had done nothing. He had looked and he had known he did not belong. A spider in the house of flies. Doctor Dupuis opens his mouth to speak. He says: I – I—

Courville speaks over the doctor's stutter. Citizens, he says. We see your desperation. A child, a lamb – most innocent of God's creatures. We pray she will be found safe. *Unspoiled.* We will join you in your search. Send riders out. We will not rest, my dear, – here he drops his eyes to the girl, Hélène – until you are reunited with your little daughter.

What of the beast? asks a porter. What of Tarare?

A bellicose murmur ripples through the crowd.

He came at night, calls out one jaundiced patient. He came to the ward and drank from our wounds, like a cat. I saw it. He is a demon. You harboured a demon with us! Do you not see?

The crowing intensifies, bubbles. One Sister crosses herself, murmuring a prayer.

Please – Courville raises a hand for silence – please! If any harm has come to the child, he shouts, then justice will be done. Justice will be done by the appropriate authorities, the appropriate means. I assure you, citizens! Now, if you go down to the kitchens, yes – then we will form search parties. Search parties. Please. Maintain order. This is a place of healing.

As they reluctantly begin to disperse, Dupuis and Courville follow behind the body of the crowd. Courville takes Dupuis' elbow. Now I know how Galileo felt, he says. Snorts. *Demons*.

But there is something – something *wrong* with him, though, mutters Dupuis. You can tell when you look at him, no? Something beyond physic.

Nothing is beyond physic, replies Courville curtly. Given time. We just need the words—

The Germans have a word for it.

Don't they always?

Unheimlich, says Dupuis.

*

They search all morning. They go to every cellar and attic, probe every crawl space, open every crate and cupboard, store and chest, bandbox and wardrobe. Bedsteads and tables are overturned, while the groundsmen comb the stippled grass for a mile all around the hospital building. The sun is like a great white scorching eye, and they find nothing. Not a single clog or lace or curly golden hair. It is as if the child never existed. For a moment, Doctor Dupuis believes this: the child never existed. It feels so like a joke, like a game, that after two years stationed in this serene place, this house of healing, the quotidian rhythms of his practice could be so arbitrarily disrupted. Then he sees the mother again, unslept and blank-faced, almost catatonic, and the guilt fills his mouth like a stranger's tongue. He forces the tragedy into the rigid shapes of reason. It makes him feel better. Children do not simply vanish: somewhere in the world, somewhere close by, no doubt, there are answers. Throbbing in the grass, dangling in the boughs. He will find them.

With the grounds exhausted, they stop soon after noon for a brief repast of bread and watered wine. They speak of riding out to search the roads, to alert the nearby villages. Doctor Dupuis volunteers himself. Before mounting his horse, he takes off his perruque to douse his aching head with water from the stable trough. The sun has burnt a mask of red on to his face, the line as clean along his scalp as though it had been painted. He looks at his reflection on the still water. Mask of red, mask of sin. His sin is pride. Negligence, he supposes, was born of arrogance. This is not a sudden realisation. He has known for a long time. But he never did anything to fix it, to humble himself. To make himself right with God and man. He never found the time. These have been busy years for doctors.

He rides south, toward Cernay. The road is empty, dry as bonemeal, suturing together two golden fields. Little brimstones flit dozily around the hedges. He drives his horse at a trot – it is too hot for haste. He likes how the dusty smell of her back mingles with the more delicate scents of summer, of desiccated grasses and madly receptive flowers. He looks out over the fields as he goes, rolling and dipping, fallow and furrowed. Alone, he feels lightened of his guilt. The cows and horses of the meadows grind their jaws. The country around the hospital is relatively unknown to him, and it is good country, he sees. He passes trees still in full blossom, hoarding snow-white flowers to their branches like a mis-seasoned snow. The heat bakes a silence into the earth that is opulent. He hears nothing, no chiming bells or voices or screaming axles. Just clopping hooves, buzzing flies, the susurrus of a silk-fine breeze over fields. It is good, he decides, to be a Frenchman. Blood and soil. All of this. He sees the blue-gold fuss, the shimmer at the horizon, where feathery spikes of wheat candesce at the feet of the sky. He sees, where the road bends up ahead, a figure all in white. He sees Tarare.

*

What is it like to eat a person? Not only a person, but a child, the holiest kind of person? Tarare knows. Tarare remembers, as he trudges the bonemeal road. Perhaps not the holiest kind of person – perhaps a priest would be holier, and eating a priest a greater profanity. But what priest would taste like that? Meat so tender it was like mouthfuls of love. He is left with only sense-impressions, remnants of the rack and madness, floating slowly to the surface of his mind. She was dead. She was certainly dead when he ate her. He doesn't remember killing her. It happened in a low place, a hidden place, he feels. Perhaps she fell? Perhaps she was already dead when he found her? It doesn't matter. What happened next, he is certain of. What happened next was the end of Tarare. Never again will he reach toward humanity. Never again will he smile his bloodied smile at the world and all its various anarchic beauties.

So he walks. He thinks of Eve. He thinks: I *am* Eve. Tasting of the forbidden. And instead of knowledge there came a great coldness. He had looked sticky-mouthed up at the silvery peel of moon and felt it condemn him. He thinks he would like to talk to Eve. He thinks she is the only person who ever lived who might understand. So now he walks, driven from the garden.

He walks south. He thinks that perhaps if he walks far enough, the grass will pale and the trees will die off into scorched carcasses, and he will have a desert, a certain white wasteland, in which to live out his contrition, circled by bald-headed vultures. Tarare's imagination was always rich. Now it is richer. No stars no roots no glow of rain. It is good to hurt, godly. It is good to be circled by vultures. Let sandstorms tear the hospital smock from his body. Let his face be slashed by blazing winds.

He walks and he doesn't stop walking when he becomes aware of the rider approaching on his left-hand. The shadow of the horse cools the side of his sunburnt face.

Tarare, says Doctor Dupuis. Where are you going?

To Hell, replies Tarare, his eyes fixed on the horizon.

Tarare—

Dupuis pauses. Tarare looks like some notably abject flavour of pilgrim or penitent. His feet are bare and white with dust. The skin on the bridge of his nose is burnt and peeling. His white hospital smock is stained brown at the breast. In his left hand he carries something equally white and stained, an indeterminate lumpy bloodied bundle. The doctor notes a frill of lace. It is a dress, a little ragged white dress. Tarare – says the doctor – *what is that?*

The bones, replies Tarare, his eyes fixed on the horizon. And hair.

The bones. *And hair.* The doctor, who, like most doctors, has a stomach of iron, feels himself overcome by queasiness as he looks at that sordid little bundle. And he wonders, why did Tarare not eat the dress along with the flesh? Tarare can and has eaten such things as cloth, as lace, as buttons. Why is it there in his hand? Why, unless as a memento, a keepsake of his crime? Why, why? Tarare is a walking *why*. The horse whickers softly as the doctor sways in the saddle, then faints. He falls sideways into the road.

*

When Doctor Dupuis comes round, he is on his back beneath the dazzling blue of the sky. He sees his brown horse serenely stripping the grass by the roadside. And he sees a cannibal, an actual cannibal, crouched over him, gazing at him solicitously.

Are you all right? asks Tarare. He is holding the doctor's water flask in his hand.

Oh, God in heaven, murmurs the doctor. He clasps his fingers over his eyes. His head reels. It is good to lie on the floor, he decides. Perhaps he will never rise again. Perhaps he will lie right here forever, in the road somewhere between Soultz-Haut-Rhin and Cernay, beginning on the twenty-ninth day of July Year of Grace seventeen hundred and ninety-three, until the grass has grown up through his bones and the birds have pecked his eyeballs out. What – really and truly – *what* is this strange and discomfiting world? Not God's work – surely not that. The nausea, novel enough in itself to the citizen-doctor, engenders a strange wild feeling. A sense, almost, of hilarity.

Dupuis watches Tarare shuffle on his heels and exhale resonantly through his nose like a sleepy dog. The cannibal is dirty: covered in dust and dried blood, reeking of sweat from his toil through the sun. Tarare, he sighs. What have you done?

Tarare turns his head toward the horizon and creases his brow as the light cuts into his eyes. I had a sister, he says. She died and we didn't tell the abbé. We took her out to the forest and covered her over with leaves. I only just remembered, but at the time it seemed I would never forget it. I was very sad. I cried.

The doctor raises himself on his elbows. I mean the other little girl, Tarare. Manon. They are looking for her back at the hospital. Her mother is distraught.

Tarare presses his lips together. I am very sorry for that, he says.

Then *why?* asks the doctor. *Why* would you do this? (He cannot bring himself to say it. He knows if he says it, says it clearly – *why did you eat a child?* – that he will laugh.)

Tarare turns back to Dupuis. I don't know, he says. I was sleeping – and I dreamed. It happens like that sometimes. When I am sleeping it overcomes me, the hunger. I cannot master myself. I can't – can't stop it – say *no* – as he speaks Tarare becomes agitated. He shakes his shoulders and neck like a mule bothered by flies. He tugs at fistfuls of his yellow hair, and fresh tears make tracks in the grime of his cheeks. It is alarming to witness. Frightening, in fact. The doctor is frightened. And no one understands, Tarare moans. No one can *know.* No one knows what it feels like. I don't want to – I don't want to cause – his words die as he encloses his knees in his arms, adopting a foetal crouching position. He rocks on his heels and a pained sound comes from his compressed body, deep and glottal.

At first the citizen-doctor believes him. Then he doesn't. Tarare, he thinks, would not be the first to clothe a naked criminality, a base lust for blood, in the rags of madness. Perhaps the wretched boy rocking on his heels before him is not so wretched at all, but in fact extremely canny. A kind of cannibal-savant, adept at affecting harmlessness when all the while atrocities swim luridly behind his watery blue eyes. Tarare, he says, reaching out a hand to touch his shoulder – please calm yourself.

The boy whimpers inarticulately, because he lives a waking nightmare.

I need to take you back to the hospital. You must understand.

Tarare raises his head from his knees and wipes his nose on the back of his hand. If I go back there they'll kill me, he sniffs.

The doctor looks at the boy for a long time. For that is what he is, really. Still a boy. Tarare – he says at last – would that be such a bad thing?

Tarare considers the doctor's words. How would it happen? Would he be taken to the gendarmerie, tried for murder? Hung, drawn, broken on the wheel? He thinks it would happen faster than that. Their vengeance would be summary. He would be plucked from the doctor's horse and beaten, and spat at, and trampled. He remembers the spring and his mock execution at Neustadt, the red sky and the black teardrop. How he had waited on the scaffold while the soldiers bayed, waited for his life to give up its meaning to him, for God to take him by the hand and lead him away in peace. But nothing had come. There had been nothing. No meaning, no love. No, he says. I'm not ready, monsieur. Citizen-Doctor.

Tarare – I cannot let you leave. I cannot – (and neither can he think of a good way to say it, but what he wants to say is: I cannot set you loose on the world. How would I live with myself? How would I sleep at night, having seen your little bundle of bones and hair, having seen the blood drying on your breast?)

Tarare rises from his haunches to stand over the doctor. Very well, he says. I am exceedingly sorry, monsieur, for all the trouble I have caused you. Long live the Republic. And then, before the doctor can answer, he takes the water flask in his right hand and strikes the prone citizen-doctor once, hard, round the head.

When the doctor comes to this second time, the sky above him has darkened to the purple of heliotropes, except for a thin

line at the bottom of the horizon, where the embers of the day –
doubtless the worst day of Citizen-Doctor Jean-Pierre Dupuis'
life – still smoulder. Clutching at his head, he takes account of
his situation. The brown horse has wandered a short way up the
road and remains ruminating serenely over the verge. But he
sees that Tarare has taken his water flask, his penknife and his
jacket from the back of the saddle.

Of Tarare himself, there is nothing left. Except the bundle.
The dirty bloodied little bundle, tied off with a loose knot,
now boiling all over with flies bewildered by the reek of it. The
doctor's head throbs.

Time has passed, hours, since he found Tarare. But how
far could the beast have got, on foot? The doctor's cheeks and
breastbone blaze painfully with sunburn, and the skin there is
hot to the touch. He knows he should mount his horse and follow after Tarare. Or else, take what is left of the child and return
to the hospital. Raise a hue and cry, call for more riders. That is
what he should do. But he does neither. An unusual – almost
heady – feeling of clarity comes over Citizen-Doctor Dupuis.
He has felt a similar feeling before only on those rare occasions
when he has had intercourse in the morning. The sour breath
of a tavern girl pooling on his neck, peeling a sheath of gut
from his cock as the milky light filters through the patched
curtains (that feeling). Of simultaneous utter seclusion from
and complete belonging to the world. It is a feeling of clos-
ure, a circle finding its point of origin. Animal, perhaps? Later,
he will write this down in his little notebook: *The operation of
instinct re. conclusion, registers in the body as dehydration, post-
coital. Not pleasure, but deeper. Sense of shapes falling into correct
positions, wholesomeness/holiness in all mundane (curtains, pubic
hair, candle grease).* Later still, he will read this back to himself

and realise he was most likely merely dehydrated, and very possibly concussed.

Plugging his nose with his fingers, the doctor takes the bundle of bones and stuffs it under the hedgerow. Perhaps it will be discovered tomorrow, he thinks. Or perhaps it will lie there for years, decades, this jumble of bones, joining the black mass of unremarked death that feeds the daisies and ripens the wheat that makes the bread. Perhaps the bones will lie there until the eschaton, when the cadavers rise in wholeness from their graves. Little Manon, limping her slight and incoherent shape behind the host of seraphim, waist-high. Toothmarks on her ribs. He must brace himself against the side of his horse as another wave of nausea passes through him. Then he mounts. That he is committing a crime does not occur to him, who for all his life has been thoroughly law-abiding. He positions himself in the saddle.

A rich dusk has fallen by the time he arrives back at Soultz-Haut-Rhin. Torches still blaze everywhere around the grounds, for the search has continued in his absence. When the porters and chars swarm around his horse, gazing up at him expectantly, he does his best to remain erect, authoritative. *Nothing*, he says, with a sad sigh. *No sign in Cernay*, he says. No Manon, no Tarare. And he is believed, because his privilege is that he always is, and always will be.

Épilogue

IV Vendée

V Vendémiaire an VII

The twelve-mile journey from Paris to Versailles can seem longer or shorter, depending on the company. Sometimes it is enjoyed, other times merely endured. Citizen-Doctor Dupuis rides compressed between a prodigiously fragrant woman carrying a blue-striped hatbox and a second, poorly dressed, who bounces a squawking baby in her arms. He looks at the baby, blowing bubbles of snot against the nurse's cockaded breast. Yellow ribbon on her tiny laced cap. It doesn't feel good to look at the baby. He doesn't like to look at any sort of baby now. They remind him of raw veal, in their glossy pinkness.

In the seat opposite the doctor, a man leans against the window, reading the *Mercure*. Dupuis scans the headlines, although he already knows the meat of them: Napoleon's glory on the waters of the Nile, General Humbert suppressed in Ireland, sons of the Republic shot summarily and tossed in mass graves outside Dublin. Blood, as ever, flows. The doctor adjusts his valise in his lap and looks out of the carriage window. Ireland. *Egypt?* Holy virgin. He is very glad he disentangled himself from the military when he did. He imagines the wounded laid sighing on rags under the serene countenance of the Great Sphinx in the bone-chill of the desert, enamel-backed scarabs large as eyes settling to their bloodied wounds. (And Napoleon's oriental jaunt has precipitated a new vogue in treatment among the moneyed: what they want, more than anything – what they ask for, for colds, for arthritis, for gleets, for impotence – is mummy powder. The bitter dust of antique cadavers snorted, swallowed, stirred into jasmine tea. He cannot speak to the therapeutic benefits of this fashionable cannibalism. He wonders if the plundered Sun-Prophets of Karnak foresaw such an end: disinterred, dismembered, ground to dust, sprinkled on the tongues of Paris lawyers who can't get it up for their cocottes any more—)

But he is not in Egypt, thank God. He is somewhere between Paris and Versailles. Raindrops vein the carriage window. The countryside beyond is palled over with mist. The shapes of hovels and windmills and trees in their last leaf swell and shrink as they reel between the sinuous rivulets. He checks his pocket watch. It is nearly nine o'clock. Today the citizen-doctor is to be reunited with Tarare.

In the six years since the citizen-doctor last saw the beast, his shape has softened in his memory to a fever-dream of the first great war summers, sordid and half-formed. He cannot remember the face. He cannot remember the teeth. But he wants to, for posterity, if nothing else. Word of the horrors at Soultz-Haut-Rhin had, of course, spread, and for a little while there came rumours of a pale apparition sighted on nearby moors and hilltops. A man who crawled over the Rhineland on all fours like an animal, tearing open the bellies of sheep. Etiolated kitchen-intruders, their mouths stained with compote. Of dogs picketed in yards found dead by morning, gobbets taken out of their flesh, gizzards smeared artfully on the ground in shapes, haruscopes, like some long-forgotten alphabet defying lucubration. In some villages they stationed night guards over the freshest graves for a little while. And then the Third Estate forgot. The medical establishment, however, has a longer memory. At the lectures and clinical symposia of Paris, in halls of old gold and purple drapery, some colleague or another will take Doctor Dupuis by the elbow and lead him aside. *Is it true?* they will ask him solicitously. *You knew The Tarare?* And the citizen-doctor will smile profoundly and say *just Tarare. No 'the'. It was his name, his Christian name.* And what follows next follows as surely as night becomes day: *you should write about him.* For this journal, or that one. *A case study.* So there it is – posterity. When Doctor Tissier's letter had arrived, he was not surprised. He knew in his bones the boy was alive out there, somewhere, chewing over his pain. He read the letter through once, then twice. He sat back at his broad mahogany desk and said aloud, to the chintz wallpaper: Tarare. He knows if anyone living can bring meaning to the boy, to the body, it is him. Rein the flesh and blood of it in reason, explain the lurid magic away. Year IX leers over the horizon: eighteen hundred, by the old reckoning. Satisfactorily epochal. Time to close the blue book and shut the monsters in. And they all lived happily ever after, *Fin.* This is how he comes voluntarily to visit with the boy he once considered killing to never have to see again.

When he arrives at the hospital, Citizen-Doctor Tissier is waiting on the stone steps to meet him. Tissier is an unfairly young and clean-cut little man with a cleft in his hairless chin like a thumbprint. He wears a russet-coloured jacket with navy braid and a glossy black perruque. His finest clothes, probably, Dupuis thinks. Tissier bows to Dupuis, low. Dupuis is not ungratified by his younger colleague's gestural and sartorial obsequiousness.

It is an honour, monsieur. I read your monograph on the use of surgical quivers in the field—

Dupuis raises his hand. Smiles. Citizen-Doctor Tissier. I apologise, but if we might forgo the customary pleasantries? We will have ample time to discuss work. Where is Tarare? If his condition is as dire as you wrote, then I would go to him sooner rather than later.

Of course. Of course. Follow me.

Through the usual chilly corridors and up the usual chilly staircase. The pleasantries are not forgone at all, in the end – merely ambulatory. How is your wife? Flourishing. Your journey? Painless. Why yes, the weather is turning. But Dupuis can tell the young Doctor Tissier's mind is equally fixed on the Lazarene creature who has fallen into his hands, to whom his chatter keeps returning. We have kept him under watch, of course, he says. Given his – given his history—

I am sure that is very wise, replies Dupuis.

And shackled to his bedstead.

Shackled?

They round a landing. Doctor Tissier glances at Dupuis. There is a soft, babyish furrow between his brows, as though he fears reprimand. Just a precaution, he says. We have a children's ward on the upper storeys. Consumptives. And such.

If you judged it necessary, then I am sure it is. Dupuis smiles again.

Doctor Tissier laughs with obvious relief. This Tarare is somewhat of an enigma, yes? he says. I have heard the same stories everyone has heard, I am sure, but it is difficult to discern what is truth and what is, well. Fantastical embellishment. Superstition. Much of it sounds like something from Perrault. The flesh-eating ghoul! He laughs again.

I assure you, Dupuis replies, a greater part is true than a rational man might wish.

What is your diagnosis, then? He is a madman, surely? Syphilitic paresis perhaps? The Abbé de Coulmier treats an anthropophage at Charenton, and has had considerable success—

Is that so? Dupuis listens indulgently. Tissier is still a very young man, he must remember. And a child of the times. Merit is the currency, and Tarare is a unique opportunity to cash in. A case utterly singular in all of France, perhaps the world. A way to make a name through a name. He wonders if he should tell Tissier about his nightmares. How he still feels charnel breath against his cheek at night, his head resting on feather pillows. How the crimson drapes at the opera house evoke an unaccountable nausea. Butchers' shops the same. The little bundle of bones and hair. Should he tell him it isn't worth it? That he should get out now, while he can? Cleave to the rim of that bottomless chasm, that bottomless man? As Dupuis is thinking this Tissier rattles on about straitjackets, special diets, purgation – until the door in front of them slams open, and a nun in a winged cornette spills into the corridor, alarm printed on her colourless features.

Doctor Tissier – thank God – the sister is gasping, breathless. The patient—

Compose yourself, Sister – Sister – Doctor Tissier frowns—

Perpetué.

Perpetué. He lifts a hand to her shoulder and presses her to one side, with an apologetic backward look at Doctor Dupuis. This will only take a moment, he says. Tarare is kept at the end of this—

That's it, says the nun. The patient is dead. Tarare is dead, monsieur.

It is Tarare. It *was* Tarare. Citizen-Doctor Dupuis feels a rush of indefinable emotion when he sees that narrow body in that

narrow bed. Already Tarare's lips have receded into the churl-
ish rictus of the dead, showing his brown corroded teeth. His
eyes – so large and vacant and blue – are fixed on a point on
the whitewashed wall. Yes, he is dead. Dupuis has never seen a
corpse quite so dead as Tarare's. Already a smell is leaking from
the pores. Tissier fusses about compressing the chest, manipu-
lating the stiffened limbs. Embarrassed.

Leave him, says Dupuis.

Tissier steps back from the bedside, biting his lip. I didn't
think – well, I thought he would last longer than – and after
you came all this way—

Dupuis waves his hand dismissively and sets down his valise
by Tarare's bony hip. He closes Tarare's eyes with his gloved
hand, because that is what you do. Don't see me, dead man.
Rest. It all seems so ordinary now. So quotidian. A corpse
ripens in a hospital bed while babies are born, doubtless, and
cats seek shelter from the rain under wheelbarrows, and the
type is set for tomorrow's papers, and hogs cool their sides in
the mud. Golden laburnum and silver rivers sparkling abun-
dantly in the high places. The sea crushing blue into stone. He
supposes other, less expected things must be happening at that
moment as well, but it is more difficult to say what those things
might be. A violin falls down a staircase. The palest green hide
of a caterpillar scabs over with silk. An Englishwoman cries as
she eats a boiled egg. Tarare is dead.

What now? says Tissier.

Now, says Doctor Dupuis, opening his valise, we look inside.

*

Of what does Tarare dream, as his body is opened like a painted
fan? Of a shallow river the colour of dogs, gently forever

wrinkled in a seemingly sourceless tender light. A handful of silver scattered on the cool of the water.

Overhead – birdsong, leaves. It feels good to him, to lie back in the torpid flow, to become one with the soft skin of the water.

The water loves and it cherishes. The water carries him – at last, on fretted silver – away.

All is perfect, and delicious.

Afterword

My intent in writing this book was not to present a truth, but to offer the most believable (and therefore compelling?) iteration of a myth. The primary source for the life of Tarare, a French peasant born near Lyon somewhere around 1772, is Pierre-François Percy's 1804 *Mémoire sur la polyphagie*, which appeared in the *Journal de médecine, chirurgie, pharmacie, etc.* several years after its subject's purported death. I accessed this through Jan Bondeson's *The Two-headed Boy, and Other Medical Marvels*. I broke from Percy's account, however, in many particulars. Citizen-Doctor Dupuis is based on Percy himself, but all the other characters in this novel, except for Tarare (and, obviously, the coterie of French Revolutionary generals and politicians who appear only briefly), are my own inventions.

I am indebted to the work of many historians of eighteenth-century France, including Colin Jones, Robert Darnton (particularly his study of French folk tales) and Simon Schama. For substance and style, respectively, Olwen H. Hufton's *Poor of Eighteenth-century France, 1750–89* and Thomas Carlyle's flamboyant *The French Revolution: A History* were indispensable. I also drew on the work of Émile Zola and the Marquis de Sade, alongside Clarice Lispector's *The Passion According to G.H.* – the best novel I know of concerning the interaction of beauty with disgust. Bonfils' diatribe against sedan chairs is based on a passage in an anonymous citizen of Montpellier's description of his home city (*Etat et description de la ville de Montpellier, fait en 1768*, trans. Robert Darnton, from Darnton's *The Great Cat Massacre And Other Episodes in French Cultural History*).

This novel's closing words – 'All is perfect, and delicious' – are taken from a description of the afterlife given by a spirit mani-festation that appeared to the Cercle Harmonique, a group of mediums working in New Orleans in the mid-nineteenth century, as described in Anna Della Subin's *Accidental Gods: On Men Unwittingly Turned Divine*.

About the Author

A. K. Blakemore's *The Manningtree Witches* (Granta, 2021) won the Desmond Elliott Prize, was shortlisted for the Costa First Novel Award, and was a Waterstones Book of the Month. She is the author of two full-length collections of poetry, *Humbert Summer* and *Fondue*, which was awarded the 2019 Ledbury Forte Prize for Best Second Collection, and has also translated the work of Sichuanese poet Yu Yoyo. Her poetry and prose has appeared in the *London Review of Books*, *Poetry*, the *Poetry Review* and the *White Review*, among other publications.